LOVED BY THE DRAGON
COLLECTION

Vivienne Savage

Loved by the Dragon is a work of fiction.
Names, characters, places, and incidents are the product of the authors'
imaginations or are used in a fictitious manner. Any resemblance to real
persons, events, and locations are coincidental or used in a form of
parody.

Copyright © PAYNE & TAYLOR 2013

All rights reserved.
ISBN-10:099038179X
ISBN-13: 978-0-9903817-9-2
www.spellboundconsortium.com
Editor: EV Proofreading
Graphic Artist: Mirella Santana

Table of Contents

SAVED BY THE DRAGON

Chapter 1

Thunder cracked overhead, a grim herald of what was to come. Barely a minute later, the sky seemed to split open and unleash a torrent of freezing cold rain. And Chloe Ellis was caught without her umbrella, clutching a rocky wall nearly a hundred feet off the ground.

Shit!

She hadn't anticipated the weatherman's predicted 20% chance of rain would come with a furious thunderstorm. Within an hour of her climb, dark clouds had swept over the topaz blue skies and eclipsed the sun. Lightning flashed in the distance.

"Well damn, what do I do now?" She wedged her body into the crack leading toward the high summit, hoping to escape the brunt of the wind and rain.

Of the three options available to her, none held any appeal. She could stay hanging where she was and hope the rain passed soon, attempt to make her way down, or keep pressing for the cliffs.

Wiping water from her face, she gazed around for an alternative. The fissure in the rock face widened several feet above her, so she made her way up and breathed a quiet prayer of thanks for the small ledge at the top. It was a place to rest safely and wait out the storm.

The narrow shelf extended farther than she'd thought at first glance. Chloe wriggled back into the crawlspace to get out of the rain. Loose grit shifted beneath her hands, skittered down a dark passage. She fetched a flashlight from her backpack and eased down the crumbling slope. Water ran in narrow rivulets from the mountain shelf behind her, plastering her hair to the back of her neck.

Should have brought Freddy with me, she thought. *Now, I'm here alone, and hiding from the rain.*

Freddy, her on-again off-again boyfriend, had practically begged to come along on this trip. He wanted to work things out; promised he'd be a changed man. They could camp and make love under the stars. Of course, he was only the most recent train wreck in a chain of failed romances.

Before Freddy, she had dated Malcolm; the hottie at the law firm where she practiced her paralegal work. Dating him had been a dream. He had a sweet personality, a stable income as a lawyer, and he seemed to love her dearly…. Until she returned a day ahead of schedule from a visit to care for her ailing father.

Chloe had walked into their shared home to discover Malcolm urging his weekend lay to hide in the closet.

Four years. She swept it all down the drain that day and refused to hear out his ridiculous excuses about becoming too drunk to say no. How he'd come out to drink with pals, who later wouldn't excuse his behavior and ratted him out because they'd warned him not to do it. Three of them broke the bro code in an effort to step in for their friend.

So she went against her better judgment and began to date Freddy; Malcolm's physical trainer, and a man with a body like an Olympian. The sex was great, and the way he treated her was even better.

Or so it had seemed.

Their first fight came four months into the relationship when his jealous persona arose. He didn't want her to have male friends because it wasn't appropriate, and no man merely wanted to be her friend. They'd want to fuck her too. They had another fight in the days prior to her little decision to go away for a weekend alone.

What made me think I could do this alone without him? It was foolish, dumb, and dangerous, Chloe thought. Freddy knew what he was doing on the mountain peaks. They'd bonded over a mutual lust for the outdoors during the initial stages of their dating. It wouldn't have been the first time they went away for a weekend in the wilderness.

The pebbles beneath her feet shifted. She slid forward and lost her balance, and in the process of attempting to regain her footing, landed heavily on her butt and slid down the cave's treacherous slope like a reluctant toddler at the playground. She screamed all the while and scraped her nails uselessly against the rocky wall at either side. Eventually, she reached the end and became airborne.

All sense of time fell away as Chloe tumbled through the air with the debris from the shaft, arms and legs flailing uselessly at the air like a baby bird falling from its nest the first time. Merciless and unyielding rock caught her, although she landed on her ankle and crumpled soon after. White-hot pain exploded through her entire leg; worse than anything she'd ever experienced before.

"Fuck!" she swore, loudly, after all who would hear. Her flashlight tumbled from her hands and rolled across the cavern floor. The wobbling light danced over the rough-hewn walls in a dizzying display until the small device rolled to a stop. She'd have to crawl to reach it and risk scraping her knees and hands to high hell in the process.

Nearly thirty minutes had passed before she was able to stop crying. Instead of feeling strong and adventurous, she felt weak and miserable. Her wet clothes and the damp environment worsened her ordeal. Of course, Chloe had also learned a very valuable lesson about adventuring without a partner.

After a while she climbed up from the ground and gingerly tried to apply weight to her left ankle. A merciless twinge, striking her joint with the ferocity of a hammer blow, forced her to immediately draw her foot off the ground again. The nearby stalagmite became her leaning post while she waited for the nausea to settle.

"Okay. Chloe, think," she told herself, while salty tears leaked down her cheeks. Her voice echoed across the cavern. "This is a popular climb. I just need to… to wait for the rain to stop and listen. Call for help."

It wasn't in her plans to die alone and in the dark recesses of some unknown cave. Unfortunately, cell phone signals wouldn't reach the outside world. She confirmed it at a glance.

Once she eased down to the cave floor, Chloe tried to pull herself together. A search through her pack produced a basic first aid kit, emergency blanket, a few energy bars, and some dehydrated meals. Being injured didn't change the fact that her activities had provoked a ravenous hunger that couldn't be sated by a tiny little rectangle of granola and dried cranberries that she had brought with her.

She rifled through the first aid kit and removed the small bottle of ibuprofen. She popped two into her mouth and swallowed them dry. The Band-Aids and antibiotic cream were useless, so she shoved the box back into her bag and leaned against the cavern wall to wallow in her misery. This vacation sucked. Freddy was probably getting his dick sucked by some ditzy bitch in a pink sports bra and booty shorts while she suffered in the dark.

"Have you become lost?"

The voice promptly shook her from a daydreaming state.

Or maybe I'm hallucinating…

The shirtless man who stepped into her field of vision belonged in a gym commercial with his rippling muscles and washboard abs. His wavy blond hair touched his broad shoulders and curled at the tips, and a reddish scruff covered his jawline. Although her tastes usually ran to black hair and blue eyes like tall, dark, and handsome Freddy, something about the fair-haired stranger lured her like a siren's call.

She would definitely make an exception for the bearded Viking in the cave.

"Are you among the hearing impaired?"

"What?" Delusions weren't supposed to speak, were they? The sudden realization that help had arrived filled her with relief. Chloe pushed to her feet and promptly cried out. Her forward stumble knocked her straight into the stranger's strong arms.

"You are injured."

"My ankle," she sobbed. She hadn't realized how cold she was until held in his embrace. The man radiated heat like the sun on a cloudless summer day. Given the dire need to become warm, she had no reservations about wriggling in against his chest. The thought did occur to her that she should ask why a random, sexy stranger was in a dark cave system - and shirtless - until she saw the incredibly heavy backpack at his feet.

Maybe he was an axe murderer hiding out from the police, and planned to kill and eat her over his own camp fire. Hell if she knew, but at least she'd get warm before he did it.

"Will you allow me to tend to you?" His words rolled off his tongue like smooth dark chocolate; deep and rich.

"I... yes," she impulsively breathed out.

The world shifted around her, bringing a wave of vertigo. The rugged stranger plucked her up into his arms and cradled her. The startled shriek died in her throat.

"What are you doing?" Chloe demanded.

"It would be rather difficult to complete my objective if you are to limp behind me as a man who has been hobbled."

"Oh," she replied. She squirmed to glance back toward the fallen flashlight and pack. "You're leaving my stuff."

"I will return for your belongings once I have settled you in comfort. I have a fire nearby."

"Alright. Fine... Do you plan to tell me your name?"

The man paused.

Chloe couldn't even see him in the dark, but he seemed to know the way and navigated well without bruising her against the walls or the hard rock. She reached out with one hand and felt the cool stone to her right. "I'm Chloe," she offered first.

"You may call me Saul."

"You're the first Saul I've ever met," she commented.

"You will also find me to be the very best Saul you will ever meet," he replied without missing a beat. Pleasant and funny, if not somewhat narcissistic.

"Oh…" Chloe nervously laughed. "So, what are you doing here?" *And why are you half-dressed?*

"I explore caves," he replied. "It is… a particular hobby of mine."

"Oh, a spelunker."

"Indeed."

"I like to climb," Chloe quickly offered. After she had said it, she could have kicked herself for sounding so very eager.

"As I have noted." His chuckle made her belly flutter, like his voice had made love to her ears and left her breathless. Chloe would have paid him to read the Yellow Pages to her.

Orange light danced ahead, yielding only the faintest outline of his features. It took many more steps before they emerged from the network of tunnels and into the open space of a cavern with a high, uneven ceiling. It extended upward toward a partially open sky revealed by a slender crevice. They were protected from the downpour, with exception of the steady stream of draining water that splattered against the rocks below the crack itself.

As promised, a fire crackled in a stone ring. It was much bigger than Chloe expected but not unwelcome. The cheery golden glow cast flickering shadows against smooth rock walls. Veins of quartz glittered just beyond the edge of the shadows, glimmering like stars as the light caught them.

"I must remove your boot. It will hurt," he warned.

"Just do it."

"As you command."

Saul set her down on a sleeping bag spread out between the fire and wall. Chloe shivered. Her damp clothes clung uncomfortably to her every curve.

Pain zinged up her leg despite Saul's careful movements. He unraveled the complicated knot that secured her laces then eased the sturdy boot from her foot.

"How am I supposed to get down the mountain like this?" The pain triggered another round of tears that she hastily wiped away.

"Perhaps the damage is not as dire as you imagine," Saul mysteriously replied. He had crouched beside her near the affected limb. Once the boot and sock were stripped away, he smoothed his palm over the top of her foot and took firm grip of her heel in the

9

other hand. The pain flared, a bright explosion that left her seeing stars. She kicked to free herself, but he had such a strong grip she didn't even budge his muscular arms.

"Ow ow ow ow! Stop!" she screamed.

The first initial spark of pain faded dimly and left a dull throb in its place. Saul didn't stop. Ignoring her, he slid the same hand atop her foot over her ankle, higher until his calloused touch smoothed over her shin beneath the damp cargo pants. His fingers curved around her calf, alternating squeezes and pressure with the occasional caress.

"What are you doing?" Chloe asked sharply.

"Easing your pain," Saul replied. He was a man of few words apparently. "Does this provide relief to you?" he asked.

His divine touch continued to spread heat along her skin. He massaged the muscle and rolled her foot, but the injury seemed oblivious to the fact that it should have caused her immense pain.

Thank God I shaved before leaving home this morning, she thought in a sudden moment of vanity. "I guess so… maybe I didn't sprain or twist it after all."

"Good." He smiled up at her from where he knelt at her feet. The smug pleasure on his handsome countenance made her want to both wring his neck and kiss him. She didn't know which seemed the most pleasing.

Kissing him would be a better use of time, she internally decided. Chloe quietly sighed. She let her head roll back and closed her eyes. "You have great hands. I haven't had a foot massage this great in years." The little Asian ladies in the salon never treated her that well during her pedicures, and she paid money for those!

"You should strip."

"Excuse me?" It wasn't everyday a man rivaling the God of Thunder wanted to get her out of her clothes.

"Would you not prefer warm attire to your drenched garments?"

"Oh!" Her cheeks suffused with heat and color, spreading down her throat toward her collarbones.

"I possess many articles of clothing which may provide sufficient alternative. Unless of course, you prefer to catch cold and perish of exposure."

He talks so strangely, she thought. *What an odd man. An odd, sexy man… Christ, maybe I did hit my head on the rocks and this is all some freaky fantasy.*

"No. I'd prefer not to perish of exposure. Thank you very much."

Saul left her side and returned with a pile of clothing. T-shirts, khaki-colored shorts, and a pair of cargo pants. All too big for her. She accepted a tee and a blanket gratefully.

Chloe began pulling off her shirt when she became aware of Saul's gaze on her. "Um... do you mind?"

"Mind?" He gave her a baffled look.

"Can you turn your back at least?"

Saul sighed as if the inconvenience pained him. "Your modesty is almost endearing, but as you wish. I will utilize this time to retrieve your belongings."

Once his broad shoulders and fine body disappeared from view into the dark crevice in the wall, Chloe stripped away her top and tossed it aside. The wet cotton fell with a plop against the dark stone floor.

"Ugh. He's right about one thing. Feels good to get all of this off." While Chloe had a change of shirt, panties, and a pair of walking shorts in her bag, she hadn't come prepared with much else. She shimmied out of her clammy sports bra and tugged on the dry t-shirt loaned to her. Then tugged the blanket up over her legs and around her hips to conceal her damp boyshorts.

Saul announced his return to the cavern by loudly clearing his throat. She glanced up to spy her handsome rescuer lurking at the fissure in the wall, clutching her bag in hand, and smiling almost shy.

"Am I permitted to return?"

"You may," she called toward him.

The hot Viking lookalike deposited her backpack beside her.

Unfortunately, enough water had entered through the flap during her moment in the storm that the tightly rolled bundles of clothing packed into the bottom of the bag were damp on top. She fished out the dry panties beneath her wet walking shorts and didn't fret over the lack of a bra, too small-breasted to feel uncomfortable wearing the man's t-shirt alone.

Her asshole boyfriend Freddy had offered to buy her tits once, promising that if she agreed to it, he'd cover the full cost of implants to bump her modest A-cups into a considerable C-cup. Chloe had declined it. She liked her shape, even if he didn't.

"Thank you, Saul, for getting that," she graciously said to him when he rejoined her on the rough stone.

"I did nothing worthy of your gratitude."

The smile began to slip from her face, but it clung precariously and lingered with renewed uncertainty. He was an odd man. Strange, but so very otherworldly and polite. His unrecognizable accent sent chills down her spine.

"Where are you from?" she suddenly asked, eager to learn more about the man in her company. Her strange savior blinked at her in surprise, as if he'd expected anything but her curiosity.

"From a land distant to this place."

"Europe?" she questioned again.

Saul shook his head. "Hardly."

Am I prying into his business? she wondered. Her smile faded, swept away by her rising uncertainty. Unwilling to bother him any further, she brought her knees up to her chest and wrapped her arm around them. The sleeping bag maintained her sense of modesty.

"Tell me about you," Saul said.

"Me? Not much to tell. I'm a paralegal. We deal mostly with family law and property disputes," she explained. "But I think I'm ready for a change. Lately…" The job lacked the rewarding qualities she once enjoyed. She wanted something fresh in a new city away from Freddy's inane insecurities and Malcolm's egotistical attitude. Chloe and her ex still crossed paths since they worked in the same building.

Recently, rumors had traveled down the office grapevine about Malcolm's new wife dumping him and finding a loophole in their supposed ironclad prenuptial agreement. She took him to the bank, and now he was on the prowl for a replacement. She confirmed it as truth when she caught Malcolm slinking around her office floor.

If the distance of a few hundred miles separated them, maybe she wouldn't feel compelled to take either loser back the next time one of them slunk into her life. She credited her best friend Marcy's support for helping her through the last rough breakup. If not for her BFF reminding her of Freddy's short fuse, she might have caved and allowed him in on her trip.

Saul was as intuitive as he was attractive. "You are unsatisfied with your work. The clientele, perhaps?"

"Sometimes. We see a lot of families come in to split up… with kids caught in the middle. Sometimes people use them like currency to hurt the other partner in the relationship. Ten years of watching people fight over things they could work out in marital counseling, and now I'm just plain tired."

"A union no longer carries the weight it once held," he agreed.

"Are you married?" she asked.

Saul shook his head. "I remain untethered."

"A happy bachelor then?" Chloe asked lightly, putting a smile on her face.

Her scruffy companion shook his head again. "It is not for lack of interest to find a better half or my failure to conduct a thorough search. She simply does not exist."

"Oh…" *Crap, change of subject, change of subject!* she thought. She admonished herself mentally for prying into the man's personal affairs, and then quickly leapt into something safely impersonal. "Do you live or work nearby, Saul?"

He shook his head again. "I work in Drakenstone Studios. Certainly not close by any means. I flew in to enjoy a fortnight away from the city's filth."

The name struck a chord in her memory. A few recent blockbuster film titles flitted through her mind, the sort with lots of action and amazing effects.

"You're not an actor though, right? I'd have seen you in something."

Saul flashed her a toothy grin. "No. I do not act."

Pity… He had the looks for it but the idea of women across the world ogling him made Chloe irritable. The out-of-the-blue surge of jealousy unsettled her.

As if sensing her discomfort, Saul leapt up to his feet and offered both hands out to her. He had agile moves, like a martial artist or gymnast. "Why have you remained stationary?" he questioned. "Come. You may resume your interrogation shortly. Put your ankle to the test."

"I dunno…"

"What concerns you, Chloe?"

"Let's just say that I don't quite trust a massage to have me up on my feet yet."

"You should make the attempt," he encouraged her.

"I'm wearing nothing beneath this sleeping bag but a t-shirt and panties, Saul. Are my pants dry?"

He sighed in exasperation. "No. Would you sunbathe in anything more while on a beach?"

"Well no, not really." In fact, her most recent swimsuit purchase consisted of two tiny triangles over the ass and crotch with patterns of bare skin over her hips. At least her hipsters provided full coverage.

"Then come."

With great patience, he took her by the hand and assisted her onto her feet. At first, she felt a vague twinge of fleeting discomfort, but once Chloe set her full weight on it, all became well again. The man had magic hands, or she'd really done less damage than she previously

13

estimated. After rolling the ankle joint, she took a few experimental steps.

"Wow! It really does feel better. But now I'm starved." By the time she had walked to her bag, her ankle caused her no further discomfort at all. It was a miracle, as if he'd laid hands on her and cast all of her pains away. "Wanna share some dinner?"

A big guy like him had to be starving. He was easily six inches taller than her and built like an Olympic athlete. He probably required as much food in one meal as she consumed in an entire day to feed those muscles.

"You would share your meal with me?"

"Well I did offer, silly. Do you want any or not?"

He nodded at her and settled on the ground again, where he waited until she gathered rainwater for the MREs. Once they were heated, she shook up the pouch and offered him two with a plastic spoon.

"You're going to want salt and pepper with that," she cautioned him.

He ignored her warning and spooned up a mouthful of soggy vegetables in beef-flavored broth. Within a matter of seconds, his inquisitive expression began to change. His mouth turned down, and he swallowed the first bite like she'd fed him pulped paper.

"This is horrendous," Saul commented, spooning through the contents of the pouch as if he expected the mirage to fade and reveal a replacement meal in its place. "How could you honestly claim that this passes for sustenance? What is this foul thing?"

"Meals Ready-to-Eat beef stew," Chloe replied.

"I neither see nor taste a crumb of beef in this ill-prepared morsel of cuisine."

"It's more than you had before I came along," Chloe shot back.

"Do you also have a preference for meat, or shall this supposed beef stew be your only meal?"

Chloe sighed wistfully. "I could go for a steak, yeah, but there isn't an Outback tucked away in this cavern, you know?"

Saul rose to his feet and offered his unopened pouch and unfinished meal back to her. "Very well. Rest. Drink. I will return shortly with sustenance of a more... edible quality."

The man disappeared into the narrow crevice again. Against her better judgment, Chloe tossed their unfinished pouches into the discarded plastic bag and settled down to rest on her side with her phone. The signal bars had forsaken her, but she at least had a good book to read.

Chapter 2

The smokey-sweet aroma of roasting meat awakened Chloe from her impromptu nap. While the digital romance novel occupying her phone had been filled with spicy sex and sensual mystery, it couldn't combat the fatigue inspired by falling into a secret tunnel and meeting her own seductive stranger.

Yawning, she propped her weight onto an elbow, and opened her eyes to find Saul crouched beside the fire. The flames crackled beneath the fragrant haunch of some animal. A deer or mountain goat maybe.

"Where did you...?" She didn't see a lick of hunting equipment in sight. Not even a damned blowgun or quiver.

"It had broken its leg. Hardly a difficult catch when one is hobbled and incapable of defending itself." His brows rose, confirming his intended double meaning. It was as if he knew she expected him to be some kind of cannibalistic, mountain-dwelling murderer.

Chloe's cheeks flushed again. "Right, but how did you even get to where there was a deer? It's pitch black and pouring outside still."

"As I said, hardly a difficult task. Deer frequent the summit and sometimes slip down the slope."

"Where's the rest of it, Saul?" she persisted. *Don't tell me he poached the leg off of that poor creature and wasted the rest.*

His proud smile diminished. "Why do you ask?"

"You didn't have to kill something just to feed me its leg."

Chloe wasn't a vegetarian or anything, but the callousness turned her stomach. Her father was an avid huntsman during his prime, and she had memories of him putting practically every inch of the animal's carcass to use. He'd create art with the antlers and sew gorgeous garments with the pelts, which he gifted to his wife and child. She gained her love of the outdoors from him before her parents split.

"I eased its suffering. What remained of the unfortunate creature became a meal for some other predator, no doubt."

"Some other predator?"

Saul scoffed. "There are larger and meaner beasts in the vicinity than this buck. Do you honestly believe it to be wasteful when another has benefitted from the kill?"

He was right, of course. Cougars were opportunistic animals who would enjoy the deceased white-tailed deer no less now that Saul had relieved it of one hind leg. It was better for the buck to be put out of its misery than to await a slow death.

Shame colored Chloe's face and forced her to look away. "I'm sorry. It was wrong of me to say that. And ungrateful."

"Apology accepted."

The meal lacked culinary finesse but Chloe had brought salt, pepper, and enough seasoning for the MREs to give the meat some flavor. They ate together in companionable silence, which led to Chloe comparing Saul and Freddy again. Her ex always blabbered about himself, his job, his clients, and his latest electronics indulgence. He rarely cared to inquire about her days.

When Saul did speak, it was to inquire about her with genuine curiosity. Where did she come from? Had she enjoyed the mountain prior to her injury? His final unexpected question drew their conversation into awkward territory again.

"Are you promised to anyone?"

Such an old-fashioned term. Chloe chuckled and shook her head at him. "No. Not really. The guy I was seeing, well, we sort of fell out right before I came on this weekend getaway."

"I am sorry."

"It's alright. He was a dick anyway." She raised one shoulder in a half shrug and tried to pass him the rest of the haunch. He waved it off politely.

"Say, would you mind taking a picture with me?"

"To what purpose?"

"First time I've had a white knight come to my rescue," she replied, grinning. "I'd like to preserve the memory. Besides, my friend Marcy won't believe me when I tell her you look like a Disney prince."

"Which prince?"

"The Beast, of course. After he turns human," she quickly added when her choice placed her on the end of his stare.

"Ah. Prince Adam."

He knows his Disney characters! The discovery whipped a twinge of excitement through her. "Though... I'd have to say you have way prettier hair."

"Hardly," he replied.

Impulse drove Chloe to touch Saul's shoulder length waves while suppressing an envious flutter. She didn't spot a single split end.

Saul was an enigma. An outdoorsman who knew his way around a mountain and a beauty salon? Come on. Those odds were one in a million.

"So… can I?" She waved her cellphone at him.

"I must humbly decline if you intend to duckface."

The most unladylike snort-laugh escaped Chloe. She shook her head quickly in denial. "No! I promise that I won't."

The photo came out perfect and just in the nick of time before her battery conked out completely. She got two perfect snaps of them in frame, with her white-blonde hair against his golden strands. She snuck a kiss to his cheek in the second picture.

Eventually, the conversation topic drifted to even brighter subjects. They spoke of movies, although he would share nothing else about his role with Drakenstone Studios. She made an educated guess that he was obligated by contract to remain silent or part of their legal department. The man had an uncanny knowledge of the law. Was he a lawyer?

He distracted her swiftly from her line of questions concerning his work by revealing his fondness for psychological thrillers and horror movies, a love they both shared.

"The mirror was beautiful… I would love to have a piece that beautiful in my home one day," she remarked fondly. "Maybe a prop replica…"

"I assume you would prefer it to lack the bevy of murderous ghosts."

"Well yes, obviously," she said with a laugh. "Oh wow, I'm stuffed."

"Here, I will prepare you a bed. A good night's rest will serve you well."

Saul didn't possess as much equipment as she anticipated. His sleeping bag spread out near the fire with the same additional blanket for warmth. She donned her dried clothing and reluctantly accepted it for the night.

"Are you sure? Honestly, I knew the risks of coming out here, I should have brought my own."

He answered with another headshake. "There is enough room to share." The man was a perplexing mystery.

For a while Chloe managed to doze, but every pop from the dimming fire startled her. Temperatures fell at night and the damp made it worse. It seeped into her bones, making sleep impossible.

"You are cold." It wasn't a question, but a statement of fact. Saul's hand rubbed up her arm over the blanket spread over sleeping bag.

"S-sorry." Her teeth chattered. The rock beneath the sleeping bag seemed to leech all the warmth away. The fire's close proximity didn't help, and hell if she knew how he wasn't trembling too. Maybe he originated from some northern climate and felt at home.

"Shall I warm you?"

Chloe nodded. Once he released the zipper on the sleeping bag, Saul slid right in beside her and snuggled up to her side. He became an oven beside her, a living radiator providing comfort she desperately craved. The shivering promptly ceased, but she became aware of how firm his muscled chest felt against her. A thin layer of cotton separated her breasts from his skin. Suddenly, she hated her walking shorts and tee. Chloe loathed his jeans most of all, and while her feet were also frigid, Saul didn't complain about her ice cold toes against his ankles.

The best way to stay warm in cold weather is skin to skin contact, she thought. It's true. His legs felt wonderful against her feet.

"I have been told that it is considered appropriate in these circumstances to shed clothing and share body heat."

It was as if he read her mind. Chloe didn't argue his logic and quickly squirmed out of her shorts and panties. She kicked them toward the foot of the sleeping bag, equally eager to remove her shirt and toss it aside onto the cold stone beside them.

He shoved his jeans off easily and settled beside her again, but with the sleeping bag flap obscuring her view, she saw only a brief flash of skin and a soft golden triangle. That hint was enough to pique her interest. His flaccid penis appeared uncut - again, she wondered if it was a certain sign that Saul originated from Europe - and his pubes were neither immaculately groomed nor wild and unkempt. Freddy liked to wax every inch of his body to silky perfection, and he had once demanded the same of her. She'd told him where he could stuff that idea. Waxing hurt.

"Thanks," Chloe muttered. Moving near to Saul was awkward at first, but they settled on their sides while facing each other. He moved one arm over her shoulders and she laid the other against his chest.

"You're so warm," she muttered, turning her cheek against his throat. A personal, human-shaped heating pad for her convenience. She threw her arms around him and burrowed into the inviting heat of skin to skin contact. Their legs twined, and modesty became a thing of the past. Her tummy pressed against his rock hard abs and she slipped a thigh over his hip. This stranger, this perfect, absolutely sexy stranger, didn't voice a single complaint.

What man would? He has a naked woman throwing herself into his arms and we've barely known one another for a day, she thought ruefully. Of course Saul wasn't going to complain. Likewise, she chose not to mention a word about the arousing presence against her lower abdomen. He'd been soft at first, but with every comfort-seeking wriggle that she made to get settled, his cock stiffened a little more.

But he remained a perfect gentleman.

"Are the accommodations to your standards?" he asked.

Chloe didn't miss the humor coloring his tone. "I find my surroundings to be more than adequate," she teased back.

His chuckle sounded like a rumble, so deep and throaty that the genuine attraction produced a natural reaction. Her nipples could have cut glass, but instead, they brushed against his sleek chest when she shifted to press her lips to his cheek.

"Thank you, Saul."

"You are welcome."

The fact that he wasn't behaving like a true creep made him as attractive as his hard body. Did he find her attractive, she wondered?

Chloe slid her fingers down his brawny shoulder and over his arm. He had thick biceps and the sort of bulky but naturally cut torso that reflected an active lifestyle or laborer's occupation. Saul hadn't shaped his body with weights and exercises in front of a gym mirror.

Taking in a deep breath, she steeled her nerves and ignored the rapid thumping of her heart. She then eased her hand between their bodies and traveled over his chiseled abdomen. She felt every muscle, every ridge, and she boldly wriggled in a little tighter, angled her ass, and encouraged the firming flesh jutting from his pelvis until it hardened even more. His body yielded the desired response. He groaned and squeezed a harsh handful of one plump cheek. He even curved his fingers into the plump curve and grinded her against him. There was no question about it. He wanted her too.

Next, she guided both of his hands to her breasts, granting him unspoken permission to fondle her however he pleased. Her small tits filled his calloused palms. The rough patches of skin scraped over her sensitive nipples and introduced her to a new sensation – a little flutter in the bottom of her belly that made her writhe toward his hands, craving more.

Saul gazed at her quietly in the dark, rising lust in his golden-hued eyes, and doubly felt in each nudge of his hips. She even heard in the way his breaths quickened with excitement. "I want you."

His growl thrilled her and frightened her in equal measure. Lust and wanting won out.

"I'm offering, Saul," she told him.

A night of hot sex with her drop dead gorgeous rescuer sounded like perfection to her and a solution to her problem with Freddy; she needed to fuck until her ex was completely out of her mind. Chloe shifted beneath him, eager and ready, already wet with her desires.

"I don't have... I didn't bring a condom," she mumbled against his bearded jaw. She warmed her cheek against his throat and restlessly awaited the next touch. God, she loved feeling the little pulse there and knowing that the quickening tempo was inspired by her.

"Is one required?"

Saul unzipped and cast back the top layer of the sleeping bag and leaned away from her onto his knees. It reintroduced her skin to the chilly evening air. Above them, the sky had gone dark; its bleak, cloud-filled sky showing intermittent spaces of midnight and twinkling stars. The rain was over at least.

"You are the most beautiful human woman to ever cross my path."

From a man who resembled a masterpiece sculpture fashioned by a Renaissance artist, that meant something. Heat spread through her cheeks. The compliment was as pleasing as it was strange, creating flutters in her belly and a shyness she'd never experienced before. Saul's hands traced her body, as if he committed her curves, her dips, and every plane to memory with his palms as well as his eyes.

She reached to give him the same attentions. The hair on his legs was silky instead of coarse. She wanted to see if the rest was the same and to feel the pulse of his cock in her hands.

It's irresponsible but... I don't care if we don't have any condoms. Marcy would kill me if I told her I walked away from this because I didn't have a rubber. She'd never forgive me. Hell, I wouldn't forgive me.

Her fingertips didn't meet round the base of his impressive dick, a discovery that awed her. He certainly wasn't lacking in the goods. She took him in both hands and acquainted herself with his length. The sounds he made, so primal and raw, covered her entire body with gooseflesh unrelated to the cold night. He was uncut, exactly as she'd suspected after her quick peek. Besides skipping on the condoms, that was another first for her.

"Chloe." The sound of her name on his lips made her melt. Saul lifted her hands from his body and pinned them back against the sleeping bag. He dipped his head and rolled forward in a sinuous movement that dragged his nose from her navel to her neck, breathing her in. Chloe's pussy clenched.

"I can smell your desire," Saul whispered against her throat. "Tell me what you want, Chloe."

"You." Nothing else was on her mind.

In a single movement, Saul flipped her over and speared her from behind, plunging his erection into her molten core. Chloe cried out sharply and arched her spine as pleasure and pain overlapped into a singular sensation, transcending all other perception of discomfort and need. It didn't matter that it hurt, as the pain was fleeting and brief. Her wet body readily accepted his sizable proportions until they pressed flush together and his heavy balls tapped against her hot folds.

Fuck, he feels good. Better than she'd expected, providing great length with the perfect amount of girth. He stretched her vaginal walls around his cock and forced her to quickly accommodate to his size. Clearly, he didn't believe in foreplay, and it wasn't necessary when she was soaked long before his cock began to press into her heated channel.

With a hand anchoring her hips and the other gripping her braid, Saul introduced Chloe to a tantalizing world of bliss bordered on torment. Her scalp stung from his tugging, but her body felt aflame. Each pistoned stroke made her yearn for more.

"Oh god… faster, Saul."

Chloe shoved back against him, rocking her hips in time to his strokes. Each time he drew his steeled length from her body she wanted to scream. When he shoved forward again, balls slapping against her clit, she wanted to weep in gratitude.

Her small breasts bounced with their frenetic movements, and her once chilly limbs gleamed with a sweaty sheen. Her entire body felt alive while Saul knelt behind her in his dominant position. Her pussy greedily tightened in expectation of the next powerful thrust. Her mind couldn't handle the image in her head, picturing Saul behind her, perspiration glistening from head to toe. His body working, his flat abdomen flexing with every forward slam.

The only thing Chloe hated about the position was that she couldn't see him and take joy in his equally euphoric features. Hearing him wasn't enough, no matter how he groaned out his delight with her body.

"Ohhhhh god, Saul. Don't stop, please don't stop. I'm so close," she pleaded with him.

Saul bent over her back and slid his hand over her hip, letting his nails drag and leave a sensitized trail in their wake. They were sharper than she'd realized, and they also left stinging pink lines wherever they touched. Eventually, his hand swept over her breast and shamelessly palmed the plump mound, molding it in his grasp. He had rough, working man's fingers that stimulated her nipple until she wished his mouth was on it instead.

"Mine," he grunted against her ear. "Tell me, Chloe. Tell me you are mine."

"Yes. Fuck yes," she panted.

"Say it," he ordered.

"I'm yours!" she cried out, readily giving her agreement. Arching against him, she shoved until his cock pressed flush in her tight little snatch and they were fully joined. From that point forward nothing else mattered, as she squealed and went wild beneath his weight, clawing handfuls of the sleeping bag. The tension within her unraveled all at once, like a spring close to snapping and then suddenly released.

Chloe had never orgasmed during doggy style before - not once - but Saul made it seem like the most natural position in the world for lovemaking. Her legs became jelly, and the loss of them pitched her face down against the cushioned sleeping bag. She shuddered again as a second orgasm overtook her. She writhed helplessly, caught in the throes of a powerful release that rippled outward from her core and seized her body in uncontrollable tremors.

"My Chloe," he growled behind her.

He drove in harder until it should have hurt, but he only delivered the most amazing quiver inside of her pussy. His growls lit her aflame with lust until she craved him even more. Until she couldn't imagine sex with another man in all of her life. The need consumed her.

"Yours!" she cried.

With her hair wrapped around his fist, Saul clamped his teeth down on her shoulder and thrust his hips forward. The hot squirt of his seed seared her like a brand and the climax continued with merciless convulsions. She milked his cock with every contraction of her womb.

It wouldn't end. The rapturous moment continued like a video set to loop, and every feeling exploded throughout her with vivid intensity.

She screamed again and the cavern seemed to spin. Her vision blurred until she slumped forward on one elbow with her upraised rump receiving the brunt of his final strokes. His name was the only sound she could make. The only word she knew.

Chloe's third climax ended with the world around her darkening into oblivion.

Chapter 3

Chloe awoke confused and disoriented, surrounded by smooth warmth on all sides. The world's best heated leather seats were her firm but oddly pleasant cushion.

"Mm... Saul?" she murmured to the open air. As she moved, she felt around blindly with her hand. It was pitch dark, and only slanted beams of moonlight fell through the narrow slit in the rocky cavern ceiling. She didn't recall the fire going out but it must have. Its reassuring orange glow was absent.

The leather mattress moved and shifted, creating a rumbling noise like the purr of an incredibly large feline. It took a breath that moved her up and down again like a kid on an inflatable play house.

The bed was moving and Saul was nowhere in sight. She couldn't feel him beside her in the dark.

"Saul?" she whispered again.

As her eyes began to adjust to the dim light, several things came into view and a couple thoughts came to mind. First, she realized something enormous surrounded and cradled her naked body, and that it wasn't a leather sectional or a mattress. It was a living creature.

Next, she recognized that this massive, leather-skinned beast had turned its head toward her and opened two golden eyes split by vertical pupils.

It's a monster. Some sort of monster lizard, she panicked on the inside. She screamed and clawed her way up to her feet, stumbled, and fell hard on one knee in the process. The monster stood, its movement allowing the moonlight to bathe it in a silver glow. It glinted off of the pair of ivory horns twisting back from its slender face and pointed ears.

It also had wings. A pair of magnificent, bicolored wings tucked against its back in a relaxed position. Black and beige feathers covered them. Staring up at it, Chloe waited for her death. Part of her wanted to flee screaming, but the rational part told her that to run might invite its predatory instincts. It might attack the very moment she fled.

It... almost looks like a dragon. Alright. This is a dream. A dream. Saul fucked me silly so now I'm passed out beside him having this nightmare because we spent half the night talking about horror movies from the 80s and giant monster flicks. That's it. It's only a dream, she rationalized internally.

"Saul?" she called out loud. If dream Saul would materialize to rescue her again, she'd gladly show her appreciation to the real thing once she awakened.

The dragon lowered its head toward her.

Chloe shrieked and nearly stumbled into the remnants of the camp fire. A few dying embers glowed. Near the abandoned sleeping bag, she found her discarded panties, his jeans, and her t-shirt.

No! Wake up! This can't be real, she thought. It was the stuff of fairytales, but Chloe's discovery that the man of her dreams was actually a big mythological creature turned it into a nightmare.

Chloe tried to awaken herself with a sharp smack across the cheek. It didn't work.

In the blink of an eye the dragon was gone, replaced by a virile naked man. Saul stepped toward her slowly. "Chloe, be at ease."

It's true. Oh my god, he's too good to be true because he's not a person. It makes sense. She backed up again and hyperventilated, terrified by the realization of what she had encountered.

"Stay the hell away from me!"

"Chloe, wait--"

She panicked and scrambled away from his outstretched hand. Lacking even a blanket for the sake of modesty, she was forced to escape him naked and exposed. The cold air had never felt more punishing than it did now.

"What have I done to upset you?"

What has he done? How the fuck is he standing there asking what he's done? "You stay back! I mean it!"

"I... do not understand. You pledged yourself to me," he said, maintaining an even tone. His topaz eyes held steady on her face. "You said you were mine."

"That's crazy. That was talk in the moment. It doesn't mean anything."

Saul's eyes darkened, bleeding the bright golden color into a flat brown. "I see." He stepped away from her, all lithe muscle and a magnificent body, flesh brought to life from the sculpted marble of an artist. He didn't wear a stitch, and he didn't need it either. "Have I done something to offend or harm you? Have I not treated you kindly?"

"You're not..." Breath shuddered from her lungs in uneven gasps. "You're not human. You shouldn't even exist." Her heart rate spiked and nausea twisted through her stomach. A dragon. She slept with a fantasy monster and she'd loved every second of it. "This isn't real. You can't be real because dragons don't exist."

25

Tomorrow she would awaken to discover the entire wild night was a dream. A feverish hallucination. It had to be.

Saul smiled sadly from the base of the rocky slope leading up. "I see," he simply repeated. He climbed to the top with ease, displaying fluid grace and natural athleticism that no human could ever mimic.

He disappeared over the top. Seconds later, a large shadow briefly obscured her view of the sky and Saul was gone.

Chapter 4

His strong fingers kneaded her breasts, molding them as an artist did clay. Even with the rough handling, heat pooled in her belly and desire prompted her to arch toward his touch. Firm lips trailed down her throat, accompanied by hot breaths that steamed against her skin. He didn't kiss, but each nibble sparked flames. The eager attentions continued downwards until he reached the curve where her neck and shoulder met. Where he had marked her.

Anticipation curled in her core and created a need so dire that she plunged two fingers between her own thighs. Chloe was soaking wet and desperate for him, filled with a longing so intense she was certain it would consume her. She wanted his bite. Craved it.

"Earth to Chloe. Look, babe, if you can't listen to the things I say to you, why are we even talking?"

The image in her mind shattered, leaving Chloe on the cusp of fulfillment.

Freddy's living room television blinked into her sight, as did the rest of his overpriced condo. She grunted and rubbed her eyes with one hand. "Sorry, Freddy. I'm a little tired. Maybe I should go home since I spaced on you."

"I know how to wake you." He scooted closer to close the gap between them on the couch. His ear nibbles didn't provoke the reaction they once gained.

When she first met Freddy at the gym, he'd seemed like a different guy. He was sweet to her, new in his occupation, and eager to build a clientele base who thrived with his services. She'd hired him, and he whipped her into shape in and out of the bedroom.

Eventually, the starving physical trainer became well known for producing results, and a modest, genuine man with a good heart was replaced by...

What a self-centered, narcissistic asshole.

They broke up, eventually they mended it in the bedroom, and then the pattern became a vicious cycle. Chloe always expected him to get his head out of his ass and to become the sweet man she met a year ago.

"I'm *tired*, Freddy. Not horny."

An exasperated sigh followed his backward lean. "You go away an entire weekend without me, don't even call or return my texts, now you don't want to get physical? What the fuck is wrong with you lately? You love sex."

27

"Look, I just wanted to hang out with you for a while now that I'm back in town. That doesn't mean I came here to get laid," Chloe said evenly.

"Are we together again or not? I thought that's why you came over today."

"We are but-"

"You don't want me to fuck anyone else when we're together, fine. I said I was cool with us being exclusive, but if you're going to keep your legs closed, too, what's the point?"

"Fine," Chloe bit back at him. She wiggled out of her skirt and pulled her sweater over her head. Her leggings and panties joined them on the floor. As she cast aside the last article of clothing, an odd sensation, a feeling of immense and horrible wrongness, swept over her.

As fleeting as a butterflies kiss, the discomfort ended seconds later. The action moved into the bedroom, where Freddy remained oblivious as he lowered to the bed and stroked his erection in one hand. He fondled his lengthy rod of flesh and patiently watched her approach.

She hadn't treated him to the sexy little strip show that he liked, and she sure as fucking hell didn't plan to jump for the chance to fellate him either. Truthfully, Chloe had a fondness for foreplay. She enjoyed giving blowjobs as much as she loved sex, and her past boyfriends had always benefitted greatly from her enjoyment. This was different. This was a point she had to make.

Instead of taking his cues to blow Freddy, she lay beside him on the vacant spot in bed and waited.

"What are you doing?"

"Waiting for you," Chloe said. She rolled her eyes and pulled him on top of her.

Freddy grunted but he didn't argue further. He grabbed her legs and bent her knees toward her chest, angling his dick for her snatch. He missed the first time then sunk home.

"Did you miss me, baby? Huh? I know you must have."

No, I really didn't... Chloe made a noncommittal grunt rather than answer. To shut him up, she grabbed his face and pulled him down for a kiss.

A pain crushed her chest, different from anything she'd never experienced before. Like cold water doused her from head to toe. It made her stop dead and go still, and she remained that way throughout the entire course of his fast pumping. Between his lack of foreplay and her disgust, there was barely enough moisture in her snatch to lubricate his hard and fast thrusts.

Good thing he wasn't a huge man, or it might have hurt even more.

"Do you have to just lie there like that?" Freddy complained. "It's like I'm raping you or something." He paused with his dick buried within her clench, and finally he seemed to realize that she needed more than a few quick thrusts to get into the mood. Too bad it was also too late.

"You wanted it. I told you I didn't. Either shut up and finish or let me go home," Chloe bitched back at him. Freddy pulled out and opted for the second choice.

"Hypocritical whore. Who were you screwing anyway this weekend?"

"Excuse me?"

"Who the fuck bit you like that?"

"You know what, that's none of your business. Especially when you were balls deep in your latest co-ed." She shoved him away and slid out of bed.

"Whatever, babe. You know you'll never find a man who pleases you as much as me and the Beast." He groped himself in a crude gesture, referring to the silly name he reserved for his dick.

The Beast... Saul's warm and easygoing smile drifted through her conscious thought.

"Actually, Freddy, you have a pencil dick and your waxed balls make you look like a child." Releasing those pent up words was cathartic; Chloe had held them in for years. "Get off the 'roids and maybe it'll be useful for something besides taking a piss again."

She dressed and left the condo without looking back.

***

"So, okay, you're over Freddy again? For real this time?" Marcy asked.

"For real. He's such a fucking dick. He seriously tried to go to town on me while I was just laying there. He didn't stop until *he* got freaked out by it."

"He's a creep. He used to be so nice, too. What a shame." Marcy sipped her tropical daiquiri and sighed. "Guess we're both single and free now."

"I guess," Chloe agreed. She sipped her piña colada and wistfully

29

glanced through the window at the busy street. A cute couple passed by hand in hand, gazing at each other with lovestruck eyes as they traveled the sidewalk in the warm spring afternoon.

Their weekend lunch socials became time to unwind from their busy professions and to trade gossip about their failing romantic lives. Marcy's equally stressful job as an accountant offered little downtime during the tax season, but the pair of roommates met every Saturday for time together away from their work loads and clientele.

"A damn shame, the way money and success turns men into absolute assholes," Marcy grumbled. "Paul did that same shit after his promotion, remember?"

"Yeah. You can do better than him," Chloe said. "His mustache made him look like a German porn star anyway."

Marcy's giggles nearly made her choke on the next sip of her tropical daiquiri. "You know how we used to troll the bars together in college and go home with any hot guy we met? God I miss those days. We should do that this weekend."

"Actually, I kind of met a hot guy while on my trip." A hot guy who, according to her memory, was also large enough to fill the cafe. To salvage her sanity, Chloe had convinced herself that it didn't happen and that they'd parted on good terms. He didn't climb out of the cavern and fly away. He didn't transform from a giant… warm-blooded lizard into a man. He was just some handsome stranger who happened to take pity on an injured woman.

He fixed my ankle. I know it was sprained. I should have limped for days. But he… he did something to it. Magic isn't supposed to exist but somehow he touched and healed me.

Marcy's brown eyes widened. "You little slut. Dish!" she ordered Chloe. "Don't skimp on the details either. I need to know dick size and everything."

Chloe choked on her mixed drink. "I twisted my ankle or something, okay? I didn't have service and I was afraid some fucking spelunker would come by and find my cold, rotting corpse. Anyway, he comes by and carries me like a superhero to his camp. Even cooked a deer over the fire."

"You're pulling my leg. He caught a deer and cooked it?"

"Yeah," Chloe answered quietly with a faraway look in her eyes, reminiscing over the quiet dinner with Saul. Now she understood why he took offense to her comments about wasting the dear. He'd eaten it, most likely in his natural dragon form.

"And? Did you get the goods or what? You're way too dreamy-eyed over this guy for nothing to have happened."

"It was really chilly and I wasn't up for moving around yet… so he kept me warm in his sleeping bag. It was amazing. I wouldn't call him hung like a horse but… he had some serious girth," Chloe sighed. "And a body like a Norse god or something."

"So, once he finished 'hammering' you, what then? Did you get his phone number? Did you at least get a photo of him for me? Why aren't you out with him right now on your Saturday?" Marcy demanded.

What am I going to tell her? That he up and flew away? "It was just a fling, Marcy. Passing ships in the night and all that."

The spicy Latina gaped. "Oh come on, Chloe! Not even a picture?"

"Well…"

"Gimme!" Marcy snatched the cellphone from Chloe's grasp and quickly slid her finger through the passcode. She pulled up the photo gallery and the most recent picture expanded onto the screen. Saul smiled uncertainly up at the two women with Chloe at his side. They were practically cheek to cheek, her smooth skin against his bearded jaw.

"Oh my god he's gorgeous! You seriously didn't get his number? Did he come off like a crazy stalker or something after it?"

"Not really…" Saul's crime wasn't that he behaved like a crazy person, but that he wasn't a person at all. She shivered involuntarily and glanced up to see Marcy frowning at her in concern.

"Was he horrible in the sack?" Marcy asked gently.

"It was the best sex I've had in, well, ever. He doesn't really believe in foreplay but… he cuddles really nice after." In hindsight, Saul's behavior made complete sense. He'd mounted her for a rough round of wild, animalistic sex, and now she knew exactly why.

"Did he say he was married?"

"No. He's single. He…"

"He…?" Marcy coached her, urging her to continue. Her friend eagerly sat on the edge of her seat, cupping her frosty drink between both hands.

"Asked me for more and I chased him off like a ditz."

"Wow. So he wanted to what? Get married? Totally creepy."

A quiet shake of Chloe's head answered Marcy's assumption. "The word marriage never left his lips, but… it was just really intense. Let's leave it at that."

"Well, maybe you're better off then. But… damn." She took

31

another lingering stare at the picture on the screen. "What's his name? Please tell me you got that at least."

"Maybe… His name's Saul. Which makes him the first Saul I've ever met. I guess it's a really old-fashioned name." Chloe sighed heavily and dropped her shoulders. "Look, we're supposed to be having a good girl time, not chatting over my latest relationship blunder."

"Fine, though I wouldn't mind the details on this one."

"Really?"

"You met a Viking god in the mountains and you've barely said a thing about him." Marcy fanned herself.

"He's sweet. And… like I said, intense. And I think he's too good to really exist. This is the first time I even looked at the selfie we took because I convinced myself he *wasn't* real."

"So maybe you need to seek him out. Here, share this big ass muffin with me, and then we can go sweat it off together in the park. The weather's perfect for a jog."

"Fine. To the muffin, I mean."

Marcy slid a plastic knife through the rich chocolate muffin and passed half of the fudge delicacy to her friend. They wolfed down their treats and sipped up the rest of their tea in silence.

Later, she and Marcy hit the jogging trail to enjoy the spring breeze and radiant sun, but no amount of running cleared the memory of Saul from Chloe's thoughts.

Chapter 5

Chloe hated to write co-parenting plans and put them into black and white, but it was a grave necessity of the job. More often than not, some jerk ignored the stipulations in the legal document anyway and decided the effort to visit his children took too much time. Or a mother hoping to punish her ex refused to allow a good father his visitation privileges.

Then the slighted member of the pair ended up right back in the law offices of Cooper and Associates to hash it out and demand his or her ex to be taken to court. It was tedious, and it broke her heart because the kids were the ones who suffered. Her mother, may she rest in peace, had been one of those women.

"Hey gorgeous." The smooth voice reached her from the doorway of her direct supervisor's office. She had a desk right beside it that allowed him to bellow orders on a whim.

Ugh. Not now. I don't need this today.

Chloe smiled through her teeth and put on a friendly countenance. "I placed the Benson account's portfolio on your desk, Mr. James."

In the year since their cataclysmic split, Malcolm and Chloe had transitioned back to formal titles. Recently, however, the man up top had transferred her up to the family law level and placed her directly under Malcolm as his assistant.

Mr. Cooper claimed it was a promotion. He'd given her a generous raise to accompany his supposed good news.

Chloe considered it living hell.

"Mister? Really, Chloe? C'mon, you don't have to be like that when we're alone. And I didn't come over about the Benson file. The father has the money, he's getting the kids."

The father is an adulterous creep who just wants to stuff it to his ex-wife.

It was another example of what she hated about her job.

"I noticed. If Mr. Benson didn't delete those photos from his wife's phone, she'd have him on those adultery claims," Chloe said dryly. "You know, and half of his money." The sly little barb appeared to fly over Malcolm's head, or he merely chose to ignore it.

The smartly dressed lawyer rounded the desk and Chloe resisted the urge to retreat. She refused to let him run her out of her own office. Wearing his most charming smile, Malcolm leaned up against her desk and raked his eyes over her. It used to make her tingle with goosebumps and feel desirable, but now it only churned her stomach with disgust.

"You're looking good, Chloe. Working out again?"

"Here and there," she replied tersely. "What may I do for you, Mr. James," she tried again, repeating her earlier words. The smile felt frozen on her face. Plastic.

"Where'd you go on your vacation a couple weeks back? You have a tan." He grinned at her and his attractive, closely trimmed black goatee only made his bright smile even sexier.

"Hiking in the Appalachians."

"With your new man?"

Freddy wasn't exactly new, and Malcolm had fired him swiftly once he discovered the two of them were an item.

Against her better judgment, she decided to answer him truthfully. "No. We broke up for good this time. He's a creep."

"Can't say I'm sorry to hear that." Malcolm placed his hand on her knee and skimmed his fingers beneath the hemline of her skirt. His fingers, brown as rich dark chocolate, contrasted against her fairer skin. Once upon a time, Chloe had been fascinated by their paradoxical complexions. Still was. It was just a shame that a cheating bastard was always a bastard, and he wasn't bound to ever change.

"You have five seconds to remove your hand before I sharpen my pencil in your eye socket."

"You're cute when you try to talk big. Always were." He slipped his touch up another half inch. "I've been thinking about you, you know."

I know what you've been thinking about, you slimy bastard.

She rose swiftly from the seat to escape him.

"I know how to file a sexual harassment claim. Do not fuck with me, Malcolm. You ended whatever we had when you decided to bounce up and down on a tramp in our home while I was away taking care of Daddy. You did that. Why come to me now? Your current post-divorce lay not floating your boat anymore?"

"Fuck you, you ungrateful bitch. I got you this job. You'd still be in the records room without me."

"No. Fuck you," she raged. "Fuck you and fuck whatever you did to get Mr. Cooper to reassign me to your floor."

"Chlo--"

"No! You do not get to come in here and touch me at your liberty like I'm whatever two-cent whore you slept around with last."

She stormed to the door and threw it open wide. The wood smacked against the outside wall. "Out. Now."

"I'm your supervisor. You don't get to kick me out."

Chloe swiftly lost her temper. "Get out!" she yelled. Every eye in the outer lobby turned their way.

"Keep your voice down," Malcolm hissed. He crossed the room and grabbed Chloe around her bicep. She jerked away and backed into the main room.

"What is going on out here?" The loud voice belonged to a rotund man with spectacles perched on his broad nose. Despite his age he sported a full head of silver hair. Jokes around the office claimed his numerous marriages and divorces were at fault for the premature graying. "Mr. James? Miss Ellis? Do we have a problem?"

"No, Mr. Cooper," Malcolm swiftly interjected. "Sorry for disturbing you."

"Miss Ellis? Is this true?"

"No. It's not."

"Chloe," Malcolm warned.

Mr. Cooper frowned. "Come to my office, the both of you."

"Please, Mr. Cooper, it's nothing to worr-"

"He fucking slid his hand up my thigh," Chloe seethed. At this point she didn't care if the whole practice heard it. "And no, I didn't invite him. He invited himself into *my* office and decided to make an inappropriate, unwanted advance." She didn't budge a step and turned her head to glare daggers at Malcolm. She dared him to lie.

"Let's take this into my office."

Half a dozen people watched the show in enraptured silence. It was as if a soap opera had left the screen and entered their office. For a moment, Chloe resented each and every one of them. Then again, they hadn't placed her in the awkward situation. One man, and one man only, was to blame for the showdown occurring in full view of all the staff.

Mr. Cooper held up both hands in a plea for silence and calm. "I am certain it was a misunderstanding," Mr. Cooper began. "You two were in a relationship at one point, were you not?"

"Once," Chloe gritted out. She resisted the man's efforts to sweep Malcolm's poor behavior out of view. "Are you trying to claim that he's entitled to touch me whenever he wants because we were once in a relationship? Because if you are, I should remind you that unwanted sexual advances may incur punitive damages in a court of law."

"Wait, wait a minute. I never said anything of the sort, Miss Ellis."

35

"You began to imply it, Mr. Cooper. I expected better of you. There's no way that you didn't know what he does in this office, and that makes you as guilty as him."

Chloe turned her back on the two men and stormed away. She returned through the doorway into her small, cramped office, and she picked up the African Violet on the corner of the desk. She grabbed her favorite wireless mouse and dropped it into the purse she claimed from the desk drawer. She packed her belongings in under thirty seconds flat and stormed to the elevator.

"I'm going to miss you, Chloe," the quiet receptionist said to her in passing. "Don't be a stranger."

"I wouldn't dream of it, Mrs. Dennis. I'll take a call from you anytime."

Later that night, Chloe sent an anonymous message to Mrs. Benson from a new email account.

'Contact your phone service provider and tell them you need to learn how to access the Cloud. You'll find what you need there.'

For the first night in a long while, she fell asleep without the weight of her job on her shoulders. Unemployed life had never felt so good.

Chapter 6

"So word around the coffee shop near Cooper and Associates is that Malcolm's looking for a new job." Marcy set down two steaming to-go cups.

"That was almost a week ago. They're only just now sacking his dumb ass?"

"Apparently some secretary came forward and said he sexually harassed her, too. Your tantrum was inspiring."

Mrs. Dennis… I never would have guessed it, Chloe thought. She shook her head and smiled in spite of the situation. "Good. That brings me a little comfort while I update my resume and search for new work."

Chloe raked her fingers through her pale blonde hair and sighed. The words on the laptop screen blurred and jumbled together into a mess of professional text listing her skills and accomplishments. She was sick of looking at it, and even more sick of phoning her contacts in search of a job opening.

"You okay, hun? You look tired."

"Hmm? Oh, I slept like crap. Dreams I guess…" Sexy, erotic dreams often awakened her in the middle of the night and left her in desperate need for her vibrator. As many times as she'd used it the past three weeks Chloe feared she was going to burn the motor out. *And I still feel achy afterward…*

"Bad dreams?" Marcy asked sympathetically. She nodded her head and smiled. "How's your dad doing?"

"Pretty good. I thought I'd have to fly out to take care of him after this recent surgery, but he has a new girlfriend. She sounded really nice on the phone," Chloe mused softly. While it had surprised and disappointed her to learn her father wouldn't need her assistance, deep down she was glad to know he wasn't alone anymore.

"Speaking of significant others, given any more thought to your mystery sex god?" Marcy waggled her brows. "

"I doubt he even remembers me. Guys that hot diddle a dozen girls a week."

"Oh please. You're a fox, Chloe. If he forgets you he's an idiot."

"You've got me beat. You're like a Latin sex goddess. Maybe you should find him for yourself," Chloe joked awkwardly in a futile attempt to change the subject. She had to play it safe. Marcy would never believe her super Prince Charming had turned into a fire-breathing beast. She didn't know if she believed it herself.

"C'mon, tell me what you remember. We'll try and look him up."

"I dunno. He said he worked at Drakenstone Studios." *Drakenstone… Drake. Dragon. Fuck. How didn't I notice that before?*

"What did you say his name was again?

"Saul."

"And does this Saul have a last name?"

Chloe shook her head. "I never asked for details."

"Hold up, check this out. According to the studio website the CEO is listed as a Saul Drakenstone. No picture though." Marcy maximized the profile on the screen and read the vague details out loud. Saul Drakenstone, age 34, inheritor of the Drakenstone legacy at the age of 29.

"You found some sort of elusive billionaire, girl. Congrats."

"I can't believe it," Chloe breathed.

"Sweetie, unless he lied about his name and stuff, this means you slept with a bigtime exec."

"He never… why wouldn't he tell me that?"

"Don't gold diggers chase after men like him all the time?" Marcy pointed out gently. She resumed her internet search in vain. Despite all of the best tricks, Marcy's work yielded no fruit since it appeared Saul lacked a Facebook page, Instagram, and all other forms of social media. No other record of him existed on the virtual world. He was a ghost who had never attended the premieres for his company's produced movies over the past five years since taking over for his grandfather.

Is that a ruse to conceal that he's an unaging immortal creature or something? Chloe wondered. She shook off the strange feeling and put on a humorous tone to playfully feign taking offense to Marcy's words. "Hey, I had no idea who he was and he's the one who wanted more from me."

"Maybe he wanted to hire you on as his professional girlfriend," Marcy teased.

Chloe chucked a pillow at her friend. The small square bounced off Marcy's head. "What should I do?"

"Um, duh. You should fly out there and see him, that's what."

"I don't know, girl…" *If I told you that I dream about him nightly, you'd think I was insane.*

"Oh come on. You quit your job so you have the time."

"I don't have money to toss around on futile flights across the country. What if he doesn't remember me? He's so hot he probably sleeps with anonymous women all the time."

"While camping in a cold, dank cave with them in the middle of nowhere? After he's hunted and killed a fucking deer with his manly bare hands for them?" Marcy dropped her brow into one palm and released a sigh so loud and exaggerated that Chloe immediately felt silly.

"You're right. Fine. Fine. I'll do it."

Marcy squealed and worked her magic on the computer. In a few short minutes she had a flight itinerary selection pulled up.

"No, no, no. I can't fly out tomorrow, Marcy, the prices are outrageous."

"I owe you money for that dress you helped me buy to impress Jeremy Peterson."

"Marceline Vargas, that was in high school! I'm not letting you buy this."

Marcy grinned smugly. "So what? I think with all the years of interest this about covers it."

"But what do I do when I get there? I'm pretty sure I can't just waltz in and ask to see the CEO."

"Why not? It'll be like a movie," Marcy assured her.

"That ends with me being led away by security."

Or in the belly of a beast.

***

"You don't understand. I'm here to see Saul Drakenstone. He knows me. We met a month ago on a... wilderness hike," Chloe blurted out to the stone-faced secretary at the front desk.

Every architectural structure in the lobby had been crafted from granite, glass, and stainless steel. The modern look clashed with her memories of Saul. It came across as cold, a stark contrast to his warm personality. The secretary fit right in with the harsh decor.

Contrary to Marcy's big plan, an unannounced arrival was not to Chloe's benefit. The receptionist at the front desk tapped a button and bellowed, "Security. Please see this young woman outside."

A portly man in a grey and black security uniform approached. The only person standing between Chloe and the a reunion with the draconic enigma of her literal dreams was a flashlight cop with a shiny badge, nightstick, and pair of designer knockoff aviator shades that he probably picked off a mall kiosk's shelf for fifteen bucks.

Chloe whirled to face the desk again and desperately blurted out, "Look, if you don't believe me, beep your boss on the intercom and tell him Chloe is here. Tell him Chloe is sorry and needs to speak to him."

"You'll have to leave the premises now, ma'am," the officer told her.

"No! I came a long way to be here and to see Saul. You'll have to drag me out."

Apparently, she had foolishly allowed Officer Chunk's girth to cloud her judgment. While his proportions were indeed sizable, they were to his advantage and only concealed the stout muscle beneath. He flexed one arm around Chloe's midsection and hoisted her up off of the floor with the sort of effortless grace that belonged on a cheer squad. She struggled and kicked her feet, too headstrong to surrender to the futility.

"Please! Just call him! Tell him Chloe's here!"

The security guard dropped her outside on the granite steps. Frazzled, Chloe raked both hands through her hair and screamed in frustration.

I knew it. I told Marcy it was too late. All this way for nothing.

Next to chasing away Saul, taking her friend's spur of the moment advice had to be one of the most foolish decisions in her life. With little else to do, she sat on the top step of the lavish building and wept into her hands.

Chloe had never been the sort for spontaneous crying, but the rush of building emotion welled within her to such a point that it hurt. It had to come out. It exploded in tears and shoulder-shaking sobs that earned the occasional glance from passers-by.

She didn't care.

Stupid, dumb, desperate thing to do for a man I only met once. A man who isn't even a man. Maybe it's for the best. Maybe I had the right idea the first time, Chloe convinced herself. Once she inhaled a few shaky breaths, she straightened and fumbled with the snap on her purse to find a tissue.

Everything about her carefully laid plan was falling apart. She'd planned every step, starting with her cute and sexy outfit. The skinny jeans and white v-neck top seemed plain at first glance, but paired with knee-high black stiletto boots and a push-up bra she had sexified the look up a notch. The two hours spent in Marcy's favorite salon getting her body waxed and buffed to a perfect, silky glow - completely wasted.

She'd never waxed for any man in all of her life.

A handkerchief suddenly hovered near her face, scaring the crap out of her with its abrupt appearance in the corner of her vision. Chloe jerked her head up and gazed into the patient features of a tidily dressed man in a traditional chauffeur's ensemble. A hint of dark, closely buzzed hair peeked out from beneath the cap.

"Good evening, Miss. I am told there is one Chloe Ellis awaiting transport from Drakenstone Studios. She would be you, I presume."

"Who's asking?" Chloe demanded. She ignored the offered cloth and hastily dried her face with the heel of her palm.

"I am Mr. Drakenstone's driver, Leiv. I am sent to retrieve you."

He has a driver? Of course he has a driver. He owns a multi-million dollar company. "I don't understand."

He extended one gloved hand to help her up from the cold steps and gestured toward the parked vehicle alongside the street. The sleek black vehicle gleamed in the sunlight, either meticulously maintained or fresh from the detail shop. Probably both. "I will take you. Come, come, Miss Ellis. Champagne?"

"Um…" *Yes, say yes!* "No, thank you."

The white leather seats were as soft as butter. Chloe sank against the plush interior and wondered if everything recent in her life was a crazy dream. *Maybe I smacked my head in that cave and I've been dreaming everything since then. Maybe I'm dead and no one will ever find my body. This is my own special little waystation between Earth and Hell, maybe even Heaven…*

The city passed by outside the windows, viewed through sheer curtains. Chloe leaned back and closed her eyes trying to imagine her reunion with Saul. A musky scent reminiscent of sandalwood and amber wafted from the vents. *Like Saul's skin,* she thought, drifting into a doze.

"Miss Ellis, we have arrived."

The driver's voice startled her from sleep. Over two hours had passed since her departure from the steps of Drakenstone Studios. Leiv, the handsome and rather stocky driver, smiled kindly at her and held the door open with his hand offered out to assist her from the vehicle. Chloe's mouth fell open in awe as she stepped from the Maybach 62. The chauffeur shut the door behind her, bowed, and gestured to the front door.

Holy shit. He's really, really rich.

"Please make yourself comfortable, Miss Ellis."

"Thank you. Leiv, right?" She couldn't identify his accent, but he definitely didn't have American origins either. It was Slavic most likely, or maybe even Russian.

"Yes, Miss." He bowed again and returned to the driver's seat.

It was the kind of home that belonged in a magazine, or on

MTV's Cribs. Once again, she felt compelled to pinch herself because nothing about her current situation could be within the realm of possibility.

The home was built into a rocky cliff face, but not cute and quaint like a hobbit hole. Two stories of glass windows and stone wall dominated the impressive landscape. To her left, green fields stretched out towards a thick treeline. Goats munched on the lush grass behind an immense fence.

Chloe pinched her arm several times along the walk to the door.

She expected a maid, or some form of servant to answer the door. She found it unlocked - who in their right mind would rob a dragon who lived in the middle of nowhere? She laughed hysterically for a moment.

This is ridiculous. Go in, talk to him. Apologize. Tell him that you can't get him out of your fucking mind.

A flurry of concerns and niggling worries harassed her to linger. What if he didn't forgive her? What if he decided she'd taste better with ketchup now that she'd refused his advances once and spurned his affection?

Courage guided her hand to the knob again. She pushed and stepped inside.

"Hello?" Chloe nervously called. Her voice echoed across the foyer, which seemed to stretch infinitely. Her heels clicked against the marble floor. "Is anybody home?"

Saul appeared at the top of a curved staircase. It came around again in a horseshoe, but it had a landing at the top that split toward an east and west wing. He didn't approach or descend the stairs to greet her.

"Chloe."

He was exactly as she remembered, naked chest and all. His jeans hung low at his hips and his feet were bare.

"Hi, Saul… Surprise." Her stiff smile died as quickly as it appeared. Saul didn't appear pleased or welcoming of her presence.

"Why have you sought me?" He maintained the distance. The realization of it struck Chloe like a knife in the heart.

"I missed you," she truthfully replied. She straightened and proudly raised her chin, unashamed of admitting her feelings. "And you stay on my mind. I can't get you out of my head. I can't stop thinking about you, dammit. I don't even know anything about you but your name!"

"And that I am a monster."

Still, he didn't approach, so Chloe did it for him. She crossed the room, aware of how much harder her heart pounded with every step. Something about his expression and the misery in his brown eyes made him seem too vulnerable, a shadow of his former, confident self.

God, she wanted to hear him laugh again.

The man rewarded her ascent up the steps by backing away when she reached out to touch his cheek. His nostrils flared and his eyes widened, distrust evident in his features. He distanced from her again, a cornered animal backing away from a predator. At any moment, he could lash out at her to escape.

"Why seek a creature you loathe?" he asked. "Why have you come here?"

"I don't loathe you. I was frightened, yes. Can you blame me? I mean... I woke up and you were.... you were..."

"A dragon," Saul answered quietly.

"Yes." It still boggled her mind. "It's not something people expect. Ever. I spent the days after our meeting wondering if I imagined you. I had your photograph on my phone, but I just... I couldn't bear to look at it and prove you were real."

"Why? Why now?" He swept her hand aside gently when she reached for him but he didn't backpedal completely.

Chloe's heart rate thrummed as fast as a hummingbird's wings. She swallowed a few times and wet her dry lips uselessly with her tongue. Her entire mouth felt like the Sahara. "Because I want to get to know you," she said. "Because in those short hours together, we were more real than any relationship I've had in years. Because I hurt you and I'm *sorry*. There are worse things a man can do than..." *Turn out to be a mythological creature.* "Forgive me."

Saul studied her in silence, revealing no change in emotion. "I wronged you as well. I knew the consequences of laying claim to you."

"Fuck the consequences. If you can forgive me, I can forgive you."

"Can you?" he questioned softly.

"Why shouldn't I?"

He didn't answer. A minute change in his facial expression gave her reason to wait, allowing Saul the time to think over his response. "Are you not troubled by our bond?"

"No. I already told you, Saul. There are worse things you could have done than want... me to be yours. I want to be yours. I want to see where this goes. Let's start over," she told him.

This time, when Chloe bridged their gap, her palm raised to his

43

scruffy cheek. He had the perfect amount of facial hair, and it was as soft under her touch now as it had been in the cave. He leaned against her hand, closed his eyes, and breathed her in with a heavy breath.

"I missed you. No day passed without you touching my thoughts. I believed... I was certain I had lost you. That my true appearance frightened you away."

"You are scary but... you're also a very handsome dragon," Chloe shyly offered.

He didn't respond, but his close presence made it difficult to breathe, like a band had compressed her lungs. She ended up taking quicker, smaller breaths instead. Those treated her to the rich, smoky scent clinging to his skin.

"I'm sorry, Saul. I'm sorry that I hurt you. Please talk to me."

"I dream of you," he replied gruffly. "It is... maddening."

"You're in my head at the worst times. I had a breakdown at work and quit my job. Every man I meet is such an asshole compared to you. I always knew they were jerks but... something about you made me realize I deserve more. You showed me kindness. You were good to me." And she'd thrown it in his face. Chloe turned her face against his throat and nuzzled him appreciatively. He felt so warm. Her own personal radiator.

"What do you want from this, Chloe? I am not human. No matter how I appear before you now, I can never become a true human."

Despite his warning, Chloe knew that if she walked away, she'd regret it for the rest of her life. "I don't care. I want you to do this to me again." She leaned back and tugged aside her top's neckline, revealing the faded bite. He'd bruised her without drawing blood and somehow, over the course of the month it hadn't quite healed completely. It remained a faded hint of yellow and green long after it should have diminished.

"You do not ask for a simple thing, Chloe." Saul's eyes flared briefly, a touch of the golden color returning.

"I don't know what it means, but you can tell me later. All I know is that I want you to trust me again. You trusted me with this secret. Trust me one more time. Please."

No more words passed between them. Saul lifted her into his arms, exactly as he had several weeks ago in the cave. His long strides took them by several lavish rooms but she paid them little attention. All her focus was where it belonged - on him.

Moonlight spilled in through a large skylight, painting the room in silver hues. As the central ornament of the expansive room, a large platform bed dominated the space with a bevy of cushions and satin-covered pillows.

Saul introduced her to the bed by tossing her on it. "Remove everything," he ordered her promptly. His hands tugged at her clothes, as if too incompetent with a human woman's garments to remove them properly. Her panties became the first casualty of their encounter, ripped by his enthusiastic hands and tossed aside. She hastily unfastened her bra to save the expensive underwire from suffering the same fate.

Apparently dragons went barefoot and commando at all times. For Saul, undressing was as simple as dropping his jeans and kicking them aside. The carved V formed by his hip muscles was a thing of absolute beauty. Bodybuilders strived to attain a figure like him.

Chloe eased a hand between her thighs. The very sight of Saul made her pussy throb. He filled her with unbearable tension and yearning to be claimed.

"God, you're so big," she breathed out.

He stood above her, his hard cock in one hand. It had been stiff and fully erect long before he shed his pants. Providing no further warning, he took Chloe by the hips to turn her on her hands and knees.

"No!" she gasped, pushing at him with her fingers. She resisted his efforts to flop her onto her belly again.

Saul froze in place, bent above her with his fingers curved over her supple skin. He released her at once and stepped back from the bed. "Have I misunderstood? You said you wished me to claim you again, Chloe."

"I do, Saul, I do. More than anything. But I want to look at you."

His bewilderment remained. "You do not like—?"

"No, baby, I loved it. But I want to look into your eyes when you take me. I want to make love looking at your face." She cupped his cheek with her palm. "Have you never had sex that way?"

His silence provided all the answer she needed. Of course not. He did what came naturally. Their sex had been primal, filled with his dominance and her willing submission. It never even occurred to him to make love to her face to face.

"Let me please you," she whispered. "I want to show you how much I care."

Wariness flickered across his stony features but Saul didn't oppose her. He remained perfectly still as Chloe slid her palms down his body, exploring the contoured planes of his shoulders and the

45

corded muscles of his arms. Everything about him radiated strength.

"Lie down for me," she requested breathlessly. Saul complied without hesitation and drew her down with him to the silk sheets. Chloe smiled and disentangled herself from his arms, rising up to lean over him.

"You're magnificent." Chloe placed tender kisses against his chest, working her way down. His erection stood tall, but when she reached it, she knew without a doubt that she'd never fit the entire thing in her mouth. She took ahold of him at the base of his cock instead and treated him to a tantalizing lick. Once he was driven to groaning out in pleasure, she teased the silken crown with tongue flicks against the tiny slit. Saul's groan was the best reward.

She wanted to give him a new experience. No. She *needed* to give it to him. Had to make amends for the hurt she'd caused him.

"Chloe," he growled. Saul's fingers fisted in the ruby sheets.

Encouraged, she flattened her tongue against the veiny underside of his erection and delivered a second slow pass. Her lips closed around the smooth pink head, taking him into her mouth. Saul's groan urged her to try and bring him in deeper.

"You are an enchantress, Chloe. A succubus or a siren."

I can live with that, she thought. She swirled her tongue around his corona, enjoying him as much as an ice cream cone. The way his body trembled, completely at her mercy, turned her on and filled her with confidence.

My dragon, she thought. *My Saul.*

She wanted to lay her claim as thoroughly as he had on her.

Her mouth came off of him with a wet pop but her hands never ceased their rhythmic pumps. Chloe ducked her head down further and gifted his baby-soft balls the same treatment, licking and suckling the sensitive bits of Saul's anatomy.

His pulse became a pounding presence beneath her hand.

"You're mine," she whispered. Then she dove forward again and plunged him into her mouth. She forced her lips to uncomfortably stretch, using them to shield his sensitive skin from the edge of her teeth. What little of him she could take in, she fucked hard and fast while using her hands in alternating strokes.

She reduced her strong, proud dragon to incoherent moans.

Just in time, Chloe placed her lips against his tender crown to catch the first burst of his seed. The sticky mouthful slid over her tongue, a perfect balanced blend of smoke and sweet. Like everything else about him, it was unique.

Dragon come. I've tasted dragon come, she thought. The ridiculous idea surfaced in her mind and sent her into a fit of uncontrollable giggles.

Saul had become so still, and so very quiet, that for a moment she feared she'd killed him. His sudden breath and strained query assured her that wasn't the case. "What amuses you so deeply?"

"Your taste," Chloe replied. Her fingertips skimmed his flat abdomen and the fair treasure trail leading to his cock.

"It is to your liking?"

"Well… yeah. You taste much better than any human man, that's for sure." And she couldn't be the only woman to taste him and determine that he was absolutely divine in every way. Unless… The answer struck her with crystal clarity. "Has no one ever given you a blowjob?" she asked incredulously.

Saul laughed weakly and declined to answer. She had grown accustomed to it, gradually coming to understand that he chose silence over revealing his embarrassments. He was a proud man. A noble dragon she longed to satisfy.

That's it. He's a blowjob virgin, she determined. "Did you… even know what blowjobs are?" Saul wasn't a small man by any means, and the term 'baby's arm holding an apple' seemed to have been created specifically with him in mind. Understandably, some women had to be put off by his impressive girth.

"I am familiar with the term," Saul answered dryly.

Chloe giggled even more at his tone. "So was that your first?"

"Yes." He shook his head. "I am familiar with the *term* fellatio, however, I find the alternate choice of name to be ridiculous. There was no blowing involved."

"You're a little too big for a proper one." She peeked down at his half-hard cock. Heat rose in the apples of her cheeks and pinkened her skin in a flush. "Improvising was necessary."

"You appeared to have no issues. I…" He paused and drew in a deep breath, moving a hand from the bed to smooth her hair from her face. "I did not know such a thing was so enjoyable. But you pleased only me, not yourself."

She kissed her way back up his body, taking her sweet time. This was her chance to become fully acquainted with him, an opportunity lost to her during their single night alone in the cavern. Shamelessly, she delivered a nibble at his hip followed by a dip of her tongue around his navel. As he responded favorably to her teases, she crawled along his body to skate her teeth over each of his flat nipples. By the time she reached his neck and straddled him, her lover's cock throbbed anew.

"This is not how it is done." Saul's hand settled against her waist.

"Maybe not for dragons but I promise you, humans find this quite enjoyable. You will too."

Chloe controlled her descent over his rock hard arousal. Or so she thought. With one hand on his chest for her balance, and the other gripping his cock, she dragged the smooth tip over her dewy pussy lips. Last night's waxing hadn't hurt as much as expected, and had been worth every penny.

Thanks to Marcy's impromptu kidnapping shortly after confirming her flight to California, Chloe had been subjected to female, ritualistic tortures. A professional with a soft voice and gentle hands had shaped the blonde curls at the apex of Chloe's thighs into a perfect, narrow and closely trimmed runway strip. Her bald snatch was sensitive to the slightest touch.

Dragging his dick over her slick folds eventually introduced him to her clit. As she groaned, Chloe positioned his tip against the hot entrance to her pussy. Saul promptly thrust his hips upwards and pulled her down, impaling her upon his erection. Her dreams over the past few weeks barely compared to the reality.

"Now who's being a naughty dragon?" she chastised, smiling down at him.

Saul groaned something unintelligible at first. It sounded like another language. "Naughty?" he echoed up to her. His bright eyes shined in the dimly lit room. Adjacent to the bed, a small nightstand held a single glass lamp with elaborately painted panels. Its soft glow cast warm light over his features.

God, he's glorious. From his smile to the shy way he caressed her hips and thighs, Chloe found every facet of the man beneath her indescribably attractive. His innocence to human sexuality made her question his origins and the life he had lived until now.

"Here…" She drew his hands up to her breasts, rolling her hips in slow and sinuous movements. "I love feeling my breasts in your hands."

"Perfect as plums," he murmured, squeezing. "I prefer them to the bouncing monstrosities decadently displayed in my studio."

The visual his words produced made Chloe giggle. She lifted from his body and nearly lost him from her tight grasp. Sinking down again resulted in the sweet harmony of their mutual groans.

"I want them in your mouth, Saul."

Saul sat up in one smooth motion. Her pink nipples budded tightly beneath his attentive fingers, but she craved the heat of his mouth.

"That would please you?"

"Yes," she breathed. "That would please me very much."

Her body clenched around him, stimulated by the playful nip and suckle of his lips to her sensitive flesh. His mouth drew away from her nipple with a pop and the hands squeezing her ass grinded her down harder atop his cock.

"It pleases me too," Saul decided. He tested his theory with the other breast, and seemed to delight when the taut muscle surrounding his cock responded in turn, delivering a delicious contraction around his swollen arousal. He alternated longer strokes with shallow grinds, plunging in and out of her with force one moment and tenderly churning within her the next.

The only constant, was that everything made her coo and moan just the same. Nothing that Saul did could displease her, especially when his lips tended to wrap around her nipple and dedicate sweet attention. Her breasts definitely pleased him.

"Are humans always this slow?" he murmured against her tit. His tongue flicked out and dragged over the taut peak at the tip. She shuddered.

"Sometimes. Do you want faster? I... I can do faster."

"I want whatever will please us both. I want to hear your cries again, Chloe. I wish to fill you with my seed and make you my own. Slow or fast makes no difference."

She trembled. The tempo of her hips quickened to match the racing pulse his words inspired, guided by the strong hand on her ass. Saul kept her close, ensuring their bodies remained joined.

"You are mine now, Chloe. No more running away." He grabbed a fistful of her hair and drew her head back to expose her throat. His nose skimmed her neck, sliding down the slender column and inhaling her scent. Every tickle of his warm breath tensed her belly. "Tell me you wish it. Tell me you accept it."

"I'm yours, Saul. I was from the start."

Pain radiated outward from her shoulder beneath his bite, overshadowed by the ecstasy that followed. Chloe lost all control. Her body was aflame; every nerve exploded with heat. She grinded her pelvis to his with anxious need and dug her nails into his muscled back. In this position, her clit received an abundance of stimulation.

Euphoric cries escaped them in unison, her name growled from his lips, and his name cried from hers. He slipped in and out, slapping their bodies together all the while, clapping skin to wet skin as she came and he spurted a messy release. His semen filled her insides with molten warmth that seemed to initiate another series of contractions.

Saul held her. If he hadn't, she might have collapsed. She was there, and she wasn't, swept away in a tidal wave of emotions and unrivaled pleasure. Physical bliss rocketed through her core in orgasmic spasms that reduced her to jelly in his arms.

No human man had ever reduced her to such a quivering state of ecstasy.

Chloe opened her eyes and realized the moon had changed position in the sky again. It was no longer directly above the glass panel over their head. Time had passed, but Saul lacked a clock of any kind to determine how much.

"Saul?" she rasped out. She needed a glass of water. Maybe a gallon.

He dragged his fingers down her back. "Hm?"

"Was I asleep?"

"For a time."

Oh my god I passed out on him. The sex was that *good this time, too.* "I'm sorry."

"You have done nothing for which to apologize."

"You kept your human form this time…"

Saul chuckled. "I would break this bed otherwise."

Chloe's laugh turned into a dry cough. Saul shifted away then returned before she could voice a complaint. "Drink," Saul coaxed her. He half cradled Chloe against his chest. A tall glass of water waited on the bedside table beside the small lamp. Once he offered it, she guzzled it down quickly.

"Thanks, I needed that."

"Rest, Chloe. The hour is late and you are deserving of pleasant dreams. Sleep."

"No. I want to know about you… I want to know about dragons. Why this bite mark on my shoulder doesn't hurt like… why doesn't it hurt me?" Chloe curiously raised her fingers to the discoloration left by his teeth. Why hadn't it broken the skin? "I need to know so many things about you, Saul. Don't rush me to sleep," she pleaded gently.

Cold fear seized her. What if everything was a dream after all and she awakened to her boring, dull bed to discover nothing had changed? The sobering possibility shook the drowsiness from her voice.

"Very well. What do you wish to know first?"

"Talk to me more. Anything." She paused and pressed lightly against the palm-sized smudge of color on her shoulder. No pain. "Maybe begin with this."

Saul's warm laughter turned her into jelly. "That is the Dragon's Brand, a mark of promise betrothing one dragon to another."

"So... if I wasn't human, I'd bite you back?"

A quiet nod provided her answer.

"How many humans have you claimed this way?"

A quiet sense of bashfulness surrounded him. His eyes cut away briefly, but they returned with his softly spoken answer. "Only you. I do not know why, but the compulsion overwhelmed me during our mating... You are the first human to ever bring me release at the end."

Renewed heat pooled at her core, initiated by his admission. No human woman had ever made him come. He'd never reached orgasm with a human until meeting her. It was an honor, a gift, and she would strive to make it happen again and again if she could.

"No other woman?" she echoed.

"I have lived in this world for many years. Sometimes I slumber, passing in and out of sleep from one generation to the next," he confessed to her as they lay sprawled together in the massive bed. It was comparable to a cloud. "But no woman has ever captivated my heart or lured me as you did in the cave. I awakened two weeks prior to our meeting, after a half-decade's rest."

Every answer spawned at least two more questions in her mind. Why had he been in a cave in the first place? "Why do you sleep so long?" she asked curiously, limiting her inquiries for the moment.

"The oldest among us have traveled this world for centuries. Were we to live each day, life would become monotonous. Dull." He ran his fingers through her hair and toyed with the sleek ends. "I know what you wish to ask. I have lived four and fifty-two years."

Four and fifty-two... He can't mean that he's four hundred *and fifty-two, could he?* Her startled gasp drew tension between them. Saul stilled again, a telling sign of what he expected from her: horror, fear, and maybe even a change of her mind.

Chloe chose her next words very carefully. "Since you must have a vivid recollection of colonial times... we will watch The Crucible one day, and you can tell me how accurate it depicts their way of life."

"A decent movie. As far as accuracy, they took many liberties."

Chloe idly stroked her foot along his calf and snuggled her face between his throat and shoulder. She breathed in the musky scent that reminded her of his dragon body. Earthy with a woodsy aroma that reminded her of the forest after a rainstorm. She shivered.

"Are you cold?"

"No." She exhaled and trailed her fingers over his chest. It wasn't as smooth as she previously believed, but the fine scattering of golden blond hairs were so fair and silky they were almost impossible to see. "Can I ask another question?"

"You may ask anything. I keep no secrets from you."

"Why do your wings have feathers? Aren't dragons supposed to be all jewel-colored scales and stuff?"

Saul snorted. "*All* true dragons are adorned with feathers. Of the scalewings, there are two breeds: our distant but inferior cousins, the wyverns, and the great wyrms who are our nemeses. Your mortal legends carry many inaccuracies."

She yawned into her hand. "Mm… tell me about them."

"Tomorrow. For now, you must sleep," Saul encouraged her.

He kissed her brow, tentatively brushing his lips against her skin as if the act were foreign to him. She'd noticed that in all of their time together, Saul had never kissed her once.

"But I'm not tired," Chloe protested. She struggled to resist the heavy, exhaustive weight anchoring her limbs to the mattress. Between his fingers sliding through her fair hair and the jet lag catching up to her, she didn't have a chance.

Chapter 7

"Saul?"

Chloe jerked up into a sitting position with the sheets pooled around her body. Her eyes opened to a decadent and lavish bedroom. Its unfamiliar walls, opulent interior, and absolute silence warred against the expectations of her own bedroom in a crowded city apartment. Saul lived away from the outskirts of Los Angeles' concrete jungle, where the green hills rolled into glorious mountains.

"Saul?" she repeated again. Her body ached from head to toe, like she'd spent the entire night out dancing in her high heels.

A crisp note awaited her on the empty pillow bearing script written in an aristocratic hand.

His handwriting is immaculate… Saul's note told her that he'd gone to make a few calls and to handle the week's affairs. He suggested for her to enjoy the amenities provided by his bedchamber and to ignore the maid.

"Okay. Ignore the maid. Why am I supposed to ignore the maid?" Chloe wondered out loud. She stepped from the bed and paid a visit to the stone tiled shower. The hot water poured without limit from an oversized shower fixture dangling above her head. And the water was soft. So very soft that she had to stand beneath it for several minutes to get all of the conditioner out of her hair.

"Huh? How'd he know what kind of conditioner I like?"

A neat row of bathroom toiletries in her favorite brands and scents lined the spacious shelf. Chloe had used each of her favorites automatically. Either Saul had acquired the information, or they shared the same feminine tastes when it came to shower products.

Chloe tucked the little nugget of information in the back of her mind and emerged from the shower. She dried off and shrugged into the cozy, hooded robe dangling from a hook beside the shower.

"That wasn't there a second ago. What the hell? Saul?" Chloe called again. "Are you playing a game with me?" She belted the plush, charcoal garment, and the color reminded her of Saul's dragonskin. A glance down revealed a personalized CD, or a possible brand name stitched in gold thread over the left breast.

He better not have given me some ex's bathrobe, she thought sourly.

She found cushioned house slippers with memory foam padding just beyond the bathroom door. Once again, they fit her perfectly.

Maybe dragons are also psychics. Chloe neither dwelled on the discovery nor shut it from her mind entirely. Instead, she simply brushed it aside for now and left the bedroom to explore. Saul hadn't told her to keep to the bedroom, and honestly, she wouldn't have obeyed him if he had ordered her to stay put.

Like a child on an adventure, she descended the stairs to the lower level, practically tiptoeing as she went. "Hello?"

Hell, I don't know where I'm going and this place seems huge. I'll be lost before I know it.

A whiff of something smoky and delicious wafted past her nose. She tried to follow her nostrils toward the aroma of bacon by stepping into a corridor beside the elaborate staircase. It took her farther away from the smell.

"Hello? Well fuck."

Chloe turned around to retrace her steps, but a tall woman stood behind her. Almond brown skin and glossy black hair were her key features, but her beautiful sapphire eyes were also very striking. She wore a gorgeous headscarf in ruby and black lace. Chloe envied her at once, then wondered who the fuck she was and why a strange woman wandered Saul's home. It took about a minute to grasp complete understanding.

"Oh! You must be Saul's maid." And not at all what Chloe expected. The tall woman brought to mind exotic models with her bronzed complexion, high cheekbones, and ebony hair. His maid belonged in an international beauty pageant.

"Such is one of my duties, yes."

One of her duties? "What else do you do?"

"Whatever Master Drakenstone needs," the woman replied primly. "At this moment, he needed me to prepare a meal for you. Do you have a preference?"

"No, not really. Whatever causes you the least trouble, Miss... What do I call you?"

"You may call me Mahasti, and it is no trouble. Please, make yourself comfortable in the solarium. The sunshine is at an optimal angle. I think you'll enjoy it."

Chloe continued down the hall as directed. Artwork ranging from paintings to elaborately carved masks lined the walls, each piece capturing her attention in turn.

Warm sunlight filled the solarium as promised. The large space occupied a top floor room at the front of the mountainside estate, facing out over the long drive and rolling hills. Glass created most of the front wall facing the open world outside. Giggling, Chloe imagined Saul curled up in dragon form like a cat to soak up the sun. The wide room provided more than enough room and the slate tile floor absorbed the heat.

A small wrought iron table with two chairs sat in the room's center, flanked by potted roses. It was both picturesque and romantic, and yet somehow lonely. She wished Saul were there to share the morning with her.

"I trust you will enjoy this."

Holy shit, she moves around without a sound!

Chloe spun about with a hand lifted to her heart. "Wow, I guess I must have lingered in the hall longer than I thought." It was the only explanation behind her meal's swift arrival.

Mahasti's lips curved in quiet smile. "If you have need of me, only call."

"Thank you."

Chloe's stomach rumbled at the sight of the food. A large Belgian waffle claimed the entire porcelain plate beneath a pile of sliced strawberries, rhubarb, and whipped cream cheese. A second plate offered buttery fried eggs and crisp bacon. Cran-raspberry juice filled the tall champagne glass beside her plate.

Every morsel could be considered one of Chloe's favorites, and she had absolutely no idea how Saul or Mahasti had known. She devoured the meal in record time and even scraped the last crumbs from the two plates. Between the food in her belly to ease her hunger pangs, the warm sunshine, and her memories of bliss at Saul's side, Chloe was in the best of moods.

"You hair reminds me of snow beneath the sun."

"Saul!"

She leapt up and flew across the room to throw herself in his arms. Saul caught her up and spun her around in a circle. Before her feet touched the ground Chloe grabbed his face and kissed him.

Saul's startled mumble against her lips charmed her as much as his other qualities. With extreme patience, Chloe guided him through the motions, slipping her tongue past his lips to explore his mouth. Her dragon learned quickly.

In the space between one heartbeat and the next Saul had her back pressed to the wall and her legs around his waist. Their tongues slid against each other in a dance as intimate as their lovemaking had been.

A snap was her only warning and then Saul's jeans dropped around his ankles. His rigid cock pressed into her wet folds. Her robe

55

allowed him easy, open access to her body.

"Mine. I wish to mate with you again."

"Yours," she agreed. "Take me, Saul, take me now. Exactly like this. We'll fit together this way, I swear." She was addicted to him, and even if their union was revealed to be only a dream, she wanted to have as much of him as possible before the fantasy ended.

A forward thrust joined their two bodies together as one and Chloe forgot everything else in the world existed. Her ass smacked against the hard wall, saved from the rough and cold stone by the plush robe still clothing her body.

"Fuck, you feel so good," she gasped.

"Tell me what you desire, Chloe." Saul nuzzled his face against her throat. "Direct me how you will."

"Oh god… fuck me harder, Saul. I can take all of you, I promise. Just… just slam in deep."

She directed and he obeyed, an eager student who abandoned his carefully controlled depth in favor of pounding into her molten core. Exhilarated, Chloe held on for the wild ride.

"Kiss me," she begged.

"Like this?" Saul's tongue imitated the in and out plunge of his cock, stroking Chloe's mouth as thoroughly. She whimpered against him and dragged her nails up his back.

"Yeah, like that," she gasped after they both came up for air. Saul's lips dragged across her skin and he delivered little nibbles that sent electric zings racing through her veins. His teeth touched against her branded shoulder and the pleasure of it nearly sent her into orgasm.

Not yet, not yet…! I have so much to show him. So much I wanna do!

"Touch me here," she ordered him next, a demanding teacher and thrilled lover all in one. He didn't need both arms to keep her suspended against the wall, so she showed him the small pleasure button between her thighs. Introducing Saul to her clit was worthwhile. His rough fingers glided over her smoothly waxed skin at their joining, gathering the slick moisture needed to fondle and circle her sensitive pearl. Once she showed him the motions, he became an expert within seconds.

"Like that, baby. Fuck yes… like that."

"So much love for so tiny a thing," Saul murmured huskily against her ear. "Later I will taste you, Chloe, as you tasted me. I will feast upon you."

Holy. Fuck. His words alone made her hotly clench and constrict around him. "I want that," Chloe blurted. "I want that so much."

The image conjured up by her wild imagination of Saul's face between her spread thighs flushed heat through Chloe's body. She clamped down around him and arched her back away from the wall, her body drawn taut. The next stroke through her tight channel pushed her over the edge and snapped the tension.

"Saul!"

Her dragon's growl reverberated through the room. His body pounded against her in a furious tempo, driving her orgasm to continue on and on. There seemed to be no end to the delicious tremors slamming through Chloe's smaller frame.

For the third time since their meeting, Saul filled her with his seed and she accepted it without question. Without regret.

She *needed* every bit of him.

If not for Saul's strong grip, Chloe would have slid to the floor in a boneless heap. They lowered to the floor together, sprawling out beneath the sunlight. Her body continued to react, occasionally spasming in climax. She writhed and groaned while palming her own breast.

"You certainly know how to greet a girl. Mm..." Her entire body felt boneless and weak, and fine little flutters of orgasm continued to ripple through her core. She giggled and squirmed in closely against him while Saul stroked his fingertips over her sleek, newly waxed skin. It was nice to remain conscious for once.

"I watched pornography while you were asleep," he confessed.

Dragons do blush. His cheeks are so red, Chloe noticed. "Saul... I'm not making fun of you, baby, but how are you so old without knowing the most common things about sex between humans."

Saul glanced away as the heat continued to sweep into his cheeks and cutely color the skin beneath his soft golden-red beard. "As I said to you before, you are the first and only female human to provide ample motivation."

Better words had never come from a fantasy monster or any man.

"I craved your touch every morning, Chloe. Every night. I would have you always at my side."

From anyone else, those words might have worried her. Saul turned them into a loving promise.

"I have two requests."

"Anything," he replied to her.

"Mating is for animals, and from what I can tell... you are very much a man right now," she teased. "Humans make love and have sex. We fuck. I'll take any of those over mating."

His laughter thrilled her and sent another series of ripples through her core. "Acceptable. What else troubles you?"

"Will you show me your dragon body one more time?" she asked quietly.

Chloe hadn't known Saul long, but something - their bond perhaps - had made him an open book. His smile faded, giving way to impassive features lacking emotion. That meant he was hiding something from her. That he was uncomfortable.

"It will only frighten you again."

"I'm sorry for hurting you. I can't tell you enough times that I'm sorry... but I want to see you. The real you. Because if we're going to make this work, I need to accept that you're more than a man, Saul," Chloe whispered. She raised her hand to her lover's cheek and quickly became elated by the way he leaned into her touch. Like a puppy or a kitten appreciating a pet from a human hand, he also pushed appreciatively against her.

"Not here," Saul finally spoke aloud to her. "First I have something I must ask of you in return."

"Anything." Chloe smiled down into Saul's face. Her fingertips brushed against his bearded jaw. "You can ask me anything."

Saul's golden eyes locked onto her gaze. He might as well have been peering into her very soul.

"Stay with me, Chloe. Move into my home and make it your own. Allow me to care for you. To provide for you."

"I…" She blinked, breath caught in her throat. *Leave my home? My friends? What would I do? Is there more than lust between us?* "I'm not hearing a question in there, Saul…" she hedged, too uncertain to answer.

Saul's palm lifted to her cheek. "Will you stay with me, Chloe?" he asked, correcting himself. "Will you share your life with me?"

What he asked was life changing.

"I…" Chloe dragged in a nervous breath. "I need time to think about it, Saul. Maybe dragons are able to make snap decisions that alter their entire life, but us humans need a little time."

"I will give you time," he agreed. Still, he was her open book and the crushing disappointment radiated so thoroughly that it swept through her and settled in her soul. She felt what he experienced, enduring the echoes of his elation, his pleasure, and even his sadness.

"I won't leave your home now, Saul. I don't plan to leave you. It's only that… I can't stay here in your home without anything to do. I like to work and do things. I have friends and a life I'll be leaving behind."

The disappointment ebbed.

"I wish only for your happiness, Chloe. If work is what you desire, then work you shall have. If you have a friend you want close by, invite them. This will be your home now, to do with as you please."

"You mean it?"

"I do." He leaned in close and stroked her cheek before pressing a kiss to her nose. The hard peck made her giggle.

"I know I have much to learn to please you, Chloe."

"You please me now, but the rest we can learn together," she said quickly. The last thing Chloe wanted was for him to feel inadequate when that was the furthest thing from the truth.

They held each other in silence, soaking up the heat from the slate floors while Chloe dozed against his shoulder. Eventually, she awakened to Saul relocating her to another room of his house. Ever so aware of her needs, her dragon carried her into the humid bathroom where a steaming bubble bath awaited. Someone had strewn the water with fragrant rose petals.

"How did you...?"

"How did I what?"

"Have a bath ready. How did you know I wanted one?"

Saul shrugged. "Mahasti." He stepped into the tub and lowered into the water without releasing Chloe. The water was the perfect temperature and just shy of boiling. Just how she liked it.

"Saul?" she asked again, unable to let the matter rest.

"Yes?"

"How did Mahasti know my favorite things?"

"She is a Djinn." Chloe's confused expression prompted him to elaborate. "Humans know of her people as genies. Anything you desire will be granted to you, although I must ask you to remain considerate. She does this of her own volition as a repayment for a kindness I once showed her."

"Oh?" she asked curiously. *Seriously? A genie?*

Her dragon cut his golden eyes away from her briefly and gazed toward a large bay window designed to overlook the expansive pasture land and forest. "I must divulge certain truths to you, Chloe."

She felt his anxiety and anticipation, which made her equally anxious to match. *I knew this was too good to be true. He's probably going to tell me the hot chick maid is his lover or something.* Preparing herself for the worst, she eased out of his embrace and into the water.

"It appears Mahasti interfered during our separation and is

responsible for our dreams. She meant no harm to you, Chloe. I apologize for the trouble she has caused while securing our reunion. I swear to you, such ploys were not devised by me."

Chloe jerked her head upward and stared at him. The hot water lapped against her shoulders and brought dewy beads of sweat to her brow. Her fair hair trailed behind her in the water and clung to her wet shoulders. Without Saul's arms around her, she discovered his tub was more of a stone basin than a bath. Practically a pool.

"She did that?"

"Yes," he admitted. "I only discovered this morning, but you have my most humble and sincere apolo-"

"Thank her."

"What?" He blinked at her.

"She led me back to you. I don't care about her reasons, or how much she drove me mad; I'm just glad to be here." She touched the colorful stain of purple and red just above her collar bone. "Tell me more about our bond. You bit me twice, but you didn't do it again in the solarium."

"The Dragon's Brand is a soul bond, Chloe, and permanent once consummated unless one mate rejects the other. Your mark faded over our distance, but I was able to rekindle it when we…" Saul stumbled over the word, but she provided him patience. "Made love again."

Saul had required only a single gentle correction since Chloe had told him she preferred the term over 'mating', which made her feel like a sassy mare waiting for a stallion to mount her.

"I never thought I'd say this but I kinda like knowing how you feel about things." She wrapped her sudsy arms around his neck and touched their noses gently. "I have one a final question."

"You may ask whatever you like. I keep no secrets from you."

"Will I get to see the rest of your home, or do you plan to keep me a sexual prisoner in your bedroom and bath?" *No complaints if you do…*

He smiled and pulled her in close. "Soon. After I have tended to your needs."

Chloe learned the true meaning of pampered. Saul soaped her back and tenderly scrubbed every inch of her body. His gentle side emerged and Chloe happily introduced him to the sweeter side of human love. She taught him kisses could be slow and decadent and trailed whisper light touches of her lips across his body until Saul was as relaxed as she was.

"I'm going to turn into a prune if we stay in here much longer. Dragons like lengthy baths I take it?"

"We do." His quiet answer sounded like a purr. "But as you wish. I have more I wanted to share with you today and your request comes in good timing."

Chloe's freshly cleaned and pressed clothes waited for her on the bed. She tugged on her jeans and top, but traded her boots for the comfy house slippers. Saul waited for her on the wide balcony without a single stitch of clothing on his magnificent form.

"I thought you said we were going out…"

Saul grinned. "We are. Do you trust me, Chloe?" He climbed up on the stone ledge overlooking a green stretch of pasture.

"Of course I… what are you doing?"

Saul leapt clear over the edge and plummeted beyond her sight. Chloe involuntarily shrieked and rushed forward onto the balcony. Her heart leapt into her throat, punctuated by the drum beat of her pulse racing in her ears. "Saul!" she screamed, expecting to find his broken body on the ground below.

An unexpected sight awaited Chloe when she reached the rail. She skidded to a halt and stared with her jaw slack.

Beneath the sunlight, Saul's hide wasn't dark as she previously believed. The dragon's leathery skin reminded her of aged terracotta, a deep and warm reddish brown color. His black-feathered wings glimmered faintly beneath the noontime sun, accented by flight feathers of gold and bronze.

"God you're beautiful," she said, breathless with awe. *How was I ever afraid of such a gorgeous creature?*

"Climb astride me."

"You can talk!" The revelation surprised her. In his draconic form his voice rumbled more deeply, but it was still his. Still Saul.

"Of course."

Thankfully, Chloe had no fear of heights. She leaned against the edge of the railing and peered down at the dragon's massive body. He sat on his haunches, much like a dog or any other four-legged animal, steadying his incredible weight on the stone exterior of his home. His large talons curved around the balcony wall.

"I won't fall off?" Chloe asked tentatively. Part of her jumped for joy on the inside, but the other part of her, the wise and prudent half of her psyche, demanded for her to show caution.

"I will not allow you to fall."

Saul extended his neck forward. That movement placed his large snout within biting distance. Contrary to his reptilian appearance, his skin felt warm and alive beneath the sun. She caressed him boldly, dragging her fingers over his nose until she reached between his eyes and patted his horned eye ridge. His head was nearly as big as her body and the teeth she spotted had to be as long as her arm. Yet she felt no fear. Only comfort and a sense of safety.

"Let me show you how it feels to fly, my Chloe."

The tour of the grounds lasted less than an hour from start to finish while Chloe rode on Saul's back. According to her lover, the incredible stretch of land was off limits to satellite imaging. Dragons such as Saul carried great weight and influence across the world, and wherever they built their homes, vast amounts of money shrouded their existence in secrecy.

"Fly again!" she cried, feeling like a little girl on her first pony ride.

Laughter shook Saul's body. Fortunately, Chloe had found the perfect spot to sit astride him between his magnificent wings. She sprawled there with her cheek against his downy soft feathers, breathing in the subtle wild and earthy scent. He smelled so good.

No one would ever believe me if I told them dragons are warm-blooded and that our fantasy stories have it all wrong, she thought.

Saul took off at a lurching jog that bounced her initially. With a secure hold of the feathery mane at the base of his neck, she remained firmly in place. Behind her, a row of spinal ridges trailed down his back until they reached the tip of his tail. The first was as long as she stood in height.

Occasionally, he treated her to moments of flight while she clung to him for security and joyfully whooped out loud while the wind blew through her hair. Saul soared above the grassy pastures and promised to catch her if she fell. Eventually her dragon landed in favor of taking an ambling pace that cruised the periphery of his property. They were nearly two miles away from his mountain home, having discovered a comfortable little grotto with a clear running stream. The deer who inhabited the area prior to their arrival bolted the very moment Saul came into view. At that moment, he tensed beneath her and his muscles wound so tight she instinctively tightened her grip.

"I will not give chase, Chloe. Relax and take comfort in the day's fair weather."

He let her down from his back by lowering to his belly, and then he approached the stream and lowered his face to sip from the cool shaded water. As fond of the untouched wilderness as ever, Chloe joined the dragon and crouched alongside him. The refreshing water soothed her throat after hours of laughing in the sun.

"Mm... I feel so good," she murmured. "Come down here and snuggle with me." When his head turned toward her, she planted her lips on the tip of his nose. "I want to hug you again and thank you properly for the ride."

His transformation from mythical beast to man happened in the blink of an eye. For some reason Chloe expected cracking bones and a lengthy change. The movies made shapeshifting appear to be an agonizing act. In hindsight she should have known better, since his leap from the balcony and his reappearance as a dragon happened in seconds. One moment he was a dragon and the next he was a naked man.

She leapt into his arms and brought them both down to the ground.

"My reward is to be tackled?"

"No, it's this." Chloe leaned down and laid a path of dainty kisses against his stubbled cheek up to his brow. She inched over and caught his earlobe for a nibble. It was a trick she'd been saving. She skimmed her teeth around the sensitive curve and dipped her tongue inside for a light trace.

"Chloe," he groaned. Saul always growled when she did something that pleased him.

"I like teaching you new things," she whispered warmly against the dampened skin. Saul shuddered and Chloe grinned, pulling back. For now.

"Doesn't the grass itch your skin?" she asked.

"No. I sowed only the finest. Try it and see," Saul urged her. In an effort to help, he tugged at her jeans.

Chloe's laughter filled the air as they worked together to rid her of her clothes. Saul tossed her jeans and shirt aside.

"I guess you don't have to worry about looky-loos out here."

Saul snorted. "None have managed to breach my boundaries, though many have tried. Our fence and Leiv's hounds dissuade trespassers easily enough. You need fear nothing here in our home."

"That's nice to know... and you're right about this grass. It's so thick and cushy." Chloe stretched her arms out above her head. "The sun and breeze feel good too. No wonder you walk around half dressed."

"It does have advantages. Some newly discovered." He rolled to his side and nuzzled his face against Chloe's breasts. "These, for example." His rough palm kneaded one perky mound.

"You're a quick learner," Chloe giggled.

"It is easy to learn when the rewards are so worthwhile. Pleasuring you delights me to no end."

"Mmmn…" Chloe sighed, content beyond all measure. Saul's scruffy jaw tickled her stomach. The continued downwards scrape stirred her arousal and her hips lifted by instinct.

"Your scent, it intoxicates me," he whispered. "Wrapped with mine, as it should always be. And your taste…"

Saul licked her waxed folds. While clumsy, the attempt sent a surge of pure, unadulterated lust straight to her core. Her pussy clenched in anticipation.

"I want more," he growled.

"Just use the tip of your tongue and suckle softly, like our bath time kisses," Chloe suggested, heart pounding. She drew up her legs and spread them wide to grant him full access. Saul readily accepted the invitation but startled and hung back when he saw the discolored bruises against her inner thighs.

"Before, in the solarium, I abused you--"

"I liked it," she countered with a grin. "But you are quite welcome to kiss my sore bits."

Saul's golden eyes flared. "I intend to."

He lapped at her like a cat, providing brief strokes of his tongue that made Chloe squirm against the ground. Saul's lazy sprawl painted a picture both humorous and erotic. She admired the length of his muscled limbs and drank in the sight of his face between her legs.

"Yes, yes!" she encouraged. "Don't stop what you're doing. Just like that, baby, yes!"

With his lips and tongue, Saul explored her wet crevice. He suckled on her smooth folds, delicately scraped his teeth over her swollen clitoris, and flickered his tongue up and down. He gathered up the first sweet traces of her sexual juices and made a sound that was part growl, part purr, and all pleasure.

"More." It was as though Saul couldn't contain his baser instincts. He rose up to his knees and dragged Chloe with him. Her body bent, shoulders and head against the ground and back angled upwards. Saul placed her legs over his broad shoulders and cupped her ass in his hands to support the awkward position. Chloe didn't care. Any discomfort vanished the moment Saul's mouth returned to her throbbing snatch.

He went wild. His long, agile tongue curled into her wet hole and stroked her insides with as much attention as his virile cock. Chloe bucked in his hold, grabbing at the grass beneath her.

"Oh god, oh god…" Green blades and rich black soil tore under her hands. "My clit, baby, oh yes, yes, yes, right there. Fuck you're amazing!"

Saul's throaty growl rumbled against her wet folds and stars exploded behind Chloe's eyes. She collapsed against the grass at the conclusion of her climax and lay overstimulated and completely out of sorts.

"Did you enjoy the tour?" Saul asked in a sensual, too smug voice.

Chloe nodded weakly and closed her eyes.

Much to Chloe's relief, Saul carried her home on his back. She lay snuggled against the warm feathers at the base of his wings, indulging her dragon lover in conversation about favorite vacation spots.

"Skiing?" he questioned in his deep voice.

"I can't believe you've never gone skiing! I think you'd love it."

Skiing was only one sport among a handful of other activities Saul never enjoyed. She quickly put together a mental list of other fun pastimes from ice skating to parasailing.

Would he like bicycling? Had he ever bicycled before? She giggled frequently from upon his back, which forced her lumbering dragon to pause and glance over his broad shoulder at her. He was built strong, a creature composed of muscle and lean sinew beneath his leathery hide. She breathed him in, enjoying a scent far superior to any new car smell.

Eventually, they reached the estate's pasture near the manor. The prey animals fled him and cleared a path, evidently accustomed to Saul visiting for another reason.

"I didn't even realize you could own so much wild space this close to LA." *Of course, he can afford it so I guess that makes a difference.* "Do you sell any of your livestock for food or milk or whatever?"

"Yes and no. Mahasti keeps the wool from our sheep for weaving. Leiv favors the goats' milk for cheese."

"And the cows?"

Saul flashed a toothy grin. "They provide excellent steaks."

"Your pantry must be impressive," Chloe replied, laughing.

"You will see that next," he promised.

Once Saul adopted his human body and they entered the house, a pair of jeans awaited him on the nearby coat rack.

"Mahasti?" Chloe asked.

Her dragon chuckled with amusement and donned the garment. While she appreciated the Djinn's thoughtful act of kindness – as she certainly didn't want to cross paths with the woman while Saul remained nude – part of her also longed to enjoy his naked beauty a while longer.

"They will not remain for long, my Chloe. Patience," he counseled her.

With Saul guiding her along, a lengthy tour of the inner structure began that took her from one bedroom to the next. They reached a personal library that appeared dated in the past, much like a gentleman's study of the Theodore Roosevelt era. The expansive desk dominated a wall near the window, flanked by two mounted hunting trophies.

"You kept their heads?" she questioned in disbelief.

"One gored me. I respected his strength and chose to memorialize his remains in honor of the hunt." Saul glanced at her. "The clever buck on the left led me on a chase by crossing through a human's camp. I could not follow. We crossed paths again many months later and I recalled his scent."

"So you rewarded him by keeping his head, too?"

The strange sentiment warmed her heart and touched her in an odd way. No part of the animal had gone to waste, devoured and enjoyed by a larger predator. She chose not to judge.

Dad would think he was amazing. Saul's a hunter, too, just of a different sort. A predator, she thought.

Eventually, they reached another modernized room with a cozy home theater. Plush leather seats spread out into recliners.

"Saul, if you live alone here, and you were asleep for the last five years, why do you have so many new things?"

"Mahasti and Leiv," he explained. "Leiv occupies a cabin on the property, but he frequents the estate for these luxuries from time to time. Mahasti chooses to live in the manor, and as you have learned, she possesses a fascination with modern conveniences."

"And updates areas of your home as needed," Chloe finished.

A quiet nod from him provided confirmation. Eventually, they came to a halt at a heavy iron door with intricate designs. It opened easily with a push, revealing the top of a staircase leading down into a dark abyss.

Chloe peeked downstairs nervously. "What's next?"

"My room."

"I'm pretty sure I saw your room already. Comfy bed, painted ceiling, amazing night sky viewing."

Saul's warm laugh coaxed prickles across her skin. "You have seen my bedroom, yes. But I wish to show you *my* room."

With their hands entwined Saul guided her into the basement level. Dry air blew past and rustled Chloe's hair.

"Go on," he urged her. "Look."

"Wow."

A single word barely encompassed the wonder and awe she experienced, but once she took in the complete sight of Saul's lair, she was struck speechless. The massive chamber was hewn from the mountain rock and smoothed to a glossy finish. Old fashioned gas lamps provided illumination. Their flickering light sparkled off the veritable mounds of treasure.

"Wow," she said again.

Chloe stepped forward, drawn to the nearest collection. Rough, uncut gems filled an old wooden chest. Thanks to movies, everyone assumed rubies, sapphires and other stones came out sparkling and flawless. Not so. The precious rocks in the chest varied in size, ranging as small as her pinky nail to as large as Saul's fist.

"You just keep these all here?"

Saul moved up behind her. "I find them on my explorations and cut them from the rock with my talons. The females of my kind favor them for bedding."

Chloe blinked. "They sleep on them?"

"Indeed," Saul confirmed. His warm hands settled over Chloe's shoulders. "They are yours now. I no longer seek a mate among my own kind. Anything you wish from this room you need only to take. What is mine is now yours."

"I..." Had no idea what to say. Chloe wandered forward through the room, pausing near each laden table and overflowing chest. Gold coins, chunks of silver ore, antique jewelry, heirloom furniture, and more filled the cavern.

"Some was passed to me by my mother. She has a fondness for beautiful things." Saul's gaze followed her. "I think she would like you immensely, Chloe."

Chloe swallowed nervously and turned a precious stone over in her hands. The unpolished boulder opal was prettier than anything she had ever seen, resembling a hunk of rounded beige rock with gleaming hues of green, gold, blue, and red shining from within deep fissures in a shatter pattern. Focusing on the object's beauty distracted her from the woozy feeling creeping into her belly.

Love. It felt like love, an emotion she would have laughingly shrugged off if he were any other man. Saul was so open, and so very trusting, that she couldn't imagine shying away from his affection.

He's trusting me with a fortune, but I'd take him even if he was penniless.

"She would?" Chloe asked in a tiny voice. If Saul was over four centuries of age, his mother had to be positively ancient.

"Yes. We are very close, she and I. The loss of her mate, my father, saddened her deeply." Saul stepped in close behind her, hands at her waist.

"I'm sorry," Chloe murmured. She closed her eyes and leaned back against him to soak in his warmth. "Were you close to him?"

"As close as a son may be to the one he aspires to follow. What of you?"

"My dad and I are very close but I don't get to see him as much as I'd like."

"Why?" Saul turned her to face him. His warm fingers stroked down her cheek to her chin, tipping her face upwards.

"He lives in a small town. Job opportunities there were, well, scarce. So I moved to the city for school and took a job a few states away. I visit him as often as I can, but I think... he'd really approve of you." Chloe blinked back a few tears and hastily raised her hand to sweep away the clear droplets that escaped. "Tell me about this place."

"My father carved this den long before the City of Angels claimed her place by the sea. A refuge for him and my mother." He turned his bright golden eyes back to his new mate. "I hope to make it a home for you as well."

"It already feels like home."

She crossed the rocky chamber and raised her arms to curve around his neck. They fit together like two pieces of a puzzle, and his warm skin heated through the fine cotton layer of her tee.

"I may go home in a few days..." *Or a week, or a month,* Chloe thought ruefully. "But I promise that I'll return to you, Saul. I can't make a commitment to move my entire life overnight. Do you understand?"

But she could never walk away from him completely. She'd never forgive herself if she didn't follow the possibility to its very end.

"Your reluctance to remain disappoints me, but I understand and support your choice, my Chloe... If you will not stay, will you allow me to return with you?"

Her throat tightened. "You'd come back home with me?"

"Chloe." He took her face between his hands, golden eyes bright. "Home is where you are."

As far as Chloe was concerned, no other option existed. Home and her dragon would become one and the same.

Saved by the Dragon Bonus Chapter: Saul

Chloe. My Chloe, the dragon thought as he gazed upon her perfect, sleeping face.

She'd shivered more than once while lying beside him in his human guise, so the natural solution had been to provide her the heat and comfort she deserved.

Saul had taken his natural shape and curled on the rough cave floor like a massive, fire-breathing feline, Chloe plucked from the blankets and settled in the dip of his immense body.

He liked watching her. The peaceful breaths, the content expression. The joy thrumming from deep within her heart even as she slept.

I have bonded with a mortal. My soul mate. My fated mate is human, he marveled. It had come so quickly that it was difficult to believe, but no less fulfilling.

Destiny had brought them together after Brigid stood him up. The spoiled dragoness had unknowingly united him with the woman who made his draconian heart sing.

Gently, Saul dipped his nose down to touch her cheek, still unable to believe she was real. There. His.

Would Mahasti and Leiv, his dear friends and trusted servants, like having her for a mistress? Would she like them?

He hoped so.

She is truly beautiful inside and out, a jewel among mortals.

As a nocturnal creature, Saul rarely slept at night. With nothing else to do but serve as her living mattress, he watched, he dreamed, and he hoped she would accept him.

Hours later as the night approached dawn, she stirred and yawned into his tough skin. "Mm… Saul?"

At last! She awakens. Excitement flooded his heart, the dragon eager to reveal his true form to her. He'd practically wanted to scream to her before their lovemaking that he would gladly be hers, and in the end, he hadn't needed to. His dragon had acted for him and claimed her, impulsive and without warning. If Chloe felt even a fraction of the bliss he received from their union, all would be well.

Saul had searched for centuries to find his other half, only to discover her in a dark little cave. He sighed, watched her, and waited as she aroused from sleep.

"Saul?" she whispered again, blinking her eyes open.

The moonlight left her nude body awash in pale light, turning her blonde hair to silver beneath the midnight sky. Hey blue eyes focused on his face and slowly widened. Where he expected and hoped to see adoration, he saw terror overtaking the initial disbelief. She screamed, darting off of his body, falling heavily onto one knee.

"Saul?" Chloe called out. She froze, still as a statue. When he lowered his head to comfort her, she screamed again, nearly tumbling into their campfire remains… not that Saul would have let her come to any harm.

He watched her slap one of her own cheeks. Startled, Saul took his human form and stepped toward her. "Chloe, be at ease."

"Stay the hell away from me!"

"Chloe, wait—" *Could it be a nightmare? Has she awakened from a terrible dream?* He paused as she rushed from him and held his ground, preferring not to pursue a terrified woman. "What have I done to upset you?"

"You stay back! I mean it!"

"I… do not understand. You pledged yourself to me," he said, maintaining an even tone. His topaz eyes held steady on her face. "You said you were mine."

"That's crazy. That was talk in the moment. It doesn't mean anything."

Crazy talk? The elation drained from Saul like a popped balloon. "I see." He stepped away to offer the trembling woman more space, afraid she'd have a panic attack. Those were not unknown to him, having seen more than one human succumb to one — usually when seated in his office at Drakenstone Studios. "Have I done something to offend or harm you? Have I not treated you kindly?" he asked gently.

"You're not…" Breath shuddered from her lungs in uneven gasps. "You're not human. You shouldn't even exist."

"I see," Saul repeated without hope, without truly seeing. Without looking at Chloe again, he climbed from the depths of the mountain and onto the cliff's edge.

I am unwanted. No woman, dragon or mortal, will ever want me.

Saul didn't think, he shifted and flew. Flew until the wind cut through his glorious golden mane and its whipping force distracted him from the heartache.

What have I done to deserve such trials?

Hours later, he touched down in the pasture outside his mountainside home, not a moment too soon, as the rising sun had transformed the predawn sky to glorious pink, orange, and aquamarine shades.

A dragon would have stood out like a sore thumb gliding above California. Like most of his kin, he preferred to fly under the cover of darkness without the risk of being sighted by humans with good eyes.

Saul made the shift to two legs before he reached the stoop of the exquisite, mountainside estate. Home. A home too large for a dragon and his two loyal servants. It was a home deserving of a family. He'd built it above his father's old horde, younger and filled with idealistic beliefs about female dragons. One day, Brigid would accept his tributes and take him as her mate.

"Welcome home." Mahasti greeted Saul at the front door. As always, she remained oblivious to his lack of clothing, accustomed to Saul's transformation between forms.

Saul grunted in reply and moved past her into the house. The djinn followed, concern creasing her brow.

"Your time did not go well? Did Brigid rebuff your offer yet again?"

"Brigid once again deceived me and failed to appear," he replied in a clipped tone.

Mahasti scoffed and swept her dark hair from her exotic features.

"Do not say you told me so," Saul groused.

"I'd never dream it," Mahasti said. Concerned blue topaz eyes gazed up at him. His immortal servant knew him well, able to read his moods whether they changed with the wind or became as stalwart as steel. "Brigid's past transgressions have never affected you this deeply."

"I met a woman," he admitted. Hiding secrets from a djinn rarely worked. "She tumbled, literally, into my path."

"Oh?"

"I have no desire to speak on the matter with you."

"I see," she murmured, hiding her hurt. Mahasti removed her hand from his shoulder and stepped away. "If you should you change your mind, you know how to find me."

He knew how to find his predictable genie. The mere thought of her name and a desire for her presence would summon her in an instant.

For the first time in their many years of friendship, Saul was without the inclination to share his thoughts with her. Instead, he retreated to the comfort of his hoard. The transformation took him mid-stride, replacing his human physique with the impressive frame of a dragon. With his wings pressed against his body, Saul wriggled through the narrow channel and into the sweet spot at the rear of the enormous underground cavern.

The horde was his shelter, a safe place filled with mementos from childhood, gifts from his mother and father, and jewels he'd acquired over his own long life. He half burrowed into the pile of gold coins and drowned his sorrows in the music emanating from each uncut gem.

Jewels sang to dragons. Each stone had its own melody, its own unique tones, but nothing chimed more sweetly than the blissful harmonies of jade.

Such irony that in his heartbreak, the symbol of his pain was the thing to bring him comfort. His pushed his snout free of the pile and opened his eyes, gazing across the room to the source.

A wasted trade. It will never see use. Saul sighed and turned away from the ornately carved jade bed. He had negotiated for years to attain it, hoping to present it to his dragon mate.

"Saul?" Leiv's voice echoed through the cavern.

Leiv was the only one who could possibly understand. For years, Saul had watched the werebear pine after Mahasti, a victim of unrequited love. Ever the good friend, Saul had attempted to encourage their relationship, but every nudge toward Leiv made her retreat further away.

"May we talk?" the Russian werebear asked.

"If you must." Saul delved into his coin pile again, submerged to his nostrils. Inhaling the scent of precious metal soothed him.

Leiv cleared a spot on the floor with his foot, moving the golden coins before he sat. "Mahasti worries for you, friend."

"I did not mean to hurt her feelings."

"She knows. Now tell me of what troubles you. Tell me what you could not speak to her."

Saul's sides heaved as he huffed out a long sigh, twin tufts of smoke spiraling up from his nostrils. "I found my mate."

The news stunned his longtime friend, who was left speechless for several moments. Unrushed, Leiv gave the matter thorough consideration. It was one of the many traits Saul admired in the bear.

"The discovery should bring joy. Why then does your heart weigh heavy with sorrow?"

"She spurned me, Leiv. I claimed her as my own, laid my mark upon her, and she called me hers. Then she denied me."

Leiv didn't offer pity or empty consolations. "Should I fetch the vodka?"

Saul huffed, a small chuckle that was sorely needed. *If only a strong drink could fill this hollow in my heart.*

***

Why am I here? Why maintain this charade, this lie, as if I could ever be accepted among them for who I am? Saul wondered. With a dour expression on his face, he watched the busy Los Angeles streets in the midst of lunch time traffic. He reclined in an overpriced executive chair, new leather cradling his body in ergonomic alignment.

He hated it.

Even the pile of manuscripts on his desk offered none of their usual amusement and distraction. He looked down at the one in his hands and resisted the urge to throw it in the face of the man seated across from him.

Ove Ball wrote the most atrocious scripts in Hollywood, but Saul had discovered most to be jewels in the rough. Whenever the dragon chose to produce and film one of Ove's movies, the contract always stipulated Drakenstone Studios held absolute authority to institute creative changes as needed.

They were always needed.

Saul tossed the script onto the desk and snorted. "Your script is shit," he said bluntly.

Ove's smile faded gradually, wavering on the indecisive divide between disappearing or waiting for the punchline. "Shit? Saul, you have always liked my scripts."

"I would tell my assistant to use it as toilet paper, but no one's ass deserves such drivel. Where is the second act?" Saul demanded.

"What do you mean? It's there, where the demon hunter frees the sacrificial maidens."

Even an idiot could guess the corny scene had been thrown in for the sole purpose of adding practically naked women.

"That is not a second act. It's gratuitous nudity for the sake of stripping our female lead. It's *trash*," he growled. "Get this shit out of my office before I place it *and you* into the shredder."

"Mr. Drakenstone?"

Saul snapped his attention to Harris, his personal assistant. The young man must have a drawer of prescription glasses each with a different frame to color coordinate with his outfits. The man had an impeccable style of dress, which he'd put to use many times by dressing Saul for last minute engagements.

His red-trimmed eyeglasses matched the silk tie around his neck. "May we speak for a moment Mr. Drakenstone? Urgent business matters."

"What business?" Saul asked.

"The kind we shouldn't discuss in front of a visitor," Harris said, gesturing to Ove.

"He was leaving." Saul paid Ove no further attention. The man spluttered in protest, but gathered up his papers and made a hasty exit.

Harris shut the door behind the fleeing screenwriter then turned to face Saul. "The Saul Drakenstone I've always worked for is a hard-ass, not an asshole," he said gently. "It's obvious you returned from your vacation last week in a foul mood, sir. We've weathered the storm before, and we'll do it again for you because your moments of temper are fleeting, but…" Harris paused. "This feels different. And I think you should take a hiatus until you recover from it."

"You are kicking me out of my own studio?"

"Your privileges are revoked," Harris confirmed with a mellow smile. "Go *fly* off to a beach somewhere and relax."

Harris was among a small handful of staff who knew Saul's true identity. He'd come with high recommendations from a friend in Texas, already acquainted with working for shapeshifters due to the werewolf pack there.

"This is what I do to relax. I read scripts. I make movies." Saul gestured to the posters on the wall, most featuring scenes of epic sword and sorcery.

"No. Currently, this is where you come to be a jerk because you're not used to showing emotion," Harris replied. "And this is where you terrify your staff because none of them are used to seeing this side of you."

"This side of me?"

Harris chuckled. "The dragon side you always restrain to be polite. You've lost your filter."

Saul sighed. After he slumped in his seat with one hand against his brow, Harris brought a snifter of brandy to him and set it on the desk. "Draft an apology to Ove and tell him I will personally rewrite his script. I exaggerated."

"There's a good plot in there, buried under the crap," Harris agreed.

He saved Leiv the three hour drive to Los Angeles and called Mahasti instead. The djinn whisked him home in a puff of jasmine-scented smoke and deposited him in the estate's lower level without a word.

"Mahasti," he spoke out loud to the still, too silent hoard.

She materialized again but kept her distance, clearly miffed.

"Forgive me for my abruptness with you, Mahasti. I was unkind."

Her features softened. "I am always here for you. Don't forget that."

"You know my wishes," Saul said in a quiet voice. "You know what my heart yearns for."

"I do, but I had hoped you would speak of it to me openly once you were ready."

Saul shrugged and glanced away. Neither his father or mother had raised a quitter, but the wound inflicted by Chloe's refusal had marked him soul deep. He sighed. "What is there to be said? She denied me, and I have learned a valuable lesson about women."

"Why don't you seek her out?" Mahasti asked. "Go to her and reaffirm your love. Show her she is yours and belongs to you." A faint smile curved the capricious genie's lips. "Or better yet, show your mate you belong to *her*."

"Her thoughts were very clear. I terrified her. I will not force my attentions upon an unwilling woman, nor will I traumatize her further." The idea of hunting Chloe down by her name had tempted him, but ultimately he'd decided appearing uninvited on her doorstep was the fast track to potentially losing her forever.

If he already hadn't.

"Then rest, my friend. Think on it for a time. Harris informed me your recent show of poor temper has earned you the nickname 'Snapdragon' from the senior staff."

Saul ducked his head, looking as contrite as a schoolboy. "You're right." He bit his lower lip. "A month or so, Mahasti."

"A month," she promised. "I will not allow you to sleep into the next century. Too many of us would mourn your prolonged absence." The woman smiled, bowed her head then vanished as silently as she had appeared.

With Mahasti gone, Saul retreated deeper into the treasure room and considered returning to a longer hibernation. Would anyone but Leiv and Mahasti miss him? Once restless sleep overtook the dragon, dreams of blonde hair and blue eyes haunted his slumber. A curved back and a slender throat beneath his lips.

Chloe.

For Saul, it had been the transference of part of his soul, his dragon recognizing the one and only woman deserving a shifter's love. For her, it had been empty words uttered in the heat of passion.

His heart called out for its mate but there was no answer. Only darkness.

MATED BY THE DRAGON

Chapter 1

Chloe muffled her yawn against the firm pectoral muscle beneath her cheek. Saul radiated warmth as usual, comforting her against the ambient chill lingering in the air. She snuggled closer and threw one arm across his chest. His hair, worn loose around his shoulders, tickled her nose to disrupt her sleep whenever his position shifted.

"Chloe," he murmured, rousing her with his voice and a firm hand circling her back.

"Just a few more minutes. So sleepy," she mumbled. She clumsily pushed his blond mane aside with one hand, batting it like a kitten.

"Chloe," Saul repeated again.

She cheekily reacted by delivering a nip against his throat. Her boyfriend startled enough to jump then a rumbling chuckle of laughter vibrated beneath her hand, felt throughout his broad and powerful chest.

"Perhaps you should open your eyes before initiating something we cannot continue in privacy."

"Hm?" Chloe groggily raised her head and blinked as the world around her gained clarity. Saul sat beside her in a gray, plush seat with floor space to accommodate his long legs. Across from them, another pair of reclining seats housed two sleeping passengers.

Chloe rubbed her eyes and took in the bizarre tableau: a flight attendant wheeled a half dozen covered dishes, followed by another attendant bearing a cart of stacked pillows. A uniformed man poured wine for their neighbors a few feet away.

The realization dawned slowly. *That's right. We're flying back home. First Class.* She was bringing Saul to Houston where her sexy dragon savior would be set loose in the big city. Giddy, she clapped her hands together then twisted to the window.

"I must have fallen right to sleep. God, I still can't believe you agreed to this," Chloe said.

Saul's brows rose. "Why?"

"Because I thought you'd pull the big alpha man thing and insist on having it your way."

Saul chuckled again. "Chloe, I have lived long enough to know that all things come in time. I care for you deeply and will neither bully you nor dispense ultimatums. Genuine desire should bring you to my home to stay as my bondmate."

Genuine desire… I do desire it, she thought. But she also had a life back home in dire need of closure. She raised the window cover and took in the rolling green hills of Texas crossed by ribbons of highway. It wouldn't be much longer to reach Houston, where her roommate Marcy promised to pick them up.

"It's funny seeing you in an actual shirt, too. I was beginning to think you only owned one set of jeans," she teased him. "I can't believe you actually own clothes, but there better be more like that in your suitcase. You're traveling a little light."

A smug smile surfaced over his bearded face. Saul shook his head. "I assure you, Mahasti has organized a sufficient amount of garments to suit my needs. I will remain clothed."

"Good."

Chloe didn't want to share the sight of her man's glorious chest with anyone. Reassured by Saul's convincing words, she settled back into the plush chair, squirmed, and inevitably ended up leaning against him again.

"Would you like lunch before our arrival?"

Where has this airline been all of my life? Oh that's right, somewhere over there in I-Can't-Afford-This Land, in the same country as the Real World — where dragons don't really exist and people work hard for a living.

Two months ago, Chloe couldn't have guessed that a limitless realm of comfort loomed in her future. Saul pampered her, treated her like a queen, and never asked for anything in return but unconditional love — affection she would have readily given even if he didn't have a dime to his name.

"Marcy wanted to take us to dinner in a few hours, but to be honest with you, I'm starved," Chloe admitted. "A little snack wouldn't hurt."

"Good. I ordered for you."

Chloe had her doubts, but the next cart of steaming hot meals brought a tangy serving of honey-ginger salmon, a side of saffron rice, and a small salad. She devoured it and would have scraped the last grain of rice from the savory sauce if Saul's gloating expression didn't make her want to punch him.

"A little snack indeed."

"Don't be a smart ass," she muttered.

"Would you prefer me to be a dumb ass?" he countered.

The plane touched down an hour later. As expected, Saul's good looks and chivalrous decision to haul both carry-ons earned Chloe envious looks from nearby passengers. She directed him with a hand on one of his huge biceps, and eventually brought him outside of the terminal to the predetermined meeting place. The humid, Houston air struck her in the face and showed no mercy to her blonde hair. Chloe ran her fingers through the frizzing strands while Saul struggled to keep a straight face.

"Chloe!" The headlights of a silver car flashed to catch their attention.

Marcy popped the trunk and leapt out of the sedan to race toward them, causing her ponytail of jet black waves to bounce wildly. The curvaceous Latina raced onto the curb and hugged Chloe tight. "So glad he didn't turn out to be a psycho killer, chica. I told you that you wouldn't end up in his freezer." The embrace ended when friend rocked back on her heels and made a show of scoping Saul out. "I guess he'll have to do. Hello, stranger. I'm going to hug you in greeting, but mostly because I need an excuse to touch your muscles."

Saul didn't stand a chance, and Chloe could only grin and laugh at the bewildered expression on his face. To his credit, he carefully folded his arms around Marcy and lifted the woman from her feet in a snug squeeze.

"No swooning, Marce, that's my job," she teased. She reached out to steady her best friend once Saul lowered the woman again.

"It is my most sincere pleasure to make your acquaintance, Marcy."

"Oooh, polite too." Marcy winked. "Okay, let's load up and get out of here before that security guard comes over here to ticket me."

With only two bags, it took under a minute to toss them in the trunk and load up. Chloe slid in the backseat with Saul after she adjusted the passenger seat to provide him the necessary legroom. While it might be amusing to see him looking like a child with his knees against his chest, it wouldn't be very comfortable.

"Really, Chloe? I feel like a chauffeur. Did you and Romeo at least bring me back a damn cap to wear, too?"

"Should I have asked Leiv for one of his?" Saul asked, mistaking their jests as truth.

Marcy's dark brown eyes peered at them through the rearview mirror. "You have a personal driver? Seriously? Is he hot, Chloe?"

"Hot and a sweetheart. He calls me Miss Ellis and nothing else."

"Is he single?"

Chloe glanced at Saul for an answer.

"Your efforts would be in vain," he replied. "Leiv chooses to exercise limitless patience seeking unrequited love."

"Damn. So, where are you from?" Marcy shrugged off the letdown and cheerfully moved into the next topic.

"Los Angeles," Saul replied.

Marcy's amused chuckle preceded another question. "Before Los Angeles, unless the hippies and surfers talk like they're from a time machine these days."

Saul and Chloe had discussed Marcy's unrivaled curiosity prior to boarding the plane. During that time, she'd warned him that Marcy would subject him to an endless interrogation.

"Ah. My father's family hails from Iceland where we own vast amounts of property." He gave the rehearsed, albeit true, answer. "I visit often."

"Brothers? Sisters?"

Fifteen years of friendship meant that Chloe could read Marcy's mind. If Saul didn't have a brother, she'd probably settle for an equally hot sister.

"You are a curious woman, Marcy."

Chloe bumped her knee into the back of Marcy's seat in a nonverbal plea for peace and quiet. The woman sighed heavily but accepted the burden placed on her. A burden of silence akin to asking a toddler to resist a plate of gooey cookies hot from the oven. She spent the rest of the drive engaging Chloe in innocent chatter about California.

"So I'll drop you two off at the apartment while I run a few errands, and then we'll go for dinner and drinks. Sound good?" She cruised through the entrance of their gated complex and drifted to their building.

Creekwood Falls, the overpriced community where Marcy rented their two bedroom apartment, was home to a dozen brand new three story buildings. Every unit was out of Chloe's price range, and if not for Marcy's generous offer to accept her as a roomie, she'd have been forced to make do on the other side of Houston and commute farther to work.

"Sounds great," Chloe replied happily. "We'll just unpack."

"Try not to wear each other out before I'm back. I mean it!"

Marcy drove away, waving with one hand before she veered her sporty little Malibu around the corner. Chloe chuckled and led the way to the stairs and their second floor apartment. While Saul toted the luggage, she slipped her key into the lock and admitted them into the spacious parlor. Back when she'd first moved into the place, Chloe had marveled over the floor plan and Marcy's way with Zen. Marcy, an avid horticulturist, made her home into a tropical paradise with a selection of small potted fruit trees occupying the balcony.

Meanwhile, Chloe had more of a black thumb than anything. She chose not to touch the plants, for fear of killing them. They added bright and cheery splashes of color that complimented the cool tones throughout the rest of the apartment.

"Well?" Chloe asked, wearing an apprehensive expression on her face.

"It is very nice," Saul answered. He set the luggage inside and shut the door behind them, cutting off the oppressive cloud of muggy atmosphere outside. He didn't seem to notice or care, but Chloe maneuvered to stand beneath an air conditioning vent.

"Is that polite dragon-speak for 'your place is a shit hole'?" she asked while turning her face toward the cool current.

Saul turned and pulled her into his arms. "I am accustomed to larger accommodations, but…" The dragon kissed her brow and inhaled the peach scent clinging to her blonde hair. Chloe had never felt secure in a man's embrace until crossing paths with Saul. Each of his hugs conveyed warmth, protection, and love. "For you, I would take residence in a cardboard box."

"Fortunately, our place isn't anything like a cardboard box," Chloe laughingly said. "Okay, mini-tour. Over there we have a kitchen, a fridge, and standing freezer. Knowing you, those are the priority locations you'll want to know about."

"Ha ha ha," Saul replied dryly.

During the week-long visit at Saul's estate, she learned his voracious appetite translated to his human side. Mahasti often prepared a covered dish of sandwiches for his late night snacks.

"We each have a bed and bath of our own. This place is really way too big for just one person, which is kind of why Marcy invited me to stay with her."

"I see. That explains much to me about your 'chick haven.' The state of the decor makes it plainly apparent no man has stepped beyond these doors until now." Saul made a show of surveying the surrounding environment.

Chloe swatted his arm and finished up the tour by showing him where they kept the remotes and how to operate the gaming console.

"You have many games and movies," Saul marveled.

"Yeah. Marcy is the gamer, and I'm the bookworm. She gets me to play every now and again though. The movie collection we both built up."

Saul pulled a colorful case from the shelf. "My studio made this one."

"We have a few, I think," she said thoughtfully. "Oh, wipe that smug grin from your face. I had those long before I met you."

"The fourth in the series is in production. When we return to California I will take you on set, if you like."

"Really?" Chloe and Marcy frequently spent their Friday girl nights together on the sofa in front of scary movies, and with Saul present that was unlikely to change. It pleased her to no end that the dragon had an appreciation for American horror. "Marcy would be so jealous."

"Then we shall fly her out to join us."

His generosity touched her. With Saul, it wasn't about flaunting his wealth or trying to impress her. He honestly wanted to make her happy, and that meant accepting and including her best friend.

"She'd love that. Me, too." Chloe put the dvd back in place then dragged Saul into the bedroom, where he tossed the suitcases onto her bed. "God, I feel gross after that flight and standing around in the airport. It's nice to see that even a dragon has to walk through TSA and stand in a few lines." During the week spent in California, Saul had spoiled her beyond measure despite her efforts to resist his lavish gifts. She plucked a thin-strapped sundress and a thong from the neatly packed bag.

"Humans have an amazing idea for what constitutes as undergarments," Saul commented. He pretended to inspect the remaining contents then held up a practically nonexistent pink scrap. "Wear this one."

"So bossy." Chloe grinned and accepted his offering, swapping nude cotton for rosy lace.

If she didn't feel like a hot mess, stripping might have led to a playful round on her bed before the shower. Instead, Chloe tossed their clothes in the hamper and led the way to her personal bathroom.

Thank God it's clean. She owed Marcy a world of thanks, almost positive the shower had needed a quick scrub prior to her impromptu flight from California.

Shared showers and baths had become another memorable perk of her stay with Saul in his lavish home. Whether in his spacious walk-in shower, sunken tub, or personal hot-spring, her dragon loved the water.

"How do you shower in this?"

"Oh, come on. It isn't that bad," Chloe defended her bathroom.

Chloe and Saul maneuvered in the narrow tub until she reached the showerhead. Their close confines brought to mind sardines packed in a tin. Failing to silence her giggles at the mental image, she scooted back and tried to angle the water spray between them.

"Was it your intention to place me beyond the reach of the water?" he asked.

"Well, no, but I was freezing when I stood over there," Chloe mumbled. "You're so tall you blocked the spray."

"And of course, you have also chosen the most frigid temperature." Saul stretched one arm past her and twisted the knob toward the hottest setting. "That should—"

"Hot, hot, hot!" Chloe shrieked. She fumbled against him, practically knocking the glass door off of its track in her effort to escape. When that didn't work, she leapt into the corner like a cat avoiding the bath as the scalding assault continued.

Saul swore. The foreign word was unfamiliar to her, but the intensity of the utterance made it recognizable. He immediately turned the hot water knob to the middle. "Forgive me, Chloe, I didn't realize—"

It hurt like a bitch, but she played it off to assuage her boyfriend's shame. "I'm okay. It's all right," she assured him despite the red splotches on her forearm. Everywhere the water had touched appeared to be lobster red. *Geez, the water heater must be set at boiling.*

"You are not okay," Saul disagreed.

His large hands glided over her wet skin, tracing her arms from shoulders to wrists. Beneath his touch, Chloe's skin tingled like a thousand sparks danced over her body. As an odd sensation spread over her burns, not too unlike pins and needles, the pain diminished and the red scald marks gradually faded.

"What the hell was that?" Chloe demanded, divided between awe and unease.

"Magic," Saul said. He wore a big smile to match the mysterious admission.

"You're… a magical dragon?" *Thankfully not green and purple,* she thought. *Or named Puff.*

"Healing happens to be of my many talents, yes." Saul's smile gradually faded and confusion firmly took its place. "Should I not use my magic to help you? I did not ask, I merely presumed it would please."

"No, it's fine." Chloe examined her arm. The flesh appeared to be good as new again without the tenderness caused by her burns. "You did this once before in the cave, but you healed my ankle then."

"I did."

For some reason, the idea of having her own personal healer turned her on. Chloe stepped forward, against Saul's chest, delivering an impulsive kiss to his lips while standing on tiptoe. Her wet skin slipped against his body and a bold nudge trapped his stiffening cock to her lower tummy. She trailed her fingers across his broad shoulders until her right hand eventually reached his soaking wet blond hair. She loved the golden shade. Beneath the water, it became the color of raw honey between her fingers.

"Fuck me," she whispered against his lips.

"I thought you would never ask."

Saul slid his hand beneath her thigh and hoisted Chloe up until her back hit the slick tile surface. After a week of mind-blowing sex that only seemed to improve with every coupling, a few hours without his dick in her seemed like eternity.

Mew. The patter of the shower failed to drown out the feline cries. A second later, two big paws touched the door and noisily scraped down the glass, interrupting them before Saul had the chance to join their bodies.

"Felix?"

"Who is Felix?" Saul's voice rumbled against her throat.

The cat cried again, making a chirping sound.

"Mommy will be out in a minute."

In a thrust, Saul filled her body with his cock. She writhed between his hard chest and the shower tiles, tilting her head back and vocalizing an impassioned plea for more.

Felix dragged his front claws over the shower door and leapt at the glass, scrambling with his hind legs to make it over the top. He tried again twice until his mewling cries urged Chloe to press one hand against Saul's shoulder.

"Let me down, baby."

"What?"

"He thinks you're hurting me, I think."

Saul gave her an incredulous look. One blond brow shot up before he glanced over his shoulder toward the shadow beyond the frosted glass. "Your feline can wait." A slick backstroke and re-entry made Chloe's needy snatch cling to his dick and involuntarily squeeze. He felt so damned good that it took another terrified call from Felix before she pushed at his shoulders.

85

"Saul, he's *scared*."

He didn't protest again, but a heavy sigh indicated his displeasure. The separation of their bodies was pure misery as Saul grunted and set her down, ensuring she was steady before he released her from his hold.

Chloe stepped from the steaming shower and jerked a fresh towel from the rack. With it wrapped around her body and secured, she crouched down and received a fond nuzzle to her cheek from her whiskered friend. "I missed you, too," she crooned to the large cat. Felix, an impulsive luxury purchase in the wake of her failed relationship with Malcolm, purred and rumbled with elation.

"I'm sorry," she apologized to Saul.

He shook the water off his body and strode past her with a growled mutter that she couldn't decipher. Felix raised his hackles and hissed at the retreating man.

It was the closest she'd ever come to actually aggravating her placid and cool dragon lover. *I'll make it up to him later.* A niggling worm of guilt slithered into her thoughts only to be suppressed once Felix tickled her face with his whiskers.

"Marcy must be home now if Felix is back from the groomers."

"Oh."

Please don't do the spoiled man-child thing and give me the silent treatment. Of course, dragon or not, Saul was still male, and no less prone to the flaws that sometimes afflicted his sex. She hadn't intended to leave him with a case of blue balls.

"He is a very handsome beast," Saul offered without further prompting.

Chloe sighed in relief. As long as Saul spoke to her, it meant he wasn't too upset. Mahasti had warned her that a quiet dragon was a brooding dragon. "He's a Savannah."

"Ah. House cats bred with their wilder kin."

The spotted feline twined between her feet all the way from the bathroom to the bedroom, even head-butting her ankles in an attempt to direct her away from Saul. He hissed at Saul and raised his black-banded tail in the air.

"Felix, enough of that." She nudged him away long enough to pull on the fresh clothes she'd laid out earlier. She shook her head when the protective feline took up a watchful post on the foot of the bed.

He's acting awfully odd. "You don't eat cats, do you?"

Saul snorted and opened the bedroom door without waiting for her to finish dressing for their evening out. The dragon walked into the next room while tugging on his t-shirt, failing to honor her question with a response.

Note to self. An irritated Saul is definitely a quiet Saul. At least he isn't pissed.

"Holy abs," Marcy called from the hallway. "Chloe! You need to put a warning label on these!"

Chloe chuckled. After she ran a brush through her damp hair, she jogged out of the room in the chosen summer dress, its folds skimming her trim body. It suited her athletic frame, showcasing long legs and toned thighs with an ideal hem four inches above the knee. It was also as sexy as her casual clothing usually came, despite Marcy's dedicated efforts to spicing up her wardrobe. Felix trotted out behind her with his tail raised in the air then he mewled for attention until Chloe lifted him from the floor.

"Missed you too, Felix." *I hope dragons and cats aren't natural born enemies or something.*

"Damn, I hoped you'd take forever doing your hair so I could interrogate your boyfriend."

"Didn't you do enough of that in the car? Honestly. You know all of the highlights already. CEO and hot outdoorsman. There's nothing else…"

A bit of a grin surfaced on Saul's face. "It is true. I am afraid anything more would prove to be a severe disappointment, Marceline."

Marcy groaned. "You told him my full name? I guess I'll accept it. Coming from him it almost sounds sexy. Come on now, no time to waste. I made reservations as soon as you told me both of you were coming home, and I'll be pissed if we're late and they give our table away."

Dinner at a local Brazilian grill allowed Saul to sample a varied selection of meat. He ate enough for three men his size while Marcy gawked in disbelief. As a dragon hiding in human form, he required frequent feedings and consumed enough meat to provide most of the sustenance needed by his magical other half.

The Latina twisted on her chair to face her friend. "Where is he putting it away?"

"No idea," Chloe mumbled around a mouthful of food. She speared a rare piece of beef from Saul's plate and popped it into her mouth before launching into an explanation. "Saul's really into fitness. You know. Marathons, hiking. All that stuff." It made a good cover story.

"I guess you two are a perfect match then... Chloe, wait, that's still bloody inside," Marcy tried to warn her, a few seconds too late to make a difference.

"It's also delicious." Chloe stole another cut of meat for emphasis. She'd never eaten a piece of steak that wasn't thoroughly brown to its center in all of the time Marcy had known her.

"Geez, Saul, what did you feed her over there in LA?"

"I did nothing. Perhaps she has finally acquired the taste for proper cuisine."

They ended the night with a tour of the local Houston area. Marcy had a day of work to look forward to in the morning, so she begged out and retired to bed early, abandoning the lovebirds in the living room on the sofa.

"I'm glad I got to meet you, Saul. Try not to eat us out of house and home until we can visit the grocery store."

Saul chuckled. "I will try. It has been a true pleasure to make your acquaintance, dear Marceline. Rest well."

"I plan to. Night, guys!"

Without Marcy's company, Chloe and Saul retired to the bedroom where she gently shut the door to keep Felix at bay. The oversized cat had entered her life first, but she planned to allow Saul the chance to acclimate to having a bite-sized animal in his presence that wasn't on the menu. To soften the blow and spare them from a night of plaintive cries at the door, she had emptied a can of tuna into the cat's dish.

"Do you not intend to allow Felix inside?" Saul asked, concern coloring his voice.

"Tomorrow night. I missed him, but I wanna give him tomorrow to adjust to having you around. He can be a little mean sometimes to new people."

"I will not eat him."

Chloe tugged off her dress and tossed aside her bra, eager to crawl beneath the taupe jersey sheets. The urgency in Saul's voice distracted her from diving into bed. "I was joking when I said that, Saul... I'm sorry if I hurt your feelings. I know you wouldn't eat him." She hoped that was the case at least, restricting Felix from the room for entirely selfish reasons. She didn't want the cat to startle her dragon in the morning and provoke his predatory instincts.

His unreadable expression made a gradual transition, alluding to a smile then finally a grin. "It is long over, Chloe. Have no concern for that."

"But since we're on the subject... remember what I said about midnight snacks and visits to the fridge," Chloe warned.

"Boxers." Saul grinned at her and set aside his jeans. He preferred to go commando, but Mahasti had cautioned him to don appropriate clothing among the humans. It wouldn't do for Marcy to step out of her room in the middle of the night to find a naked Viking look-alike in front of the fridge, even if it would probably be the most thrilling moment she'd had all year.

Once Saul joined her in bed, she scooted in close against him and tugged the sheets over their nude bodies. The entire month in his company felt a dream, but the reality of sharing her bed with a mythological creature struck her as absolutely surreal.

"Saul?" she whispered in the dark.

"Hm?" His arm circled around her shoulders and kept her close. The secure presence of his body warmed her more than the sheets, a perfect contrast against the cold air circulated from the ceiling vents.

"Thank you for coming home with me."

"You told me this once before."

"But I want to thank you again. I think Marcy really likes you."

"Your friend is a generous and likable woman." His fingers traveled over her spine, a repetitive circuit that began anew at her nape and ended near the small of her back. She shivered beneath the touch.

"I'm going to miss her."

"My affection comes without a time limit, Chloe. You are neither required to leave at this month's end, nor will you be forced to abandon all you know and love. I will wait with you for as long as Marcy accepts my presence."

"She'd keep you here forever, I think. But I'm glad you two get along. It'll make things easier in the long run, and she can always come and visit."

"She is welcome whenever you desire." Saul continued his strokes down her back until he reached her ass and kneaded the soft flesh.

"That feels nice." She stirred beneath his touch and lifted her rump, sliding one knee under her body. She next drew the second beneath her and angled her backside into the air.

"Chloe..." Saul's hands circled her ass with firm pressure and his breath quickened.

"I want you to take me like our very first night," she whispered huskily.

"I presumed you did not favor the position."

89

She pressed her ass into his palms, hot and needy. "Sometimes I dream about our first night in the cave, Saul. I may not like the position, but I like the way *you* do it."

Freddy had always made it a position of domination, preferring it especially whenever she indulged his desires for anal sex. Saul made it feel different, tender, loving, and wholly natural. It was a vital part of who he was, a mighty beast masquerading as a man.

"Will there be another interruption from your feline?" A touch of humorous warmth filled his voice.

"Saul, please. I'm sorry. I'm sorry, all right? I didn't mean to make you angry."

"I was never angry, Ch—"

"Then just fuck me already!" All she could think of was having his cock buried inside of her. She didn't just crave his touch, she needed it. Chloe had been hot and achy all day, a discomfort inspired by his every touch and as well as the longing looks he'd given her over dinner. She'd frequently wanted to rip his clothes off.

She didn't have to ask again. For a large man, Saul moved with agility when the mood struck him. He snaked into position behind her and took her hips in his hands, his possessive hold securing her in place to receive the forward nudge of his pelvis.

"Always so wet for me." His voice thrilled her, a sensual growl against her ear accompanied by the close proximity of their joining bodies. Together, it was undeniable bliss.

"Always! Fuck yes, please," she cried in satisfaction, urging him to continue. His cock filled and stretched her in all the right ways and every thrust stimulated her clit, which felt hypersensitive to even the most minor touch.

Whenever Freddy stayed overnight, Marcy slept with earplugs and her alarm set on the highest volume. Chloe had no doubt that her best friend had adopted the same practice again.

The headboard slammed against the wall while Chloe clung to it, the helpless recipient to the hard thrusts bringing their bodies together. She wished she could see him and even hungered for the joy of watching his features contort in bliss, but the deeper penetration came at a price.

A mirror. I am buying a goddamn mirror if this is going to become normal for us. The mere thought of seeing him behind her, muscles rippling as he fucked her, caused Chloe to clench around him. Saul groaned and increased the tempo.

Every stroke slapped his balls against her clit, and when Saul grinded to the full depth of her tight pussy, the world around her spun. His mouth sealed over the mark on her shoulder to deliver a suckling kiss.

"Harder, baby, harder."

"I do not wish to harm you."

Chloe reached back and grabbed a harsh fistful of his hair, anchoring him close. "You won't, baby. But if you don't fuck me hard and deep right now I'm not responsible for what I do to you."

Her dragon's chuckle raised goosebumps over her skin and ran a delectable shiver down her spine. "As my lady commands." His hand ascended her flat stomach and palmed one breast. The nipple responded to his touch and stiffened.

She lost all sense of the world around her. Nothing mattered but the movement of their bodies and the indulgent gratification it brought. Chloe moaned out, withholding nothing.

"I'm so close," she whimpered, rocking back against him frantically. Saul dropped a hand between her thighs and slid his calloused fingertips over her clit. A single flick against the sensitive nerve bundle was all it took. She cried out his name, lost all control, and surrendered to her orgasm. The climax spasmed her muscles — harder than she'd ever experienced in all of their many couplings, nearly forcing his dick from within her tight snatch. Saul's feral growl vibrated through her ear, and then he slammed forward through the unyielding resistance.

"Fuck!" she cried, drawing out the word on a long groan. "More, baby, more."

Saul's hips pistoned forward in powerful, churning rhythm that pushed her orgasm beyond normal limits. Or maybe she was having multiples, each rolling into the next, too closely to be differentiated from each other. "Harder!" she screamed at him. The next thrust rocked Chloe physically against the headrail and pressed her cheek into the cool wood. Her climax became a pattern of starburst explosions, each blissful shudder radiating through her core.

Chloe collapsed against the sheets. Ever since her soul-binding and mating with Saul, she no longer recalled the meaning of mediocre sex. She shuddered and snuck one hand between her thighs where his come created a slippery mess. A shower seemed like the next logical step, and would be, if she didn't feel like someone had attached lead weights to her limbs.

Multiple orgasms were a thing of fantasy in bad pornography and erotic novels. For Chloe, it had become a reality that left her drained and useless afterward. "Does... does that ever stop happening?" she murmured up to him drowsily.

"No." He flashed her a sated grin and slipped out of bed. He returned moments later with a dampened, warm washcloth from the adjacent bathroom, and unlike any man of her past decade of sexual activity, he tenderly cleansed her body of the mess he'd made.

Chloe felt like a queen.

"What makes that happen? I know I've had a month or so to ask but..."

Saul slipped from the bed to dispose of the cloth into the laundry bin. When he returned, his fair brows rose with curiosity. "I explained this to you but poorly, so you must forgive me. It is... you may think of it as natural selection. When a male dragon performs a soul bond with his mate, certain changes occur to produce young."

"To produce... young?"

"We are magically inclined to gift one another immeasurable pleasure. As a result, you would submit to me more often, enhancing our chances of bearing little ones."

"Little ones?" Chloe's voice cracked. *Relax, Chloe, I'm pretty sure he's not expecting babies right this second. Can I even have them? Don't dragons lay eggs? I can't lay eggs!* Her inner worries approached hysteria and shattered the euphoria left in the wake of their sex.

"What is wrong?" His abrupt question pierced through her frantic line of thoughts.

"Nothing," she lied while searching for a valid excuse.

"Your heart races. I feel your anxiety, my love. Have I upset you? Have I said the wrong thing?"

"No, Saul... It's nothing you've done. I was thinking."

"Your thoughts appear heavier with each passing moment. What troubles you?" When she failed to answer, Saul persisted again in a gentler tone. "I am your mate. If I am not the one to whom you air your grievances, then what good am I to you?"

"Why didn't you talk to me earlier after the shower? You were upset but you didn't speak," she blurted out.

"You did not ask."

He had her there. She'd assumed her preferential treatment to Felix angered him and let it go without inquiring. A nervous giggle slipped past Chloe's lips as she burrowed into him for comfort. She loved him even more for his cool sense of logic and rationale.

"What about us? I mean, I'm human. Can we have children

together?"

"I am unaware of any successful dragon and human breeding, Chloe. For all intents and purposes, we are sterile together. Does this upset you?"

The knowledge didn't soothe Chloe's heart. If anything, his words bore an insidious sense of despair.

He's sacrificed so much for me, and I can't even give him a child. Why does he want me? she wondered. *Did he only settle because he's unable to find one of his own kind?*

"Did you... want children?" For all that she knew, he had no desire to father a child, and all of her concerns were the product of a tired mind.

Saul chuckled in the dark. "Once I did, but that is an interest long lost to me. Females of my kind are few and far between, and those with a good heart even more rare to find."

His words confirmed Chloe's darkest fears.

"Okay," she whispered.

"My love, I am happy as we are." He tucked her in close to his body, an arm wrapped her waist and his cheek atop her head.

She should have been comforted. So why did she feel so uneasy instead?

Chapter 2

Marcy was absolutely smitten by Saul, and if they weren't such close friends, the Latina might have been jealous that she hadn't found him first. At some point during their visit, Chloe had wanted to confide the secret of his true nature but couldn't bring herself to admit that the sexy Viking was a giant fantasy monster.

To their immense relief, Saul adjusted easily to Houston, claiming his life to be no different in the girls' shared home than his day-to-day activities in California. In the mornings, he and Chloe slept in, and by the afternoon they roused to walk Felix and sight-see local attractions. She even took him to the Houston Zoo, where he became an eager child, thrilled at every new sight.

"You've never visited a zoo?" she asked in disbelief.

"Many of these creatures are food to me. I have never pondered their existence beyond the taste of their flesh," Saul replied, his honesty taking her by surprise. He glanced at a nearby giraffe stretching its neck toward a branch bearing green leaves. The creature remained blissfully unaware of the predator observing its mealtime.

"And now you do?"

"You are a poor influence on me, my love. My behavior would shame others of my kind."

"Why's that?" Saul rarely spoke of his people. Between his scant clues and the information Chloe dragged out of Mahasti, she understood Saul to be a rarity among the great dragons in the world.

"My kind prefer solitude, and most certainly wouldn't mate with a human or live in her domicile for any extended time."

"If dragons prefer solitude, why do you have a company, a home, and friends like Mahasti and Leiv? Why befriend and care for me after I hurt my ankle? You could have left me there."

"A corporation is viewed as an extension of my horde, but as I said, I am considered eccentric among my kind. Perhaps Mahasti's presence has given me more freedom to live so openly."

Chloe considered that possibility and nodded. "I guess a djinn is handy to have around. But still, you have a job."

"I was curious, I admit. Theater amused me in my younger years. Mahasti encouraged my fascination by presenting it as a challenge. A test, if you will. Her powers can grant me the physical possessions to accompany humanity but they cannot make *me* more human. To learn their nuances, I had to walk among them."

Laughter filled the air between them. "Oh wow, I can almost picture it. So you went out, liked what you saw, and started your own business. But you kept a distance, too."

"I did, but nothing about this world intrigued me or held my interest for long. Before you, I visited my office when necessary. I did not make friends beyond the company of Leiv's father Ivan and Mahasti. When Ivan died, I understood how it felt to mourn for a mortal and felt comfort when Leiv took his place. They are both servants, and yet they are my closest and dearest friends," Saul said quietly, his breath a soft tickle against her ear. He snuck his arm around her waist and tugged her close.

"But I thought…" Chloe's voice trailed, a pause allowing her the time to search her memory. "You made it sound as if you'd taken other women to bed before me." In her mind, she had imagined a bevy of women flitting in and out of Saul's life, each of them fucked to the point of absolute bliss and left hungering for his prolonged company. She had pictured a playboy in search of a mate to fulfill him, and had taken profound pleasure in knowing she was the first to bring him to orgasm.

"On occasion," he admitted. "But only to sate an urge. I did not linger for sweet words and soft touches, and I never experienced the same satisfaction."

"You made it sound like you didn't come either," she pointed out.

"I did not. It was deeply irksome."

"Okay, okay. We're going to have to talk about this later when we're not surrounded on all sides by strangers attempting to muscle past us to see the okapi." Chloe had the sudden itch to find a secluded spot and show her man all the wicked things she could do to him to achieve his release.

God, I am such a nympho lately.

"Very well, but only if we go to see the camels. I promised Mahasti we would take photographs."

"Deal."

***

The morning at the zoo transitioned to an afternoon on Galveston Island. Marcy's current boyfriend, Antonio, met them at Hotel Galvez where they'd arranged for an overnight stay in one of the expensive spa suites. Saul had insisted on covering the rooms but had to promise to let Chloe, Antonio, and Marcy handle the rest.

Chloe dressed in beach attire beneath her summer dress and twirled in the mirror. "Tomorrow we go for a harbor tour," she explained.

"And this eve?"

"The aquarium, the beach, and then dancing around the town. Is that acceptable?"

"I do not dance."

She skipped over and tickled her fingers up Saul's delectable, bare chest. "Is that because you don't like dancing, or you don't know how?"

"I do not understand the purpose," Saul admitted. "From what I have observed in movies, human females prefer to perform awkward mating dances, each one adorned in plumage more ridiculous than the last."

Chloe attempted to maintain an even expression, but his serious features shattered her efforts. "Because it's fun, and *yes*, because it's sexy. Do you need a better reason?"

Saul grunted and said nothing further about dancing, much to Chloe's amusement. To prompt a reaction from him, she tugged the Velcro closure of his board shorts and loosened the tie.

"What are you doing now? Marceline and her suitor await us."

"Ever heard of a quickie?"

"I am a dragon. I do nothing quickly and perform all deeds with the utmost regard—" Chloe's decision to turn around and bend over the mirrored bureau distracted Saul mid-sentence. She flipped up the skirt of her sunny orange dress to expose the tiny swimsuit beneath.

"Wanna find out?"

She released the left hip-tie of her bikini bottom. It slipped down her thigh and tumbled to her ankle as she spread her legs. Sex with Saul had been on her mind since their provocative talk at the zoo, and hell if she planned to miss the opportunity. *Oh, who am I kidding? I've been wanting to jump him from the moment we woke up.*

To provide a little inspiration, Chloe trailed her fingers between her legs, gliding them between her slick folds until the returning stroke found her easily stimulated clit. A single touch made her core clench in anticipation, desiring his cock's deep penetration.

"See how wet I am?"

Saul's nostrils flared. His gaze focused on the path her fingers took, tracking their movement. The low rumbling sound he made in his chest aroused Chloe and tightened her nipples.

She watched in the mirror as Saul fucked her from behind. It was even sexier than she'd dreamed of, and about ten minutes later they determined that dragons did things quickly enough when given proper motivation.

Afterward, they freshened up to meet Marcy and Antonio in the lobby. As promised, the group's path led to the island's prime attraction for an afternoon of marine animals and rainforest exhibits.

"I'm so glad I bought this new camera, girl. These photos are going to be gorgeous," Marcy commented. She had crouched to angle the camera between the slats beneath the bridge railing. A white-faced monkey fastidiously groomed his dark fur on a nearby branch.

"Can you believe we've both lived in Houston all this time and never come down this way?" Chloe asked.

The two women chatted animatedly about the biospheres within the glass pyramid then continued their exploration from one exhibit to the next. With Saul at her side, Chloe listened to his tales of visiting the cloud forests of South America in his youth.

"I'd love to visit one of these places in person outside of a regulated habitat," Chloe said.

"If it is truly your wish, we will visit. I have a dear friend who lives in the Yucatán Peninsula. Teo would be thrilled to entertain us for a time before we continued farther south to Bolivia."

"You're going to take me to Bolivia? Saul, you're the best!" She threw her arms around his neck and clung to him in the middle of the walkway.

"Most women celebrate when you bring them wine or flowers. This one wants to hike in a muggy forest," Antonio muttered.

"I love the tropics," Marcy defended herself. "Did you forget what I told you about my family? I grew up on the beach in Mexico."

"I like flowers just fine," Chloe argued. "Is it bad that I want to see them in the wild and thriving instead of in a vase and dying?"

"Whoa, whoa, whoa. Okay." Surrendering, Antonio raised his hands like an outlaw facing the cops. "My bad, ladies."

Saul chuckled.

"See, Saul knows to keep quiet," Marcy said.

By the time they completed their tour of the various rainforests around the world and admiring a gorgeous ocelot beyond the glass, Marcy's wavy black hair was a frizzy mess. The group escaped into the cool, air conditioned hallway and settled at a table near the food court so that Chloe could wrangle her friend's hair back into a single plait.

"I told you that wasn't enough hair spray... there. You look

97

fabulous again," Chloe said as she fastened a band around the tip.

Antonio shook his head. "All of that effort for her to get in the water at the beach in an hour."

"Hey, looking this fabulous takes work," Marcy laughed as she returned to his side. Chloe caught the disapproving glance she gave when Antonio wasn't looking, and didn't need to read minds to know what Marcy thought — Antonio wasn't working out to be as fun as she'd hoped for. His tendency to complain was putting a bummer on the entire outing, whereas Saul went with the flow and never fussed.

Dinner in the adjacent restaurant afforded Saul the chance to see an all-you-can-eat buffet for the first time. He marveled over the assortment in passing on the way to their table then pulled back the seat for Chloe to sit her like a gentleman. Antonio shot the pair a bewildered look, especially after Marcy stared him down for failing to do the same. Chloe almost felt sorry for the poor guy. Almost.

"I'm going to miss you so much."

"Wait. What?" Marcy paused with her fork halfway to her mouth.

"I... made up my mind today. I'm going to go back to California with Saul." Part of Chloe had known what she wanted from the start, but she'd needed to make sure before making a drastic change to her life. The interaction between Saul, her oldest friend, and even Felix, gave her everything she needed to know. Her new lover had passed the test.

"But... I'll never get to see you."

Saul spoke up before Chloe had a chance to comfort her morose friend. "You may always come to our home to visit, Marceline."

"I guess," Marcy agreed quietly. She stirred the food on her plate in silence without looking up again. Antonio excused himself to ravage the buffet for a second helping, and Saul wisely followed his example, leaving the two women alone.

Why'd I have to pick now to tell her? Chloe sighed and dropped her head, overcome with guilt.

"Sorry, Marce. I didn't mean to be a bummer."

"Nah, it's all right. I sort of figured, I guess." Marcy looked up with a smile, but her eyes were watery. "Plus, it's not like I can disapprove of Saul. He's great. I mean, really great. I'm happy for you. You deserve better after Malcolm and Freddy."

"I can still help cover rent 'til you find someone else."

Marcy waved her off. "No, don't do that. I paid the rent just fine before you moved in, chica, and I can do it while you're gone. That's not a big deal."

"Are you sure? It's not like Saul allows me to pay for anything. When I told him that I wanted to work, he told me he'd hire me on in his company's legal department." Chloe shook her head and chuckled softly.

"You'll be a glorified housewife, basically?"

"Not even that. He has a housekeeper *and* a driver, so I'll have no idea what to do with myself. But you bet your ass I don't plan to sit around his giant mansion on my bum every day."

"That's right. You tell him. You're a strong, independent woman." Marcy picked up her glass and clinked it to Chloe's. "I'll fly out and see you this Christmas, girl."

"If you wait until Christmas, I'll start to think that you don't love me." Chloe blinked away the moisture in her eyes. "Saul's gonna take us on set, remember? You can bat your lashes at the leading actor and steal his heart." She waited a moment before she whispered, "Because Antonio sucks."

They both laughed over the idea, which had the intended, comforting effect. Once Marcy cheered and Chloe didn't have to worry about losing her best friend, both men returned like a masculine third sense told them the coast was clear.

The decision to take a stroll down the beach followed dinner. Jokes ensued in the car ride to the seawall about whether or not Chloe would sink like a stone to the bottom of the gulf after appearing to compete with Saul's ravenous appetite. She showed her friend and boyfriend up when she shed her dress and boldly raced Marcy for the waves.

"This was a great idea!" Marcy called to her minutes later.

"Remember how gross the water was last time we came out here?"

"Ugh, don't remind me. Hey Antonio! You coming in or what?" Marcy called out toward the beach.

"Where'd Saul go?" Chloe asked.

Hands grabbed her beneath the water and tugged Chloe under. Spluttering, she resurfaced and slapped water at her grinning mate, but he evaded her playful attack like a dolphin. His uncanny grace and impressive lung capacity held an unfair advantage over the rest of them in their water play.

If he didn't already tell me that he breathes fire, I'd think he was a water dragon.

Chloe discovered her dragon didn't excel at beach volleyball when a group of college coeds invited her, Marcy, Antonio, and Saul to join

99

their game. Eventually, after he missed enough serves and passes, Saul excused himself from the game to spectate instead, much to everyone's relief.

"Your boyfriend definitely needs to remain on standby as eye candy until we can teach him to play," Marcy teased.

"Well, at least he's a damn good distraction. Their back corner player keeps ogling him instead of watching the ball," Antonio commented.

With Saul gone, their team won the next game. The loss of the sun brought in a cool breeze from the gulf and visitors on the beach thinned. It turned out that a long day of touring Southeast Texas' attractions and waterfront athletics had worn them all out. Dancing was off the agenda.

"Wanna stop for snacks to take back to our rooms? Room service is a little too rich for my pockets," Marcy commented on the way to Antonio's SUV.

"I don't want to look at anything else to eat for the rest of today," Chloe muttered. "I think I'm good." Chloe lay down in the rear seat and set her head upon the beach towel covering Saul's lap. A half hour later, she awakened to find her cheek against his shoulder.

"Tell Chloe we'll meet you both for lunch tomorrow if you want. Me and Antonio plan to visit his family before we meet you both for the harbor tour."

"Of course. Have a pleasant eve, Marceline."

"Night, Marcy," Chloe mumbled.

"Shit, sorry. We tried not to wake you. Sleep well, you two."

Marcy flounced away to join Antonio in their hotel room. Once Saul and Chloe showered off the salt water residue, a strange sense of vitality seeped through her veins. It hit her like a shot of adrenaline and quickly shed her exhaustion.

"Saul?"

"Yes?" He sprawled beside her, silent but peaceful in appearance with his golden eyes shut. He often feigned sleep but rarely dozed off before her.

"Are dragons nocturnal?"

"Most are. Why do you ask?"

"You always get up to go snack and stuff."

"Many centuries ago, my kind once awakened with the arrival of false-light and hunted freely. Many of my ancestors delighted in setting villages ablaze until the flames could be seen from miles away," he admitted. "I have adapted over the years and overcome my natural inclinations. It allows me to pass for a human more easily."

"I certainly appreciate it. No wonder you always snore until noon. You must be rubbing off on me because I can't sleep either." All of those long nights of cuddling and drifting off just prior to the sunrise took their toll on Chloe's circadian rhythm. "This problem is all your fault, so you can fix it," she teased.

Once he stifled his laughter, Saul kept her entertained through the night with tales of his ancestors. He told her about his mother's gentle heart, the contrast between his parents' personalities, and how she had tamed the worst of his father's habits only just before the dragon's demise. Even his ruthless grandfather was a beast feared so greatly that the legendary St. George slew him, among many others, and yet Saul had inherited neither male dragon's tendency toward violence.

"So what you're saying is that it's a good thing you guys have adapted to other methods of conquest that don't involve fire?"

"You misunderstand, Chloe. Our disguises are a necessity in these modern days of missiles, tanks, and jet planes. But yes, you are right. Many of my kind do prefer to manipulate humanity from behind our corporations."

"And the government," she murmured while clicking through the cable channels on the television.

"The silver dragons are especially fond of politics, yes," he chuckled.

"Silvers?" Chloe perked.

"Quicksilver dragons, my love. Otherwise known as storm dragons."

"They sound pretty. Are all of you organized by color?" She reached over his shoulder and into the bag of cheesy nacho chips on his nightstand.

"Mmhmm." His fingers trailed through her hair, an absent stroke that continued down her back. The ridiculous reality show on the television faded into the background.

"Oh come on. Don't clam up on me now. What are you?"

"Bronze," he answered absently. The models on the catwalk distracted Saul more easily. She rolled her eyes and poked his bare chest until he coughed up more information. "The product of a quicksilver and volcanic dragon, Chloe. Hardly anything special. I can't say that I've inherited my mother's love of political scheming."

"So volcanic must be red. Tell me about reds."

"They're assholes," he said bluntly.

Chloe almost inhaled her chip. "Okaaay," she said, drawing out

101

the word. "You going to clarify that any?"

"There is little else to say about them."

"Where did you pick up that language anyway?"

"I learned it from you," Saul said, an amused tone accompanying the cheeky smile on his face. "If you must know, my father and grandfather were both volcanic dragons, although I feel no such inclination to dwell in a pit of lava myself."

"Because you take after your mother?"

"Possibly."

Chloe didn't press Saul anymore about his family or the mysterious red dragons he seemed to hold in disdain. Bits and snippets of conversation alluded to a love/hate relationship between her lover and his male progenitors, one she certainly understood thanks to a failed relationship with her mother.

"Do you think I'll ever meet any of your fellow dragons? Or are you all, you know, a solitary sort?"

"Do you wish to?"

"Maybe one day." Chloe shrugged and snuggled in closer. "Hey, do you think room service has a midnight menu?

"Did you not tell Marcy that you would prefer not to see food for the rest of the day?"

"It's past midnight. It's a new day," she argued.

Saul sighed and reached for the phone. One thing remained certain — Chloe knew how to train a dragon.

Chapter 3

The days after their weekend in Galveston passed like a blissful dream. Thanks to her savings and Saul's generosity, Chloe treated unemployment like an extended vacation. After an enjoyable jog on the paths cutting between the residential complex and adjacent park, she showered and fell into a pleasant sleep while Saul perused her bookshelf and watched television. She dozed in and out of her nap, awakening once to the sound of Saul asking if she'd like Marcy to bring home a pizza, and a second time to a ruckus outside.

"Who the fuck are you?"

No. Oh god, no. Freddy's loud voice carried all the way to the bedroom and interrupted her attempt to resume napping. Saul must have answered the door, as he often did whenever Marcy or Chloe were unavailable. The two women had even returned one day to find him entertaining a pair of Kirby salesmen, who had easily convinced him to buy three of their vacuums and complete accessory kits before Chloe ran them out of the apartment. She managed to snatch the check from their hands in the nick of time.

For a dragon, Saul had a soft heart, and if he couldn't chase two door-to-door salesmen away, she had little hope of him running off Freddy.

Chloe scrambled from the bed, driven to hurry by the sheer outrage in her ex-boyfriend's voice. Felix ran past her on his way to hide in the closet; her cat had never liked Freddy.

The reason for Freddy's ire became apparent when Chloe stepped from the hall. Saul didn't wear much, accustomed to Marcy vacating the home between the hours of 8 and 5. He must have visited the facility's pool, as he stood half naked in only a towel, like some bronzed and gleaming Adonis. Or better yet, her new manservant.

"Chloe, tell this jackass to get his clothes on and get the fuck out. We need to talk."

"Uh, no. *You* get out." *I don't need this right now!*

Freddy ignored Saul *and* her indignant cry by stepping over the threshold. "I thought I'd give you a chance to apologize for what you did, baby. I know you can be a little unreasonable sometimes, and I get that. But I'm still willing to take you back."

"I do not believe Chloe wishes to speak with you." Saul placed himself between Chloe and her ex. "Leave or I will escort you from the premises."

"Are you serious? Who the fuck is this guy? Tell the Fabio wannabe to hit the road so we can talk about this like adults."

Yes, who is he? How do I introduce him? Boyfriend sounds so trite and simple. Chloe sucked in a long breath and slowly released it through her nose. She could do this.

"Baby, meet Freddy. Freddy, this is Saul, my…"

"Betrothed," Saul offered in the silence following her falter. "Chloe and I are to be wed."

She expected Freddy to make fun of Saul's formal speech pattern, or at least question it, but his steroid-deteriorated mind latched on to the wedding announcement instead. He laughed.

"Good one, sweetcheeks."

"No, we're serious. I'm flying back with Saul to Los Angeles in a week. I came back to handle my life and pick up Felix."

Saul stared at her while Freddy looked between the two of them in disbelief. "Like hell you are. You can't marry this asshole."

"Excuse me? You're not my fucking father, Freddy." Saul opened his mouth to speak, but Chloe whirled on him and poked her finger into his bare chest. "I can handle this myself without you butting in, thank you very much." Saul shut his mouth and stepped back with both hands up. By then, she'd already returned her attention to the jerk in front of the door. "I meant every single word that I said to you."

Freddy's cheeks mottled. "You ungrateful little slut. Is this the thanks I get for taking your beat-up pussy after Malcolm got tired of you?"

It didn't surprise her even a little that Freddy resorted to name calling and insults. Color flushed over her cheeks and turned her face into a blazing inferno of shame and anger. It hurt, cutting deeply no matter how much she told herself that he was only a bitter, lonely man who would never see beyond his own ego. She blinked away the stinging tears and drew in a slow breath.

And then she launched her right fist into Freddy's face. The blow laid him on his ass just before the welcome mat. The satisfying crunch that could have been his nose breaking didn't faze or stop Chloe's furious tirade.

"Fuck!" he cried from the ground, holding his nose. His eyes watered with tears and blood leaked from his nostrils.

"I am not a slut, but *you* are an asshole and no woman will *ever* stay with you. No one! You'll always be a lonely asshole, but I have someone who loves and cares about me now. Now get out of my house before I kick your ass and let him fuck up whatever is left of you!"

"You fucking crazy bitch. Keep her, dude, just fucking keep her!" Freddy raged as he climbed to his feet and vacated the apartment, too much of a wuss to risk further physical confrontation.

With a deep frown lining his face, Saul shut the door behind Freddy and turned to face Chloe. "I am sorry, my love," he apologized as if he were the one in the wrong. He guided her to the couch and settled a blanket across her lap before stepping away into the kitchen. He returned a few minutes later with a sandwich, chips, and a tall glass of sweet tea.

The food tasted like sawdust in her mouth, and despite that setback, Chloe forced herself to eat the lunch prepared by her considerate mate.

"I think I'm gonna go take a shower."

"Would you like me to wash your back?" Saul's offer held no hidden innuendos. That was another thing she loved about her generous dragon: he knew when to ignore his randy libido.

Chloe shook her head. "No, but thanks. I just need a few minutes alone."

"Take as much time as you need."

***

Chloe rose from the bathtub floor and tilted her face up into the hot spray. The tuna had tasted awful coming up the wrong way; so awful she'd reached an arm out of the shower and snagged her toothbrush from the nearby counter. The mint paste helped rid her mouth of the sour taste but the usually refreshing scent was off-putting.

"Chloe? Sweetie?" Marcy knocked on the bathroom door before opening it. "Geez, woman, turn the fan on. It's a sauna in here."

"You home already?"

"Already? It's the same time I always get home." Marcy flipped the switch for the fan. "You okay, hun? Saul told me what happened. We've been waiting for you to come out."

"Sorry. Just a sec, okay?" Chloe scrubbed soap over her face a final time, rinsed, and shut off the water. A towel hung beside the frosted glass door for her to wrap around her shower-reddened skin. Ever since Saul had scalded her, she had acquired his strange tolerance for boiling water and preferred it.

105

"Hey, your dad called, too, and wondered if you were still planning to visit for the Fourth of July."

"Dad's too busy with his new girlfriend to miss me at the barbecue. Besides, I don't want to intrude."

"Sam misses you plenty. Even if he does have a hot girlfriend half his age to take care of him now. Hey, are you okay? You look horrible, chica."

Chloe shook her head and tightened her grip on the towel. Felix snaked in between her wet ankles to deliver a round of loving mrowls. "It's nothing."

"It's something. You know you can't lie to me. What's wrong? Is it Mr. Moneybags? Did he do something to you? I swear, I will fuck his world up if he—"

"No, it's nothing Saul did."

"Freddy then? Honestly hun, don't let that prick upset you. He's so not worth it and from the sound of things, you chased him off good this time. I wish I'd been here to see you bloody his big nose."

"It's not that. It's…" *Please no, don't let me be pregnant. Please, please no.* Chloe paced in a short line and raised one fist to her lips. She bit her knuckles fretfully.

"Chloe, it's me. You can talk to me about anything."

"I think I'm pregnant," she blurted out, interrupting whatever else Marcy intended to say.

Her friend stared at her with wide eyes. "Holy shit. What do you plan to do? Is Saul okay with that?"

"It's… it's not his." Chloe bit her lip.

"Are you sure? You two have been at it like rabbits for the last couple of weeks."

"No. Marcy, you don't get it. Saul can't… he's had a vasectomy," she lied, erring on the side of caution to avoid spilling the truth. "You know, rich and wealthy, wanted to keep women from using him for his money."

Marcy gaped. "No, sweetie, no. *Please* don't tell me you let Freddy go bareback in you."

"He didn't come! I didn't even want to have sex. I told you that."

"Well…" Marcy bit her lip and fidgeted. "Those vasectomies, they fail sometimes, right?"

Fresh tears wet Chloe's cheeks. She didn't want to be pregnant, but the likelihood of Freddy being the father outweighed the chances of Saul impregnating her with some sort of magical dragon spawn. *I saw the hesitation on his face. He's disappointed that I can't bear him 'young'. Disappointed that I'm human, and hell, I was disappointed too I guess.* It was one thing to decide on her own to enjoy life without a child, but another for circumstances to dictate the choice to her.

"I'll run out to Walgreens and get you a test," Marcy volunteered.

"I can't ask you to do that. You just came in from work after a long day."

"Are you serious? Give me thirty minutes to make it there and back. Saul's a little worried about you, so you might want to pop out and say something to him. He thinks he pissed you off by trying to jump in to your rescue."

Chloe nodded. "Sure. Yeah. I'll get dressed and go talk to him. Just hurry back, okay?"

"Of course." Marcy stepped backwards from the humid bathroom and pulled the door with her.

"Marcy?"

The door hesitated, cracked an inch. "Yeah, babe?"

"Thanks."

Once Marcy was gone, Chloe smoothed her fingers over her belly and tried to imagine some tiny life forming within it. She'd had a false alarm in the past, a result of foolishly forgetting her birth control while dating Malcolm.

Dismissing the thought, she retreated from the bathroom and stepped into the open foyer to greet Saul with the towel wrapped around her drying skin. She met him halfway and stood on tiptoe to accept a sweet kiss. He had dressed while she showered and donned a t-shirt with a casual pair of khaki shorts.

"I'm not upset at you, silly. What happened to asking before assuming?"

"Perhaps I have begun to adopt your human ways."

She poked him in the ribs before stepping back. "Hey, I'm still not feeling so great. Would you take Felix for his walk?"

"Of course I will, but may I ask a question first?"

"What is it?"

"I was under the impression that a litterbox serves that purpose, and yet we walk him each day."

Despite the gravity of her worries, Chloe chortled a quick, sharp laugh. "We aren't walking him to poop, Saul. It's because he needs the exercise. Besides, Marcy went to get me some medicine from the pharmacy."

"Ah. Very well then. As I said, it is no trouble. I was merely curious."

Saul clipped a leash to Felix's harness and left without argument. She loved that man and appreciated his sweet personality.

How do I tell him I might be carrying another guy's child?

Chloe lit one of her handmade candles and breathed in the soothing clary sage and geranium that wafted toward her as the wax melted. Marcy and her mother made scented candles with organic essential oils, so Chloe had reaped in the therapeutic benefits for years.

While waiting for her pal to return, she dried her hair then tossed on plain yoga pants. She spent the rest of the time sitting on the bathroom sink while waiting for Marcy to return.

Thanks to the evening traffic, Marcy's thirty minute trip to the pharmacy dragged into an hour. Chloe practically snatched the plastic bag and shut the door in her friend's face. Minutes later, she opened the door with the answer held in one hand. Marcy bounced on her toes and fixed Chloe with an expectant look.

"Well? Don't keep me in suspense, chica. What does it say? Are you good?"

She wordlessly held the pink plastic wand out for Marcy's inspection. A big (+) stood out darkly against the white background in the little oval window.

"Oh damn…" Marcy blinked, rubbed her eyes, and then looked again. "Oh sweetie, you're going to be a mommy."

Chapter 4

Despite Marcy's insistence, Chloe succumbed to disbelief and refused to schedule a doctor's appointment to confirm the truth. As the rest of her vacation days in Houston dwindled, both women began the tedious packing process. Chloe's initial guess of five boxes proved to be too few, so Antonio volunteered to visit his job site for more while the girls and Saul got her belongings together.

"Chloe?"

Chloe turned to find Saul holding up a semi-translucent slip of shell pink lace and silk. The tiny babydoll nightie was a favorite during her relationship with Freddy. She hadn't worn it since.

"Why do you never wear such things? It is very attractive."

Marcy, seated on the floor amidst a sea of porcelain, butterfly-winged unicorns, chortled out loud and continued to wrap newspaper around the delicate baubles. "The man has a good question. Didn't you pay a lot of money for that?"

"I'll go shopping in LA for new ones. Those you can toss in the trash bin over there."

Saul's disappointed expression brought a smile to Chloe's face. *I'll get some special ones just for him. Not these used leftovers.*

When Marcy headed out for work the next day, Saul summoned Mahasti for the veritable mountain of boxes. It was as simple as wishing them away to his home. They would tell Marcy that they had a delivery service retrieve them.

"Finally. With all of that gone, I can find Felix's carrier."

"Why must we place him in a tiny box? Would he not be happier in your arms during the flight?"

"That's for human babies only, Saul. Some parents pay for the extra seat and bring the baby carrier but most just hold them in their lap." Chloe's expression darkened, unbeknownst to her until Saul shrank back a step. The mirror behind him revealed the severity of her frown and brought her glaring expression into focus.

"Have I asked too many questions?"

"No. No. Sorry… I don't mean to take it out on you. I'm tired," she explained.

"Enjoy a nap. Felix and I shall enjoy a walk around the block."

Chloe kissed him in apology. The moment Saul and Felix disappeared out the door she hurried for the bathroom.

Maybe the first test was a fluke.

It wasn't. Like the first, the stick depicted a positive result.

The next week passed in a surreal haze, fueled by Chloe's disbelief. What would she do, how would she tell her family, and most importantly, how could she break the news to Saul? On the final day of their visit to Houston, she and Marcy held each other tight at the airport security gate.

"If you ever need to come home, you always have a place to stay with me, Chloe. I mean it. No matter what," the short-statured Latina told her fiercely with tears in her dark eyes. "Both of you." Marcy wasn't referring to Chloe and Felix.

"You better come visit for Christmas like you promised," Chloe whispered back.

"Nothing could keep me away." They hugged tightly again then Marcy even squeezed Saul around his broad shoulders. "Be good to her. Don't give me any reason to come to California to kick your ass, buddy."

"I would not consider myself worthy of Chloe if such a visit became necessary, Marceline. Travel safely."

An uneventful flight delivered Saul, Chloe, and Felix to Los Angeles where Leiv retrieved them from the airport. As usual, her every wish seemed to be his and Saul's command. He drove her to a Wendy's for a Frosty and the greasy burgers she craved, allowing her to introduce Saul to the frozen chocolate decadence for the first time.

Still, things didn't quite feel right, and it took a minute for her to figure out what the anomaly was. There was silence from the front seat.

Something must be wrong with Leiv. He's never so quiet.

The odd, taciturn change of personality warred with her memories of the chatty bear shifter. He was polite as ever as he helped her from the car, but the sparkle was missing from his eyes. Reluctant to intrude, she left him alone and retreated to her bedroom with Felix's carrier. Saul promised to join her after he checked in on the household affairs.

"This is home now, at least for a while," Chloe murmured to the curious feline. If Saul allowed them to remain once she made her confession. It felt foolish to move blindly into his home, but the wistful, crazy-in-love part of her wanted to trust nothing would change.

"Go on now. Have fun, baby," she coaxed the cat, urging him from the carrier. Felix scrambled across the polished floors and slid beneath the bed. He ran circles across the room and leapt into a window sill to peer outside into the golden afternoon.

By the time Saul arrived with her luggage and personal items, she had sprawled across the bed with Felix nestled beside her. He was bored of investigating his new digs but intrigued by the gold silk tassel on her pillow case.

"What's wrong with Leiv?" Chloe asked. She absently teased Felix and giggled at his batting paws.

"Matters of the heart, Chloe. Mahasti is similarly pensive."

"Looks like they took advantage of our absence."

"Indeed," he replied without elaboration.

Fine. I'll have to ask Mahasti about it then, Chloe thought, brimming with curiosity that her boyfriend wouldn't sate with information. Since her arrival, she and the djinn in Saul's service had developed a girlish camaraderie.

After she abandoned the bed, Chloe crouched beside the luggage pieces brought up from the car. Part of her wanted to lounge away the afternoon to enjoy the comforts of bed, but a desire to behave like an adult drove her to get an early start on establishing her professional career in California. She wouldn't settle for being his low-maintenance human pet, a rent-free occupant of the manor who happened to share his bed. For Chloe, it was more than a mere desire to pull her own weight — she had worked her entire adult life and couldn't fathom staying at home.

"Mahasti will unpack for you."

"I can empty my own things, and I'm not unpacking right this moment," she replied. She returned to the bed with a slim leather case and removed her laptop. "How do I access the internet here?"

Saul rattled off a complicated password that Chloe asked him to repeat twice. *Jeez. Dragons are all about security. How the hell does he have that memorized?* The long string of special characters, numbers, and letters looked like gibberish to her.

"What has you typing so busily?"

"Working on my resume. I need to update it."

"That is unnecessary," he told her with a chuckle.

"I mean it, Saul. I didn't come here to be a trophy wife like one of the gems in your vault. I want a job."

"Don't be silly, Chloe. You will work with Drakenstone Studios."

"As what?"

"You are a paralegal with many years of experience. Arrangements will be made for a new supervisory position—"

"I will not."

Saul paused to stare at her and raise an inquisitive blond brow. "You will not do what?"

"Accept some management position handed to me. Everyone will know why I'm there! I'll be a laughingstock. The boss's new girlfriend given a cushy desk job to sit on her ass and collect a salary."

"Why would I pay you a salary?" Saul's quizzical expression deserved a punch, if not for the unveiled sincerity on his features.

"Are you teasing me? Saul, the entire purpose of employment is to receive a paycheck."

"No." His brow furrowed. "Did I sound as though I were jesting?"

Chloe sighed and rubbed her fingers against her temple. "Saul, I need a job. Income."

"My love, it is common among dragons to combine hoards once mated. What is mine shall also become yours. We are not humans to maintain separate bank accounts and financial means."

The bottom of her belly seemed to drop to her feet. Chloe stared. "Combine... *hoards?* Saul, I don't have a hoard. I haven't brought anything."

"You have given me you. That is sufficient." He paused, seemed to consider something, and then thoughtfully added, "And you have brought Felix."

The tears flooded from Chloe all at once. Saul, who remained completely oblivious to the inner turmoil surrounding her secret, merely hugged her close and pressed his lips against her brow.

"Saul, you're too good to be true."

"No, I am a dragon."

Chapter 5

"There we go, all set up." Chloe stood back with her hands on her hips and regarded their tent with satisfaction. After Saul's cavalier declaration of combining their holdings, Chloe had come to a single conclusion.

He needed to know about the baby, and she wanted to treat him to one fantastic night before she broke the news to him. Before she jeopardized their relationship and risked losing his trust.

Saul rumbled a noise of disapproval. "Am I not an improvement over a sleeping bag?" Her mate towered above her in his draconic body, seated on his haunches beside the tent.

"You're great to sleep on. But you don't keep mosquitos away and they love to bite on me."

"I never notice them."

"You have dragon skin," Chloe pointed out dryly. She tried to pinch his hide between her fingers. Contrary to popular fiction, dragons lacked scales, and had the exterior of a lizard like a chameleon or gecko. After a soak in Leiv's big fishing pond, Saul's flesh resembled velvet, but it was thick and impervious to most damage. She loved to stroke her fingers over his face and through the silky mane at the base of his feathers and around his throat.

A plume of smoke accompanied his irritable huff. "I cannot fit inside."

"Not like this you can't," she laughed. "But you can't enjoy my skimpy underwear in this form either."

For a giant creature, Saul had impeccable reflexes. Out of his dragon skin and into his human body in the blink of an eye, he swept her close and dipped her back into an exaggerated kiss. The playful flirt received the intended response and lulled her into a relaxed state in his arms.

"Come inside with me."

A day ago when they visited the local town for an impromptu shopping trip, Chloe had beseeched Leiv to drive past the local sporting goods store. The brand new pads and sleeping bags filling the snug space were part of the surprise. Chloe kicked off her shoes and stepped inside the family-sized tent with Saul right behind her. She had the advantage, able to ogle every magnificent inch of his body since the shift had already bared him for her pleasure.

"Zip it up behind you, please," she called over a shoulder.

Chloe spread a blanket over the sleeping bags and crouched down to power on the mp3 player. Smooth orchestral music whispered from the speakers once she set them to a low volume for ambience. "C'mon. Sit down in front of me. No, with your back to me."

Saul's bewildered expression was priceless. "Is this a new position? How will I—?"

"No, silly." She failed to hold her giggles at bay. "This isn't for sex. I'm going to give you a massage," she explained once the obedient dragon lowered himself to sit in front of her.

"Why?"

Chloe bit her lower lip, divided between confessing her selfish motivations and keeping him completely in the dark. Uncertainty filled her almost at once, doubting whether Marcy's idea to put him in the best possible mood would help. "To relax you."

Saul looked back over his shoulder with a smug grin. "I know exactly what will make me relax."

She rolled her eyes and pushed on his cheek to make him face forward again. "Trust me on this. Breathe in a deep breath and slowly let it out. If you really hate it, I'll stop."

As if he sensed the longing in her voice, Saul silenced his complaints and became still as a marble-carved statue. Her own personal David, but warm and alive beneath her hands. With a backpack of goodies within reach, she dragged it closer and unsnapped it with a hand.

I hope dragons aren't allergic to anything, she thought. She uncapped a small, navy blue bottle and poured fragrant oil into her hands.

"What is that?"

Chloe nervously bit her lower lip again. At this rate, she'd die of an anxiety attack long before she had the child. "Something I hope you like," she whispered.

"The smell is pleasant. Did you bring mint tea?"

"Not tea. Something even better." *I hope.*

A surge of confidence overtook Chloe as she drizzled the oil onto one cupped palm and warmed it between her hands. After smoothing her fingers across his broad shoulders, she kneaded a path down his back with alternating pressure until the tension in his spine released. She swept his hair aside and brushed her lips against his nape. Saul purred as loudly as Felix, and the mental comparison made her giggle despite her best efforts otherwise.

Chloe stole a peek over Saul's left shoulder to see his sexual interests hadn't waned. His big cock stood tall in arousal, the very sight of it encouraging her body to match his reaction. Her core clenched and her dampening panties became an uncomfortable hindrance. She wanted him and had become practically insatiable when it came to satisfying her recent lusts.

Swallowing, she settled again with her bottom against her heels and slipped her hands down his sides until every drop vanished into his skin. Her dragon became like putty in her hands, a low groan escaping his half-parted lips. Another lean to the side revealed his serene features in profile, a man at complete peace who easily lay down once she moved from his path and coaxed him back against the blanket.

Chloe knelt alongside her lover to skim her fingers over his muscular chest, kneading his pectoral muscles, glossing him with scented oil, and anticipating him more with each breath.

"You're gorgeous," she finally murmured.

"Hm?" Saul finally opened his eyes to gaze at her.

"How are you so beautiful inside and out?"

"Dragons are superior in every way." His warm grin and sparkling eyes eased the offense from his arrogant reply

With her willpower exhausted, Chloe climbed to her feet and pulled her shirt over her head. Saul caught the hint and sat up quickly to help. "I've become fond of your human ways to make love," he admitted.

Saul unsnapped her jeans and yanked them down her thighs to discover a scant blue thong. His appreciative, rumbled growl sent her heart into excited palpitations. Thank goodness he loved her choice, as evidenced by the twitch that flexed his erection and the hunger in his eyes. During her last night in Texas, Marcy had swept her away on an all-evening girl-hunt for sexy attire, leading to a substantial increase in Chloe's lingerie collection. Every night with Saul would become a surprise if her secret didn't drive a wedge between them.

"Well?" she whispered.

Saul responded by shoving his face against her panties. He flicked his tongue against her freshly waxed mound through the delicate lace pattern while his strong fingers kneaded her bare ass cheeks, delivering his own massage.

"This color suits you," he mumbled against the lace, following up with another flat press of his tongue. "A shame it must come off."

"Watch and learn," Chloe whispered. "The great thing about thongs is they can be shifted aside."

The tiny triangle bunched up easily when Chloe pulled it to one side, and with Saul's help, she sank upon his cock to receive the satisfying stretch she craved. Chloe shuddered once he reached full hilt then leaned forward to rest both hands over his oiled chest.

"You are the beautiful one, Chloe. You."

She started slow with a roll of her hips that made Saul's eyes glaze over. If this was to possibly be their last night together, she wanted it to last. To savor every moment. She watched anticipation tense his muscles and felt the twitch of his cock inside her. Every rise of her hips was one stroke closer to orgasm. He held her hips and directed her with care, groaning at times as his balls slapped against her ass.

And then she slowed and lay against him, touching tender kisses on his lips. She loved him. If there had ever been any doubt in her mind, she knew it now. She loved him for sharing his life and the secret of his draconic nature with her. For giving her a second chance. For nurturing her ills and befriending her closest lifelong pal.

The first hot tear slipped down her cheek and splashed against Saul's bearded face. Her surprised dragon raised a hand and dried the wet trail with a wipe of his thumb over her skin.

"What is it?"

"Nothing," Chloe lied. The knife stabbed her in the heart again, as if punishing her for the falsehood. "I'm just... so happy to be with you."

Saul rolled, tucking her body in beneath his. "I cherish you, Chloe. You know this, right?" A slow backstroke withdrew his dick until only the sensitive crown remained, and then he drove forward again until their bodies met in a solid union. She shifted beneath him, threw her head back to expose her throat and groaned.

"Show me how much."

Whether it was the beast in him or the man, Saul took her words as a challenge. Her lover learned quickly and knew exactly where to touch to make Chloe tremble or sigh. He nipped her ear in a playful bite that sent electric zings down her spine and gripped her thigh, drawing her leg up towards her chest.

The eucalyptus and mint oil tingled, transferred from his body to her skin. "Faster, Saul."

Their bodies slapped together, the frenetic pace sped, and Saul didn't dare to stop fucking her until her pussy squeezed his cock and shuddered with the arrival of orgasm. Chloe came hard. Every spasm was a delicious tremble around his dick, and through it all, he never slowed. Saul reaffirmed his place as her unstoppable and never tiring dragon lover while her snatch massaged him to the very end, coaxing him to join her in orgasm.

And somehow he denied the greedy spasms around his cock. It wasn't just sex, it was an adrenaline-fueled claiming, as if some subconscious instinct drove him to assert his dominance again. Renew the act that made her his girl and his mate.

Another orgasm ignited the next series of contractions around Saul's dick. She buried her fingers against his broad shoulders and wildly clung as the world spun. Chloe was soaking wet long before he spent his seed.

"My Chloe," he rumbled against her jaw. "Mine."

"Fuck, I love you," she rasped on a heaving breath.

"Me or my cock?" he teased on a shallow backstroke.

Chloe arched beneath him and raised her hips, burying her toes against the blankets. The resulting grind of their bodies stimulated her clit and initiated another hard clench. "Both... I love it when you talk to me that way, too." Saul had taken her occasional teases seriously regarding his use of the word 'manhood' and obliterated it from his vocabulary.

"There is definitely something to be admired in human slang," he agreed.

"Now how am I supposed to get clean? You made a mess of me." *As if I could even move on my own after this.*

"How do you think humans washed before the invention of the bathtub?" Saul asked? Clever as usual, he carried her outside to the cool stream that snaked through his property.

"When the sun sets I will hunt a proper meal," he said as he waded into the water.

"Okay. God, I can't believe how clean the water runs here. It must be an advantage of living so far away from the city I guess."

Once they lounged against the edge of the stream, her head against the grassy edge, Chloe had no desires beyond a glass of wine and a picnic basket. She tilted her head back to gaze at the colorful sky fast on its approach toward twilight.

"Would you like me to wash you?"

"Mm. I'll be fine. Go do your manly thing. Hunt. I want to lay here and enjoy the water." Chloe shooed him with her hands and splashed cold stream water at the approaching man. Chuckling first, he leaned close to kiss her brow then rose from his seat beside her to leave the narrow stream. Once he reached a safe distance from their tent and supplies, he transformed into a powerful beast, spread his wings, and took to the sky.

She didn't know what came over her. Luckily, the sobbing began moments after Saul's great wings carried him away, otherwise she would have never peeled him from her side to capture their dinner.

I don't want to end this because of Freddy. Because I was stupid again.

Chloe dried off inside the tent and sprawled on the floor to rest. The realization of possibly losing her dragon haunted her the whole while that she lay beneath the eucalyptus mint scented blanket until, eventually, exhaustion claimed her completely. She fell asleep wishing her baby would have Saul's golden eyes.

***

For the second time in their relationship, Chloe awakened to a succulent aroma wafting through the mosquito net of their tent. She crawled from beneath the quilted blanket and unzipped the flap to look outside.

In his dragon form, Saul tended the campfire fire by exhaling brief bursts of a fiery steam from his open mouth. The unfortunate goat skewered on a branch had been seared golden on all sides.

Animal welfare would be all over him for this, Chloe mused. At least his livestock were fat and healthy animals, free to roam hundreds of acres of pasture before becoming a meal fit for a dragon's consumption.

"Ah. You have awakened at last. Good eve, my love. How did you rest?" he inquired.

"Great," she replied with a big smile. She forced it for his sake and moved toward him. When she tilted her face up for a kiss, the dragon lowered his head to touch their noses. "Do you need any help?"

"Sit. Let me tend to you now."

"I don't think I've ever had meat cooked like this before."

His shift from mythical beast to man happened in a blink and like every time before it, Chloe was fascinated. Without a wince, Saul took the roasted meat in his bare hands and pulled it apart.

"Did your mother not cook for you?" He set a leg down on Chloe's paper plate.

"My mother wasn't much of a mother," she confessed to him quietly. "We stopped speaking a long time ago. She was…" Chloe searched for a word. "Toxic."

Saul raised both brows.

"My mother wasn't a nice person. She was manipulative and self-centered to the end and not really a great person to be around. I moved out when I was old enough to get away from her and lived with my dad until it was time to go to college. She's gone now." Her mother had coked herself into an early death years ago.

"You deserved better," he murmured, gaze distant. "I miss my own mother greatly, but I meant what I said. She would approve of you, Chloe. It was from her that I learned to treat humans with respect and dignity. To hold you on the same level as our own kind."

For a while, she ate ravenously, providing little input to the conversation. Saul had clearly eaten to satiety while hunting, as he sat beside her with a smaller portion of food than usual.

"Is she very different from most other dragons?" Chloe finally asked around a mouthful of meat. Even without spices the goat tasted succulent.

"Very. In the middle ages, war between our species became quite common. My father told me stories when I was a young pup of the days when knights would challenge him from horseback. My mother is different. She counseled great men and diffused wars while my father... sated his baser appetites."

Chloe wiped down her hands on a towel and reached for a bottle of water to wash down the meal. Practice and patience improved Saul's fireside cooking from their first dinner together.

"Have *you* ever eaten a person?"

A wolfish grin spread over his handsome features, revealing every white tooth. "Occasionally, I have indulged in a particularly cruel mortal to whet my appetite."

Chloe shivered. "I don't know if that's hot or terrifying."

"Hot only if I decide to use my dragon's breath first."

She glowered at him. With a full belly, she eventually sprawled amidst the grass on her side. The dancing flames mesmerized her but ultimately failed to distract from the worries festering in her heart.

I have to tell him soon.

"Chloe, will you tell me what weighs on your mind? You have been off in your own thoughts these past few days."

Leave it to a dragon to notice what most men would ignore. "Actually, there's something I've been wanting to tell you. I've just been trying to decide how."

"You may always speak with me, my love. Nothing you could say would upset me."

God, I hope that's true. "I'm pregnant, Saul."

Chloe wiped her face again and struggled to control her breathing. The air tore in and out of her lungs, and fear seemed to compress her

119

chest with every heartbeat. Her frantic pulse filled her ears with pounding bass.

"Pregnant?" he repeated. "But I... How did this happen?"

Chloe didn't insult his intelligence by leaping into an explanation about the birds and the bees. Sniffling, and also very aware that he didn't move closer to comfort her, she looked away toward the fire. "After we met at the mountain, I went back home and hooked up with my ex. It was stupid. We didn't finish but—"

"It was enough," Saul interrupted.

"Yes." Chloe drew her knees to her chest and wrapped her arms around her legs. She hid her face against the blanket. "I'm sorry."

"How long have you known of this and kept it from me?"

"Two weeks," she replied without raising her head.

Saul remained still and quiet beside her, his silence as damning as the thoughts in her head.

"I'll leave tomorrow. I just... wanted one last night with you." The pain became an unyielding band around her ribs. Her lungs hurt again, and her throat felt too tight to comfortably swallow back the bad taste in her mouth. She couldn't breathe.

"Do you love him?" Saul finally asked.

"No. God, no." Freddy had become everything she hated in a man. Cocky, emotionally abusive, and arrogant. Her self-serving ex would have never set aside his own ambitions for a child. "I never want to see him again."

"Then do not leave."

Don't leave? Chloe raised her head. Saul's distorted shape shimmered in her vision. She rubbed her eyes as he moved closer and lowered one arm behind her shoulders.

"Stay with me."

"Why? Do you mean it? Stay?"

"I will not force you to remain by my side, Chloe, if I am no longer wanted. I may not like your choice, but I will respect it."

"The baby?"

"We will raise it together, of course."

The weight lifted from Chloe's chest. For the first time since her admission, she could breathe again. "You'd really do that?"

"Did you expect otherwise?" He cupped her cheek in his palm. "Could you truly expect anything else of me after I have brought you into my home and my life? You are my mate, Chloe. My treasured mate. Nothing short of my own death or your rejection will ever chase me away."

"I thought you wouldn't... wouldn't want another man's child in your home." She gasped in another full breath once the shaking stopped. She'd had the worst thoughts about him, jumped to horrible conclusions, and she couldn't bear to voice a single one out loud. "And... I've seen how men can treat children that aren't theirs."

"Ah... I see. I may be a dragon, but *I* am no beast to cause you or a little one harm, Chloe." Males of certain species tended to kill the offspring of a chosen mate in order to place her into a heat cycle again. A morbid part of Chloe wondered if it was true of dragons, and if Saul was the exception.

"I shouldn't have thought..."

"My only regret is that I failed to observe your troubles. I could have spared you this pain." Saul dragged his fingers through her blonde hair. The touch brought her comfort and eased the inner turmoil bubbling in her gut.

"I love you, Saul. I was so afraid. So afraid you'd be furious with me. I love you so much and I couldn't tell you because I thought... I thought you wouldn't believe me if you knew."

"I know," Saul replied. He pulled Chloe onto his lap and kissed her brow. Within moments, her dragon's loving embrace soothed her spirit, a balm following the two cruel weeks. "No. To be honest, I always expected we would one day adopt a human child to call our own when the natural inclination of motherhood came upon you. If it ever did. I know some women have no such aspirations."

"You're too good to be true. Do you mean it?"

"How could I not love a child of your blood, Chloe?"

Part of her waited to awaken from her dream. Speechless, Chloe pulled him down for a kiss. The only thing that could improve her life was the one thing she could never have.

I wish this baby was his.

Chapter 6

Chloe always screamed whenever Saul came down for a swift landing. With his majestic wings spread, an effortless glide carried them across the green pastures. The wind whipped her hair into a tangled mess but she didn't care, not when she was filled with so much joy.

"Hahaha."

"You did that on purpose!" she accused.

"So I did," Saul agreed. His hearty chuckle warmed her as much as the radiant summer sun. That morning, they had awakened to the chirping of the birds. Saul hunted a pair of rabbits for their breakfast and they reminisced over the memory of her MREs.

The fear of being cast aside into the real world, a world without Saul, became a thing of the past. Naturally, the next big decision regarded whether or not she would share the news with Freddy, or leave him forever in the dark.

"Hey. You didn't go and do something silly like buy me a car, did you?" Chloe perked up at the site of an ivory and gold Rolls Royce occupying the circular end of the drive.

"I most certainly did not."

Chloe dismounted from his back and walked to the front door. Her naked mate joined her a second later in his human body. "Are you planning to greet your visitor with a salute?" She glanced down at his semi-erection.

"Anyone bold enough to visit my home without invitation has seen it before," he replied. "And I know who has come to visit me."

"Point." Saul's estate was so remote that she couldn't imagine any normal person paying him a visit. According to Saul, only certain members of the production company knew his secret.

"You have a guest in the parlor," Leiv informed them at the door. His disapproving grimace made Chloe shrink back a step behind Saul until she remembered Leiv was as gentle as a kitten.

"I am aware, but thank you, Leiv. I would like to take Chloe out for dinner in town tonight. You and Mahasti as well."

The grimace was replaced with a surprised blink. "You want to take both of us to dinner with you?"

"You are beloved members of my household. Of course I would

enjoy your company over dinner."

"Thank you." Leiv opened his mouth to speak again, but he promptly shut it and stepped away, appearing to carry something heavy on his thoughts.

Saul grinned and tugged Chloe by her hand, pulling her with him through the house.

"Dinner?"

"Yes. A night out with our companions. Is that acceptable?"

Hugging his arm, everything in her world seemed right. "I'd really like th—"

"Saul, darling, there you are." A lyrical voice interrupted Chloe, its sensual tone as seductive as a 40s era lounge singer. Heels clicked against the floor in a staccato beat as a female stranger crossed the room. The woman greeted Saul with a kiss that belonged behind closed doors, even threading her fingers through his golden hair.

Chloe stood to the side, arms crossed and stomach twisting. *Maybe kissing is normal for dragons? The French kiss cheeks, right?* Except the French usually weren't naked. Somehow, Chloe resisted the urge to draw the attention to herself by clearing her throat.

Saul broke from the embrace and stepped back, appearing genuinely shocked. It was a plus in his favor and relief to Chloe that he never returned the sensual gesture. "Chloe, this is Brigid. Another dragon." He cleared his throat, fell back until he reached Chloe's side, and possessively curved his arm around her shoulders. "Brigid, Chloe is my mate."

Brigid, Chloe repeated the name to herself. In her black, overpriced heels, Brigid towered above Chloe. She wore an ebony crocodile skin purse upon her arm, a perfect match to her slim fitting pants suit.

"Do not tease me so, darling." Brigid tossed her sleek red hair over her shoulder, looked Chloe over, and then promptly dismissed her. "Is humor your new tactic in our courtship?"

"Our courtship ended five years ago, Brigid." Saul's attention flicked from Brigid to Chloe, as if assessing her reaction to the events. "We will speak of this privately at another time. Perhaps for now, it is better if you return to your home."

"Home?" Brigid's voice raised to a sharp pitch and indignant color spread across her cheeks. "How dare you send me away like some lowly human trollop. We had an arrangement, Saul. Your father and mine promised us to one another. I waited for you."

"Your behavior during our last meeting implied otherwise," Saul stated evenly. His golden eyes practically flashed with anger. "I made

123

an offer, you refused. There is nothing further between us worthy of conversation at this moment, so I must ask you to leave my home at once."

Chloe rubbed her sweaty palms against her jeans. She felt plain in Brigid's presence; a frumpy and pregnant mortal.

"I smell a bastard whelp inside of her. Has my absence made such a desperate dragon of you that you'll accept a *human* plaything that comes to you harboring spawn? Don't make me laugh."

"Bastard? Fuck you," Chloe spit back at the dragon. The words tore out of her before she could bite her tongue then Saul's grip tightened. "Who the hell do you think you are, coming in here and insulting *my* baby and *my* mate?"

Brigid's brown eyes flashed molten red, as vivid as fire beneath the generous sunlight spilling through the windows. In a step, she placed herself in Chloe's face and snarled.

Saul's reflexes nearly threw Chloe off balance as he pushed her behind him.

"You will leave. Now," Saul growled in a low voice. The mirrored surface of a display cabinet revealed his hardened features, the warmth gone from his golden eyes and replaced with deadly intent. Saul was both glorious and terrifying, poised before her like a Roman gladiator preparing to battle a lion. Under better circumstances, Chloe would have appreciated his flexed muscles, but imminent danger promptly made her cower behind him.

The dragoness straightened and promptly composed herself. The furious color leached from her naturally ivory skin. Flawless might be an understatement, as she had the polished look of a model who spent hours before a makeup artist. "My father will be notified of your refusal."

"Excellent. Tell Maximilian I humbly await his correspondence." Saul angled his body to remain between Chloe and Brigid when the latter passed by on her way to the door.

"You have not heard the last of this." Brigid seethed. "Keep an eye on your pet. It would be such a shame if anything were to happen to her."

The woman moved fast in her heels. She strode out of the home without a backward glance or even a thankful utterance to Leiv, who held the door open for her.

Saul turned to face her immediately. "Chloe, forgive me, I was never told to expect Brigid's arrival."

Chloe nervously bit her lip and glanced toward the door, where Leiv stood with an apologetic expression on his handsome face. He bowed and hurried away, too eager to be away from the room. "You never told me you have a mate."

"Promised one. Not a mate. Brigid has had a century to accept my claim to her. Over a hundred years to accept that our parents intended a mutually beneficial arrangement between our families. Even among dragons that is no small drop of time."

"Why would she show her face now?"

Saul quieted. Time alongside her newfound mate had given her the uncanny ability to judge and read his changes in mood. Silence could only mean one thing.

"Were you looking for her when you met me?"

"I was," he admitted.

"Oh." *He was looking for his dragon lady and stumbled across me. He settled for less than he wanted.*

"Chloe, you wear your worry on your face, but most of all, I sense it here," he told her, placing his hand directly above her heart.

"She's just so... so..." She struggled to release her self-esteem issues.

"Beautiful and vain," Saul finished. He closed his arms around her and kissed the top of her blonde head. "Brigid was my father's choice. She is capricious. Selfish."

"Sounds like a dragon," Chloe said as she attempted to smile for his sake.

Saul chuckled. The smile upon his face seemed fragile, fatigued by the brief exchange with Brigid. "Perhaps some. When I came of age, I sought her out to fulfill my part of my family's bargain and she rebuffed my advances. For one hundred years."

"Do you... mean it... that you would prefer our relationship over someone of your own species? I don't mean to..." Chloe gulped in a lungful of air. A quick wipe of her palm dried away the fresh tears on her face. "To question you over and over about it. But she seems to want you now, and she can give you things I can't." *A child of his own,* she thought.

"Yes, I did seek her when I awakened, in hopes of discovering her feelings for me had changed. Meeting you has altered that course, Chloe. I do not want her, and I am quite satisfied with how circumstance has entwined our lives. I will change nothing about this, nor would I change it for anything."

"You chased her for a century, Saul."

"I did, and had I not sought her out one final time, I never would have found *you*, Chloe. You."

Chloe opened her mouth to protest, but then a subtle ringing noise escaped her pocket. "It's my dad."

Lifting the slim cellular device to her ear, she accepted the call and forced some cheer into her voice. "Hey, Daddy."

"Hey to you, too, sweetie. I wanted to see if you'd changed your mind about the barbeque tomorrow."

"Actually, I'm in California visiting my boyfriend. Remember?"

"Bring him along then."

Chloe glanced over at Saul. "Maybe next time."

"I can fly you out if money's the issue and it's too far a drive," her father offered.

"No, Dad, don't do that."

"Southwest has a good deal right now. A pair of tickets won't cost much."

"It's not about money, Dad. I didn't think I'd come out this ti—"

Saul plucked the phone from Chloe's hands. "Mister Ellis, I presume?" Swinging one hand out, she tried to swipe the mobile phone back from Saul. She failed when he pivoted on a foot to avoid her, placed a hand atop her head, and held her away at arm's length. "It is my deep and profound pleasure to at last make your acquaintance. Chloe and I shall drive to your familial reunion post haste. Expect our arrival by the morrow."

"*Saul*," she gritted out between her teeth.

"I look forward to introductions as well. Good afternoon, Mister Ellis."

"You big jerk! Why did you do that?" Chloe demanded.

Saul dropped her phone into her open palm, apparently oblivious to her angry words. "A road trip! This is very exciting. Are you not anxious to begin our adventure? I certainly am." Without another word or even an apology, Saul strode from the room as if they were preparing for an epic quest. She sighed and dropped her brow into one palm.

Too bad pregnancy meant booze was off the table.

Chapter 7

Mahasti packed their bags while Leiv prepared the car. Chloe and Saul arrived in the garage in time to find him standing mournfully beside the spotless vehicle, as if he had been denied his one true joy. Chuckling gently, Chloe slid into the driver's seat and accepted the keys from the distraught man.

"Are you certain you do not require a driver?"

"Chloe is quite capable behind the wheel," Saul cheerfully replied. "Enjoy your time alone with Mahasti. Please."

Chloe adjusted the rearview mirror as she drove away. Mahasti had leaned against the side of her bear shifter lover as if to console him. "Christ. You'd think that we stole his baby from him."

"He often feels that he does not do enough for the estate."

"What? If he did anything more for you, he'd be sleeping with me at night, too," Chloe muttered.

Saul snorted to conceal his amusement. The thought must have crossed his mind at some point. Grinning, Chloe glanced over to appraise her boyfriend. He didn't know the first thing about selecting human clothing, but she and Mahasti had put him together well. An unbuttoned, maroon shirt revealed a grey t-shirt beneath it, worn over his dark jeans. For the first time since she'd first met him in the cave, he'd pulled his hair back. It suited him, even if she did long to run her fingers through his golden strands.

Saul made good company during the ride. He teased and sated her curiosity about his earliest attempts to masquerade as a human, and inevitably queried her about the human race in hopes of perfecting his act.

"You should know everything there is to know about us by now, Saul. Aren't you over four hundred years old?"

"The opportunity to learn is ever present, Chloe. Anyone who claims to possess all knowledge proves they are only a fool."

"It's so hot when you look at me that way." God, she loved his cocky, uneven grin and the way one corner of his mouth raised a little higher than the other.

While Saul remained awake for most drives and even their flight, he slept hard as a baby most of the drive to Vegas and only awakened when Chloe sped off the main road for a stop at a restaurant her father introduced to her during her most recent visit over the holidays.

"What? Where are we? Is this Las Vegas?" he asked blearily.

"Even better. It's El Rey Burger."

The Mexican-influenced diner, a sinful delight that featured deliciously tall hamburgers, held local renown for its special salsa and condiments. She stretched her legs and graciously took the chance to fill her belly.

I wonder if as many other couples bond over food the way we do? He'd be a thousand pounds if he wasn't a dragon, Chloe thought while snickering into her drink.

"Will you not tell your father we have arrived safely?" Saul inquired. He studied the ridiculously tall burger and took a large bite, a pleased expression surfacing over his rugged features a moment later. The chimichanga burger received the dragon seal of approval.

"No, he'll only demand for us to come over and see him right now, and it's kind of late. Besides, after that drive, I feel like shit."

Saul immediately became apologetic. "I should have allowed Mahasti to bring us, or even let Leiv drive."

"No," Chloe insisted. "Being pregnant doesn't mean I'm a delicate flower to be tended, Saul. I just need a li'l time to adapt." She grinned at him.

Saul's dramatic sigh brought a big smile to her face. She'd won the verbal match without a struggle. "You're correct," he agreed.

At the conclusion of their meal, Chloe treated Saul to a romantic walk down the Las Vegas strip. They held hands and occasionally kissed beneath the glittering lights. Exploring the city with her mate was like a dream, too surreal to be true. Was it possible to fall so completely in love with a man who had been a stranger to her no more than three months ago? The old Chloe of a year past would have said no, but every time he turned his ochre eyes toward her, she tingled all of the way to the bottom of her toes.

I deserve this. I deserve to be happy with a man who treats me as an equal instead of a servant. I deserve every single second of happiness with him, she realized. The niggling thought had been at the back of her mind all along, but it wasn't until she gazed up at him, and saw his features all aglow with the light from the casino, that the vast reality set in. Saul belonged to her as much as she belonged to him.

Saul had told her that she'd never have to see Freddy again. The decision to reveal her pregnancy to him would remain hers and hers alone, but it was too early to make such a lasting decision without pondering the probable consequences.

She shivered.

"Are you cold?" Saul asked. Their joined hands disconnected in favor of Saul sliding his arm around her shoulders. He brought her close and smiled down at her. One smile melted her knees and turned them to jelly.

"No. No, I'm fine," she assured him. "Let's turn and walk back to our hotel. I think I'm ready for bed now."

"As you wish." Saul extended his arm to her, ever the classic gentleman, and together they returned to retrieve their vehicle from the diner and check into their hotel. She leaned against him during the elevator ride up and placed her ear against his chest. As a dragon, his slower heart rhythm continued in his human form, strong but powerful beneath his muscular chest.

"I love you," Chloe whispered.

"You are the air I breathe," Saul replied.

His words struck her as genuine, and yet the hilarity made her giggle against his shirt collar. "We sound like a terrible romantic comedy."

Saul chuckled. "I may or may not have borrowed the line."

Chloe parted from him and stepped from the elevator. "It's the thought that counts. C'mon. Let's see what fancy room your money got us at this place."

Sometimes when she looked at her rugged, nature-loving boyfriend, she forgot that he was accustomed to lavish accommodations. His choice of lodging reflected his expensive preferences and tendency to spend great sums of money on a whim. Their suite at the Venetian was the most opulent hotel room Chloe had ever seen. She walked into the room and stared.

"It's as big as Marcy's apartment," she marveled. The king-sized bed lured her over, fluffy pillows and memory foam cradling her travel-weary body. She tried not think about the large collection of relatives, or that her many single cousins would descend like a cloud of piranha the moment Saul stepped into view.

By the next afternoon, Chloe had developed full-blown doubts about introducing her boyfriend to the family.

"Are you really going to be able to pretend to be human?"

"Did I not convince Marceline?"

Chloe tightened her fingers around the steering wheel and stared through the windshield. The car remained in park while she babbled out her worries to her new mate, airing out every niggling concern that surfaced in her mind.

"You did," she agreed lightly. "But Dad is different." Her heart thrummed in her chest, a frightened hummingbird desperate to

129

escape. She tried to take in slow, even breaths, but the rising hysteria wouldn't allow it.

"Do you fear that I will embarrass you?"

"No!" she blurted out.

"Do you believe your father will hate me?"

"He's hated everyone I've ever dated before." *Especially Malcolm. He hated him on sight and I should have listened to him. And I don't even want to remember the things he said about Freddy after meeting him. Dad shouldn't know so many swear words.*

"You have dated many dicks before me, but I am a dragon and thus perfect," Saul said, his placid tone an odd contrast to his choice of words.

Chloe stared at him. Waiting for her reaction, he stared back.

"Am I wrong?"

She wanted to slug him, and she wanted to kiss him. Choosing the latter option, Chloe unfastened her seatbelt and flung herself at him in the passenger seat. "Thank you for coming. You're right. I'm overreacting."

Saul circled his palm over her back and held her, a tender embrace that eased her panic attack and returned Chloe to a rational state. Once she programmed Sunset Park into the vehicle's GPS, she cruised Vegas' streets until she reached their destination and pulled the car into an empty space. The renewed tension in her frame and clenched jaw prompted Saul to touch a hand to her cheek.

"Will you be okay?" he asked.

"Fine. I kind of want to punch you in the nose sometimes for remaining so calm all the time, but I'm glad we're here now. I miss Dad."

"Do you normally avoid your family functions?"

"No. Only when I'm pregnant and dating man-eating beasts," she replied.

"I have not eaten a human in years," Saul insisted.

"Try to refrain from it this afternoon, even if my cousin Jimmy bothers the hell out of you."

Her reservations all faded into obscurity the moment Chloe spotted her father at the grill. He gripped a cane in one hand and a pair of tongs in the other, and she might have successfully crossed the park grounds unseen if her Aunt Susie hadn't blown her cover.

"Chloe! Sam, Sam, look, she made it after all!" Her father turned to greet her, prompted by the energetic wave from her aunt.

"Chloe!"

"Daddy, I missed you!" Chloe ran to her father and threw her arms around his neck.

Saul caught up to her as the embrace ended, arriving just in time to fall under her father's scrutiny.

"Daddy, this is Saul."

"I am honored to meet you, Mr. Ellis." Saul shook her father's hand.

"Call me Sam. It's a pleasure to meet you too, Saul. Thanks for convincing Chloe to attend the reunion. This would have been the third that she's missed in four years."

Saul glanced at her and raised one skeptical blond brow. "Her tenaciousness will not allow her to admit that she would have mourned the missed opportunity this time."

"You know her well."

"Dad."

Sam ignored her in favor of waving a hand toward the nearest picnic table. "Come on now. If you're going to stick around for a while in Chloe's life, I may as well get to know you."

"Just like that?" Chloe had expected resistance, or at least a varying degree of the cold shoulder. From the moment her dad first came in contact with Freddy, the two loathed each other. She should have taken that as the first clue to dump him and never look back.

"Yeah. You can go."

"Huh?" Chloe asked.

"You can go," Sam repeated, dismissing her. "How can I talk to the young man if you're going to hover?"

Saul provided no help whatsoever. Instead, he grinned and shooed until she gravitated toward the drink station where an enormous barrel-shaped ice cooler held her Aunt Judy's special cherry limeade.

The feeding frenzy began as anticipated once Saul and Chloe separated. While she allowed him the chance to bond with her father, curious gazes fastened on Saul and observed his every step. One of her cousins approached with a pie under the guise of offering slices to her dad and the new arrival.

"Chloe! You made it!"

Chloe spun on her heels to face the fast approaching woman. Her father's new girlfriend drew her into an enthusiastic embrace. "Hi, Annette. Nice to finally meet you in person after all of these Skype calls."

"Sam was worried you wouldn't come after all." The woman was only a handful of years older than Chloe herself, yet genuinely attracted to her dad. If not for Annette's loyalty, Chloe would have had to take off work to help him recuperate from his hip replacement. "I'm so glad that you changed your mind," Annette said.

"Saul wouldn't let me back out of it this year." Chloe laughed and stole a glance toward the barbecue pit. The two men sat opposite one another, each holding a cold bottle of beer. If she strained to listen, a hint of Saul's hearty belly laugh reached her ears despite the distance.

"Good man there," Annette answered. She nudged her sunglasses to the top of her head, revealing one blue and one brown eye. "Come sit with me. I've been waiting weeks to get to meet Sam's daughter, and you're finally here."

"Weeks to meet me?"

"I've heard so much about you from Sam that I feel as if I already know you," Annette admitted.

They settled at a table away from the rest of the boisterous group. Giggling children played and frolicked while a game of soccer traveled up and down the green field. It turned out that Annette had anticipated Chloe's disdain due to her and Sam's differing ages.

So they chatted and became reacquainted beyond a first name basis. Annette owned the small bakery across from Sam's favorite diner, where he took supper every evening alone.

"You both sound like a romance novel," Chloe commented, laughing.

"I guess we do. I don't know what made me do it, but he looked so sad sitting there that I had to take him a pie." Annette craned her neck, keeping Saul and Sam within her sight. "They seem to be getting along well. So, how'd you meet him?"

"In a cave, of all places."

While talking love, romance, and men, Chloe and Annette shared the remainder of a pecan pie left on the picnic table.

"Your dad won't ever admit it, but he's been worried about you. Misses you." Annette smiled and refilled both of their glasses. She stole another look at Chloe's father, allowing her pensive expression to linger a few seconds longer.

I've been away too long. "Now that I'm moving to Los Angeles, I'll be closer for visits at least. It wasn't so bad a drive, even if Saul slept the last half of the trip." The memory of his serene features coaxed a smile to Chloe's face.

Annette's brows furrowed above her mismatched eyes. "Are you sure about this whole moving thing? I mean, it all seems so fast. Do you know enough about him?"

"Saul? He's amazing, Annette. Honest. I wouldn't have brought him to meet you guys if he wasn't 100% better than Freddy. I know Dad's probably talked your ear off about him."

"Sam had a lot of things to say about your boyfriends, but I told him it wasn't up to him to judge. To, you know, give this new guy a fair chance. Not that he'll listen to me either way." Despite her words, Annette appeared unconvinced, and her eyes returned to the two conversing men. "So tell me about him then. Is he a model?" she asked.

She's barely any older than I am and she's giving me the third degree about my boyfriend? What the hell is this? Chloe opened her mouth to blurt a rude retort, but the words died on her tongue.

Her own mother wouldn't have given a damn, and for just one second, it was nice that someone did. According to her father, Annette was as loving and kind as they came.

"No, why?" Cautious, Chloe feigned ignorance. She sipped her lemonade and stole a glance at Saul and her father. They appeared to get along without her present. Every time she checked on them, one or both of the guys were laughing.

"He's drop-dead gorgeous, that's why," her cousin Sarah spoke up in passing. "No wonder you weren't going to show up. If I had a man that hot I wouldn't trust him around you bitches either."

Chloe choked on her drink. "That has nothing to do with it."

"Hey Chloe, want a beer?"

Shit. "Nah, I'm good. I've been pretty dehydrated lately so right now this lemonade is like ambrosia." *If I tell Uncle Dan before Dad, he'll never let me forget it,* she thought. Her uncle was the family's gossip. If a secret touched his ears, he was bound to share it to any relative willing to listen. If none were available, he phoned them.

"So what does this mystery man do besides charm everyone with his toothpaste commercial smile?" Annette asked. Her warm smile put Chloe at ease until Sarah's rabid interest placed her right beside them.

"I know this is practically hurling chum into the water, but he's the CEO of a movie studio in LA," Chloe said dryly. "He inherited it from his grandfather or something." She waved her hand and feigned boredom with the discussion.

"Tell me you're joking," Sarah said.

"Nope."

"Does he have a brother?"

"No, but he has a butler," Chloe replied.

After a moment of hesitation, Sarah asked, "Is the butler hot too?"

"Very. And *taken.*"

Sarah muttered.

"I know. Marcy was bummed too."

Annette interrupted, "Oh look. Maggie's dragging your boyfriend away to the playground. Five bucks says he returns covered in sticky handprints because she leaves him with her brats and goes to smoke and have a few margaritas."

Chloe crinkled her nose. "He's not her personal babysitter. Should I save him?" On one hand, she felt pity for Saul, but on the other, it made excellent practice for when her little one arrived. For a terrifying nightmare creature of myth and legend, he displayed kindness toward her young relatives above and beyond what some humans were capable.

"Hell no. Let them have fun with him a little. You know their dad doesn't give a damn about them. He's probably the first man to pick Mikey up in weeks," Sarah said while shaking her head. She and Maggie were sisters and only a couple years apart. While one remained childless, the other had birthed four children within six years to a deadbeat.

Saul's relaxed posture indicated that the children hadn't upset him yet. After deciding to keep tabs, she nodded in agreement. "You're right. I'm going to go talk to Dad some now and see what he thinks about my guy."

While Saul was occupied with her younger second cousins, she maneuvered beside her father at the grill and helped him to turn the meat. A delicious aroma wafted toward her nose. Beer bratwurst and smoked cheddar and mushroom filled burgers.

"Daddy, if you're done here for now, can we talk for a few?"

"Sure."

Ever the observant father, Sam didn't waste a moment once they distanced themselves from the reunion and left earshot. "What's on your mind? I knew something was wrong from the moment you two arrived."

Chloe gauged the distance again between them and the rest of the party. She sighed. "I'm pregnant," she blurted without further suspense.

"I…" Sam stared at her, completely at a loss. "That was fast," he commented lamely. As far as her dad knew, she'd only broken up recently with Freddy.

"Well…" Ever since childhood, Chloe had never been able to successfully lie to her father. "It's not Saul's baby, but he wants to help me," she admitted.

"Oh, sweetheart." Her father sighed and hugged her close. "Is it that asshole gym trainer's?"

"Yeah," she replied in a shaky breath. "He doesn't know, and I don't think I'm going to tell him."

Her father was quiet for a moment, wearing an indecisive expression on his face. "Now, Chloe, don't you think he deserves to know?"

"No, Daddy, not really. Freddy wouldn't be any better than Mom was to me. I don't want him involved in my life at all."

"Yeah… yeah. No child deserves that." Sam leaned back. "You know that I'll support whatever you decide. Now, what is this about moving to California? Saul says that you're going to take over as executive assistant at his company. Sweetheart, I'm impressed."

Chloe sighed. "We discussed that I *might* take over as executive assistant. I don't want to steal someone's job."

"According to Saul, he's creating the position just for you. Honestly, Chloe? Go for it." As she leaned back to scrutinize her father through narrowed eyes, Sam laughed at her. "I know, I like one of your boyfriends for once, and I'm excited to see this movie studio he's invited Annette and me to visit. Now tell me about Saul."

"You just talked to him for an hour, Daddy."

"I want to hear more about him from *you.*"

It didn't take long to summarize her meeting, whirlwind romance with Saul, their separation, reunion, and recent vacation in Texas. By the time she reached the end, her dad had begun to nod his head in approval.

"You found yourself a good man there, Chloe. Damned shame he didn't beat Freddy's ass. I would have."

"With your cane?" she teased him.

"I'd give him a well-deserved whoopin'." Her father wisely steered the conversation to a sweeter topic: the child itself. "So when's my grandbaby due? When do I get to hold him? Or her?"

Chloe toed the ground nervously. "I haven't gone to the doctor yet. Sort of just found out in Texas, and only told Saul… yesterday. But he's okay with it. I kind of thought I'd take it one step at a time, you know?"

"Punkin…"

"I know, I know," Chloe sighed. A first pregnancy should have been giddily reported to her mother. Her mom should have chastised her for failing to seek care and whisked her off the next day on a journey to purchase maternity clothes, stretchy pants, and little dresses with bow-tied ribbons beneath her tits.

But Chloe's mother had been a self-absorbed drug addict who thrived on sucking the life out of others. Nearly a decade had eclipsed between their last meeting in person, and then two years ago, Chloe found out her mother overdosed on coke.

"Tell me, Daddy, what do you really think about Saul?"

"I think he's great. He's the first person I've met from Iceland, but his parents raised a fine young man. Have you met them?"

Chloe shook her head. "His father died when he was a child, and his mother... travels a lot. The adventuring sort. She wouldn't have cell phone reception wherever she is."

According to Saul, his mother had hibernated since the loss of her mate, and there was a high possibility that she wouldn't awaken during Chloe's lifetime at all.

"Sounds like a woman I'd like to meet."

Chloe swatted him. "You have Annette."

"And I love her. I really do, Punkin. I know it hasn't been long but—"

"Daddy. Considering how fast I'm moving with Saul, you don't have to explain anything to me." She hugged her father tightly again and breathed in the cool scent of his cologne. For as long as she could remember, he had always been her protector. "I like her. I see she shares your love of the outdoors too."

"We'll have to take you and Saul out to the cabin sometime."

"That'd be fun."

Her father's unconditional acceptance eased the tight knot in Chloe's chest. *Everything is going to work out. Everything.*

"Speaking of, here comes your man now." Her father squeezed her fingers then passed her hand over to Saul. "You take care of my li'l girl."

"Nothing would please me more," Saul replied. "Save for one thing."

"Wh—"

"Chloe Ellis." Saul lowered to one knee and produced a small black box from his jeans, mimicking the fantasy proposals in every romantic comedy she'd ever dared to show him. "Be my wife."

Oh my god! Chloe's limbs became uncooperative and refused to move.

"In the short time since you entered my life, I have come to realize how empty my existence had been without you. You have brought me joy and shown me a new world of immeasurable wonder. Do me one last honor, Chloe. Marry me."

After her mouth opened and shut a few times, she turned toward her father.

"Well don't look at me," Sam said, smiling. "I gave him my blessing to ask, but the answer has gotta be on you, sweetheart."

"Yes!" She screamed the word louder than intended, and received a few chuckles from the observing crowd. Golden light danced over the ember-hued jewel at the center, and a tiny circle of black pearls gleamed around the fire opal. "It's beautiful, it's so beautiful."

Before Saul could rise to his feet to embrace, or possibly kiss her, as seemed to be his intent, Chloe threw herself into his arms. A smaller man would have toppled back onto the cement ground, but he remained upright and caught her in his powerful embrace.

"I love you," she whispered against his ear.

"Then we shall not waste a minute. I am told Las Vegas is the Mecca of weddings."

"Now?" Chloe's voice squeaked.

"Tomorrow," Saul said.

It was something out of a dream, all of it. From the first moment she and Saul met to this instant in time, Chloe expected to wake from the fantasy. But the new weight on her finger was real, and the warm arms around her held her close to her soon-to-be husband.

I'm marrying a dragon and I have never been happier.

Chapter 8

Saul never turned his cell phone off, but he did often lay it within Chloe's reach to satisfy her Candy Crush addiction. The first time that she'd lost all of her lives and sent an eager plea to Marcy for assistance, Saul had groaned, reclaimed his device, and bought her several more.

The game wasn't nearly so frustrating when an eternal being willingly purchased more power-ups.

He's so damned generous, she thought while laying the iPhone onto the bedside table. *My family loves him. Dad really thinks he's a great guy. Hell, he is a great guy.*

Of course, Saul wasn't actually a guy. He was a dragon, an immortal who would long outlive her, her child, and everyone he graced with his noble presence at the reunion. Would he feel the same way about her as she grayed, curved at the spine, and eventually succumbed to the cruelty of old age? Would he still love her as much on the day she died as he did now?

Chloe swept those thoughts aside and laid her head against the pillow to sleep. Thanks to her family wearing him out with exhausting activities, Saul snored beside her and remained dead to the world. By nature, dragons were light sleepers, but they adapted to the presence of a trusted person in their domicile. Mahasti and Leiv's movement never awakened him if they entered his vault during hibernation periods.

A thief on the other hand...

She peeked over her shoulder at her sleeping fiancé. Despite his lack of spontaneous dutch-ovens and other gross bedroom habits associated with men, he slept beside her like any other spouse-to-be. Chloe considered that a blessing.

"Mm... this is going to be great when winter comes," she mumbled as she edged close enough to rest her cheek against his shoulder.

A subtle chirp interrupted Chloe's sleep and grew progressively louder in volume until it threatened to hurt her ears. Her moan of protest led Saul to disentangle from her embrace and reach over her to pluck the phone from the table.

"Hello?"

Who's calling him at...? Chloe peeked at the digital clock on the table. The glowing display told her it was nearly five in the morning. If it was an urgent matter, Mahasti would have appeared in a plume of jasmine-scented smoke. After the troubles that plagued his residence during their last vacation, Saul had made it abundantly clear that they were contact him at any time, no matter how obscene the hour, if another plague of vampires attacked his home.

"Maximilian. Greetings," Saul rumbled quietly beside her.

Definitely not Mahasti.

The bed shifted then footsteps indicated his path to the window where heavy, gauzy curtains concealed their view of the Las Vegas Strip. Saul parted them and gazed out into the electric, pre-dawn night.

"I am pleased to know Brigid passed my message to you with haste. It is true. I have mated, thus I shall no longer pursue your daughter." Saul paused. A throaty chuckle warmed Chloe's blood and eased the dread filling her gut. "It was not intentional, I assure you, but perhaps you should find a better use of your time by asking why she refuted my claim to her for so long? The time has come to move on."

Chloe smoothed her pale blonde strands away from her face and watched him. Worry gnawed the pit of her belly. As if sensing her apprehension, Saul turned to flash her a nonchalant grin.

"Does Brigid feel slighted? Surely you did not expect me to court your daughter for another century. Be reasonable. No, I shall not consider it. The matter is closed, Maximilian. I thank you for returning my call, but your promises of intervention are too little and too late. I bid you to have a good day." Saul lowered the phone from his ear and ended the call.

"What's happening?" Chloe asked immediately.

"Nothing to concern you."

Coming from another man, she might have taken offense to the dismissive phrase, but from Saul, the words were spoken with genuine innocence. She smiled and raised herself onto an elbow. "Maybe I want to be concerned."

Bathed in the Las Vegas lights, Saul's nude body resembled a piece of art. Better than the finest Renaissance sculpture. Hotter than Michelangelo's David. With open arms, Chloe beckoned her dragon to return to the bed, where the sweet bliss of their love making melted away their worries.

Tomorrow, she would be his wife.

***

While Chloe doubted in the likelihood of a wedding venue on short notice that didn't involve a fat man dressed like Elvis, Saul surprised her with his investigative preparation. Or, at least, Mahasti's preparations.

As a child, Chloe had never dreamed of a fairytale wedding with hundreds of guests, expansive tables of catered food, and a $500 an hour photographer. She'd only wanted the man of her dreams — a good man who loved her unconditionally and cherished her as she deserved. Malcolm and Freddy hadn't been worthy of her.

In her sundress, she stood before the judge and held Saul's hand while her father, Annette, Mahasti, and Leiv witnessed their union. Afterward, she kissed him chastely, then they gathered for a family dinner at an upscale restaurant. Saul insisted on covering the bill.

"Leiv and your father's beloved appear to have become friends." Saul glanced at her.

"She's sweet." Chloe smiled and leaned her cheek against Saul's shoulder. *My husband. Mine.*

"I admit to some surprise," Saul murmured, his words for Chloe's ears alone. "She is remarkably calm, all things considered."

"Should she be otherwise?"

"Many smaller creatures become nervous when in the presence of larger predators."

Chloe nearly spewed out her virgin daiquiri. She coughed into a napkin and waved off a concerned glance from her father.

"What do you mean?" Chloe whispered. Turning her attention toward Annette revealed that the woman watched them from the corners of her eyes.

In fact, Annette had watched Saul since meeting him.

Saul had the good grace to appear guilty. He cleared his throat and feigned fascination with his bourbon. "Forgive me, I should not have spoken out of turn."

"Would you excuse us for a moment?" Chloe practically dragged Saul out of his seat. Annette and Leiv, embroiled in a deep conversation about the many uses of honey in baked goods, barely noticed their departure. Her father chuckled at Saul's helpless expression.

Once they rounded the corner and stopped near the public restrooms, Chloe released him and placed both hands on her hips.

"Spill it."

Saul gave a long suffering sigh before he glanced around their immediate area to confirm a lack of snooping mortals. "Annette is a shifter, my love," he finally admitted. "I knew the moment we arrived at the park that one was nearby."

"Are all shifters not as cavalier about dragons as Leiv?"

Her husband chuckled. "Hardly. Though many submit to our service, those unfamiliar with dragons keep a safe distance. Rightfully so. She has watched me very closely, but appears to be more at ease with Leiv," Saul said.

"So... can you tell what she is?" *Smaller than a bear. A wolf maybe? No...* Chloe's thoughts turned over a hundred possibilities, from an exotic tiger to a long legged deer.

She peeked around the corner and ogled Annette. The gorgeous woman had long legs and an exquisite figure suited to running, but Annette's odd, tri-colored hair and gentle eyes drew memories to the front of Chloe's mind. With startling clarity, the truth struck Chloe in the next instant. *She's a dog. She's a dog shifter. I know it.*

"Ah, judging from your expression, you no longer need my answer."

Chloe swatted him. "Why didn't you tell me at the reunion?"

"I did not know it mattered."

It didn't. If anything, the divulgement of Annette's identity inspired a sense of relief for Chloe. Her father deserved a loving companion who would stick by him through thick and thin.

They returned to the tail end of her father's thoughts about a recent vacation to Dubai before his hip replacement. "Dubai was a beautiful place. Annette and I plan to visit again in the fall," Sam said.

"Come with us next time, Chloe."

"Ahh... I don't know." Chloe rubbed the back of her neck. While she had taken her father aside to share news of the baby, she hadn't told the rest of her relatives. "I'm pregnant, and I'll probably be too big for a plane by then," she fessed up.

Annette's mouth fell open. Her mismatched eyes flicked between Saul and Chloe, working out the obvious truth: the baby clearly had been fathered by another man. "Congratulations. To both of you," she said, words spoken in a cautious tone. "I'm so happy for you, Chloe. A new husband and a new baby. Oh goodness. There's a small shop near my bakery with the best little clothes."

"When we find out what we're having I'll plan another trip over here to shop with you," Chloe said. "It'll be fun."

"Excellent. And now that you're on the west coast, we're only a

141

drive away," Sam reminded her. "Any time that you need me."

Chloe didn't miss the pointed look directed at Saul, but her kind dragon lover feigned ignorance and twisted to chat with Mahasti. She patted his thigh beneath the table. "And the same goes for you two, Daddy. Come out and visit us sometime. You'll love hunting on Saul's property."

Annette studied Saul again, using only the corner of her eyes. "I'm going to run to the ladies room," she excused herself from the table.

Recognizing an opportunity to get the canine shifter alone, Chloe quickly rose to her feet. "Hey, wait for me, Annette. All this water is going right through me."

"Sure."

As they left the celebration party behind, Chloe overheard Leiv playfully taunting Mahasti, asking if she planned to disappear to the women's room too. Contrary to the myth about women all leaving in flocks, she remained behind with the men.

There's no gentle way to do this, Chloe realized while washing her hands. Annette emerged from a stall to do the same, prompting her to let the words rush out in an awkward tumble before the chance was lost. "Look, Annette, I just wanted to say that I'm really happy my dad has you." Chloe studied Annette's reflection in the mirror and smiled when their eyes met in the glass. "And... I know what you are."

Annette's mismatched eyes widened in surprise and a hint of color crept into her cheeks. "You do?"

"Yeah..." Chloe almost felt bad for springing it on her like this. The faucet automatically turned on when her hands reached beneath it, jetting out tepid water.

Annette sighed. "I figured it would come out, all things considered."

"It doesn't matter. Not to me," Chloe assured her. "But... do you think you'll ever tell Dad?"

"I could ask you the same thing."

Chloe laughed, nervous beneath Annette's knowing look, and snagged some paper towels. "Somehow I think dragon is gonna be harder to swallow. I mean, how do I even start that conversation?"

"Well maybe I can ease him into the idea for you. So as for your question, yes, I do intend to let him know. But..." Annette glanced to the door and parted her lips to speak, only to shut her mouth and clam up. The silence between them thickened the air until an undercurrent of anxiety swarmed in Chloe's gut. Being around Saul and Leiv had granted her an exceptional awareness at reading shifters' emotions.

"What is it? We just broke the ice about the hard stuff, right?"

"Right," Annette agreed. She inhaled a deep breath. "Are you sure about what you're doing, Chloe? With a dragon?" The dog shifter's brows rose, allowing Chloe a brief instant when she saw past the human facade and into the loyal soul beneath. Instead of irritating Chloe, Annette's concern touched her in a display of genuine compassion. The love her mother never showed her.

"I love Saul, Annette. He doesn't scare me and I feel safe with him. Cherished."

"He does appear to be nice," came the woman's reluctant agreement. "But do you know him well?" Annette wrung her hands together and severed their eye contact. "Do you know dragons and their rules? I do, and they're not friendly. They're never friendly without something to gain from it."

This is none of her business, and I want to be mad, but she looks so damned worried about me. "I'm learning about them," Chloe replied, opting for full disclosure. "He's not trying to keep me in the dark, if that's what worries you. It's just a lot to learn, but I have Saul, Leiv, and Mahasti to help me. No one has kept any secrets from me. Not a single one."

"Okay." Annette forced a smile. The uncertainty clashed with her failed attempt to appear cheerful. "I don't mean to pry."

"It isn't prying. I would have been upset if I later found out you knew about him but didn't try to warn me."

"If you ever need to talk…" Annette offered.

Chloe followed her gut instinct and pulled Annette into a tight hug. Her father's new girlfriend wasn't the mom she'd needed growing up, but in as few as two meetings, Annette's compassion surpassed the memories of the cold, selfish woman in Chloe's childhood memories. "Thanks. I mean it."

They headed back to the dining room arm in arm. True to his gentlemanly nature, Saul stood to greet her when she returned to the room. The sight of him sped her pulse, making her breath catch.

I hope I never stop feeling this way about him.

"I believe it is time to retire and, if my memory serves me well, it is a tradition to carry the bride." Saul scooped her into his arms, much to the delight of their guests. Even her father clapped and laughed.

Diners all around the room joined in, tapping silverware on their wine glasses or clapping as Saul carried her out. Red-cheeked, Chloe turned her face into his shoulder and giggled. In his arms, she was a princess, fancy wedding dress or not. A bellhop held the elevator for them and the moment the doors closed, leaving them in seclusion,

Saul's lips came down over hers. Neither of them came up for air until the elevator dinged its arrival on the top floor.

She remained in his hold down the hall and into the room, only released when Saul lowered her with gentle care to the bed. Not that she allowed him to move far. Her fingers fisted in his shirt, keeping her dragon close.

"I love you, Saul, more than anything, and I'm so happy to be your wife."

Chapter 9

Despite Chloe's great love for her family, the return to the estate came as a welcomed treat. She collapsed on the sofa shortly after their arrival and napped long into the afternoon, until Mahasti awakened her.

"Mmm... How long was I asleep?" Chloe asked. A kittenish stretch accompanied her twist amidst the cushions.

"Several hours. We all thought you could use the rest. Come, join us on the veranda for a while. The fresh air will do you some good. Are you thirsty?"

Chloe readily accepted the glass of lemon-infused water that materialized in Mahasti's hand and drained it within seconds. To her parched mouth, it may as well have been ambrosia.

Outside, they chatted over drinks with their friends, shared a bottle of freshly pressed apple cider, and caught each other up to date on recent developments.

While Mahasti normally handled business matters concerning Drakenstone Studios, several conflicts among the crew of a potential blockbuster led to a prized actor walking off the set.

"Actors," Saul snorted as disdain twisted his features into a grimace. "Does nothing please them?"

"Cocaine," Chloe suggested. She then ducked her head a few seconds later. "Sorry, that was in bad taste."

"I, for one, am relieved you thought to clarify, Miss Ellis. Otherwise, he may have sent me to the darker parts of Los Angeles to collect drugs," Leiv muttered.

Chloe twisted in her seat to face her husband. He shrugged.

"Anyway, didn't I tell you to call me Chloe, Leiv? We're all friends, and I plan to be here a long time."

"Yes, you did. I am having trouble remembering. It is habit," the bear shifter replied, thoroughly abashed. Hints of red color spread over his darkly bearded cheeks.

"Besides, she is a Drakenstone now," Mahasti reminded him.

They toasted again, and after Chloe drained her glass she snuggled against Saul's side. As the others talked, her eyelids grew heavier.

"Chloe?"

"Mm? I'm okay, just tired is all," she mumbled in reply to Saul's concerned voice.

"But you woke only a short while ago." Saul's brow crinkled in confusion.

"Hey, I've got a bun in the oven. I'm allowed to nap whenever."

"Ah." Saul nodded. The mere mention of pregnancy-related issues shut him up without a fight. He hadn't yet seen her at her worst when susceptible to the hormonal imbalances of PMS. The idea made her grin and shake off the drowse.

"Okay, so prepare me for what I need to know about Drakenstone Studios. What should I expect?"

"Plenty of bowing and scraping," Mahasti quipped. She refilled Chloe's glass.

"Come on. What's it really like at the studio."

Leiv grimaced. "Very much like what you witnessed the day you first arrived in Los Angeles. It is very busy, very loud, and there are rude people everywhere who will not listen to reason unless you are him." He gestured toward Saul. "As you are to be the assistant executive, you will not face such troubles again."

"I hope not. That was sort of horrifying until you showed up to drive me here. I had never been so embarrassed in all of my life. The man carried me out of there kicking and screaming."

Saul chuckled. "I reviewed the security footage the next day. You put up quite the scene."

"Damn straight. I didn't come all that way to be turned around."

Even if her childish tantrum didn't land her a visit with the head executive of the studio, she'd met up with him later when Mahasti answered their mutual wishes. Chloe's despair and Saul's loneliness culminated in an irresistible wish the genie couldn't – and hasn't wanted to – deny.

"I can't thank you enough, Mahasti."

"I did what was right. I saw Saul's suffering and I saw your heart. It may be beyond my power to make two souls fall in love against their will, but the two of you had already fallen for each other. I only had to nudge you back together." Mahasti waved off her praise. "So I sent Leiv in the car to retrieve you."

Once all jokes were set aside, the trio gave Chloe the rundown on the senior staff and the peons directly beneath them. Saul treated all of his employees with dignity and respect, but he'd somehow gained a terrifying reputation after traumatizing a former employee.

"Okay, okay. So you scared this guy so badly that he didn't return to work for a few days. What the hell did he *do?*" Chloe asked.

"He paid a lesser wage to my female employees," Saul answered in a matter-of-fact tone.

Chloe continued to wait for the rest of the reason. When none came, she prodded him with a finger. "Well?"

"Well?" he echoed. The confusion drew his brows close.

"Saul, my friend. You must explain to her why this is a criminal act," Leiv spoke up.

"Ah, I see. It is theft. They were not paid adequately for work they had performed. A dragon does not steal from the hoard of another being, dragon or otherwise."

"So after Saul adjusted their salaries, he had his accountants pull employee records and issued checks for the difference accumulated over their months of employment at the studio. He even issued checks to women who were long gone."

His motivation had nothing to do with feminism and everything to do with draconic honor. Despite that, Chloe laughed good and hard until her belly ached and tears stung her eyes.

By the next morning, she'd come to dread their arrival. After she dressed in an impeccable suit with a mid-thigh length skirt and sassy heels, Mahasti braided her hair into a business casual updo. When it came to hairstyles, Chloe was all thumbs. A ponytail and a bun were her limit, but she and the genie had bonded over the weeks and acquired a familiar level of comfort. Enough comfort that she received the entire lowdown on Mahasti's budding relationship with Leiv.

"He's a good man, Mahasti. I'm happy for you."

"You're not upset that Saul no longer owns my lamp?"

"Pffft, no." She admired her reflection in the vanity then held up a hand mirror for a better look at the back. Small, black pearl pins secured her braided bun. They stood out, a stark contrast against her white-blonde hair. "Maybe some other women would be mad, but I'm just glad to see you're both happy. I don't need a genie at my beck and call."

"Now that Leiv holds the lamp, I'm limited in what I can do for you and Saul, but I will continue to do whatever I can to ease your days. Calling my name three times will be sufficient." Mahasti smiled. "It's an honor to serve you both."

The drive to Los Angeles gave Chloe the time to rehearse her introductions. Saul laughed at her again along the way then assured her that she fretted for nothing. He urged her from the vehicle and escorted her up the building steps.

"Why is everyone staring?" Chloe whispered. Did they remember her tearful pleas to see Saul a month ago?

They didn't. As implied the previous night, Drakenstone Studios

147

had its fair supply of drama to overshadow the miserable five minutes Chloe spent at the receptionist desk before a security guard dragged her out of the building. The same man smiled and courteously greeted her today without an ounce of recognition in his eyes.

"I rarely come to the building, my love. As the company executive, I leave the business matters to friendlier individuals unless absolutely necessary. My company is an extension of my horde, as I mentioned last eve."

Something told Chloe that dragons didn't mess around when it came to their possessions and wealth. She didn't want to see Saul's bad side.

"They're all scurrying around." She resisted the urge to twist and watch the hurried movements she caught from the corner of her eye. Saul's amused chuckle gave her something better to focus on.

"They did not expect me."

They're probably alerting the other big wigs upstairs. Hell, I'm surprised someone hasn't run up to offer him coffee yet.

As if summoned by Chloe's thoughts, a well-dressed young man veered over and presented a snifter of cognac to Saul. Electric blue framed eyeglasses perched on his nose and lent color to his otherwise pale face. He reminded Chloe of an albino mouse, an amusing likeness that made her giggle inappropriately and receive a curious stare from her husband.

I hope he isn't another shifter, too.

"Good afternoon, Mr. Drakenstone."

"Harris." Saul accepted the snifter, then seemed to reconsider after a glance at Chloe.

"We didn't expect you today, or your guest."

"My wife, Chloe," Saul introduced. "Today seemed as good a day as any to acquaint her with the office. My apologies for failing to provide forewarning."

"It's no trouble, sir."

It seemed as if every set of eyes on the office floor had turned to ogle her sexy dragon in his suit. Her most paranoid thoughts convinced her that the dozen or so female employees were mentally appraising her every aspect like a snake measuring prey.

"Pleasure to meet you, Harris," Chloe spoke up despite her shyness.

As she offered her hand for a shake, Harris' eyes dropped to the precious jewels decorating her ring finger. Confirming Chloe's suspicions, some of the hustle and bustle near them quieted as curious employees strained their hearing to eavesdrop on the conversation. 'Wife' must have been the magic word.

"Congratulations, sir. I had no idea." Harris recovered from his surprise swiftly and gave Chloe a courteous smile followed by a firm handshake. "Can I get you anything, Mrs. Drakenstone? Coffee? Tea?"

"Water for her."

Chloe nudged him sharply in the ribs with her elbow. Saul's soft grunt indicated she hit the right spot. "Don't speak for me."

Saul held up both hands. "My apologies. Order as you will, my love."

After a pause, Chloe sighed. He was right about the water and until she knew the upper limits of what his personal assistant could acquire, she didn't want to ask for something more exotic like a pomegranate and mango smoothie, no matter how great that sounded. "Water will do." She whirled to face Saul before he opened his mouth. "Don't start," she warned.

"I have started nothing," Saul said in his defense. The smug expression remained. "I plan to tour Chloe around the studio."

"No troubles. I'll catch up to you, sir."

Harris left their company to retrieve her drink then Saul guided her further into the ostentatious building. Friendly employees and clerks uttered respectful greetings in passing that Chloe returned with a shy smile. Of the many people present, none approached Saul directly, and when he exuded such an intimidating aura, Chloe couldn't blame them.

God, he looks fantastic in a suit. Mahasti really knows how to get him dressed properly. Despite a hundred years of walking among humans, Saul couldn't pair colors to save his life. And while he did understand the fine art of self-grooming, his golden hair hung loose around his shoulders, courtesy of Chloe's fondness for brushing it each morning.

"At the moment, we are filming the indoor scenes for Malignant. Would you like to walk onto the set?"

"Hell yeah!" Chloe exclaimed. A few heads turned her direction. Heat rushed to her cheeks and she dipped her head to avoid meeting any curious stares. While speculative eyes burned holes through her, Chloe clung closer to Saul's immaculately dressed torso and tried to walk with grace.

The power suit lent him a strong resemblance to an Armani model, but Chloe fretted over the tight buttons around her own midriff. She had tried to suck it in a few times in front of the mirror

149

while Saul laughed and taunted her with Leiv's homemade bear claws. She wolfed down two of the gooey treats before they left for the office.

"We must be quiet during the filming, but we will stand to the rear near the director," Saul instructed her.

The director of the film, a petite, pixie-sized young woman with red hair, flashed them both a cheerful thumbs up when they approached to stand beside her. Saul placed his arm around Chloe's shoulders and watched the action.

Chloe's favorite actress, a sassy brunette named Mia Patrick, ducked for cover as the ceiling fan groaned in protest and shook. Green screens dominated the back wall with a partial set built on the stage. Mia and her male counterpart hurried through the apartment setting, fleeing an unseen assailant. Carefully timed pyrotechnic blasts destroyed small knickknacks on shelves and a motorized construct flipped over the living room table.

Pissy ghost I'm guessing. Or a demon. I forget what the premise was on this one.

Mia rushed to the apartment door and tugged on the knob to no avail. They were trapped inside.

"Cut!" the director cried. "That was perfect! Take a break, we'll pick up from there in five." As people began to disperse for water breaks and snacks, the young woman immediately whirled on her stool to face Chloe and Saul. She hopped down and put out her hand. "Hi. You must be Mrs. Drakenstone."

"Uh... Yeah. But how did you know?"

"Word came in when you arrived at the studio. A pair of good eyes spotted that." She pointed to Chloe's left hand where her fire opal gleamed.

"Oh!" Chloe's eye-catching engagement ring rarely left her fingers, but she adored their matching bands the most. A single circle of titanium revealed he was off the market. "We heard there were troubles on one of the movie sets, and Saul wanted me to see how it works behind the scenes. I'm excited to be here."

"Excellent. You picked a friendly one this time, Saul. I like her."

Saul grinned. "Chloe, meet Abigail Parker. My favorite director."

"Thanks for letting me watch," Chloe said as she offered her hand. Abigail had a firm grip and a friendly smile.

"What did you think of it?"

"It wasn't as scary as I thought it would be," Chloe confessed.

Between the green screens and the animatronics, it was almost lackluster.

"You married Saul. Of course it wasn't as scary."

Saul twisted his face into a grimace. "Abigail, you make me out as if I am a monster. My reputation holds no weight compared to your movies. As for the film, special effects will be added later of course, Chloe. But I think the set holds a rather despairing air, don't you?"

"It's a little creepy, yeah. Mia's a good actress, too. Really compelling performance."

"She is," Abigail agreed. "We'll have her new co-star up to snuff soon. This was his first scene on set and I think he'll rise to the occasion. Jordan's walk-off was a blessing in disguise, Saul. We'll only have to reshoot two scenes."

"Let us hope so. I agreed to accept a video conference call between Jordan and his agent this afternoon. My expectations are minimal at best, and experience has prepared me for excuses that lay blame at the feet of all parties involved but his client. If he believes—"

"Does it take so many words to say he's a dick?" Chloe asked. She didn't know what came over her. She blurted it out and stopped Saul mid-rant. "Sorry."

"No, please. Chastise him again," Abigail immediately said. "Please keep her around. Pretty please, Saul. I like her."

He grumbled something under his breath.

"He told me he was a grouch on the job, but I never would have believed it if I didn't see it." *It's like someone shoved the stick right up his ass when we arrived,* Chloe thought, turning her amusement internally to avoid disparaging her husband again.

"Yeah, he's a real dragon on the set sometimes." Abigail winked and glanced back at the crew without waiting for Chloe's reaction. Saul had never mentioned whether or not his business associates knew of his true nature, so Chloe was unsure if Abigail was being literal or not.

"Yeah... he is."

"Anyway, it was a pleasure to meet you Chloe. I need to get these folk back on set."

Saul guided her back into the main building. Along the way, he pointed out people and offices of interest, naming titles and confirming familiar faces. From the first floor to the top, he showed her every aspect of the studio, introduced her to the legal department and to his direct subordinates in the business. Along the way, Chloe counted a handful of Hollywood stars and struggled to maintain her decorum.

Harris caught up to them as they stepped off the elevator on the top floor. "You have a video call waiting for you in the conference room, sir."

"Excellent. Thank you. My office is beyond that door, my love. Make yourself comfortable and I'll be with you in a moment." Saul kissed her brow and followed Harris through an adjoining door, so Chloe let herself in to the indicated office.

The huge space housed only the necessities, holding a sprawling desk, executive style leather chair, and a pair of cushioned chairs. An exquisite view of the world below caught her eye. In a way, it was almost comical that LA's gritty streets attracted her more than his empty barren room. *It feels so cold and impersonal,* she thought. *Intimidating.* Which, she supposed, was the point. He didn't call people up for tea and crumpets.

With Saul gone, she slid behind the desk into his chair, leaned back, and let both hands rest against the hint of tummy beneath her blouse. Sometimes, when all became silent, Chloe imagined she could feel her little one moving.

But it was far too early for that.

"I wouldn't get too comfortable if I were you."

Chloe jerked her head up toward the silken voice to see Saul's ex framed in the doorway. The door behind Brigid closed with a soft snick as the immaculate female dragon moved toward her. Every red hair was in place, her makeup perfectly applied, and not a single wrinkle or smudge marred her pristine ivory outfit.

"Saul's in a business meeting," Chloe said tersely. *I won't be intimidated by her, dragon or not. She won't harm me here in a building filled with people while Saul is a few yards away. Only a couple rooms. Don't be afraid,* she thought, giving herself a pep talk.

"I know." Brigid's catty smile unnerved her. "I know everything about his schedule and his business."

"Good for you. That doesn't at all make you sound like a stalker."

Brigid's eyes narrowed. "Saul belongs to me, little girl. He will always belong to me until I release him, and I don't see that happening any time soon. We are Promised to one another. Our fathers struck a blood bond over fire and ash. Draconic Law says he is *mine.*"

"Why do you even want him if you don't care about him? What's in it for you?"

Brigid slid her fingernails over the back of a plain leather sofa by the windows. "Saul is a well-sought after dragon, my dear. Didn't you know? Born of fire and storms… bronze dragons are a rarity among our kind. Prized as mates. Powerful. We'll have a strong cub once we're bonded."

Chloe rose from her seat. "He's bonded to me," she spit out. "Saul told me how it works. He can't have two bonds at once, and I'm not letting him go either."

"Oh? I think he could be persuaded."

"He's my husband, Brigid, whether you like it or not." Chloe thrust her hand out for Brigid to see the sparkling jewel, a priceless gift from Saul's treasured hoard.

The redhead's chuckle turned Chloe's blood to ice in her veins. "Your mortal laws mean nothing. If you're lucky, perhaps I'll let him keep you and your bastard around as pets. Dragon males have large… appetites. Allowing him a toy will be my gift. And should your whelp be a girl-child, well, she'll serve him nicely as well when you've gone all wrinkled and grey. I'll train her myself in how to properly please him."

All of Chloe's hatred and fury boiled to the surface at once. She flew across the floor as the office door exploded open, practically knocked from the hinges. Instead of clawing Brigid's eyes out, she collided with Saul's muscular chest. He caught her before she reached her target.

"You fucking bitch! I don't care if you're a dragon. I don't care!"

"Control your pet human, Saul."

"I'm his *wife!*" Chloe launched herself at Brigid again, unsuccessful for the second time. Saul remained between them but slid back across the sleek tiled floor. He grunted and spun Chloe around into the sofa, where he planted her firmly and held her down by the shoulders.

"Chloe, stop!"

"How charming. No better than a wild animal."

Brigid's husky chuckle renewed Chloe's anger. Saul's grip tightened against her shoulders, burying his fingers into her skin.

"Leave, Brigid. I will not ask you again," Saul growled.

"As you wish, my promised one. Never say that I am cold-hearted and completely without remorse." Brigid stepped toward the door. "Keep your pet on a leash, Saul, lest she get hurt. I am not to be held responsible for what happens if she chooses to behave like an unruly child." The she-dragon's laughter lingered in the air like a foul odor long after she was gone.

"I am sorry, Chloe. When Harris told me Brigid arrived to see me, I did not realize he sent her to my office with you. This is my fault."

153

His hand lowered to Chloe's shoulder. She jerked from it instinctively and twisted, placing her back to him as she cried. Uncontrollable sobs shook her entire body.

"Why are you protecting *her*?"

"She baited you. She wanted you to strike her, and had I not arrived in time, she would have killed you without batting a lash. Chloe, please. Look at me."

She swiped at her eyes uselessly. "I wanted to hit her! She should have her tongue ripped out for the things she said."

"Nothing is worth death—"

"You don't know the things she said! She told me she would take you away... that she..." Her breaths came rapid, and despite her great effort, Chloe couldn't force herself to repeat Brigid's words.

"Brigid can't have me, and you have my word that I won't leave you for her. Nothing in this world could convince me to end our bonding."

"She told me that you're required to by Draconic Law." Chloe wiped the tears streaming down her face and sniffled until Saul crouched beside her with a handkerchief in his hand. For every tear that she wiped, two more took its place until Saul's tender strokes dried her cheeks for good.

"I love you beyond the worth of my own life, Chloe. Brigid will neither harm you nor lay claim to me. I swear this to you." After taking a seat on the sofa beside her, the dragon pulled Chloe onto his lap and held her close. She lowered her cheek to his shoulder and breathed him in. The subtle scent of his natural musk never failed to soothe her.

"Okay," she whispered.

"Do you wish to go home?"

"No." Chloe shook her head and drew in a steadying breath. "I want to learn more about what you do." *Screw her. I'm not gonna let her drive me away.*

"Come with me then. Let us find an adequate task for you to perform."

Saul carried her to the desk where he set her in the high-backed leather chair. With one hand, he pecked out the password to open his desktop menu. "Harris scans each screenplay. I review new arrivals once a week to give the final approval."

"So what will I be doing, exactly?"

"My job." Saul guided Chloe to the enormous seat. "While I

delegate much of my authority to Harris, Mahasti, and my other subordinates, I would like you to become accustomed to my work."

"Saul, I'm a paralegal. Not a big honcho executive." She laughed and settled into the oversized chair. Luxurious leather stretched over expensive cushions and molded to her unique shape in a comforting embrace. Despite her intentions to merely humor him, she relaxed and closed her eyes.

"You are far more than a paralegal. That life was beneath you. Now you are my partner in *all* things and that includes the maintenance of my hoard."

"So I get to swim around in the vast ocean of jewels you keep beneath the estate?"

"If you so desire. Now, as I was saying, Drakenstone Studios produces no less than a dozen movies each year. As you know, we specialize in fantasy..." His voice trailed as Chloe dissolved into a fit of giggles. "And horror. What amuses you so deeply?"

"You're so *serious*. Come on, baby, can you really imagine me sitting here behind your desk pretending to be you, doing whatever it is you really do in this room?"

"Yes, I can," Saul insisted. "Trust in me as I trust in you, Chloe."

Their gazes met and held, his golden eyes twinkling with warmth, reassurance, and love that she'd never experienced before with another man in all of her life. At times, it was so funny to Chloe that a dragon could give her the world and succeed where so many human men failed. "Okay, so I read these and tell you if I think they suck?"

"Never read the entire screenplay unless you are truly riveted by the plot," Saul said. "Read the first and last ten pages. If that fails to intrigue you, the middle will be an absolute waste of time."

"Really?"

"Really," he told her. "While I have employees dedicated to this role, I prefer to give every submission my personal attention. Sometimes my staff passes over one that has hidden potential. A diamond in the rough, as you might say."

"So this is what I always see you reading at home when I wake up at night."

They devoted the morning to Saul teaching Chloe the ropes of his big-time executive job. When Harris brought them lunch around noon, it took every ounce of willpower Chloe possessed to wait for the man to leave before she attacked her plate. She was starving and the bacon-wrapped steaks smelled divine.

"No wine for you, Mrs. Drakenstone?"

"Chloe, please, and water is fine." She dipped her head, tucking her chin briefly. It wouldn't take long for her to become known to the public eye. People would see her swelling belly and know. Secrecy could only protect her for so long. "We're expecting," she confessed.

Harris opened and shut his mouth twice before he articulated an appropriate response. His eyes cut over to Saul first, no doubt gauging his boss' reaction to Chloe spilling the beans. "That's terrific news. Congratulations to both of you."

When Chloe turned to Saul, his satisfied expression surprised her and lured a smile to her face in return. "Thank you, Harris. We are thrilled to await the little one's arrival. Kindly keep this news to yourself for now."

"Of course, sir. I'll be outside if you need me."

Harris played gatekeeper for the rest of the day, canceling most of Saul's appointments while Chloe became accustomed to everyday life at the office. By evening, she didn't want to read another line, meet another actor, or hear another audition. She slept most of the drive to the estate, sprawled on the backseat while Saul rode in the front and engaged Leiv in casual conversation.

Once they hit the open roads away from the Los Angeles traffic, Mahasti sped their way home.

Chapter 10

Contrary to Chloe's initial expectations, she took enjoyment in learning the role of an assistant studio executive. Over the course of the week, she helped Saul draft documents with her superior typing speed, and they giggled together at terrible storylines. She also coaxed him into sex on his office desk and scandalized his assistant when her hand landed on the intercom button.

"Many of these recent submissions are beneath our standards," Saul muttered. "Unfortunate."

"Oh come on. You should make this one, baby. It's so horrible it'll be funny. It's like a parody of a true horror movie."

"Perhaps." Saul stroked his chin. "But it was not intended as a parody."

"Okay, what if I tell the writer that if they intentionally cheese it up a little more, we'll produce it for them?"

"Excellent idea. You have complete autonomy. Do as you will."

"One of these days you're going to say that, then I'm going to greenlight a big budget porno flick with a dozen kung fu transvestites shooting cocklasers."

Her words scandalized Saul, but he left her at the helm during a meeting with his casting director. She spent the rest of her morning chatting with Harris until Saul returned at lunch. Her husband's personal assistant excused himself from the room to partake in his own lunch break and left them alone.

"I have a private meeting to attend this afternoon with Brigid and her father. You may remain here in the studio or go to the estate with Leiv and Mahasti."

"But I want to go with y—"

Saul cut her off. "No you shall remain here or at the estate. You have proven thus far that you are not to be trusted in Brigid's presence."

"Fine," Chloe snapped. "I'll have Leiv take me home now then."

"Chloe—"

"Go deal with your dragon politics." She brushed past him on her way to the door and didn't stop until she reached the elevator. Leiv greeted her at the front doors and escorted her to the waiting car.

"Hi, Leiv. I want the full drive home please... No magical rushing," Chloe mumbled from the rear seat, where she laid her head against a silk-cased pillow. Sometimes, the feeling of movement eased her nausea. Saul had given her countless rides around the property and confessed to enjoying it.

"Of course. Will we make a stop for your usual?" Leiv asked.

"No Wendy's today."

It didn't take long for guilt to gnaw more than her appetite away. Thirty minutes later as they left Los Angeles behind, Chloe pulled out her mobile phone.

I love you, she texted him. She added an apology to the next message and waited, holding her breath, for his response.

Saul: You were forgiven before the words left your lips. I love you, Chloe. Take the time to unwind and enjoy the use of our bank account. Spend frivolously.

I don't want to spend frivolously. I want you to hold me, she texted back.

Saul: I must attend to business with Maximilian and Brigid. Once our negotiations are complete, I will return to share the news.

Okay. Love you, she messaged, before putting the phone away again.

Leiv's concerned face peered at her through the rearview mirror. "Is something the matter, Chloe? You seem very changed today." Despite all of the time Leiv had lived in America, he still struggled with English at times.

She chuckled quietly against her pillow, a humorless sound that didn't assuage the cold dread spreading through her chest. "I'm worried about Saul."

"Bah. Brigid and Maximilian are harmless. The only danger Saul faces is that perhaps Maximilian will talk him to death. Fear nothing," Leiv assured her. He glanced back at her and flashed one of his boyish smiles.

"Have you met them?"

"I have met Brigid many times. She would come to abuse Saul's good nature and generosity. She was much like… like a parasite," Leiv said in his thick accent. The driver shook his head, disgusted. Chloe had noticed that as he became accustomed to her company, his natural speaking voice became all the more prominent. "He courted her desperately."

"What happened to make him hibernate for five years? He won't tell me."

Leiv silenced. The bear shifter's loyalty to Saul touched her deeply, but the secrecy created an urgent need to delve to the heart of the matter.

"Please, Leiv. What did she do?"

"She took another dragon lover. Another volcanic dragon."

"That's cheating!" Chloe's outrage flared, filling her with white-hot hatred.

"Not in the eyes of Draconic Law. It is not to be considered cheating until a bond has occurred," Leiv explained.

"So it's allowed but…" *She hurt him. She refused him, wouldn't take his mark, and then she fucked some other dragon instead.*

"It is a very dick move to make," Leiv said, speaking the words for her.

"Very. So what is this? She's done with her play toy and decided she's ready to accept Saul?"

Leiv nodded from the driver's seat. "So it would seem. She likely came that first day to toy with him, but your presence threatened her."

"I threatened a female dragon?" Her incredulous voice rose sharply. He had to be joking.

"Female dragons are not kind creatures," Leiv said.

"Why can't we wish her away? If I asked Mahasti—"

"A djinn may not take away another living being's free will, Chloe. Trust me, were it so simple, Mahasti would do as needed to aid you both. Our hands are tied."

The disappointment leached the remaining life from Chloe's bones. She slept until their arrival when Leiv gently called her name, waking her, then they chatted for a while in the garage while Leiv wiped down the front of the car and cleaned the windows.

"Ah, I blame you. Mahasti drops hints daily about babies. She is excited about the idea of becoming a mother now that she knows it is possible. Yesterday she told me, 'Leiv, if we have our baby now, Chloe's child will have close friend.' And I am the bad guy because I say we should wait."

"Aww. That would be sweet," Chloe said, a wistful smile on her face. "But that shouldn't be the main reason. You and Mahasti can cuddle my baby if you want. Consider it practice."

Leiv laughed and nodded. "Yes, that is a fine idea. Now go on inside, Chloe, before you catch a chill. I will be in shortly."

"It's summer. I'm far from chilly. You just want time alone with your baby," she teased him as she passed through the door.

Once inside, Chloe helped herself to a bubble bath. She soaked away her troubles, gave herself a pedicure, and painted her toenails an obnoxious shade of pink. Saul didn't know any better, and had on impulse purchased her an amazing number of toiletries and feminine products, some she would never use, and others that were just…

strangely colored.

"Hrm... That color isn't really so bad," she mumbled out loud.

She brushed out her hair, braided it, then brushed it out again in a fret. Once she decided on a ponytail, she jogged down the steps to find a snack. Had she been smarter and less angry at Saul, she would have made the usual pit stop for a Frosty instead of waiting until her stomach cramped from hunger.

"Mahasti?" Chloe stepped into the empty kitchen and frowned. She's probably with Leiv, she realized. According to Saul, calling the djinn's name thrice would summon her, but she didn't want to interrupt a possible nookie time.

Especially if he changed his mind about babies. She doubted it. According to Saul, Leiv and Mahasti had centuries together... a djinn's lifetime. She envied them.

I wish... I could be with Saul forever. She sighed. It was a foolish wish to make, although it would fortunately go unheard. Such whimsies were beyond Mahasti's power to grant.

"Ugh, I don't even know what I'm in the mood for," she grumbled, searching the well-stocked refrigerator. She twisted the cap off the chocolate milk and guzzled it straight from the quart. Rich liquid cocoa distracted her for a while at least until a garlic-scented aroma reached her from the fridge shelf.

Mahasti's curry beef marinated in a deep dish with a thin plastic sheet over the delectable cubes. Chloe peeled the edge of the saran wrap off and inhaled.

Between her and Leiv, I'm going to be four hundred pounds by the time this baby is born.

After a glance over her shoulder, Chloe surrendered to impulse, scooped two pieces from the dish, and shoved them in her mouth. The curry spices danced over her tongue, improved by the tender cuts of meat.

It didn't taste raw in the least.

What the hell am I doing? This isn't cooked.

Part of Chloe wanted to freak out, but deep down, she couldn't stop herself, like a crack addict hungering for the next fix, she plucked another cube and quickly devoured it.

"Chloe?"

Chloe whirled with one hand to her mouth to find Leiv bearing a basket of glass jars filled with dark, golden-amber honey. "Uh... How much of that did you see?"

"Enough to know human women do not normally eat raw meat. Is that not bad for you and the little one?" His dark brows rose. "Mahasti."

Her prompt appearance meant that three utterances of her name weren't required for Leiv. "Yes?" The scent of jasmine wafted through the kitchen, smoky tendrils of the djinn's essence circling around her semi-translucent body. Without waiting for Leiv to answer, she turned to face Chloe. "You shouldn't eat that. It isn't cooked," she stated matter-of-factly.

"Um... she is aware," Leiv said. "That is why I called you."

"I'm sorry, I couldn't help it. They smell so good and look so... so juicy..." Chloe trailed off and eyed the plate with longing. Mahasti delivered a light smack to her reaching fingers.

"I will find you a doctor," Mahasti said.

"Aren't you overreacting a little? A doctor because I ate some meat?"

"Saul would never forgive me if I did not take you to a physician, Chloe. I am not an expert in human medicine, so I would prefer to be safe than sorry."

"Saul can heal wounds with dragon magic." Chloe rolled her eyes. "I'm not really concerned. If something's wrong and I get food poisoning or *E. coli*, he'll fix it up and we'll both be fine. It was only a few bits of raw meat. I'm not going to collapse and die right this moment, Mahasti. Honestly. The two of you are behaving as if I swallowed Ebola."

Mahasti didn't answer her. She pulled out a phone and dialed.

Half an hour later, the genie and bear shifter had bundled Chloe into Saul's car and embarked on a drive to a spur of the moment obstetrician's appointment. The fancy building outshined any doctor's office Chloe ever visited before, complete with marble floors, a waterfall, and a Zen garden.

The receptionist welcomed them with a smile and asked them to have a seat. They didn't even ask Chloe for her insurance information.

"What hoops did you jump through to arrange for this?"

"Saul and I spoke of it when you returned from Las Vegas. Ultimately, he wanted the choice to rest with you, but given the circumstances..."

"I waited long enough," Chloe finished for her. "You're both right. I should have handled this when we returned from Vegas, but I've been so nervous about it that I put it off time after time."

Mahasti smiled, attempting to ease her worries. "Trust me, Chloe, this is the finest OB I found. And now that you and Saul have married, you'll be covered no matter what options you take. The receptionist tells me their sister midwifery center has a birthing pool if such is your desire."

"Ugh. I don't think I'm ready to discuss this part yet. Let's take baby steps, Mahasti." *Baby steps*. At least the pun was unintended.

"All will be well. You'll see."

"Maybe… I wish Marcy was here too," Chloe sighed. She tilted her head back and shut her eyes, mourning the recent events missed by her best friend.

Mahasti's sympathetic hand rubbed her shoulder. "You'll see your friend again soon, Chloe."

"Sorry. That was kind of rude of me. I really am glad you're here. Really, it's just—"

"What's happening? Where am I?" a shrill voice cried from the restroom.

Chloe turned her head toward the sound. "That sounded like…" *No, it couldn't be.*

Marcy emerged from the small room, dressed in shorts and a tank top with unruly dark hair hanging around her shoulders in need of a brush. Her incomplete makeup made Chloe giggle once the horrifying realization passed. She had wished her best friend into the obstetrician's office while she applied hangover cover up. Dots of concealer under Marcy's eyes revealed her attempt to hide a long night.

She looked absolutely ridiculous. One lined brow contrasted against its unfinished twin.

"Chloe? Shit. I must have really passed out hard last night." Marcy turned around a few times and craned her neck to gaze at the world beyond the office windows. Sunny Los Angeles greeted her, the office yard decorated by top notch floral landscaping. "Usually I dream about shopping sprees and sexy dudes on the beach."

Should I let her think it's a dream?

"I mean, I thought I was up, but maybe I laid back down…" Marcy pinched her thigh, doubting in the reality around her.

The office door opened and a nurse in pink scrubs leaned out to flash a friendly smile. "Chloe Drakenstone," she called.

"That's me." Without responding to Marcy's bewildered speculations, Chloe grabbed her friend by the hand, laced their fingers, and dragged her into the back.

**

With her two best friends present, Chloe answered a series of personal questions about the state of her health while the nurse took notes. Afterward, the chipper doctor squeezed cold goop onto Chloe's bare midriff.

"KY Jelly? Really?" Marcy asked. "Probably the only time you've ever needed the stuff, huh? As much as you and Saul went at it, you clearly don't need any."

"*Marcy.*"

Mahasti snickered from her seat by the wall where she had settled to remain out of the way. The very moment the appointment ended, Chloe and Mahasti were going to have a stern conversation about granting inappropriate wishes. As much as she adored the genie, a little warning would have been appreciated.

"Okay, Mrs. Drakenstone. Are you ready to see and hear your jellybean?" the doctor asked. Her obstetrician was a spritely woman with a short bob of brown hair and a freckled nose. Doctor Thompson's reassuring smile melted some of Chloe's apprehension.

"I'm ready."

"This is so weird," Marcy muttered.

I'm going to have to tell her when we leave. Tell her what's really going on. She still thinks she's dreaming all of this in her bed while she sleeps off a hangover.

Moments after the doctor placed the funny probe to Chloe's tummy and moved it through the slick field of lubricant, a rapid 'whoosh whoosh whoosh' sound began. The doctor slid the probe left then right as the black and white picture came into focus.

"There's your baby's heartbeat. We don't normally hear that unless the pregnancy is beyond the seven or eight week mark."

"Is this good then?"

Doctor Thompson didn't answer immediately. "Hm… Interesting," she muttered.

"What is it?" Chloe jerked her eyes away from the ultrasound screen to the doctor.

"Are you positive about the date of your last period?"

"Um, yeah?"

"She was a real grouchy bitch," Marcy added cheerfully.

"Why? Is something wrong?" Chloe's throat tightened. Mahasti squeezed her fingers in reassurance and Marcy rubbed her shoulder.

"This fetus is rather large for gestation. I would have estimated a conception in March or early April."

"So my baby is too big? What does that mean?"

"I wouldn't say too big. The development appears appropriate for this size as well. Everything is there. Fingers and toes. If there's any cause for concern, I'll let you know," the doctor assured her. The woman smiled again, but this time her sunny disposition failed to ease Chloe's growing anxiety. "Your labs are a little unusual, so I'd like you to come in for a complete fasting blood work tomorrow. No food after midnight, okay?"

After wiping the goop off of Chloe's tummy, Doctor Thompson printed a few photos and saved a digital video to a disc. Chloe left the office feeling numb and terrified, with an appointment to return. Her elation dwindled to a cold knot of fear that twisted her belly with nausea.

Marcy pinched herself again. "I don't like this dream anymore." Like Chloe, she looked scared and nervous. "Why can't I wake up?" She pinched the back of her left hand and paced in a circle.

"It isn't a dream, Marce."

Saul's sleek silver vehicle pulled into park. Leiv left the driver's seat and opened the door for the women to pile into the spacious rear. Marcy hesitated at the door until Chloe pulled on her hand to coax her inside the vehicle.

"Come on, Marce. We gotta talk." *And close the damned car door before more cold air gets out.* Chloe fanned herself and positioned her body to receive maximum current from the vents. Cool air rustled her hair, a godsend for a pregnant woman.

"Okay, chica, spill it. What the heck is going on?"

"You aren't dreaming. All of this is real. You're in California with me, but an hour ago you were back home in Texas, probably about to flat iron your hair and finish your makeup."

"How the fuck did I get here?" Marcy demanded, her voice shooting up an octave. "Chloe, I don't get it. How am I *here?*"

"I am to blame for your current whereabouts," Mahasti answered, calm and unruffled as ever.

"Who *are* you?"

"I should have introduced you. Marcy, Mahasti is Saul's um…"

"I am a djinn."

Marcy's eyes crossed. "A whatsa?"

"A djinn," Chloe replied. "She's a… a genie, Marcy. That's how you got here. I said I wished you were with me and Mahasti made it happen."

Silence. Marcy stared at her as if she'd grown a second or third head.

I need to prove it to her. She's never going to believe what's going on until she sees it for herself. "I wish we were home right now."

The world beyond the tinted windows shimmered and faded until the congested Los Angeles streets became the winding driveway leading up to Saul's estate. The vehicle cruised effortlessly to the garage while Marcy held a white knuckled grip on the door.

"She just…"

"I wished us back home."

"I am so drunk," Marcy whispered. "Someone must have spiked my drink. LSD. Something."

"C'mon, Marcy, let's go inside and I'll pour you a glass of water. Then I promise to tell you everything."

Once they reached the veranda, Chloe decided to blurt out the truth. It came easily, like ripping off a Band-Aid. "Saul is a dragon in a human body."

"A dragon?" Appearing faint, Marcy quickly lowered into the chair before she lost her balance. "You're surrounded by creatures out of a bad paranormal romance." The woman rubbed her face then released a hysterical laugh. "What's Leiv then? A werewolf?"

"Uh, bear, actually," Chloe said.

"Christ, Chloe, are you serious? This is crazy!"

"I know… I felt the same way. God, at least you're taking it better than I did. I freaked at him and chased him off."

Understanding dawned in Marcy's brown eyes. Her jaw dropped slightly. "That's when you came back from your weekend away!"

"Yeah. I hurt his feelings."

"So where is he now?" Marcy asked.

"He went to handle 'very important dragon business' and said he'd be home this evening for dinner," Chloe said. She shrugged her shoulders and nervously settled into the lounge chair. The veranda provided a small comfort to her, and with a clear sunny day casting warm sunlight over the green pastures, the calming atmosphere was exactly what she needed.

Something may be wrong with my baby… Is this what I get for refusing to tell Freddy? Is this my punishment?

Tears stung her eyes again, bringing an abrupt end to Marcy's laughter.

"Oh no, sweetie. What's wrong?"

"The baby… I'm scared," Chloe admitted. She rubbed her wet cheek with the back of her wrist. "I finally got used to the idea of being a mom and… now you know why I knew Freddy was the father.

165

Saul's not even human. And now it turns out I was probably pregnant before I even met Saul…"

As Marcy squeezed beside her into the chair and held her close, Mahasti arrived with lunch. She offered Chloe a handkerchief then poured peach-scented tea.

"I do not believe your former lover fathered this baby," Mahasti said.

Chloe dabbed at her eyes. "What?"

"Who else could it be?" Marcy demanded angrily. "Chloe doesn't sleep around and she's already said that Saul can't have babies with her."

"As a djinn, I see many things, but even some truths elude me," Mahasti admitted. "I can see your love for Saul, and I can know your heart's truest desires, but my hands remain tied until a wish is made. And even then, some gifts are beyond my ability to grant. When Saul wished for a mate who could love him for who he truly was, I took steps to guide you back to him — but I could not make you love him. That came from within you, Chloe. I believe Saul conceived with you in the mountain."

"You think… No. He said it isn't possible." *I want it so bad. I want this baby to belong to Saul, but is that even possible? Can a dragon and a human conceive a child?*

Mahasti shook her head. "Few things are impossible in this world, Chloe. What Saul should have told you is that it's not *probable*. Leiv and I have begun to research what we can in the library." A wistful look crossed her features. "If his mother were awakened, we could ask her," Mahasti said.

"Does that mean what I think it means? His mother is a…" Marcy's voice trailed off.

Chloe frowned. "A real hibernating dragon. He's never told me where, just that she's slept for decades and probably won't even budge while I'm alive." Her fingers traveled over her barely visible tummy curve. According to the doctor, her active lifestyle and tall build worked to her advantage.

"Holy shit. Dragons and genies. This is a lot to digest," Marcy said.

"Is it really possible that Saul could've fathered my baby?"

Mahasti's bright smile widened, reassuring Chloe within seconds. "I believe so… I remember vague stories of a man known for his courage and half-dragon blood, born from a storm dragon and mortal man."

"And you think my baby is like that…" Chloe closed her eyes and dragged in a deep breath. She remained that way until long after Mahasti had vanished to continue her research, leaving Chloe and Marcy to enjoy their evening tea. "I want it so bad. It seems too good to be true."

"Holy crap, chica," Marcy breathed out. "Your kiddo is going to be a superhero or something."

"I guess so. If they're right."

"This is all so crazy," Marcy muttered again. She drained her glass and set it aside.

"Marcy… I'm sorry for dragging you into this. Do you want to go home?"

"Hell no. I'm in this for as long as you need me." Marcy patted her hip for her cell phone then groaned. "Dammit. I need to text Antonio and let him know tonight is canceled. And… I really hope my styling iron isn't burning down the apartment 'cause I had it heating up while I did my makeup."

"Mahasti?"

The genie reappeared moments later with an iPhone in her hand. "I secured your home."

"Thanks." Marcy accepted the phone with tentative fingers, reluctant to take the device from the genie's fingers.

"She's not going to burn you or anything if you touch her. Mahasti is harmless."

"You can never be too sure. I saw the movie *Wishmaster*." The Latina flashed the other woman an apologetic smile. "Sorry," she apologized to Mahasti.

Chloe sighed. While Marcy was her oldest pal, the developing friendship between her and Mahasti meant that she didn't want to risk their uncertain, new relationship over a misunderstanding.

"It takes much more to offend me, my friend. There is no harm done. But please, there are more important matters at hand. While in the library, a passing thought came to me regarding how we could prove your child is dragon-blooded."

Marcy and Chloe both stared at the genie. "Well don't keep us waiting in suspense, chica. Come on," Marcy encouraged her.

"What I am about to share with you is a closely guarded secret among dragonkin." Mahasti fixed both women with a stern glance. "Can you keep this a secret?"

"Of course, Mahasti," Chloe assured her. Marcy promised the same.

167

The djinn's smile lit up her entire face. "Good. As you know, all dragons maintain a vast hoard, but they don't come by their riches by chance. Gemstones and precious metals... call to them, for lack of a better description. They're attracted to it like iron to a magnet. It's their greatest weakness, and also their curse, so to speak."

"They can't help themselves."

"Correct," Mahasti confirmed for Chloe. "I think if we take you down to the hoard, we might see if the same phenomenon occurs."

"I dunno, Mahasti. I think I'd know if I was drawn towards, you know, diamonds and rubies and stuff."

"How many diamonds and rubies have you been around recently?" Marcy demanded.

Chloe glanced at her engagement ring and tungsten band. Neither had a single diamond or ruby, but the precious black pearls and lovely opal made her smile. Given from the heart, even a piece of glass from Saul would have exceeded the worth of her ex-fiancé's diamond.

"I'm not going to run over and dive into his collection like I'm Scrooge McDuck, am I?"

Mahasti laughed. "The effect would be weaker with you."

"We haven't visited Saul's hoard since returning home from Texas. Is he going to be okay with this?"

"You're his trusted and beloved mate, Chloe. Trust me when I say he approves wholeheartedly of your entrance here, whether he is present or not."

"What about me?" Marcy asked.

Mahasti glanced at the lone outsider, a speculative look pursing her lips. "Leiv and I are Saul's closest friends. As the same remains true between you and Chloe, you are entrusted with the same honor. Enter, but touch nothing without Chloe's permission."

Citing that Mahasti's mode of rapid travel made her experience morning sickness too, Marcy requested for the two women to lead her to the underground chamber via their own feet. At the bottom of the stairs, the candles came alive with flames, shifting hues of blue that cast their shadows over the walls.

"It's so damned cold down here," Marcy muttered.

"Yeah, I thought that too the first time he brought me down. You get used to it."

Chloe led the way into familiar territory, a massive cavern carved beneath the house, in the depths of a mountain, with smooth worn floors polished to a perfect gleam. The occasional lantern burned to reveal their winding path amidst Saul's belongings, old and new treasures displayed on shelves, beneath glass displays, and sometimes piled haphazardly over tables or overflowing from chests.

"Holy shit. What *doesn't* he have?"

"You tell me," Chloe murmured. "Though it's been a while since I last came down, and I guess he must have acquired some new things. Sounds like he has some wind chimes in here now."

"I don't hear anything," Marcy said.

The mellow notes continued, each lyrical whisper louder than the last, leading her deeper into the chamber until the blue-flame lanterns reflected over gold coins spilling from the rearmost room. Beyond the open archway, the sight of Saul's jewel-laced stash took her breath away. It sparkled in rainbow hues, luminescent under the thin ribbon of daylight that slanted through a clever skylight.

"This must be worth millions. Maybe more than millions." Marcy whistled and crouched to peer at a perfect star sapphire amidst uncut rubies. "I promise not to take anything but can I touch—"

"Yeah, go ahead."

She left Marcy sifting through sparklies and followed the melody into the back of the room where the lantern glow dimmed. There, in the darker corner of Saul's sanctuary, the meager light bounced off the edge of a four poster bed tucked near the wall.

"It's beautiful." The ghostly lullaby calmed Chloe's senses until she surrendered to her instincts and perched on the edge of the platform bed. She stroked the cool gemstone beneath her with one hand, tracing the fine whorls of pale green streaked throughout the dark texture.

Mahasti remained a respectful distance behind her. "It's carved from a solid block of jade. Saul traded for it several years ago with a dragon from the east."

"I'd feel like a queen sleeping in this. With a mattress though."

A thin, memory foam mattress materialized beneath Chloe's rump, speckled with blue cooling gel beads. A split second later, high thread count sheets in her favorite gold color whooshed into place, accompanied by body pillows.

"You're spoiling me, Mahasti." And she wouldn't change it for the world. "It's like lying on a cloud surrounded by my own personal string quartet. What song is that anyway?"

"I hear nothing, Chloe. You must hear what the dragons hear," Mahasti said in her placid tone. "Which means that you must have dragon blood within you."

Chloe traced her belly's subtle curve and closed her eyes. Saul had

169

gifted her a treasure beyond the worth of any gem in his hoard. He'd given her his child, and he'd granted her awareness of the magical world. For the first time since discovering her pregnancy, Chloe felt tears of absolute joy. They streaked down her cheeks as relief flooded her soul and lifted away the apprehensions of birthing Freddy's child, confessing the truth to him, and accepting he was bound to her life.

Mahasti gave her privacy to enjoy the precious moment and stepped away from the carved niche at the rear of the horde. The subterranean space's acoustics made it easy to overhear the djinn's discussion with Marcy. She passed on stories regarding a few of the spectacular pieces in Saul's collection as if she were a museum curator.

Marcy's here, getting along with my new friend. This baby is Saul's. Life just couldn't be any more perfect.

After their treasure room explorations, the girls made a reluctant exit to return upstairs. Marcy exchanged a few texts with Antonio, canceling their plans for a movie date while she wolfed down her share of their afternoon snack. Upon receiving sufficient nourishment and rest, the two friends went for a tour of the grounds.

"Are these cows and sheep all for what I think they're for?"

"What do you think they're for?"

"I'm thinking of the T-rex scene from Jurassic Park."

Chloe laughed. "You're right. He doesn't do it in front of me, but we snuggled in his hoard a few times to let him stretch out in his true form. We tried it out here and the bugs ate me alive."

"Am I going to get to see him?" Marcy demanded.

"That's up to Saul." *Like he'd miss the chance to show off his wings. He's as vain as a preening parrot,* Chloe thought.

"What's that cabin over there?"

"Leiv lives there. You didn't really get the chance to talk to him, but he's a great guy."

"So he's a chauffeur slash groundskeeper?"

Chloe chuckled. "Among other things, yeah. You should have seen how sad he was when I drove the car to Vegas. He's like the man of the house when Saul isn't here, or when Saul goes into hibernation."

"Him and Mahasti are boning, aren't they?"

"Yep."

"So are you going to, I dunno, lay an egg?"

The absurd question made Chloe laugh. "No! I think the doctor would have mentioned an eggshell in the ultrasound. Honestly."

"Oh yeah, right." Marcy rubbed her neck. "Sorry. The whole time in that room I was convinced I was having some fucked up dream. I kept thinking 'I can't wait to wake up and tell Chloe about this freaky nightmare.' Shit… after touching enough jewels to fill a museum, I'm not convinced I really did wake up."

Grinning, Chloe hooked their arms together and guided Marcy from the veranda. "You'll really think you're dreaming once you see Saul's aquatic garden. Leiv convinced him to spring for a natural pool and it's fantastic!"

"I don't have a swim suit! You know I need that special one I bought if I'm going to fit—" Marcy patted her generous bottom. "—All this ass into a suit."

"Mahasti has you covered. Trust me."

The two friends tittered at the intentional pun and continued forward to their next adventure.

Chapter 11

Saul returned while Marcy and Chloe soaked in the sun alongside the pool. Clothed in his expensive Armani suit, he walked out onto the stone and crossed his arms. Both bikini-clad girls peeked up at him, almost in unison.

"Greetings, Marceline. Mahasti informed me that you came for an impromptu visit."

"Oh yeah. Making myself at home." Marcy's lopsided, half-drunk smile made Chloe giggle. "Leiv makes the best drinks." She sipped her tropical daiquiri and noisily sucked up the brown layer of rum from the bottom. A hangover wasn't enough to discourage Marcy from imbibing enough for both of them.

"That he does," Saul agreed.

"Hey, it isn't too late to change my mind and move in, right? You guys will need a nanny or a babysitter. I'm also a great math tutor. Come on. Once you get that kiddo in school and see what the kids are doing these days, you'll be screaming at Mahasti to bring me back."

"Your presence is always welcome, Marceline." Saul grinned. "But for now, I have been sent to fetch you both. Dinner will be ready shortly."

"Do I get to see you au naturale?"

She's taking this ridiculously well, Chloe thought. "Leave it to you to get straight to the point. I thought you'd at least stuff your face with food before you asked my husband to strip."

Saul glanced at Chloe for approval, and when she shrugged, he loosened his tie and began unfastening his shirt.

Crap. "Saul!" Chloe cried, interrupting him. She swatted his hand as he reached his belt.

"What?"

Marcy covered her eyes. "Not looking! I meant au naturale as a dragon, not sexy Viking warrior and cock and stuff!"

"We didn't mean for you to strip naked right now," Chloe blurted out. She hadn't yet acquired her husband's lack of modesty. While Leiv and Mahasti regarded nudity with a similarly cavalier nature, she couldn't bear to allow them to see her in anything less than her bathing suit.

"Oh. I misunderstood," he said, abashed.

Marcy peeked from between her fingers. "I saw enough of you when you were strutting around the apartment half naked, Barney. You're hot and all, but I think I'm happy without seeing all the goods."

"Barney!?" Saul's incredulous tone drew a peal of laughter from Chloe. "I am not a purple dinosaur."

After dinner, while Marcy and Chloe chatted over herbal tea in the solarium, Saul startled them both by peeking in through one of the enormous windows. Marcy screamed and threw tea everywhere. A splash of the hot liquid scalded Chloe's leg, feeling more like tepid water.

"Holy shit, he's huge!"

"I warned you!"

Without picking up her teacup, Marcy darted to the balcony for a closer look. Saul settled on his hind legs and propped one forearm on the balcony edge, showing Marcy his massive claw.

"Oh my God, oh my God, he's huge," she repeated, trapped between feeling terror and awe. Clearly, she chose awe and reached one trembling hand toward the nearest maroon talon. Her fingers slid over the smooth, curved claw.

"Would you like a ride? Chloe has grown very fond of flying," Saul said.

The dragon's ability to speak caught Marcy off guard and stumbled her back into Chloe. She lost her balance then nearly toppled onto her ass until Saul adjusted his claw to catch her against the leathery paw pad.

"He won't hurt you. I promise, he's exactly the same guy he was before."

"I'm not freaking," Marcy replied quickly. "Not freaking." Nor was she breathing. Her motionless body tensed from head to toe, but eventually her muscles relaxed and she dragged in a lungful of air. "He's beautiful."

"Yeah. He is." Chloe smiled up at her golden-eyed dragon, expecting him to preen with pride. His magnificent wings fanned out to reveal their full span, while Marcy's eyes widened even further.

"Fuck yeah, I want a ride!" Marcy finally cried out once the initial terror faded.

An hour later, once Marcy finally had enough of the wind whipping through her hair and the gorgeous expanse making up Saul's thousands of acres, he deposited both ladies by the front door. They watched him amble off in search of a meal.

"He kind of smells like Felix when he's fresh from the groomer." Marcy sniffed her shirt, searching for Saul's lingering scent.

"You know, you're right." Then Marcy shoved her. A playful nudge of both hands made Chloe stumble a step to the side. "What was that for!?"

"For not telling me about this when he came to my place for a month! I can't believe you didn't tell me."

"I didn't know how to tell you. I mean, if I outright said he was a mythological creature, you would have made some crack about his sexiness being magical and ignored me."

Marcy grumbled a reluctant agreement, "I guess you're right. Okay, as pleasant as that was, I feel a little scummy from the pool."

"I'll show you to one of the guest rooms. The bathrooms here are awesome. Mahasti will provide you with whatever clothes you think you need."

A desire to soak away the morning's stressful ordeal divided Chloe and Marcy for an hour. They chatted over the household's intercom system from their individual bathrooms and met again in the room designated as the future nursery. Chloe brought her laptop along as directed and connected to the estate's WiFi while Marcy marveled over the room's design. Felix, ever curious, followed them and gave the space a thorough inspection. He explored the walk-in closet, batted at the drapes, and then made himself comfortable on the wide window ledge.

"Girl, you have an awesome view." Marcy peered out while giving the large cat scratches beneath his chin. "I bet we could put a rocking chair right here... and I'm sort of envisioning the crib over there. Since we have access to Genie Airlines, I can come out whenever you're ready to help paint."

"You'd do that?"

"You're my best friend. You bet your ass I'll be here to help. I'll get Mom's brushes and stencils." Marcy scanned the nursery's barren interior and cream walls. She had always been the one with the artistic talent.

"I love you, Marce. I really, really do." Grateful tears misted Chloe's eyes, and without warning, she threw her arms around her friend.

Foresight or the gift of perfect timing allowed Saul to arrive at the conclusion of their heartfelt moment. The oblivious dragon passed Chloe his credit card without uttering a word.

"Seriously? He just hands off his platinum card and that's that?"

"I don't even argue with him anymore. 'What's his is mine.' He says the same thing about that massive treasure room of priceless crap we showed you."

"Crap?" Saul demanded. He crossed his arms, scandalized features drawing laughter from the two women.

"Uh. Beautiful relics," Chloe corrected herself. He grinned and took a seat on the floor while they perused high-end baby stores online.

"Look, this crib converts into a toddler bed, then a full-size." Marcy pointed at the laptop screen.

"It's a good thing they don't have a one-click feature," Chloe muttered as she ticked the item off into her wish list for later comparison. "What do you think about this bed set, Saul?"

"Ah…" Both girls giggled at his befuddled expression.

"Men are always hopeless with baby stuff, Chloe, you know that."

Saul cleared his throat. "The color is fetching. If you like it, my love, then I'm happy."

A frenzied internet shopping spree ensued. As the evening dwindled, an unnatural silence fell over Saul until he no longer participated, aside from the occasional curt nod. He excused himself from the impromptu three-person baby shower and retreated to the movie den where Chloe found him seated in front of an old black and white film an hour after his disappearance. He loved King Kong, and she'd watched it countless times with him since their reunion.

"What's wrong?" she called.

"Many thoughts on my mind."

This is as new to him as it is to me, Chloe thought. "About the baby? You'll be an amazing father, Saul." She scooted sideways onto his lap and set one arm around his broad shoulders. Her long legs went over the arm of the recliner once she slouched down to rest her cheek over his heart. She'd counted them once, a powerful but lazy rate of thirty-two beats a minute. Too slow to sustain a human, perfect for a dragon shifted into a smaller body.

"Perhaps."

The brooding continued, a sour stain on Chloe's mood that she longed to wash away with her good news. "Saul, there's something you need to know. About the baby."

"Is something the matter? Mahasti told me she convinced you to visit a physician. I hope all is well."

Chloe bit her lower lip. His patience must have rubbed off on her, otherwise she would have never held the secret so long. The old Chloe would have blurted it out the moment he arrived poolside.

Sitting up, she studied his face and touched her fingers to his golden beard. Slim digits caressed the soft velvet, and then she kissed his lips. "You're going to be a father."

"We established this, Chloe. I will adopt your little one."

"No, Saul. This baby is yours. You fathered our child. Your blood."

For the first time in their relationship, Chloe witnessed Saul stunned into speechlessness with his gaze lowered to her belly. Guiding him with gentle hands, Chloe brought his left palm to her subtle bump.

"*Our* baby, Saul," she whispered.

"That cannot be possible... I've never heard of such a thing."

"It is. While you were gone, Mahasti took me into the hoard to your gold collection... I never saw anything so radiant in all of my life. Now I know why I sleep so well with you in your vault, Saul. I do because our baby wants to be there. The gems sang to me. I always thought I heard sounds at night but... it's so beautiful now. I can't describe it."

Still as stone, Saul failed to utter a word, but an underlying sense of his happiness snaked into her senses. "Mine?" he finally whispered.

"Yours," she confirmed.

"I never thought... how is this possible?"

"Mahasti told me there are legends of a dragon warrior born from a female dragon and a mortal man."

"My father always told me those are only stories and tall tales to frighten us... or I wouldn't have given away..." Saul swallowed and gazed beyond her, through her, revealing thoughts of great importance weighing on his troubled mind. "That matters none at the moment." The abrupt change in his mood treaded a fine divide between thrilled and morose.

"Saul?" she whispered again.

"It is merely difficult to believe... This news pleases me greatly, my love." Saul dipped his head to place his bearded jaw against her smooth cheek and sighed. "I am undeniably happy."

"Then why are you so distant now? What happened?"

Saul inhaled a deep breath. In the little time since their relationship began, reading his emotional state became a fine art. Her new husband was an open book, wearing his feeling on his sleeves. "Trouble. But you have suffered enough worry this day. Now is time for celebration."

"Don't protect me like I'm some delicate flower. What's

happening?"

The silence told Chloe all she needed to know. When he turned his head away, she raised a hand to his face and directed him back to her. Eyes the color of rich liquid gold gazed down at her. "I met with Maximilian and Brigid. It did not go as planned."

"I'm here to listen to you," she reminded him. "That's what being married is about."

"They will not accept the cessation of our betrothal. Rather, Brigid will not accept and her father has no inclination to dissuade her from pursuing this to the end."

Cold swept over Chloe, an icy kiss leaving goosebumps over her arms. "What does that mean? Why won't they?"

"Her father does not consider our union as a true mating bond," he spoke slowly.

"He can't be serious. You told me that you chased her for decades while he said nothing."

"Indeed, and he said as much during our meeting. He is a mediator in this and nothing more. Maximilian was quite fair, all things considered, but Draconic Law is indisputable. Once pledged, both parent and child must release me. He is willing, but she stands firm in her decision to have me, and he will not force her."

"What if you told them that I'm carrying a half-dragon child?"

Saul shook his head. "I am reluctant to share as much with the rest of my kind. We are a traditional lot, set in our ways, and easy to anger. Change becomes terrifying when it is not guided by our own hands."

"In other words, you're afraid they'll try to kill me."

Saul nodded his head. "And I would lay down my own life before I allowed harm to come to either of you."

Chloe blinked away the hazy field spreading over her vision until her eyes no longer stung with impending tears. *I won't cry and worry him even more. I won't.* "What happens now, Saul?"

Saul's weary sigh and reluctance to speak became clear with his next words. "Our baby has changed everything, so now we wait for Brigid to make her next move, and we prepare for the worst. According to our laws, you have usurped her claim by breeding with me and she would have every right to issue a challenge if you were also a dragon."

"But I'm pregnant!"

"To a female dragon, that means nothing, my love. But because you are human, we have the right to refuse. She cannot force you to obey our laws." His strong arms squeezed her close, conveying the security she craved, but how could he possibly protect her from an envious fire breathing dragon?

"I'm terrified," she breathed out on a shaky breath.

"So am I, but we will weather this storm together."

Chapter 12

Saul and Chloe celebrated their good news in the morning, surrounded by their close friends. Amid laughter and jokes, they were able to ignore the threat overshadowing the joyous occasion.

After breakfast and tea, the two girls stole Mahasti and Leiv away for a day of exploring Los Angeles together. Saul remained true to his word by arranging for Marcy to walk onto the set of a movie as an extra, and she caught a passing glimpse of one of her favorite male actors.

"Damn, he's sexier in real life than he is photoshopped and airbrushed."

"Definitely," Chloe agreed.

They stopped for haircuts, visited top landmarks, walked Hollywood, and caught a double matinee feature. Eventually, Marcy googled a boutique on her phone and dragged Chloe away to shop for leggings, slip-on shoes, and little dresses with ribbons and elastic beneath the tits. Half an hour into their shopping spree, Chloe realized she was ecstatic to tell the world about her child.

I'm so glad she convinced me to come out with her.

"You're rocking that new haircut, too, chica. I didn't think you'd ever cut it like that."

Chloe ran her fingers through her short bob of blonde hair. "Thanks. It's nice to splurge and not worry about money for once."

"This is the life. The stuff we always dreamed about in high school," Marcy sighed in contentment and gazed out the car window. "I'd go bonkers if I had to drive in all that city traffic. It's worse than Houston."

"Leiv and Mahasti make it pretty easy to arrive in style."

"They're an awesome team. Thanks," Marcy called to the front seat.

Leiv chuckled. "You are very welcome. Ah, now, Mahasti. This is a good time to take us to the estate."

"With pleasure."

They're such lovebirds. If he spent any more time moon-eyeing her, he wouldn't be able to drive. Chloe giggled and whispered her thoughts to Marcy. She nodded her agreement.

The genie whisked them away from Los Angeles to the secluded driveway leading up to the estate. As Leiv angled the car for the garage and hit the automatic remote, a sporty convertible cruised down the lane toward Saul's home.

"Oh man, is that a Ferrari?" Marcy pressed her face against the window.

"It is trouble. Only trouble," Leiv muttered.

Chloe swore under her breath when she recognized Brigid in the driver's seat. Her wind-tousled hair gave her a Just-Got-Fucked look that Chloe couldn't pull off. Without prompting, Mahasti transported Chloe and Marcy both inside the house. The moment the mist dissipated, Chloe bolted for the front door. She beat Saul to it.

"Why are you here?" Chloe demanded after she jerked the door open. Saul attempted to budge her, and in a fit of childish pique, she drove her elbow into his ribs. His audible 'oof' assured Chloe that she was stronger than she appeared.

"I came to see my betrothed," Brigid answered, snide tone filled with as much venom as a coral snake.

"Then we will speak outside. You are no longer welcome within my home. Chloe, stay inside."

Chloe followed Saul despite his warning for her to keep clear of Brigid. She didn't trust the female dragon. Not one bit.

"I have spoken of this, Brigid. My mind will not be changed," Saul growled. "Chloe is my wife. My mate."

"She is an insect. An inferior—" Brigid cut herself off abruptly and her nostrils flared. She inhaled deeply and twisted to face Chloe. "What have you done? What manner of atrocity did you commit to pull this off, Saul? This mortal smells of dragon's blood."

Crap! Why didn't she notice that before?!

Unlike Chloe, Saul didn't seem worried about the revelation. He drew himself up, proud and strong, and met Brigid's gaze without a flinch. "The child she carries is mine, Brigid. The cherished result of a true mating."

"An abomination," Brigid hissed between her teeth.

The deplorable insult stabbed Chloe in the heart. She opened her mouth to fire a retort, but Saul beat her to it.

"A child," her husband said. "A beautiful child I will raise, love, and treasure alongside a woman who is every bit your superior. Now leave us."

Brigid trembled with rage. A hot flush swept over her porcelain cheeks as fury curved her teeth and elongated her claws. Instinctual self-preservation drove Chloe to fall back a step. "Slay her at this moment, Saul, and all shall be forgiven. It isn't too late to make amends for this. You can make things right in my father's eyes."

Saul didn't budge. "Maximilian and the rest of the Conclave know you for what you are: a self-absorbed child. Be gone from my estate."

The change took place in an instant. Leather slacks split and white linen burst at the seams. Ember red dragon's hide covered Brigid from head to toe as she towered above Saul's human body. As she dove forward, Saul caught her with his own considerable bulk. Shreds of his jeans fluttered to the ground. He had transformed in the blink of an eye.

Somewhere behind Chloe, Marcy shrieked as the two behemoths tumbled across the ground. They snapped and bit at each other, raking their claws like brawling lions going in for the kill.

"Saul!" Chloe screamed.

Snorting, snarling, and tearing up sod, the two beasts twisted upon the ground, each in a bid to gain the upper hand. Chloe watched as a helpless bystander until wisps of jasmine smoke surrounded and whisked her away. After the dizzying teleportation ended, she stood with the door between her and both draconic beings.

"It is unsafe to stand outside while they fight," Mahasti told her gently. "For your safety, please stay indoors this time, Chloe."

"What if she kills him!?" A tight vice constricted her chest, hindering her breaths until each inhalation took more effort than the last. Her lungs burned and tears fell easily down her cheeks. "Mahasti, do something, please."

"Can't you make them stop?" Marcy asked the genie.

"She won't kill him, Chloe, I promise. It's not unusual for dragons to fight to release aggression, and Brigid isn't stupid enough to risk it. To kill Saul on his own property would be to bring the wrath of the Dragon Conclave down upon her. It would be murder."

"Conclave?" Chloe asked.

"The Dragon Conclave. They're a council of the eldest and most ancient wyrms. They construct Draconic Law."

"She's smaller than he is. She's barely putting a dent in him, look," Marcy murmured. Fires flared and lightning flashed in the waning twilight. Saul exhaled a mighty breath that left stars in Chloe's eyes, releasing a storm of jagged bolts that seared Brigid's red flanks.

She's beautiful. Even as a dragon, she's beautiful. But she isn't the one he wants. All of that beauty and it's wasted on a black soul, Chloe thought as she squeezed beside her friend to watch. She held her breath and remained glued to the small glass pane in the sturdy wooden door.

"Get her, Saul. Get her," Marcy said under her breath. "Kick her fucking ass."

Both girls cheered him from the safety of the house and seemed to give Saul the motivation he needed. His talons ripped down Brigid's ribs. She reared back and made her prompt exit from the battle, quitting the field by placing yards between them. Saul advanced on her, but Brigid quickly scurried to keep the massive stone fountain between them. Her actions lent a hilarious resemblance to two kids using a parked vehicle to stave off an after school fight. It was the most ridiculous thing Chloe had seen in years.

"That thing gestating in her gut should never see the light of day!" Brigid shouted. Her labored breaths continued as she licked her wounds. Ash-colored flight feathers dangled from her wings, glistening wet with blood.

Too bad Saul didn't rip them off completely.

"It will. That is my child. Come near my mate again uninvited and I will finish what I began this eve, Brigid. *I will skin you.*"

Brigid's wild, amber eyes flicked between Saul and the door. They narrowed when she saw Chloe spectating. Then something sinister happened.

She smiled. A smile on a dragon's face could be a truly fascinating thing, or it could be terrifying. Saul often smiled when she stroked his stomach, pet his wings, or even when she sprawled upon his softer underbelly and slumbered to the slow rhythm of his powerful heart. She lived for it and treasured his elation, but Brigid's toothy grin terrified her.

"Hear me now, human waif. In accordance with Draconic Law, I challenge you to a duel to the death. The winner takes Saul as her mate."

"And what if I don't accept? You can't make me fight you."

"That is where you are wrong, human. You carry a dragon's spawnling in your gut, and thus you also have a dragon's blood in your veins. Your bastard has legitimized my challenge."

Saul's growl raised the fine hairs on Chloe's nape. His motionless figure towered between the two women, an intimidating presence covered in Brigid's blood and little of his own. "I will die before I allow you to harm a hair on Chloe's head."

"Then die and take those within your household to their deaths as well, knowing they will leap to your defense and suffer for it. I will have you or no one shall." A plume of smoke drifted out from between her sharp fangs. "But if you and your bitch kneel to me now, I may allow her to remain as your consort. Warm her bed when I have no use for you."

Chloe thrust open the door and moved onto the stoop. "I won't share him."

"Then you accept."

"Chloe, don't acknowledge the challenge. This is unprecedented, she cannot make you—"

"Once the Conclave declares your union to be invalid, I will fuck him every night as you watch. You will have my scraps and the mere honor of licking his cock clean once I have finished. Or will you fight like a woman?" Brigid's forked tongue snaked over her lips, as sinister a gesture as her terrifying grin.

Impulse swept Chloe into their world, and left her incapable of voicing more than a single word. "Yes."

***

"Okay, there has to be a way you can get her out of this, right?" Marcy sat beside Chloe, rubbing her shoulders while Saul paced a groove in the priceless Persian rug decorating his library floor. He wore jeans without a shirt, revealing the jagged wounds decorating his shoulders and back. Most of the injuries inflicted by Brigid's claws and sharp teeth were already in the early stages of healing. Mahasti said he wouldn't recover completely until he hibernated a day or two underground.

"No. No. The acceptance of a challenge remains binding until death."

"She's pregnant. She got upset in the heat of the moment and her hormones made her say something stupid. There's no way anyone can expect her to fight a giant fire-breathing dragon like this. What's she supposed to use anyway? Her bare hands against that bitch's skin? Would they make her fight if she were a dragon like you?"

"Pregnancy is no excuse to escape a fight among our kind. While I did fight Brigid, I would not tangle with a brooding female wyrm for any amount of treasure," Saul said. "However, Chloe is not a dragon."

"Perhaps we can use this to our advantage. Chloe is human. She has a human's thin skin. No claws. A fight between her and Brigid is suicide," Leiv said. The bear shifter sat on the floor while Mahasti perused the pages of an ancient tome beside him.

"If she had only listened to me," Saul growled. "We would not face this problem." The anger in his voice made Chloe wince and flinch back.

"I'm sorry," she whispered. "I didn't mean to make things

183

worse."

Saul's failure to answer her cut deeper than any knife. He became all business, the suit-and-tie executive of Drakenstone Studios instead of her husband. "I will appeal to the Conclave. Call in allies; those who can be trusted. Perhaps they will call off the fight once we plead our case."

"And if they can't? Or won't?" Marcy asked.

Saul dragged his palm down his face. "If Chloe refuses to fight, then the Conclave will attempt to execute her for breach of her verbal contract. Anyone who defends her will be dealt a similar fate."

"Wow, you guys are really strict," Marcy said.

The dragon shrugged and settled heavily into his desk chair.

"If I'm going to die then I'm going to die. Would they at least allow me to wait until the baby is born?"

"Unlikely. As I said, the Conclave may view our child as a threat to draconic values. Our traditions have always… discouraged human and dragon relations."

"Now we know why. If a dragon can impregnate a human, it means there'd be a lot of race mixing going on," Marcy muttered.

Like her friend, Chloe viewed the events with mixed fascination and horror. She feared what was to come, but each minute of conversation yielded something new about Saul's world.

"Who am I kidding? The Conclave will never reverse Chloe's acceptance," Saul growled. "There is only one solution. I must kill Brigid. If I move swiftly, they will believe I have acted on my own, and the Conclave will be without reason to discipline the rest of you."

"Saul, no," Chloe spoke up. "*No.*"

"Here!" Mahasti suddenly called. "I have a solution." The genie rose from her seat on the floor and crossed to Saul. He met her halfway and looked down at the pages.

Then he laughed. A deep, mirthless laugh filled with resentment. "Of course. This surprises me none."

Chloe's eyebrows rose toward the top of her head. "What is it?"

"Mahasti, you know as well as I do that I no longer have it," Saul said.

"What is it?" Chloe asked again. Her voice shot higher as they continued to talk around her, ignoring her. Saul gestured with one hand toward the open pages, muttered an incoherent utterance and thrust the book away from him in frustration.

"Appeal to him for its return, Saul. Now is not the time to

become frustrated," Mahasti said.

"She is right, friend. We will contact him. Talk. Tell him what is the matter and perhaps he will allow Chloe to borrow it," Leiv said. "You cannot make this decision alone."

"You have forgotten one very important thing: it is a fairytale. Its magic is a fucking *legend*," Saul scathed.

Saul rarely swore, despite his claims of inheriting the awful habit from his wife. Marcy and Chloe exchanged curious glances. "Dragons are fairytales too," Marcy pointed out, fear for Chloe prompting her to speak. "What's happening? Please tell us."

"Don't ignore us like we're not sitting here. Tell us what's happening!" Chloe cried out.

Leiv and Mahasti said nothing, but their intense gazes suggested the two had a way of conversing without voicing their thoughts out loud. Chloe had wondered about them for a while, convinced her knowledge of Mahasti's supernatural powers didn't scratch the surface.

"Saul, tell her," Leiv urged.

"Fine," the dragon growled. "It was once your desire to meet other dragons, Chloe. It seems that you will receive your wish. Mahasti, contact Watatsumi. Tell him I would like to discuss our most recent transaction."

"Of course."

"Watatsumi?" Chloe repeated.

"One of my father's oldest comrades. I traded him a very special gift five years ago from my father's hoard," Saul said, his dry tone an unconcealed sign of his displeasure.

"What'd you trade him?" Marcy asked.

"A sword."

Marcy snorted. "So, like, what? Excalibur or something?"

"No, Marceline. It was the sword Ascalon, the relic of Saint George, and I foolishly traded it away."

Chloe's mouth fell open. "You mean, the actual sword from the stories? The one he used to kill the Welsh dragon or whatever the damn story says?"

"The sword used to slay my very own grandfather among many other dragons in our history. I loathed my grandfather's legacy and wanted no reminder of his uncivilized behavior, so as you can imagine it took little convincing for me to part with it. When Watatsumi named it as his price, I accepted the offer... and now Chloe's survival depends on its return."

"Do you think he'll give it back." *Will he help us?* Chloe prayed that

185

he would.

    Saul's expression had never looked so grim. "Let us hope so."

Chapter 13

Chloe stretched upon the cool sheets, enjoying her preferred state of nudity whenever she slept beside her slumbering dragon. Her reaching fingers encountered only open air.

"Saul?" she whispered, before jerking upright in the jade bed. The absence of Saul's body heat spawned an initial moment of fleeting terror until her eyes adjusted to the pitch black surroundings. Since Brigid made her challenge two nights earlier, he'd been edgy and moody in their bedroom. With hopes of soothing him, and herself, Chloe had suggested sleeping deep below the estate in his hoard.

I can see perfectly in the dark now. When did that happen? The answer eluded her. Like many other subtle changes to her body, it had crept in to take her by surprise.

After dragging herself from bed, Chloe pulled on her silk robe, belted it in front, and padded barefoot over the smooth polished floor. She found Saul easily in the main house, but he wasn't alone. His voice carried down the hallway from the library. With the door ajar, she picked up the incredulity in his guest's voice.

"This is madness, Saul."

"Have you come to dissuade me from my path as well?"

"Why would you pursue such a foolish endeavor for a half-breed and a... a *human*? Please. Listen to reason, my friend. Consider these choices. I came this eve hoping to find these stories were lies wrought by a bitter shrew. To know that you risk infuriating the Conclave over—"

"My child, Teo. My cub and *the mother* of my cub are worth my life and any other sacrifice I may pay to protect them. I will not oppose the Conclave outright, but I will plead to them for aid."

The other man sighed. "I did not travel such a distance to argue with you."

"Then let us not argue. Celebrate with me. I am soon to become a father, and if I recall, you once told me you'd beat me to the task long before Brigid submitted."

"How could you celebrate when—?"

One of the dragons sniffed. The other mimicked him and inhaled.

"We are not alone, my friend," the stranger said.

Following a brief pause, Saul spoke up, "Come in, Chloe. Teo does not bite."

"I find the taste of mortals unpalatable."

Chloe nudged the library door open completely and stepped inside, thankful she donned a robe prior to tiptoeing around the estate.

Teo's green eyes startled her, bright and bold within a face that reminded her of Central American natives. While Saul's golden blond locks fell in sleek waves, his friend had glossy, pin-straight ebony hair down past his shoulders.

"Teo, allow me to introduce you to Chloe." Saul wrapped his arm around her waist and drew her in close. His lips touched her hairline, imparting the relief she'd sought since waking alone.

"It is a pleasure to meet you, Chloe. Your beauty is indeed as radiant as Saul proclaimed in his letters. I am Teotihuacan, but you may call me Teo for short."

"Happy to meet you, Teo." Chloe pasted a polite smile to her face then turned to gaze up at her husband. "You wrote about me?"

"Why wouldn't I?"

"Fair point," she muttered. "So… uh. Did I interrupt something? You both look a little stressed. Do I need to leave before any fire-breathing happens?"

"No, señorita. Hardly. Saul is my oldest friend, a brother to me. We were merely having a discussion about his troubles and… the best way to deal with the matter." Teo's green eyes lingered on Chloe, too intense to bode well for the topic of their prior conversation. His scrutiny made her feel like a bug.

Chloe shivered and chafed her hands down her arms. It didn't help. With only a thin silk robe to cover her, she felt exposed to Teo's occasional wandering glances. Did he find her attractive, or was he merely sizing up the mortal?

"Saul, would you fetch my Snuggy? I'm freezing."

"Of course." He kissed her cheek and left the room, preferring not to interrupt Mahasti for every minor request.

A minute of awkward and uncomfortable silence passed. Teo made no effort to speak with her and, in fact, barely even seemed to acknowledge her presence.

"You don't approve of me, do you?" Chloe asked bluntly.

The handsome dragon jerked his green eyes back to her. They dropped to her tummy and gradually rose to her face. "I have nothing against you personally, señorita."

"Just against humans in general? My name is *Chloe* by the way."

Teo frowned. "I came here this evening to convince a good friend to do what is right."

"Which is?"

"To send you away for your own safety, of course. If you go, Saul lives, and you and your... child will also survive this ordeal."

This prick, she thought, smoldering on the inside. "You speak as if my baby isn't good enough."

Teo held both palms out toward her. "Please. I meant no offense."

The change in attitude took Chloe by surprise. She stared at him and maintained a distrustful distance. *I wonder if the males are the only ones who learn manners. Saul makes it sound like their females are all a bunch of catty bitches.* "You have immaculate manners for a dragon, you know. Compared to Brigid. I was beginning to wonder if Saul was the exception and not the rule."

"I may not approve of the choice Saul has made, but I will not disrespect you in his home."

Well, there's that much at least. Chloe sighed. "Do you know Brigid well?"

Teo snorted. "She is known by many. A beautiful and cunning dragon."

"If you admire her so much why don't you go court her?"

The toothy grin Teo flashed unnerved her. "I considered it once, but her temperament does not suit my preferences for a mate."

"Okay, I'll bite. What are your preferences for a mate? After meeting Brigid for the first time, I wasn't sure if it was her personality or a... dragon thing."

Teo's warm chuckle reassured her. It was rich and warm, his mannerisms as relaxed as his bronze friend. Saul kept excellent company.

Marcy would lose her mind over seeing him. He looks like an Aztec god. I wonder if dragons like him and Saul are where all of those myths and stories come from. "Come on. Tell me. What are other female dragons like?"

"I pursue another black dragon of a more subservient nature—"

In only a few words, he dashed her positive outlook toward him. "Subservient? *Really?*" Chloe groaned. *He's probably like a draconic Freddy.* "Is that what you're into?"

"I prefer a quiet existence — a pleasurable one without the noisy distractions Saul finds endearing."

"Uh huh. So what do you do then? Live in a cave?"

"An island."

"Oh. Well that must be sort of nice. Sandy beaches and all the surf you can handle." *And now I'm making small talk with a dragon.* Frustrated with the awkward situation, Chloe sighed and glanced at the door. "Are you going to help us or not? I know you don't owe anything to me, but I care about Saul."

"I can see that. I believe you care, but if he chooses to oppose the Conclave, he has no chance of survival. They are many elder dragons, more powerful than he and I could ever hope to become in your mortal lifetime."

"Then give us another option!"

Teo flinched. "The sword, if tales are true of its power, is the only way a mortal could even hope to try and win. *Try*, señorita. It is no guarantee that you will triumph."

Maybe it was his doubt, or maybe it was the condescension snaking into his tone, but Teo's words incited the worst of her anger. Common sense warred against rising fury, until her temper surged like an irrational tide. "My fucking name is Chloe, not señorita." She stepped forward and poked her index finger at Teo, jabbing him hard in the center of his chest. "What kind of fucking dragon are you? You want a subservient woman but you're not man enough to stand by a friend who needs you?"

Teo drew himself up, shoulders stiff. "It is an honorific of respect." His eyes narrowed and he studied her in silence. The look churned her anger further. "Saul did not speak of your temper. Or your strength." He took her by the wrist and lowered her hand, gentle fingers warm against her skin.

"Shit. I'm sorry. I'm really sorry… I just… I don't know what comes over me sometimes. I get so angry." And then she wept. Her fleeting outbursts of uncontrollable fury left exhaustion in their wake and a strange sensation of disconnection as if she were floating. She wanted to return to bed.

"You are worried for your cub and thus in an understandable position."

Teo guided her to a chair with an awkwardness he hadn't exhibited since his arrival. He patted her on the head and glanced back to the door with a worried expression. "I will fetch Saul for you."

"N-No. I'm fine. I'm just…" Chloe sniffed and swiped her cheeks. "I'm fine. Sorry. I shouldn't have… shouldn't have poked you like that."

"You caused no lasting harm."

Saul returned seconds after Chloe pulled herself together. She ignored the blanket-robe hanging over his arm to focus on her husband's wooden expression instead. "What's wrong?"

"Forgive my delay, Chloe. A visitor arrived."

"Who the hell shows up in the middle of the night?" Chloe groused, shooting a sour glance at the grandfather clock in the corner. "Rude."

"We are dragons," Teo reminded her.

"Right. Nocturnal. So who was it then?"

"That was Brigid's retainer to bring news of the Conclave's decision. They voted in her favor. We are to expect her arrival three days hence."

"What the hell for?" Chloe bolted to her feet.

Saul crumpled the letter in his fist. "She will be moving in to initiate our mating."

"Over my dead body!"

"Brigid moves fast. Always has." Teo shook his head and sighed. "Saul, I would like to offer my aid since it seems your mind is set. If you allow it, I shall remain here a time to maintain the peace. Brigid has no quarrel with me and may listen if I intervene."

Saul looked up in surprise. "What changed your mind?"

"Your mate." Teo turned his green eyes in Chloe's direction. "She has dragon's blood. It is as the legends claim, Saul. Your Chloe is not as mortal as you think. Not anymore."

A turbulent storm of conflicting emotions assailed Chloe's senses, spilling fresh tears down her cheeks. "Not mortal... does that mean...?" She twisted to look up at Saul.

"It means that if we are able to appease Brigid, you and Saul may have a long life ahead of you," Teo replied.

Together... a long, immortal life together with Saul. In all the time that Chloe had coveted Brigid's draconic existence, wishing their places were exchanged, Saul had inadvertently blessed her with a gift unique to her alone. Once Chloe failed to stall her sniffles, she leaned into his palm, savoring every second his warm skin caressed her face.

"We were meant to be together, my Chloe." Saul stroked her cheek and stared deep into her eyes, his features heavier than she had ever seen them.

"What do we do?" she asked in a whisper.

Saul bowed his head, touching their brows together. "I will have Mahasti return to Watatsumi, tonight, and request his presence here immediately. There is no time to waste."

Golden streams of sunlight slanted through the library windows into Chloe's face. The warmth against her cheek stirred her awake, then it took a moment to gain her bearings.

That's right. I dozed off on the couch while Saul and Teo were planning. The two dragons had poured through ledgers recording Saul's hoard in the hope of finding something to trade for the sword.

With neither dragon in sight, Chloe made her way to her room and cleaned up for the day. A peek into Marcy's room revealed her friend was still dozing. And snoring. Chloe giggled, closed the door, and retreated back to the library.

"Good morning, Chloe," Teo greeted her. The shirtless look appeared to be a draconic trait. Teo wore only his white linen pants, no less immaculate in the daylight than the previous evening. She stared.

Where's Saul?" *And where's the señorita at this time?* she wondered.

"He went below to gather treasures to offer as a trade to his guest. Come. Eat. Since his djinn is occupied with her task I took the liberty of preparing you a meal."

Chloe dropped a dubious gaze to the desk where a plate of dry eggs and hard toast awaited her. "Thanks. Really. It looks great, Teo." It was the effort that counted, or so she told herself as she stared at the mess on her plate. Saul and Teo must have graduated from the same chef academy. His culinary repertoire began with peanut butter and jelly sandwiches and ended with tuna fish on crackers. She didn't trust anything else from him unless it was an animal seared by his dragon's breath.

Despite the torturous amount of salt, Chloe smiled through every bite and guzzled two glasses of water to stave off choking. Something told her that Teo didn't know the Heimlich maneuver and she didn't want to give Brigid the satisfaction of arriving to find out that her opponent had died by toast asphyxiation.

"The time comes to excuse myself for a hunt. Your guest has arrived."

"Thanks for the breakfast, Teo."

She waited until he was out of sight before she scraped the remainder of her plate into the trash. A quickly muttered wish under her breath resulted in the prompt removal of both the trash and her dishes. *Thanks, Mahasti.*

The clean-up came just in time. Voices drifted down the hall to announce the impending arrival. Chloe expected to meet an ancient, wrinkled old man able to give Confucius a run for his money, but a dignified figure strode through the double doors alongside her husband.

"Chloe, I would like you to meet a good friend of my father, Watatsumi. Watatsumi, meet Chloe, my beloved bride," Saul introduced them. His voice brimmed with pride.

"It is my profound pleasure to make your acquaintance as well, Lady Drakenstone."

Pitch black hair streaked with fine lines of silver was pulled back from the Asian man's unlined face into an elaborate topknot. His dark blue and gold kimono resembled a wardrobe piece from a historical movie or art museum, exquisite down to the last silk thread. Chloe had never seen something so beautiful on a man before.

Twin servants followed the regal dragon, each woman garbed in similarly extravagant, identical kimonos. Against their fair skin, the mercurial silver and deep blue brought out the rosy undertones in their cheeks. Chloe envied them immediately for their slender frames, effortless grace, and immaculate appearances. She felt like a pig by comparison, even if Saul and the others claimed she hadn't yet begun to truly show.

"Gifts for the newly bonded," Watatsumi announced.

"Gifts?" Chloe echoed, stunned. Were the gifts a nonverbal form of approval?

"It is customary for a dragon visiting another's domicile to come bearing gifts," Saul explained.

"Mariko, if you will."

"Hai."

Mariko, the girl on the right, stepped forward with a garment box in her arms. A respectful bow brought her lower to the floor as she presented the gift to Chloe. The exterior wrapping had to be as gorgeous as the gift bound to be inside.

"What is it...?" Chloe asked.

"Open it and you shall see," Watatsumi said.

Chloe untied the ribbon and carefully peeled the decorative paper, afraid of ripping it. She lifted away the top to reveal a gorgeous amber and gold work of art. With a trembling hand, she caressed the cool silk and felt the vibrant cord. The kimono reminded her of Saul.

"It's beautiful," she whispered. Tears stung her eyes that she quickly wiped away with the back of her wrist. "Thank you."

"Of course, there is more, but we shall get to that in time. Let us get to the heart of the matter and our reason for this meeting."

Watatsumi drew a sheathed sword from thin air, parting reality as if there were an invisible curtain unseen to Chloe's eyes. Awestruck, she stared in silence as he drew the weapon from the black scabbard. The blade glimmered in the sunlight streaming through the high windows.

"You've taken excellent care of it," Saul commented.

"Of course I have. I remember the day you offered this treasure to me in trade, desperate to provide Brigid with the one gift that would earn her affection." Watatsumi chuckled and restored the blade to its sheath. "Now you wish to have it back to earn another woman's favor. What price will you pay?"

Saul sighed. "I searched high and low for an adequate offer, but we both know that you have come with something in mind, Watatsumi. What do you desire?"

"To speak with your mate alone."

Saul crossed his arms. "Absolutely not."

"Do you no longer trust in me or the validity of our friendship, Saul? I would sooner swallow lava from your father's volcano than harm this woman and damage my honor." Watatsumi scoffed. His twin servants shrank back a step.

Chloe laid her hand on her husband's arm. "Go ahead, Saul. I'm not afraid of him."

Her husband balked, but once she convinced him to leave the library, she shut the door. A niggling feeling told her they'd need privacy.

"Excellent choice, Chloe. I am pleased you are willing to hear out my offer."

"Let's hope it was a good idea. What did you need to say to me that you couldn't say with my mate here?"

The dragon chuckled. "I have known Saul since he was an impetuous cub, quick to respond with emotion. I wished to know your thoughts alone. After all, the child grows within *your* womb."

Chloe's hands went automatically to her small baby bump. "My thoughts about what?"

"An offer I have in mind," Watatsumi continued serenely.

"And what offer might that be?"

"The baby. I will grant you the sword in exchange for your infant."

"My *baby?*"

"Yes. Such a rare creature has not come into birth in centuries." The dragon's lips spread into a wide grin, revealing each of his sharp teeth. His human guise melted like a wax figure revealing hints of the true form beneath. According to Saul, his father's old friend was an ancient being among the eldest of their kind.

And none of that mattered to her. "Get the hell out." Indignance quivered Chloe from head to toe. She snapped her arm out, finger pointing at the door. "We'll make do without your sword."

"Are you not a young and fertile female? Saul is a virile male. Young. You can make another in time."

"You think you can come in here waving your offer around in exchange for *my* baby? Well to hell with you. I'll find another way because this baby is mine and I'm not going to just trade her off like a piece of meat at the market."

"Will you not consider it? Sleep on it, as you mortals say."

"Abso-fucking-lutely not," Chloe spat. "Get out. Get out now."

Watatsumi bowed his head in respect. "Saul has chosen his mate well. You are a courageous woman, Chloe."

"Get the — what?"

"I admire your tenacity. In all of my years, few humans have stood up to me. You defend that little one, and yet there are many dragon mothers who might consider my offer to vastly expand their hoard. You put our female kin to shame."

Chloe swallowed the hard lump in her throat. Pressure compressed her chest with each inhalation. "I don't understand. What was this? Some sort of test? Why?"

"Your mate intends to sacrifice himself to save you and the child. He *will* murder Brigid when they next meet, and by doing so, violate one of our oldest laws. He has called Teotihuacan here to bear witness that his act comes without provocation from you or any other resident of this home."

"That's why we need the sword. So I stand a chance against her."

"Do you know the tale of Ascalon's original owner?"

"St. George? I know a little of the story from bible school as a kid," Chloe admitted.

"Quite different from the truth scribed in our history. He was born of a union not unlike the love between you and Saul, his mother a dragon and his father a Roman officer. Like many storm dragons of her temperament, she dabbled in human politics and mingled through their society."

"So, I don't get it, if his mother was a dragon why isn't it in any of the history books?"

"My dear, we write history as we see fit. My kind have done this for centuries to protect our secrets. The modern world is not ready to discover the truth."

Chloe shivered. If the leaders of the world knew about shadowy draconic figures pulling their puppet strings, they did an excellent job of hiding it. "Did he really die as a martyr?"

"That he did. It broke Theia's heart to lose her human lover, but the murder of her son at human hands became an unbearable pain. Centuries have passed and yet she still slumbers. Such is what occurs when one of our kind loses a loved one. We sleep. We dream of better days and time spent with them."

"He was killed because he wouldn't convert faiths, right?"

"Ah, so you are not completely ignorant to the old stories. What else do you recall of your Roman history?"

"To be honest, I think I know more about Greek than Roman. I, uh, binge-watch a couple of old TV shows when I can't sleep."

Watatsumi chuckled and gestured Chloe to a seat. "The eldest of us once chose divine guises among the mortals and inspired the very tales that grace your textbooks and television shows."

"And movies," Chloe mumbled. "But this doesn't explain why Saul doesn't believe in Ascalon and thinks this is all some kind of weird folktale for your people too. He told me he traded the sword because he doubted in its power."

"You are part of our world now, Chloe, and you must understand one important aspect of our natures. We do not tolerate change well. When Theia birthed her son, many elder dragons sought to make an example of her. She hid him among the humans as a normal child."

"But why?"

"She had a mate. A tidal dragon like myself, chosen for her in the same manner as Brigid was chosen for Saul. Of course he was angered by Theia's perceived betrayal, and swore vengeance against the mortal who spoiled her."

Chloe leaned forward on her seat. "This is as good as a soap opera."

"Her son grew up among the humans but she always kept watch over him. When he came of age, she forged him this sword with a piece of her soul and a mother's love. A means to defend himself. He proved its worth when a dragon sought him out and he slayed it in one-on-one combat."

"The dragon from the legend?"

"No. That was only his first."

Holy crap. Saul and Mahasti did *say that he killed more than one.* "So the one in the legend...?" she prompted when Watatsumi delayed to imbue dramatic suspense.

"Theia's mate," Watatsumi told her. "The rest is as told in your stories. In his rage, he dried the city wells and claimed the only remaining spring as his lair. The people pleaded and begged but he was not swayed. He demanded tribute for use of his water."

Subtle changes differentiated the stories from what Chloe learned in school. "So that's when George arrived?"

"And slew him, yes."

Chloe eyed the sword in Watatsumi's hands. *It's true. It's all true...* "Will you help us?"

"Ascalon is yours." The Asian dragon bowed at the waist and offered out the sword on his upraised palms. Chloe accepted it gingerly. In its sheath, Ascalon felt weightless and featherlight.

"Just like that?"

Watatsumi's grin spread wider, losing the predatory gleam that once traced ice down Chloe's spine. Mischief lurked in his expression, like a child eager to one-up his betters. His chuckle eased her heart until eventually, a nervous laugh escaped her.

"Saul has offered me several tempting treasures in exchange."

"I don't know the first thing about using a sword," Chloe whispered.

"Ascalon knows all that it must. Trust in it, and it will guide you, Chloe."

One effortless tug drew the weapon from the scabbard. Sunlight danced over the silver edge and inner luster gleamed through the metal as if moonlight were captive in the blade. Magic. A dragon's magic given from the heart, turned against her kin and fellow wyrms. It felt right in her grip, as it if belonged.

A mother's gift to her son. And now, another mother was destined to use it to save her own child.

"Watatsumi, will you arrange for the duel to take place tomorrow?" Chloe asked.

"It shall be done."

***

"So now there's three of them on the estate?" Marcy asked.

"No, Watatsumi is away with Mahasti arranging for the duel to take place tomorrow. He has to pull some strings with their weird dragon council."

"So, it's Saul and his friend. Is he hot? Do you think—"

"He doesn't like humans much. I think he's only tolerating me because I'm the magical baby oven."

"Hopes dashed." Marcy snapped her fingers and swore, "Damn."

"Sorry to bust your bubble."

"So where are they?"

"You can look outside and watch them recreate a scene from The Lost World if you want—" As Chloe spoke, Marcy's face nearly turned green. "Or stay here and drink coffee with me."

Marcy joined her at the table and poured black coffee into a mug. "I don't know if you're any better after what I just saw you eat. Raw meat, Chloe? Ugh. What is this child doing to you?"

"Ha ha," Chloe said dryly. "Anyway, all kinds of dragons are supposed to begin flying in soon. Saul's inviting the ones he trusts. Brigid may be able to force her way into the house, but she can't stop him from having guests."

"And if she tries to harm you beyond the rules of the duel—"

"It's an insult to their laws, and they get to kill her."

"Almost makes me wish she *would* try something," Marcy muttered.

Chloe snorted. "Yeah, well, if everything goes to plan she won't get the chance."

Marcy pushed back from the table and crossed to the window where she dared a brief peek outside while she sipped her brew. "Looks like they're done rounding up breakfast. I see them chatting in the driveway and... holy crap! Saul's buddy looks like those hot Colombian drug lords in the movies. How the hell does he keep a white suit so clean when he was just snacking on goats in a field?"

Balancing her cup of herbal tea, Chloe left the table and joined her. "I know. It's totally unfair, right? Saul says most dragons are power players in business and politics. I guess Teo owns a resort somewhere on some island in the south."

Marcy whistled. "Do you think he'll at least f—"

"Marcy. No. What happened with Antonio anyway?"

"That movie date I cancelled—"

"You mean the one I stole you from?"

Marcy grinned. "Yeah, that one. I was going to end things anyway. This just sped things up a little... he didn't like it when I canceled."

"How come?"

"Eh." Marcy shrugged. "Turns out he's a real mama's boy and that woman, I met her when we were in Galveston, remember? Well, she is *very* opinionated and he always goes with what she says. It's frustrating as hell when your boyfriend blows off what he promised you because his mommy says otherwise."

"Oh no. Yeah, fuck that. I guess I won't have that..." *I can't say that's not a problem anymore,* Chloe realized. *If I was going to live a normal mortal life, I'd never have the chance of meeting Saul's mom. But if I win this duel with Brigid, I'll meet her one day... While Marce grows old. Fuck.* The stark reality of her new situation took the wind from Chloe's sails and cast a dismal cloud over her mood.

Unless, maybe...

A fleeting, improbable thought slithered through Chloe's mind. Another glance at Teo dashed her hopes. He made his thoughts about humans and half-breeds clear. There wouldn't be a magical matchmaking session in Marcy's future.

"Let's go greet them. A couple more dragons should fly in this evening. I guess they do most of their big moving at night. Some of them have to board planes to make it to the States, though."

"Wait, what? Dragons are coming from other countries too?"

"Oh yeah. I guess news about the baby has brought them all out of the woodwork. The oldest ones haven't seen anything like this in centuries, and the young ones like Saul didn't know it was possible." Chloe wiped her clammy palms against her pants. Saul didn't know about her deal with Watatsumi yet, and she dreaded telling him that the timetable had been moved.

Please let everything go okay.

In hopes of softening her mood with some light conversation, Chloe changed the subject and led the way to the stairs. "How do you like that dress Mahasti picked out for you?"

Marcy scoffed. "It fits like I wished for it." Marcy's vintage-style cream sundress fit snugly at the torso, sporting a built-in corset that enhanced her already fantastic breasts.

"It looks great on you."

As predicted, Teo barely acknowledged Marcy's presence beyond a cordial greeting. Chloe frowned and allowed it to slide.

"I need to speak to Saul for a moment, Teo. Alone. Think you can handle this, Marcy?"

"Yeah, I'm fine." Marcy's frown deepened. Chloe reassured her with a smile before moving off a ways with her husband and leading him to the kitchen.

"Good hunt?" she asked, while guiding him to a seat at the cozy

199

dinette table. She poured a glass of lemon water and pressed it into his hand. The pitcher and four glasses weren't there a minute ago.

"I'd forgotten how much I enjoy sporting with Teo," Saul admitted. "He is an expert hunter."

A hilarious image surfaced in her thoughts. She pictured Saul and Teo, two enormous dragons, crouched down outside of the cow pasture and whispering in cartoon fashion. Two draconic Elmer Fudds. "It can't be that hard to track your own livestock."

"We ventured off for wild game. Now, what did you wish to discuss away from our friends?"

"It's about my talk with Watatsumi…"

"He said nothing of what you discussed beyond accepting my bid for the sword."

"Yeah. I asked him to let me give you the details." Chloe sucked in a deep breath. "I asked him to use his clout with the Conclave to set up the fight. For tomorrow."

"Tomorrow? Chloe, have you lost all of your senses?" Saul shoved both hands through his tawny hair. "You are not prepared. You know nothing of wielding a sword."

"We spoke about it and according to your laws, I'm the one challenged so I get to set the date. Brigid knows that and I'll just bet you she expects me to wait until the baby is born. And in the meantime, she'll be here, living in *our* home, trying to make us miserable. Trying to…" She swallowed and forced herself to say the words despite the pressure it exerted on her heart. "Mate with you. I'm not going to let her spend even one day here."

"Chloe, no. I cannot be swayed and you have nothing to fear of me mating with Brigid," Saul said.

"I don't have a choice, Saul! If I don't fight, I'll lose you to her."

"I'd rather die," he hissed.

"And I won't let that happen. I won't let my child grow up without knowing you, and I won't let a flock of dragons dictate my life. *I won't!*" Chloe screamed. She swept the glasses from the table and rose from her seat as fragments scattered across the floor. "I won't… I won't let it end this way. As long as I succeed, we can stay together."

Saul left his chair to place his hands on her shoulders. "I cannot watch you die, Chloe. Please… don't do this to me. Brigid is brutal, and I do not trust in the power of this sword. I would rather lose you and know you are well than watch you d-die." A choked sound, suspiciously close to a sob came from Saul, shaking his muscular shoulders.

Not once in all of their weeks together had Saul ever revealed so much emotion. Not when she rejected him in the cave, and certainly not when she returned. A surge of protective instinct prompted Chloe to hug her dragon tight. She kissed his cheek and smoothed her fingers through his golden strands. "I love you, and I'm not going to let anyone ruin our happiness. I'll gut her before I let her take you away."

"Now you are sounding like a female dragon."

"I *feel* like one."

Saul slid his hand down her side to rest his palm over her stomach. "He gives you strength."

"What makes you think it's a boy?"

"Or she," Saul amended.

"Watatsumi says to trust in the sword and it will protect me. I have to place my faith in it, Saul. I have to. It's the only way to keep you and our baby safe."

A flurry of angry Spanish echoed down the hall, interrupting whatever else Chloe had to say. She and Saul exchanged looks then hurried out the door.

"You're a pretentious asshole," Marcy seethed from the main room. Her voice traveled despite the vast and open space between the entrance parlor and kitchen.

Chloe sped up to a jog and hurried into the foyer where she found Marcy stalking to the door. "Wait, what? What happened?"

"I'm going... fuck I don't know, for a walk. To get away from your husband's jerk friend." Marcy stormed outside without another word.

Chloe and Saul both whipped around to stare at Teo. Nothing about his behavior seemed to imply anything occurred in their absence. In fact, he had withdrawn a tablet-sized phone and appeared occupied with swiping across the screen. "Teo?" Chloe asked.

"What?" he asked, looking up from the device.

"What happened?"

"I will go to soothe Marceline," Saul volunteered.

Teo's green eyes flicked to Saul's retreating shape, clear disbelief apparent on his chiseled, handsome features. "He goes to comfort a human?"

Without hesitation, Chloe stalked up to him and put herself in Teo's face. "What did you say to my best friend?"

"I said very little."

A niggling feeling in Chloe's belly told her that was the precise problem. However, Marcy wouldn't have lost her cool so easily over

201

a handsome man ignoring her.

"What. Did. You. Say?"

"I gave her honesty."

"Seriously? You couldn't even be civil with her?"

"Do you suggest that I acknowledge the ants on the pavement as well?" Teo asked.

Chloe slapped him. "Marcy was wrong. You're worse than a pretentious ass. You're an insufferable, egotistical brute."

The red imprint of her hand glowed upon Teo's cheek like a beacon.

"I—"

She cut him off before his defense began. "You are *nothing* like Saul. You're not a quarter of the man or dragon that he is, and you should feel ashamed to bring your foul opinions to his home. To our home," she corrected herself. "On your island, you may be the boss who makes all the rules, but you're a guest in our house right now. That is *my* friend you chased off with your rude bullshit, and you will respect her while she's here."

"Understood," Teo gritted out. He strode the other direction, a man-child in a fantastic ivory suit, too spoiled to take responsibility for his abysmal manners and issue an apology.

Without donning her shoes, Chloe stepped barefoot onto the porch to find Saul with his hand on Marcy's shoulder. He offered her a handkerchief with the other. Their whispers didn't extend to Chloe's ears, despite her strained attempt to pick up more than a word resembling her name.

"Is everything okay out here?"

Marcy nodded wordlessly. Saul lowered his hand and exhaled a deep, rumbling sound, the noise more inhuman growl than anything.

"I will have a talk with Teo," Saul began.

"I already did. It's taken care of," Chloe assured him.

"I'm sorry for making a scene."

"Marcy. You didn't make a scene. We're not out in public and this is our house. Nothing harmed."

"It's just... when he said I had no right to be here, I lost my shit. I was so awed that he was a dragon..."

"You have every right to be here. Teo was beginning to grow on me, but he's shown his true colors again."

Her proud friend sniffed and dabbed her eyes with Saul's handkerchief. "Now I feel like a fool. Crying over a verbal altercation like I'm in high school again."

"What'd he get all high and mighty over?"

"The silence felt awkward, so I tried to ask about his resort. I just thought… after this was all said and done maybe all of us could go away for a weekend. I wanted to surprise you. A honeymoon."

"Oh sweetie," Chloe sighed. She threw her arms around Marcy and hugged her.

"I asked how I could go about setting up a weekend getaway, and the jackass told me I could never afford it. I j-just wanted to surprise you."

Chloe squeezed her even more tightly. "Don't listen to that jerk."

"I guess he just hit a raw nerve. Your stupid duel is tomorrow and I'm terrified it's the last time I'll ever…" Another ragged sob shook Marcy's body. "When he told me I was useless, I was already feeling it. Then he demanded to know my purpose for being here, Chloe."

"You're my best friend in the entire world, and I love you. That's your purpose for being here."

The embrace ended after Marcy got ahold of her emotions and dried her face.

"Come on. Leiv made a strawberry honey cheesecake just for us, and food makes everything better. Let's demolish it together."

***

With each passing day, the supernatural melody had become more distinct to Chloe's ears. The draconic obsession with gems and treasure never made sense until she spent a night sprawled atop her new bed, allowing it to lull her into peaceful dreams. For the first time since her pregnancy began, she began to sleep without fitful tossing and turning.

But Saul wasn't beside her and she longed to feel his arms around her. He had a house full of dragons, with one more to arrive during the long night. Mahasti and Leiv had agreed to greet each one personally, but her dragon remained on the main level to welcome his guests. Meanwhile, Chloe lay alone while Marcy snored in a guest room with the help of sleeping aids and Felix's rumbling purr.

Chloe pulled on her clothes and journeyed upstairs to find him. When she had retired for bed, Watatsumi, Teo, and Saul were alone. She now found the den occupied by three more unfamiliar faces: a fair blond man with a golden-red beard, a woman with skin the color of obsidian, and a wizened old man with a bald head who reminded Chloe of a Buddhist monk.

"Hello… Am I interrupting?" She hesitated in the doorway, aware of their inquisitive expressions. The woman appraised Chloe from afar with coal-colored eyes. She wore a revealing, wrap-style dress with one bared shoulder, its caramel hue attractive against skin as dark as night. The close crop of her black hair suited her angular facial structure.

"You have interrupted nothing, friend. Have we kept your mate from you for too long?" the unfamiliar woman said.

"He's taken so long to come down," she admitted from the doorway, reluctant to enter and disrupt their pow wow.

"I will be down shortly, my love."

"Will you not introduce us to your mate? After all, it is for her that we come to show our support," the bald man rumbled.

"Ah… so this is the young woman? I concur with Vasuki. Introduce us," the blond man said as he rose from his seat. Of the three dragons, he was the only one to resemble Saul. They both had the same muscled frame, golden eyes, and proud stature.

"As you wish." Saul sighed. "Chloe, please enter. No one here will cause you any harm."

While she couldn't process why, a strange sense of animal instinct had allowed Chloe to come to that conclusion on her own. When she moved to Saul's side, he placed one arm around her shoulders and kissed her brow. His tender display brought an approving smile to the black woman's face.

"Friends of my mother and father have come to bear witness to tomorrow's duel."

"More than mere friends," the blond grunted.

Saul rolled his eyes. "You would call this one my uncle. Thor, allow me to introduce you to my mate, Chloe."

Fucking Thor? "Really?" Chloe blurted, staring after her inelegant query. "*Really?*"

The two dragons exchanged a glance. No doubt Thor thought his nephew had mated to a dimwitted human. "I do not own a hammer, contrary to the myths and legends. I used my tail to bring the thunder."

Holy shit, it's Thor. Chloe wanted to laugh hysterically in a corner, but instead, she stared at him until the next realization struck her. He was laughing, too.

"Your feline has formed an attachment to me," Thor said, with a nod of his head to Felix.

"Felix, what are you doing here? You're supposed to be with Marcy."

Felix arched his back and purred, rubbing his face against Thor's jean-clad leg the whole while.

"If you're Thor, do I even want to know who the others are? Are there anymore dragon gods in the room right now?"

"Chloe, meet Vasuki and Nefertiti. They are members of the Conclave who voted in our favor."

Chloe's eyes widened. Teotihuacan and Watatsumi were prime examples of dragons inspiring certain myths and legend, but she never expected to meet Nefertiti, Queen of the Nile.

"I am the only female dragon to oppose Brigid's claim." Nefertiti made a disgusted sound, its noise reminiscent of a hissing cat. "I see it for what it is — an inhumane act of greed. She has had many decades to accept Saul's offer and I, for one, am pleased he has found you."

"I... thank you," Chloe murmured in appreciation, awe and gratitude bringing heat to her cheeks.

"May you fight with a true warrior's spirit, Chloe," Thor said.

"Excuse me, maybe I'm being silly but... I thought... I expected everyone to be upset. You're not upset about our child?" Saul's worries had led her to believe she would be ostracized and loathed for carrying a half-breed.

"No one can halt the winds of change indefinitely, young one. It was bound to happen eventually," Vasuki said. "Many of us intermingle in human society, some more than others." He shot Saul and Thor pointed glances.

Saul's uncle clapped Vasuki on the shoulder. "Sitting in mountain temples may be fun for you, my friend, but not for all of us."

"Go with her, Saul. We are not children to be entertained," Nefertiti encouraged. "You have fulfilled your duty as host for the evening."

"It was nice meeting you all. Thank you for coming out in support." *Maybe this will all go well after all...*

They bid their guests goodnight and left them to the comforts of the library. As diverse as dragons were, they all appeared to share a common love for books and learning. Saul's vast collection would keep them entertained.

Chloe laced their fingers together as they descended the wide stairway into the lower level. Felix didn't follow, too intrigued by his new friend to follow Mommy to bed.

"Are they what you expected?" Saul lifted her hand to his lips and kissed her knuckles.

"No. Yes. I dunno." Chloe blew out a breath and laughed at herself. "They seem so nice for dragons. After listening to you and Teo, I thought all female dragons were bitches like Brigid."

"Most are quite cruel," he agreed, confirming her original thoughts. "Nefertiti and my mother are special exceptions to what is typical of dragons. Females among the earth and storm dragons are a rarity, but they are known for their compassion toward humankind. Teo has pursued Nefertiti for quite some time, but…"

"She won't have him?" Chloe snorted. "Can't blame her with that attitude of his." *Subservient woman my ass.*

"He is many centuries her junior and a cub by comparison."

"And also a pig," Chloe pointed out.

"That as well."

Once they reached the lair, Saul shut the doors behind them and led Chloe to the rumpled bed. He straightened up the sheets from her tossing and turning, then turned to face her with a smile.

"My apologies, Chloe. I did not realize the hour or that you would remain awake for me."

"It's fine. I'm glad I came to find you, or I wouldn't have met those three."

Chloe unbuttoned Saul's shirt and smoothed it back from his shoulders. Whether it was the influence of his friend Teo, or the arrival of so many other dragons, he had dressed business casual and foregone the usual laidback 'jeans and nothing else' look. She unfastened his slacks and pushed them below his hips, delighted to find he wore nothing beneath them.

"Now it is your turn," Saul announced. He took joy in tugging her robe sash until the multilayered silk garment fell open.

"I traded Watatsumi the sword for this bed," Saul confessed as he stroked his fingers through her hair. "Jade has the sweetest notes and is prized among my kind as being the finest stone for breeding females. I thought it would encourage Brigid to accept me. To move into my home and begin our life together."

From another man, in another relationship, Chloe would have taken offense at receiving a gift intended for another woman but she had claimed it without asking his permission and made it hers. "Do you regret doing it? You know… for her?"

"I'm glad *you* are the one using it, Chloe. I never offered the bed to Brigid. It had been my intention to do so, but she flaunted her dalliance in my face and I shut myself away."

"That's not what I asked."

"No, I do not. How can I when the jade's song is what led us to the truth? Seeing you here, I feel as if this bed was always meant for you. For us."

Saul guided Chloe to the bed to lay her amidst the soft cushions, and with only tender kisses and his fingertips, he traced over every inch of her body.

"Saul?" she whispered up to him. His mouth closed around her tightly budded nipple.

"Shh... I wish to make love to you."

Gone was the dragon who took her with one powerful stroke after the next, mounting her in a dark cave on the night of their first meeting. Saul revealed a new side to himself that she never experienced. A gentle side of a sweet man who took his time, unrushed and unhurried through their lovemaking.

"No matter what happens tomorrow, you will always be my Chloe."

"And you will always be my dragon. My Saul."

With the jade's song gently whispering in her ears, Chloe later drifted to sleep with her head against Saul's chest, pale blonde hair fanned over his chiseled muscles. It was the perfect end to what may be their final night together.

Chapter 14

"They're all dragons?" Marcy stared out from the balcony, standing with her arms wrapped around her middle. "Wow."

"Yeah, I know." Chloe gazed down at the assembled guests, over a dozen dragons and their retainers waiting for the main event. They came from all over the world and represented only a fraction of the dragon population. "At least they're all in human form."

"For now. Pretty soon you're going to have a pasture full of fire-breathing dragons."

"Nah, some of them blow acid or ice and stuff."

Marcy gaped. "How are you so calm about this?"

"Because if I think about how scared I am, I'm afraid I'll run away pissing my pants."

"Oh, Chloe…" Marcy pulled her in close and hugged her tight. "I'm here with you, no matter what."

"Stay with Mahasti, all right? If anything happens…" Chloe swallowed back a sob. "She'll make sure you get home safe, okay? Promise me."

"I promise."

"Your friend will not come to harm." Watatsumi and Teo entered the room behind the girls. "As Saul's supporters, she will have our protection as well," the tidal dragon assured her.

Teo didn't add a verbal agreement, allowing his presence to speak for him. At least, Chloe hoped he remained supportive and wouldn't let her friend suffer a squishy fate under an angry dragon.

"Go ahead," Marcy said. She put on her brave face and smiled for Chloe's benefit. "I'll be fine with my own personal bodyguards. You go and kick that bitch's ass."

"You bet."

I'm going to see her again. We're going to share virgin daiquiris at the pool tomorrow and laugh about this.

Chloe dried her tear-streaked face as she left Marcy behind on the balcony in safety. Saul escorted her the rest of the way with their hands clasped and fingers entwined.

"It is not too late to back out," he whispered to her.

"And let her claim the victory? No way. We're ending this now." Saul and Nefertiti helped her dress for the face-off. She clutched

Ascalon in her hands while she focused on every tiny bit of knowledge the two dragons imparted to her about fighting their kind.

"Do you remember when I fought Brigid on the lawn? Her stance lowers whenever she plans to exhale her fire. Remember that, Chloe."

"Lowers her stance before breathing fire. Got it." Chloe nodded. "So, how do I look?"

"You wear the armor well," Nefertiti complimented, pleased with the finished result.

"I feel like Xena... or a sexy cosplayer," Chloe muttered. She twisted to have a better look in the mirror. Light chainmail seemed inadequate against dragon claws, but the leather molded against her curves and clung in all the right places. She bent her arms and knees to test the resistance against her joints, only to discover the pliable material didn't restrict her movement. "What is this?"

"Scalewing skin. Thor brought this for you as a gift," Saul replied.

According to the history lesson she received from Saul once, scalewings were also known as wyverns, and were mutually hated by all dragonkind. Chloe shuddered. It didn't surprise her that she would be sent into battle wearing the flesh of their enemies.

Mahasti appeared in a hazy mist to interrupt her worried ruminations. "Brigid awaits you," she reported. "Saul, I'm sorry, but I am to bring you immediately to the elders in the circle."

"I will... we will see one another again soon, Chloe."

"I know."

Before he left, Chloe yielded to impulse and tangled her fingers in his golden hair. She kissed him hard with all of the passion she had in her soul, and when he walked away, she forced back the stinging tears that threatened to spill down her cheeks.

She had to be strong.

The rest of the preparation passed like a dream. She was led from the house to the rear pastures where Leiv had cleared the livestock to another field. Their battleground, as large as a football field, had a line of spectators on each side. Ancient wyrms, alive at the start of the millennia, glowered from where they waited to watch Chloe become a charcoal briquette.

"Breathe, Chloe," Mahasti told her.

"I am breathing," she whispered. "Don't forget your promise."

Mahasti's serene smile reassured Chloe. They hugged, then the djinn moved off the battlefield to stand between Saul and Leiv.

A dragon in ornate white robes strode onto the field with Brigid not far behind. The dragoness moved to the opposing side of their designated battleground to stare her enemy down. Chloe shivered, chilled by the hateful vehemence in Brigid's stare.

"In accordance with tradition, Brigid of Éire has issued challenge to the human Chloe Ellis. The fight shall commence and continue until one female lies dead. The victor shall be afforded all mating privileges as dictated by law without reprisal. All here will bear witness."

Frowning faces glowered from the edge of the field, but one stood out among the others. The stark resemblance between Brigid and her father was undeniable. Her masculine, red-haired duplicate watched from the sidelines as a dispassionate, silent observer to the event.

If Saul was anything, he was predictable. Without warning, he lurched forward, elongating and expanding exponentially with each second. Ripping cloth revealed his muscular upper back as bronze dragon skin spread where human flesh belonged. His teeth gleamed beneath the sun and opened to release a ferocious snarl.

"Now, Mahasti!" Chloe screamed.

The genie and bronze dragon vanished before the change completed, effectively ruining his plan of self-sacrifice. In the end, Saul's honor wouldn't allow his wife to face Brigid, although the consequences of his gallant act would have forfeited his life. He would have slain Brigid and accepted his execution from the elders.

A low murmur of discontent traveled down both sides of the field from supportive acquaintances of either lady. Saul's uncle smirked.

"Well then. As there are no further interruptions…" The official seemed to glide from the field.

Prior to the preparations, Thor and Nefertiti gave Chloe a crash course in draconic manners and law. Honor was everything to them, at least when there were witnesses to their actions.

She turned her back to Brigid, despite her senses screaming for her to keep the predator in her field of vision, and strode ten useless paces away from her opponent. It did little good. While the monstrous dragon had taken ten steps of her own, not even a vast ocean would have provided the safety Chloe needed.

A thunderbolt split the sky to signal the start of the fight. Chloe whirled on her heels in the nick of time as Brigid bounded toward her with jaws open wide. Screaming wasn't an option. It was too late to cry and plead, and she couldn't depend on Saul to be her savior this time. Instead, Chloe had to rescue both of them.

The sword whistled through the air and proved Watatsumi right.

It became an extension of her arm, exhibiting prowess Chloe didn't possess prior to taking it in hand. With its guidance, courage flooded through her, creating an unnatural sense of confidence.

She didn't need muscle to block Brigid's attacks. The sword did all of the work for her with a blade fine as a scalpel's edge, too sharp for Brigid to tolerate its touch. The edge parted her durable dragon hide and flayed open her snout. The backstroke cleaved across Brigid's descending claw. It laid open the skin to the bone.

Brigid screamed, and it became apparent she'd underestimated her opponent. Within seconds, the blood glistening over the silver blade evaporated, the metal too thirsty for dragon's blood to tolerate the presence. Chloe had no time to admire or marvel over the magical act — it prompted her to jab forward, but it missed the mark when Brigid scurried away at a limp. It wouldn't be so easy to strike her again now that she'd felt Ascalon's bite.

Left, right, forward and back — Chloe's rising sword clanged against Brigid's claw. Pieces of talon flew like wood chips in a mulcher, shattered by the enchanted weapon that had become Chloe's defender. The dragoness snarled and lunged forward for a bite, and had Chloe not jabbed out with the sword and pierced the beast's nose again, Brigid would have made quick work of her.

No time to think. Just move. Just move. Chloe spun and evaded every strike Brigid threw her way, using battle reflexes she'd never realized she possessed. The dragon hissed her frustration and snaked around her human prey for a rear assault. According to the rules set by the elders, flight was the one advantage Brigid had been denied. That small favor was the only reason Chloe wasn't already a smear on the ground.

Tired of playing cat and mouse keep-away, Brigid swapped her tactics. She kept back out of the sword's range, braced her legs, and lowered her body.

Shit, shit, shit!

A blazing inferno rushed at Chloe, faster than she expected. There was no time to dodge. No time to duck and roll. She trusted instead in instinct and raised Ascalon before her like a shield. It sliced through the fire and parted it to either side of her body, creating two blazing jets that scorched the earth around her. Her skin tightened within seconds. Ascalon may have protected her from the fire, but it couldn't save her indefinitely from the heat.

I need to do something. I can't just stand here until she's out of juice. What do I do!? she panicked.

Someone sane of mind would have fled from the fire, but Chloe did the opposite. She charged into its source.

Flames hurdled past her in an unrelenting stream but Chloe pressed onward. She broke through the wall of oppressive heat and came up beneath Brigid's chin. The dragon's ruby eyes widened.

"No!" Brigid screamed as she scrambled back.

Chloe lacked any desire to show mercy to her opponent. She swung upward with all of her strength, and when she connected, the miraculous blow slid neatly through Brigid's throat. A hot knife through butter wouldn't have been as efficient as Ascalon. At the completion of her stroke, Brigid's head tumbled through the air and struck the ground, creating a fountain arc of blood.

Absolute silence reigned over the pasture. Stunned faces, human and draconic, stared out at the limp corpse.

"Fuck yeah!"

Marcy's outburst broke the oppressive lull. Thor joined her cheers next, followed by the rest of the ancient beings in her spectating section. Solemn faces in varying stages of grief and disbelief watched from the other side.

I can't believe it. I did it. I did it. She repeated the victorious mantra in her head a dozen times over, unable to move and unable to accept that it was safe to sheathe the bloodstained weapon in her hand.

Mahasti and Saul appeared again. Chloe's struggling husband broke free from his genie friend's embrace to tear down the field.

"Chloe!"

Ascalon dropped to the blackened earth as Chloe stumbled into his arms and sobbed tears of happiness, overcome with immense relief that their ordeal had ended. The nightmare was over.

I killed a dragon.

She wept into Saul's throat and hugged him tight. "We did it!"

"No, Chloe. No. *You* did it. I should have never doubted you. Not once." As she raised her palm to his damp cheek, Saul gazed down at her and smiled. "Now you are truly Chloe Drakenstone." And in the eyes of his prestigious Conclave, no one could ever threaten to take that away from her again.

Once, many months ago, Chloe Drakenstone was saved by a dragon. Their story ended with her rescuing him.

Mated by the Dragon Bonus Chapter: Saul

"Take me back now," Saul demanded in a growl.

He and the djinn stood atop a mountain peak in his father's native Iceland. Waves from a cool waterfall crashed to the world below them, sending a refreshing mist drifting heavenward.

Saul had never liked Iceland. He hated it more when his presence on the island placed over 4,000 miles between him and his family. It would take him days to fly it, and his Chloe had only minutes. Seconds.

"No," Mahasti said quietly.

"Return me at once!" Saul's baritone boomed across the wide open space.

Raising her chin in defiance, Mahasti stood her ground as Saul threw the draconian variant of a child's tantrum. He screamed, raged, thrashed his tail and roared fire, but she waited until at last, he collapsed to the smoldering ground.

"Why… why would you do this to me?" Not his Chloe. Not his child.

"Chloe would not want this. Do you not understand her love for you is equal? Do you believe for a moment she has any desire to see you torn apart by the Conclave for your insolence?"

"I——"

"Do you?" Mahasti pressed without sympathy.

"I don't care," Saul said hotly.

"You should. It would kill her to have you ripped away. You men are always willing to make the ultimate sacrifice, but unable to see it done for you in return." Mahasti's features softened, then one small hand came to touch his snout. "I promised her, Saul. Here is where we will wait."

"Please don't do this to me."

The minutes passed in agonizing silence, each second weighing on his soul.

Would he feel the moment of her death through their soul bond? The macabre thought slithered into his mind and racked him with guilt. Chloe's death would always be over his head. By bonding to her, he had signed her death warrant. He'd murdered her.

"Come," Mahasti said quietly. Her features betrayed nothing, filling Saul's heart with dread. "It is done."

I will slay Brigid myself if she still breathes. I will never forgive the Conclave.

They appeared moments later in the very place where the shredded remnants of Saul's clothing littered the ground. He expected to see Chloe's mangled body or even her funeral pyre, and had prepared himself to unleash unholy vengeance on the surviving dragoness.

Instead, wide blue eyes met his across the field.

"Chloe!" Relief nearly overwhelmed him and his heart felt as if it could fly from his chest.

His wife dropped the sword and ran toward him. He met her halfway in his human form and swept the singed woman into his arms. The smell of blood and fire clung to her skin, but underneath it all, she was still undeniably Chloe. His mated. His beloved. The mother of his unborn child.

Our child still lives. He breathed her in, delighting in the scent that was unique to her and their cub beneath the stink of Brigid's putrid blood.

"We did it!" she cried happily.

"No, Chloe. No. *You* did it. I should have never doubted you. Not once." Gauntleted fingers rose to his tear-stained cheek. Never in his life had he shed so many tears for anyone. Not for his deceased father, nor the loss of his mother, nor for Brigid's many dismissals.

Chloe was worth every tear.

"Now you are truly Chloe Drakenstone. They can never part us." His hand curved against her belly. "Any of us."

"I can't believe it's over," Chloe whispered.

Their embrace continued without interruption, her cheek to his bare chest and his fingers threaded through her pale blonde hair. Over and over, Saul whispered his thanks to his ancestors.

As Saul finally turned to lead Chloe from the field, he saw members of their community standing idly by, the line queueing to pay last respects to Brigid's body, or to congratulate the winner.

A tall man with dark auburn hair approached the couple first, his face an impassive mask.

Shit, Saul thought. Chloe's victory over Brigid hadn't come without a price. Few were closer to her than her father, and even fewer could tolerate her acidic personality for long.

"My apologies that it has come to this, Maximilian. Mahasti will take Brigid's remains wherever you wish. You need only say the word."

"To Mount Shasta. It... my volcano was beloved by her. It will suit as her final resting place." Maximilian bowed his head to Saul then turned his heavy gaze on Chloe. "You fought bravely, child. May that strength serve you and yours in the future."

The elder fire dragon strode away and Saul released his pent-up breath. Deep inside, he had expected Brigid's father to take the loss poorly. Brigid may have been many things, a manipulative bitch among them, but she had still been his only child. The last of his line.

He and my father were close friends once. If things had gone differently in the past, he and Brigid would have long ago celebrated the birth of their first cub. Their fathers had dreams for them. Hopes of uniting their families.

Three women crossed toward them and Saul briefly considered steering Chloe toward the house before the trio could reach them. But he couldn't. It would appear cowardly, and would only throw fuel onto the fire. Brigid's buddies were as scathing and shallow as their deceased friend.

They appeared as three breathtakingly beautiful ladies in their mid-to-late twenties. The two redheads were fastidiously groomed and clothed in cocktail dresses, as if they'd attended a ball instead of a duel to the death. The third wore nothing, a sign of recently transitioning from her dragon form. Pale strands of platinum hair fell in sleek waves over her shoulders, spilling over the tips of her perfect breasts.

"My, how low you have fallen, Saul Drakenstone, reduced to accepting a simpering mongrel," a fire dragoness purred as she slipped by. "Did anyone offer Brigid the same benefit of using a weapon?"

"Brigid would have toasted her if she'd fought as a true woman," the platinum blonde said. Saul never did understand what the white dragoness had in common with the reds. Her attitude revealed itself to be the common factor.

"And now our cousin lies murdered. This is a terrible day in the history of dragonkind," the second fire dragoness said. "What a pity for Maximilian to lose his only child."

"Our dear uncle will likely never have another. Brigid was a contract cub after all."

"How does it feel knowing you have taken everything from a man, murderess?" the second hissed.

Chloe weathered their barbs with dignity and raised her chin. "It feels as if I have protected my unborn child and secured *my* mate. And as I am one for one today, I'm feeling really, really lucky right now if one of you cunts is in the mood to fight me in her honor."

The three women wore matching expressions of shock, their mouths agape and their words silenced. The blonde spluttered while the two redheads seethed, their cheeks mottled with hot color.

"Come. It is clear he has mated a savage." The ice dragon sniffed daintily and pulled her two friends along. Saul waited for steam to spill from their ears.

"I love you," Saul spit out impulsively to his bride. He took Chloe into his arms again, never tiring of how she molded against him.

"Because I shut those bitches up?"

Saul laughed. "For that and more. You are a hundred times the dragon they are.

"Do you think they're going to be a problem after this?"

Saul's uncle stepped up with Watatsumi closely behind, both clearly among those in the group of well-wishers. "Heh. Pay them no mind. It brings back memories of the dark ages for many of them, when humans with sorcery and magical weapons could hold their own against us," Thor muttered. "You fought with the honor she lacked in life."

"This was a humbling, necessary reminder of our own mortality," Watatsumi said. "I congratulate you, Chloe Drakenstone. You have earned this peace and the prosperity soon to fill your life. It is as I have foreseen."

"You predicted this outcome?" Saul demanded.

"If you knew I would win, why didn't you tell me?" Chloe cried.

The old dragon smiled. "Too much confidence is as detrimental, if not more so, as not enough."

The gathered assembly of dragons took their leave in turns. Some by car, others by Mahasti's magic, with the genie spiriting Maximilian and the mourning party away to the volcano. Eventually, the field outside of his home cleared until only a few close friends remained.

A tense silence fell over the fire-scarred pasture. Thor shattered the somber mood with his booming voice, turning to raise both arms above his head as he shouted, "And now, the time has come for celebration!"

"Um, first, can we put some clothes on my husband?" Chloe asked.

"Mahasti."

Chuckling, the genie fulfilled Chloe's wish and provided a replica of Saul's shredded clothes. The cotton t-shirt was cool against his skin, fitted to his upper body. Snug jeans appeared on his lower half with another pair of casual boots.

"And now the revel begins!" Thor called happily.

The dragons cheered.

"Don't I get the chance to bathe and clean up first?" Chloe asked.

"Uh, no," Saul murmured. "It is actual tradition to celebrate while covered in the blood of one's enemy."

"You have to be kidding me."

"If only."

***

"This feels so much better. I had no idea dragons could party that hard."

"We have been known to carouse for days at a time."

"A few hours were enough for me. I almost feel guilty that we ditched when we did. Almost," she added slyly with a peek over her shoulder and into his face.

Saul cradled his wife in his arms while they both soaked in his massive bathtub. He'd suggested the personal hot spring, but Chloe had quickly dismissed the idea. After a fight to the death, she wanted nothing less than fragrant vanilla bubbles and bath salts. While Saul had personally prepared her bath with a variety of favorites summoned by Mahasti, Chloe washed the blood away under the shower.

"Saul, I'm curious about something."

"Yes?" He paused in his washing of her back, a natural sea sponge held in one hand. He set it aside and rinsed her with his bare hands, preferring to feel her silky skin against his skin.

"Why did those three classless bimbos say Brigid was a contract cub? What's that?"

"Finding one's true mate is not always an easy thing, my love. Sometimes dragons enter into breeding contracts."

"So Maximilian didn't have a mate?"

Saul recognized the guilt-stricken tone in Chloe's voice. He kissed the top of her head and hugged her close against his chest. "No, he did not. Brigid's mother, as I recall, was a much older dragon who passed away shortly after she weaned her daughter and passed her to Max."

"That's so sad."

"Indeed. He spoiled her rotten, a fact he discovered far too late." Saul shook his head. "Despite Maximilian's loss and my heartache for him, my soul also feels lighter, as if all worries were vanquished with

217

Brigid."

"They *were* vanquished with Brigid," Chloe said. She twisted around his hold until she straddled him, her slim thighs positioned on either side of his hips. "Worrying is now a thing of the past. Vindictive dragon skank defeated. Concerns gone. Poof, gone."

"Is that right?"

"It is," she replied. "It is one hundred percent correct, Mr. Drakenstone, and I dare you to tell me otherwise." Chloe leaned in for the kiss he'd craved since the end of the festivities, parting their lips and thoroughly claiming his mouth.

"Mm... one would think you had devious intentions, Mrs. Drakenstone," Saul spoke against the corner of her mouth. He dragged her closer by a grip of her ass, introducing her to his hardening dick. Her wiggling trapped it between their bodies then she nipped his shoulder playfully. "I certainly do."

"Oo!" she cried sharply, flinching.

Her sudden outburst instantly killed the mood, like popping a bubble. "Did I hurt you?" Saul dropped his hands from her.

"No. Not you."

"Were you injured during the fight? Why did you not—?"

"No," Chloe repeated, shaking her head. She seized Saul's hand and moved it to her abdomen, gliding his palm over the gently curving bump beneath the water. Something touched his palm in return. A gentle something, an indescribable flutter of pressure.

"Is that...?"

"It's our baby," Chloe confirmed with tears in her eyes. "I was startled, not in pain."

"He has a vigorous kick." Saul slid his hand over her belly, searching for the baby's elusive foot again. "We will have a strong and robust son to carry on the Drakenstone name."

Chloe aimed a big grin up at him. "It's a girl."

"How can you know so soon?"

"I know," she insisted. "She feels like a girl, and I've been talking to her and calling her a girl."

A daughter, he thought in wonder. In seconds, his idealizations of the perfect son vanished, replaced by visions of a little girl with Chloe's smile. *A precious baby girl as beautiful as her mother.* "Then what shall we call her?"

"She needs a special name, for a special girl," Chloe mused. "Do you have any ancestors you want to honor?"

Saul grinned. "You would not wish their names. They are a mouthful, much as Teo's is, or Watatsumi. I was quite fortunate and born of a generation who chose to move away from such traditions."

"Point." Chloe giggled. "Okay then, what about Freya? Or is that name already taken and used by someone?"

Thor's mother would never forgive us if we named a halfbreed after her. Or perhaps it would honor her. He considered it, but ultimately shook his head. "The true Freya is a mighty white beast who slumbers still in Scandinavia," Saul said with caution. "As a rule, we avoid reusing names. We are each unique."

"Fair enough." Chloe pursed her lips thoughtfully. "What about the name Astrid?"

"A name worthy of Norse royalty and our little one."

Chloe's fingers wrapped around his thick cock beneath the sudsy water. It twitched eagerly, always responsive to the slightest touch or moment of her attention. "Now, where were we before Astrid interrupted?"

"We will disturb her rest," Saul protested.

"Shhh…" Chloe silenced him with a touch of her fingers to his lips. "She's floating in her own little pool and absolutely clueless about what's happening in our world out here."

Saul's head fell back as his wife directed him into her waiting channel. Hot and exquisitely tight, she was all his, her inner muscles clenching around him as if by reflex. They joined in a puzzle-pieced union, and once she was full of him, Chloe's hips began to move to a rhythm of her own choosing. Saul was swept along for the ride, absolutely lost in each rise and descent.

At the end, once Chloe tensed against him, fingers grasping at his chest, Saul dragged her head back by a handful of hair, kissing her roughly until the last shudders left her body.

Then he made love to her again on his own terms, both of her hands on the lip of the tub. Afterward, the dragon washed his wife again, toweled off her sore and aching body, then took her with him to the bed where they snuggled amidst the thick comforters and found steaming mugs of hot cocoa awaiting them on the bedside table. Beyond their bedroom window, the party continued into the night, revelers from the paranormal community celebrating in honor of Chloe's acceptance into their world.

"I love you," she whispered dreamily against his shoulder.

"And I love you. Forever and always, Chloe." His fingers glided over her curved stomach. "If you are my heart, then Astrid will certainly be my soul. I will never allow either of you to come to harm or know threat again."

TAMING THE DRAGON

Chapter 1

Marceline Vargas lay in the driver's seat of her sporty little coupe with the back of her hand over her eyes. It was an evening ritual after a stressful day on the job in a career she'd come to loathe. Working as the regional finance manager of Burke Brothers Department Stores had become a demanding drain on her life.

"Maybe Matt's made dinner for me," she mused.

Hell, it wasn't like he had work or anything, since he'd lost his job and spent most days at home on her computer. He assured her he was actively seeking new employment and submitting applications. It was only the middle of the second month of his unemployment, but she'd strangle him with her own stockings if things didn't change.

Groaning, Marcy stepped from the car and climbed the stairs to her upper level apartment. Bass pounded from inside, greeting her with the thump of hard rap. She tore down the printed sheet of paper taped to the door and scanned it before entering.

Ms. Vargas,

Under the stipulations of your rental agreement, you have agreed to refrain from excessive amounts of noise that will constitute a disruption to the peaceful environment expected by your fellow tenants.

We are writing to inform you of numerous complaints received by this office since our second and last written warning on the date of March 14, in regards to your failure to adhere to the noise policy of your rental agreement. Further infractions may lead to disciplinary action, leading up to eviction.

Remember that you are allowed to entertain guests on the property, but ultimately their noise is your responsibility.

Numerous complaints and another written warning? Marcy spun on her heel and stormed down to the main office in time to find the clerk closing up for the day.

"Excuse me?"

"Oh, hello, Ms. Vargas."

"Don't 'Ms. Vargas' me, Julie. What is this about?"

Julie averted her gaze. "Well… I wrote you two other notes, Marcy. Everyone is complaining about the noise during the day."

"Two other notes? This is the first note I've had," Marcy gritted out.

"Really?"

"Uh, yeah. I wouldn't be down here waving this about in your face if I received another, don't you think? If there were problems, why didn't you call me?"

"We made calls to the apartment and Mr. Jones said he would pass the message on to you."

Molten red flashed before Marcy's eyes and became a furious curtain over her vision. Her head pounded like the music thundering from her apartment. "This will be remedied post haste, Julie. Next time there's a problem, you come to *me*."

"I'm sorry, I thought—"

Marcy whirled and exited the office. Less than a minute later, she'd run in her heels up the stairs to her walkway and charged into her unit. Her boyfriend didn't budge from the couch to greet her. He reclined with a bag of Doritos on his lap, her laptop on the table, and a bowl of hot cheese on the coffee table beside it. He was playing Candy Crush. She breezed by him and snatched the television plug out of the wall.

"What the hell are you doing?" she demanded.

"Relaxing? What's up?"

She shoved the paper in his face. "Third warning?"

"Oh, yeah. About that…"

"What about it?"

"Hell, I forgot. It's not like it's loud anyway, baby. They're trying to scare you."

"Well consider me scared and pissed off. Get off my computer and pack."

"You're going to kick me out because they wrote you a little letter?"

"No. I'm kicking you out because you're a slob and I hate living with you. I'm kicking you out because my place looks like a cyclone hit it. I've seen accident scenes less messy than this living room," she hissed. His clothes were usually left on the floor until she came home to tidy up. Enough was enough. "You aren't even trying to find a job."

"I look for work all day when you're gone."

"No, you don't. I've looked at my internet history. You spend all day looking at porn GIFs on Tumblr!"

Half an hour later, Marcy had finished bagging Matt's stuff into trash bags and setting them on the walkway outside. He shuffled away to his van like she had betrayed him.

"Time to retake my life. I don't need him." *Or my damned stressful ass job,* she thought. With Matt gone, she settled at the computer and wrote out her two weeks' notice. She signed the printed resignation and placed it in her briefcase for the morning, then trudged into the kitchen to look at the pile of dishes overflowing from the sink. How had one man turned her kitchen into a disaster zone in a single day? Things had never looked this bad when Chloe lived with her.

The phone rang as if on cue. She picked it up and saw the Caller ID: Saul Drakenstone. "Hi, Chloe."

"Hey, girl. I'm not calling too soon after work, am I?"

"No, not at all."

Marcy returned to the kitchen and fetched dinner ingredients from the fridge. She balanced the phone between her ear and shoulder while she chopped them on the cutting board.

"A little someone suggested now would be a great time to call you about an idea I had," Chloe said.

Marcy grunted. The "little someone" was probably Saul and Chloe's genie friend Mahasti. "Yeah? I'm listening."

"You, me, and Astrid enjoying two weeks in the sun on a white sand beach at a resort on a private island. Blue waves crashing clean ocean water onto the shore. Hot guys in speedos. Bahama Mamas. Wild and casual sex. Uh, for you, not me. Saul, stop looking at me like I'm a naughty girl." The dragon shifter chuckled in the background.

"I don't know… a visit to an island right now, Chloe?"

"Saul is overworked and busy. Come on, Marcy. I'm begging you. Besides, Astrid misses her *tía.* She's going to grow up behind your back. You'll miss everything," Chloe stressed. Her best friend knew how to lay it on thick.

Marcy rolled her eyes. "Your daughter ages half as quickly as normal children, chica. Don't give me that bullshit. She'll look exactly the same in a month when I visit as she did a season ago."

"I know, but I really think you need some time away from your shithole job."

"It's not a shithole," she sniffled into the phone.

"You're not happy there. Are you crying?" Chloe demanded with worry.

Marcy scooped the diced onions into a bowl and discarded the knife into the dishwasher. "No, I'm cutting onions. My job isn't worth tears. Yet. So anyway, tell me how Astrid's doing."

"She's doing great. We were going over colors together outside with the chalk today, and she spelled her name."

223

"No way. You helped her right?"

"Nope. She spelled her name out all on her own." Chloe's enthusiasm made Marcy beam with pride, too.

"That's amazing. Man, I miss you guys."

"So... you'll come?"

"Maybe. Oh, who am I kidding. I planned to put in my two weeks' notice tomorrow."

"What? You're actually quitting?"

"I'm tired of the BS, Chloe," Marcy replied, sighing. "You're right, I'm ready for a break."

"Then come. I'm supposed to represent some of Saul's business interests since he can't attend. I'd really love it if you attended these stupid functions with me."

"When is it?"

"I have to be there Saturday."

"Count me in then. I can have Mahasti send me back to Houston for work by Monday if Howard won't let me have the time off. Now tell me about this resort and where we're going."

According to Chloe, the resort was owned by some billionaire friend of Saul's, located off of the Yucatán Peninsula. They would be expected to attend a banquet to celebrate both the advancement of local conservation efforts and a giant merger between two organizations striving for environmental protection of the rainforest. Saul was a donor.

"I dunno... sounds a little shady, doesn't it? How can you own a mega resort and also claim to support the environment? They're probably dumping tons of trash into the ocean every day, and can you even imagine the electricity usage going on there?"

"Actually, no. 90% of the island is run by solar power. The rest is wind-generated. Eco-resorts are actually a thing now," Chloe said. "Anyway, I can hear your belly grumbling through the line. Go eat, and I'll talk to you again soon. Love you."

"Love you, too."

After ending the call, Marcy tossed together the makings for fajitas then enjoyed a soak in the tub with her favorite book. The silence without Matt was bliss, and she knew without a doubt she'd made the right choice.

Fixing her life began at home, and in the morning she'd have one more change to make.

"Marcy, you can't leave us. You've been with us since the beginning. Years," her boss emphasized.

Gee, thanks a lot. Way to rub it in, Marcy thought. She'd seen the company through its shaky, fragile start all the way through its booming success. "And now it's time for me to step down."

Howard Burke frowned, concern etching his brow. The salt and pepper haired man rose from his seat behind the desk and moved to take the chair beside Marcy. Her boss was a robust, middle-aged man in his late fifties. The father she'd never had and an all-around sweetheart. Leaving the job had nothing to do with him and everything to do with the rigors of performing her duties.

"How could we ever replace you? Do you want more money? Is that the problem? I'll increase your annual pay by twenty-five grand. A bonus right away. Buy yourself a new car."

Marcy sighed and twisted a strand of her hair around one finger. He made a tempting offer. "It doesn't have to do with the money. I'm ready to move on, Howard. I spend too much time working for this company in *and* out of the office. I need time to actually live my life and enjoy it." What good was her massive savings if she rarely had time off to spend it?

"A vacation then. How long do you need? A week—"

"Would not be enough," she cut in gently, laying a hand on his arm.

"Two weeks paid beginning Monday, and if at the end you're not rested, I will allow you to go with no more questions asked and a glowing recommendation letter for any future employers."

"Howard… Are you sure?" She considered the upcoming vacation with Chloe and chuckled.

"I am," he assured her. "Go on. Go home, and enjoy your vacation with Chloe. Take as long as you need, and when you return we'll speak about it again."

"Howard, I need a time frame, or you may not get me back until winter."

Her boss waved at her and returned to his desk chair. "Katie is your assistant, and she's eager to show some responsibility by taking more duties. Take a month. At the very least, it'll give her time to prove herself without relying on you. We'll survive."

The remaining two days of the week passed with relative peace. By the time Saturday arrived, she'd packed her clothes and informed the apartment office staff she'd be away for at least two weeks of fun in the sun.

Chloe phoned at half past noon. "We're coming."

"O—" Kay, she intended to say as her blonde friend appeared in the center of the living room. Marcy laughed and ended the call. "Hi, guys."

Chloe looked as youthful as ever, forever frozen at the age of 29. In her arms, she held a squirming toddler who immediately began to kick and fight for freedom.

"¡Tía, tía!" Astrid squealed until Chloe lowered her to the floor. Her child had the appearance of a kid half her age, but the mental awareness of a four year old.

"Ah, come here, *mi corazón.* I've missed you so much." The child made a beeline for Marcy and raised her arms to be picked up. She acquiesced and swept Astrid into her arms for exaggerated kisses to her face and golden-haired head.

"She speaks more Spanish than I do because of you," Chloe grumbled. "Why don't I get hugs and kisses like your auntie? Huh?"

"You want hugs and kisses?"

"Maybe I *do.* I want to feel some love, too."

"Well I am so sorry you were left out." Marcy leaned in a placed an exaggerated smooch against Chloe's cheek.

They had a laugh together then finished gathering the rest of Marcy's vacation belongings, running off a mental checklist that included her makeup kit, favorite beach cover-up, camera, and art supplies.

"Got everything?" Chloe asked.

"I think so."

"Okay, Mahasti, we're ready," Chloe spoke aloud to the air.

The world around Marcy shimmered and spun, whirling out of control until her stomach seemed to rise and fall in her gut. She would have staggered if the bonds of magic didn't anchor her firmly in place. The dizzying arrival deposited them in the middle of a lavish hotel room with enormous windows spanning half the wall. A fifth floor view overlooked the resort grounds and lush greenery bordering the beach below.

"I'll never get used to flying Air Genie," Marcy muttered.

Air Genie was her fond way of referring to the instantaneous travel Mahasti the Djinn used to teleport them from one location to the next.

"I mean, don't get me wrong, it beats airport security and cramped seats by a long shot, but I always feel nauseated afterward. Thanks, Mahasti."

"It is nothing," Mahasti's disembodied voice replied.

Astrid clapped her hands together. "Again, please! Wanna do it again!"

"I think you're alone there, Marce. I feel fine."

"You both also have the blood of a dragon in your veins," Marcy pointed out, giving a disgruntled grumble. "That probably negates magical teleportation motion sickness."

Chloe grinned at her. "Well, Saul's Uncle Thor is always in the market for a new concubine... He usually goes for shifters but will make an exception and take a human only if she's as hot as me."

Marcy tossed her purse onto one of the queen size beds then waved her hands around. "I'm not having a baby for a shot at eternal life. This womb is closed for business."

"How can it be closed if it's never been open?"

Within seconds, they had both burst into a fit of giggles.

"Down, Mama, down." Astrid kicked her little feet until Chloe set her on the floor. She immediately ran and leapt onto the bed to roll upon the soft coverlets. As her child played, Chloe stepped over to her friend and hugged her tight.

"I'm glad you're here. You know, I'm joking right? About the baby thing?"

"I know," Marcy replied. "But you almost died, chica. It was the most... terrifying experience of my entire life, thinking you would be gone forever."

"I couldn't have made it if not for you and Saul," Chloe admitted. "It's a good thing he inherited his mother's ability to cast healing spells."

Until five years ago, Chloe had never intended to become a mother. It all happened by chance when a one-night stand with a mysterious man resulted in her life-changing pregnancy. Of course, all pregnancies were life altering, but Chloe's was more special than most.

She'd conceived with a dragon named Saul, and in bearing his child, cemented her own immortality. The blood of the dragons flowed through her veins, an irreversible and magical change that made her as strong as the ancient being she had married.

And one day, her best friend Marcy was bound to grow old, wither and die. It was a sobering thought that brought them together so frequently for visits that Marcy may as well have packed up her home and moved in with the dragon family.

227

"I already unpacked everything I brought for Astrid and me," Chloe explained, gesturing around the big suite. "You can take a moment to do the same then I'll show you around."

"Sounds good," Marcy said, moving her clothes from her luggage into an empty dresser. "So, tell me why you made me bring my flirtiest dresses."

"There's going to be lots of rich and influential people around for the opening festivities. A few actors from Saul's films also accepted Teo's invitation—"

"Wait, what? *Teo's* invitation?" Marcy interrupted.

Chloe hesitated. "Well, Marcy, whose island did you think we were visiting? I told Teo the two of us were coming on Saul's behalf. He isn't really a fan of hobnobbing, and too many people in the business have long memories. If they recognize he's the same man they met thirty years ago, we'll have problems. So I'm here instead as Teo's personal guest."

"Ugh. You mean *he's* going to be here?"

"Well, it's his island, silly. Seriously though, I doubt he'll stay long. Teo will probably put in an appearance then soar off to his place."

"Yeah, well good riddance," Marcy grumbled.

Chloe sighed. "You guys had that spat five years ago. Are you seriously still pissed?"

Marcy leaned over and pressed her hands over Astrid's ears. "Once an asshole always an asshole. If I knew we were going to be hanging with him, I'd have spent my vacation at home."

"He doesn't really like people, so it's not like you'll see him much."

Marcy stuck her tongue out, and the childish gesture made Astrid giggle. The little girl scrunched up her nose and imitated her aunt, leading the two into a silly face match-off.

"You win, Astrid, you win."

"Even when she's being silly or naughty she's adorable," Chloe said with a laugh.

"So, has she done any freaky dragon stuff yet?"

"Nothing yet. We don't really know if she'll ever shift like her dad or not. Saul says he was born as a dragon cub and never took human form until he neared adulthood. It could be the same for her."

"I guess it's a good thing. It might raise some brows if she changed in preschool. Speaking of, how're you going to handle the whole school situation if she ages so slowly?"

"We decided to homeschool her with tutors, but if she does one day want to be around other kids, I'll say she has a condition. I mean, she really does, when you think about it. She's going to be my little girl for a long time." Chloe plucked Astrid up and kissed her tummy. "And I don't mind at all."

"She's gorgeous. She really got the best out of you and Saul both."

Chloe smiled down at Astrid before looking back at Marcy. "Come on. Let's change and hit the beach. I promised Astrid we'd build sand castles and have fun before tonight's banquet."

"Are you bringing her to the banquet?"

"No, Mahasti said to give her a call and she'll come to babysit with Nuri. She and Leiv have been thinking through the whole baby thing more, so she wants some actual hands-on practice whenever she can get it."

Once Marcy finished unpacking her delicate, easily wrinkled items, the trio of ladies tossed on their beach dresses and rushed to frolic on the sand.

***

With VIP passes firmly secured around their wrists, Marcy, Astrid, and Chloe hustled onto the electric rail line for their tour of the island. Within minutes of their boarding, the doors shut and the sleek vehicle pushed forward.

"You weren't kidding when you said this place was environmentally friendly. Christ, it must have been expensive."

"He's a billionaire. What do you expect?" Chloe asked.

"You don't see Saul owning private islands and throwing money around into the environment."

"He does actually. He's just not so flagrant about it as Teo and he runs a lot of dummy corporations to funnel money into conservation efforts."

"Look, look!" Astrid shouted, interrupting them. The little girl crawled onto Marcy's lap for a better view through the open window. "Birds!"

"God, that's lovely," Marcy commented.

The sprawling island contained more than a resort with its strict guidelines for beach usage. It also held a massive sanctuary dedicated to the owner's favorite rainforest animals. Majestic trees towered above a perfect reconstruction of the Amazon, a verdant landscape teeming with life.

"Mama, I wanna go there! Wanna go there!" Astrid cried, clutching double handfuls of Chloe's dress bodice.

"So do *I*," Marcy admitted.

The tour looped around the vacation hot spots, visiting attractions of varying interest, some designed for families, others for party-goers and lovers, then a few targeted toward children. Chloe held on to her daughter extra tight, fearing Astrid would leap through the window when she saw the colorful cartoon character themed rides.

A delicious aroma wafted through the train as they passed a high-end restaurant. Chloe and Marcy salivated and circled the location on their maps.

"Tomorrow."

"Yes, definitely," Marcy agreed.

"Saul told me you're not allowed to cover any of the bills this trip, so we're heading to the shopping outlet to get you a swimsuit that's actually *sexy*. I saw the rag you brought in your suitcase, girl. It's hideous."

Marcy rolled her eyes. "He does realize I have money of my own, right? Still…" Saul didn't throw his money around to impress them. Generosity toward friends was an integral part of his draconic nature. Marcy remembered the fact whenever they paid visits to each other and Saul leapt to catch the bill without fail.

"Let's make his eyes bulge out when he reviews the bank statement."

Marcy laughed at Chloe's impish expression. "I think you'd have to buy an island of your own to faze him!"

They disembarked from the monorail when it arrived to the shopping center and walked the rest of the way. With seven hours to spare before the evening banquet, they hit up a fashionable, top name outlet catering to a diverse range of sizes. Despite childbirth, Chloe remained slim and willowy in build. She and Marcy hadn't shared clothes since their high school days.

"Ugh," Marcy groaned. "I think I need to go on a diet. I'd totally raid your closet for your dresses if I could."

"Woman, you don't need to lose weight. So what if we can't steal clothes from each other anymore?"

"I'm aware… I've been thinking about it lately, you know? There's no harm in being healthier."

"Healthier doesn't always mean skinnier. If you're serious about getting in shape, Mahasti will teleport you out to jog with me each evening. Oh, oh, we can go rock climbing on the property—"

"I said I want to get in shape, not do extreme sports!" Marcy protested.

Casual back and forth jesting continued for the duration of the shopping trip. The two women chose outfits for each other and Astrid until they reached the beachwear section. Chloe shoved a stretchy black piece of ribbon into Marcy's arms.

"What the hell is this?"

"Your new swimsuit. This is your size, right?"

"This wouldn't fit Astrid and she's a toddler," Marcy argued. "Chica, if I put this on, I'll be escorted to island law enforcement because no one will think I'm wearing a swimsuit at all."

"It will fit you fine."

Once Chloe shoved her into a spacious changing room, a reluctant Marcy stripped out of her dress and pulled on the skimpy garment. The one piece resembled a generous monokini with wide black strips crossing in front to cover her ample breasts. A diamond cut out in the abdomen revealed her tummy, its lowest point three inches below her navel.

"Okay, you've been in there long enough. Let me see."

The door opened to allow Chloe and Astrid to wriggle in through its opening. "Tía Marcy pretty!"

Chloe echoed the sentiment while her baby girl clapped. "You look amazing."

"Do you really think so?"

"It hugs you in all the right places. It's still modest, I mean, you aren't showing anything more than a two piece. Your tits also look phenomenal."

"Okay, okay. I'm convinced."

Their multi-thousand dollar bill was charged to their account, and their goods packaged for delivery to the room.

"Salon visit time! I didn't make an appointment, but when I picked up our VIP bracelets at the guest services pavilion, I was told these should get us instant bumps to the front of any line."

An employee painted Astrid's little digits bubblegum pink and read her stories while Chloe and Marcy received a series of spa treatments.

"I can't remember the last time we've been pampered together like this," Marcy said. She and Chloe were submerged to their necks in matching mud baths.

"Mama, look at my toes!"

Chloe glanced out of the tub and grinned. "Those look great, baby. I love it." She twisted to peek at Marcy beside her. "I can. When I recovered after Astrid's birth, you swept me away for a full day, remember?"

"Mmn, yes. It was nice, too."

A wave of nostalgia hit Marcy. She smiled at her friend and reached for her hand. "I'm glad I came with you for this. Jerky billionaire or not, we're going to have a rocking good time." Marcy shifted in the mud pool. "Even if I have my doubts about this mineral bath. It feels funny."

"It feels amazing," Chloe disagreed before wriggling her greenish-brown toes out of the muck.

"At least it smells nice," Marcy grumbled. "I'm looking forward to the massage. I can't believe how quiet Astrid has been." A glance revealed Astrid seated on the floor nearby with a pile of plastic building blocks.

"She's a good child. It's funny, but I've heard so many horror stories about toddlers that the reality of having one was kinda disappointing. She doesn't color or paint on walls. She has no interest in eating things off the floor. Uh, anymore."

"Maybe it has to do with her maturing differently, chica. She's incredibly smart for her age."

They emerged with an hour to help each other into their slinky cocktail dresses.

Mahasti appeared in her characteristic puff of smoke to assist with eyeliner and makeup application. She always managed to apply the perfect smoky eye look.

"I feel like Cinderella on her way to the ball," Marcy commented, "and you're the fairy godmother."

"Ah, but *I* will not send you away in a pumpkin," Mahasti replied.

Chapter 2

Patrons in their best Black Tie finery mingled in the opulent banquet hall. Round tables covered in black tablecloths set the background for bone white china and crystal stemware. Orchid centerpieces added a touch of elegance.

Waiters in white jackets carried silver trays brimming with hors d'oeuvres and champagne glasses, moving from group to group with their delectable offerings. Marcy expected one of them to drop their burden at any moment, but they weaved in and out of the crowd with effortless grace.

The two women had flitted among the varying guests, with Chloe spending the most time with the professionals from Saul's studio. Marcy met two of her favorite actors before Chloe introduced her to a producer from a sister studio.

"Burke's is one of the fastest growing department stores in the southern United States. There are plans in the making to expand to the eastern coast," Marcy boasted about her job. Maybe Howard was right about the vacation after all and she'd only needed a break from the routine.

"Quite a bit of responsibility. You wouldn't happen to be in the market for another job, would you?"

Marcy shot a skeptical glance at Chloe. As nice as the change in scenery would be, a big Hollywood business mogul offering her a job coincided suspiciously with her decision to leave her old career behind. "I may be in the near future."

"Excellent." The gray-haired businessman extended a card to Marcy. "This is a direct number to my personal office line. Call me if you're up for a change." He then excused himself from their company.

"Nice attempt," Marcy whispered once they were alone.

"Huh?"

"You put him up to it, didn't you? You or Saul."

"No, I didn't. Sweetie, you helped make Burke's into a billion dollar company. *That* is your resume, and you don't need me to vouch for you. Did you think old man Burke was only blowing air up your ass because he likes you?"

"No," Marcy admitted reluctantly.

"Good, because — oh, look, there's Teo. Try to be cordial."

Marcy turned her head to follow Chloe's line of sight. The handsome billionaire owner of the island approached them in a fashionable black tuxedo. His sleek black hair spilled past his shoulders, framing a brown face with chiseled features and bold green eyes.

"Good evening, Teo. It's so good to see you again," Chloe replied. She stepped forward to kiss his cheek.

"Good evening, ladies." Teo bowed deeply, a perfect gentleman despite Marcy's expectations. She swore internally at herself for wanting to stroke the immaculate waves resting over his shoulders.

Holy shit, he's sexier than I remember. Marcy plastered a smile to her face. "It's a pleasure to meet you again, Mr…" Hell, she didn't know if all dragons had surnames or if Saul was the exception to the rule.

"Arcillanegro. But you may call me Teo, as all my friends do."

"I see." Chloe and Marcy exchanged uncertain looks.

"How do you find the island?" Teo asked, aiming the question at them both.

"I didn't expect the kid stuff, Teo, I have to admit," Chloe replied. "Astrid is so excited."

"It made good business sense to expand this resort into a more family-friendly environment. My other will remain as it is. Exclusive."

He means for rich people, Marcy thought. She resisted the urge to roll her eyes and offered a polite smile instead. "It's very pretty."

"Mrs. Drakenstone," a merry voice called. An older woman with rosy cheeks hurried up to them on unbelievable stiletto heels. "What a pleasure to meet you in person." Her bright eyes turned to Teo and Marcy as if they were an afterthought. "Teo, when you told me you had invited only the best to participate as donors, I never dreamed the Drakenstones would be present."

Teo's flat expression twitched, suppressing the emotion he wanted to display. "I did inform you Mrs. Drakenstone would be among the party attendees, Mrs. Valance."

"Um, excuse me… You seem to be familiar with me, but I don't recall meeting you," Chloe said.

"Cordelia Valance, dear. I knew your husband's grandfather. We attended a benefit together many years ago. Such a shame to hear he passed." She sighed, her lovestruck eyes telling Marcy everything she needed to know. The older woman took Chloe by the arm in the fond gesture of close friendship. "Where is he?"

"Where is who, Mrs. Valance?"

"Your husband, young lady."

"Saul didn't attend. He, ah, was feeling under the weather, so I've come in his stead to support his interests here." In other words, Saul feared someone would find the striking resemblance between him and his "deceased grandfather" to be more than coincidence.

"Such a shame," the older woman said. "Well then, I suppose we must become acquainted."

"But—"

"I insist," Mrs. Valance said as she hauled Chloe toward another group. The helpless blonde shot an apologetic look to Marcy and was swept away to socialize.

"So…" Marcy sought a topic for conversation when it became apparent Teo planned to stay. He lingered beside her with his characteristic, neutral expression firmly in place. "Your orchids all flourish here. I was telling Chloe I wish I could get mine to grow so large."

"If you have an interest in botany, then you will certainly enjoy a tour of the hotel's indoor garden. Shall I show you?" Teo offered his arm.

Marcy froze in place.

Damn Chloe for abandoning me for that pushy broad, she inwardly seethed. *Now what?*

"Are you afraid to be alone with me?"

The question stiffened her spine. "Absolutely not."

"Then let us go."

Marcy shot a look over her shoulder toward Chloe. Her friend was trapped in an awkward conversation about her elusive husband.

"Chloe will survive. They are harmless, if meddlesome mortals," Teo assured her.

I guess he probably feels the same way about me. He's stuck playing tour guide since one of his guests stole Chloe.

"Shouldn't you stay here for your guests? I'd think they would want to rub elbows with the host."

Teo shook his head. "I will return once it is time to dine. Until then, I am free to socialize with my guests as I please. You are a guest, are you not?"

"I suppose when you put it that way…" With her hand above Teo's elbow, they walked side by side through the magnificent banquet hall and deeper into the hotel. Eventually, they reached a set of double doors with gold-trimmed glass windows. Her gentleman escort held one open for her to breeze past him into the humid environment.

Thank God for hairspray, she thought. Self-conscious, she smoothed a hand over her sleek updo and proceeded forward. As if

235

capable of reading her mind, Teo plucked a red hibiscus from the branches dangling overhead and tucked it into her hair, grazing her ear with his warm fingers. Her whole body became hot with sensation.

"Gracias," she murmured. *I won't be charmed by a damned flower. If he thinks kissing ass with a garden makes up for being a prick five years ago, he has another thing coming.*

Teo led the way down a curving path of multihued river stones. Smaller trails branched off toward private nooks in the lush growth.

"Your gardens are beautiful."

"My workers take the utmost care," he replied with his usual haughtiness. "As is their job."

The predictable arrogance crept into his tone. Marcy sighed. "Ah. Well, thank you for showing them to me, but I think I should let you get back to everyone else."

"I have not shown you the best spot."

His words intrigued her. "What spot?"

"There." He gestured with one hand toward a glass wall ten feet away.

Marcy's mouth fell open when she read the bold print above the translucent door.

"You have a butterfly garden!"

"Indeed. I have cultivated a habitat to sustain over seventy varieties."

They stepped through two sets of screened doors into the inner habitat. Verdant plants filled the domed space and blossoms in multiple hues scented the air with sweet perfume. Marcy recognized most of the plants, excluding a handful of unfamiliar specimens. She leaned in toward a mossy tree and sniffed one of the strange white flowers dangling from its many vines.

"Ghost orchids," Teo offered.

"Yes, I know," she said. "I've heard of them, but I've only seen pictures. They're much prettier up close."

"You like flowers..." he ventured.

"I do. Chloe is the one with the black thumb, though Leiv is teaching her how not to kill the garden he set up for her. Every time I visit I bring her a new plant."

"I have noticed. I paid my visit to Saul only a month ago and found her despairing over several dying plants. She did mention one came from you... Be still," Teo said, staring at her.

Marcy blinked. "Excuse me?"

Teo stepped aside. "Look," he urged. With the arrival of night, the garden's glass windows had become mirrors. At first, her questioning eyes rose to Teo, but when Marcy caught sight of her reflection in the glass surface she saw a butterfly resting upon the red flower Teo had placed in her hair. Another one joined it, then a third descended to rest on the narrow strap of her dress, resembling the world's most beautiful living brooch.

Marcy held her breath, mourning the missed photo opportunity of the year. She was torn between marveling over the delicate creatures and irritation for her lack of a camera. "Shit," she muttered under her breath. The picture would have looked amazing on her blog.

"It is an omen."

"An omen." She raised her eyes to Teo's stoic features. He stared at her in return.

"Yes. Even we dragons have our own beliefs." He didn't elaborate.

After a few moments the butterflies abandoned her and returned to the greenery. Disappointed, Marcy watched them fly away. "I'll probably never have this kind of luck again," she said. "It would have made the perfect profile photo."

"Profile photo? What is that?"

"I take it you don't go on the internet often."

Teo shook his head. "For what reason do you require a profile photo?"

"For my blog," Marcy said. "My picture goes on it near my name."

"What is the purpose of this blog?"

"Well, I write articles and post things I'd like to share with my readers. Sometimes I post cooking recipes or the art I make."

Teo's impassive features never changed. "Do all mortals pursue such trivial internet hobbies?"

Marcy's improving regard for Teo evaporated. *Trivial? My hobby is trivial?* "Right. I should go join my actual friend." She brushed past him to return to the banquet hall in search of Chloe.

"Marcy, why do you leave?"

"I need to pursue some other *trivial* matter," she replied. The stunned dragon watched her exit the garden, an unmoving figure behind her.

Serves him right. Nobody deserved to listen to his smug attitude.

After coordinating their meeting by text, Marcy met Chloe in the restroom where the blonde had gone to hide.

"How was your chat with Miss Stilettos?"

"Let's just say I met one of Saul's oldest living admirers," Chloe said dryly as she primped and checked out her reflection.

"Huh?"

"Remember how I told you he toyed around with humans but didn't know what to do with them in the bedroom? Yeah... well. The old lady was a mountain of TMI."

Marcy's mouth fell open. "No!"

They were both in stitches by the time Chloe finished the sordid tale. Many years ago, as a dragon fresh to walking with humans, Saul had attempted to become intimate with women and often ended the act in frustration. Chloe was the first human woman with whom he'd ever finished sexual intercourse. Apparently, he'd left admirers hoping to meet him again.

"So, where'd you get off to? I'm sorry for leaving you with Teo. Did you flee and abandon him after I was dragged away?"

"No, not really. He showed me the indoor garden here."

Chloe's mouth fell open. "So he was polite?"

"For about ten minutes, then he said my hobbies are trivial."

Chloe winced. "Say no more. He does the same thing to Saul, if it makes you feel any better. You don't know fun until you've seen two dragons rolling across the yard clawing at each other. I imagine it's like watching two siblings putting each other in a headlock when mom isn't looking, except there's... fire. And claws." Chloe frowned. "And acid pools on the grass."

"If it's anything like your dragon duel, I'll pass. Thanks."

They settled at a round table where small cards announced the seating order. Marcy admired the elaborate centerpiece and stroked her fingers down the glossy green leaves. Someone had arranged each one with love. "These flowers aren't cut."

"Does it matter?" their dinner companion asked. A man settled opposite them with his wife. Neither seemed to be impressed by their surroundings.

His wife, a slender living trophy half Chloe's size, appraised the two friends with indignance in her eyes. "I was under the impression we would share a table with Saul Drakenstone and his wife.

"I *am* Chloe Drakenstone," Chloe said evenly.

"Ah. I expected a younger woman."

Bitch, she's younger than you, Marcy thought.

"And who is this?" the husband asked. "We are Archibald and Helena Galway. I handle the financial aspect of Mr. Arcillanegro's foundation. To whom do I owe this pleasure?" His eyes dropped to Marcy's cleavage and remained there.

Chauvinistic pig. Marcy wondered how Chloe put up with snobs like the Galways.

"This is Marcy Vargas," Chloe introduced. "She is a close friend of mine and my husband's."

"So I gather from her presence that your husband was unable to attend? Such a pity. We had looked forward to a meeting with the elusive Saul Drakenstone," Archibald said. "I must say, though, the change in company is rather pleasant."

Helena glared at her husband then turned her haughty eyes toward Marcy. "Are you anyone important, or merely a plus one?" she asked.

"She is *my* honored guest." Teo's voice came from directly behind Marcy. His hands lowered to her shoulders, sending an electrifying tingle burning through every nerve until it reached the tips of her toes.

Helena's mouth fell open, and her husband managed to tear his eyes away from Marcy's generous bust for the first time since the couple joined them.

Chloe smirked. "How nice of you to finally join us. Teo is a close family friend, and godfather to our little girl," she explained to the gaping woman. "He and my husband are practically brothers." She then took Marcy's hand and laced their fingers. "And Marcy is my sister. We've been best friends since childhood."

"I wished to remind you of our lunch plans tomorrow," Teo said. His thumb made a single stroke over Marcy's shoulder then he released her.

Lunch plans? What the fuck is he talking about? Marcy thought. She tilted her head to gaze up at him with her mouth slightly slack. When her eyes lowered to their dinner companions, she saw Helena's glare had chilled to Antarctic levels.

"Lunch sounds great, Teo, thanks," Chloe replied, smiling as she played along.

"I'll meet you both at noon by the cove. I think Astrid will enjoy the calm waters there," Teo said.

"We'll see you then," Marcy murmured. Her shoulders felt cold without his hands on them.

After Teo's departure, their dinner companions became more amicable. Marcy wasn't fooled by their change in tune, but at least it made the time less uncomfortable.

Charitable donors made speeches prior then servers visited each table with artfully arranged dinners. The expensive plates held

239

succulent cuts of medium-rare steak, grilled asparagus spears coated with a layer of savory butter, and the cheesiest mashed potatoes Marcy ever sampled. The miniscule serving size of the creamy side dish was enough to fill her stomach. The night ended with a performance by talented dancers. For show, Chloe broke decorum and penned her check at the table, adding enough trailing zeroes to make Helena and Archibald stare.

"Holy crap, that was intense. I didn't know snobs could backpedal so quickly," Marcy said as she and Chloe stumbled into the elevator, giggling crazily together. "I've now had my first taste of rich people wine. I wonder how much of the money they raise went into supporting that shindig?"

"Barely a fraction, girl. Which is why all of the portions are so tiny and rich. They fill you up with bite-sized morsels and microscopic steak filets so you don't have room for a lot of their expensive wine."

"I really am full," Marcy agreed. "Even though I think I had only a bite of food. I wish I had the recipe for those asparagus spears."

They rode to the top and entered their shared suite. Inside, they found Nuri curled upon the bed fast asleep. Astrid had cuddled against her nanny, clutching a blanket in one hand and burying her face against the wolf's rust red pelt.

"That is too adorable." *And too cute to pass up.* Marcy dug out her camera and clicked a few photos with the flash off.

"Nuri is a godsend," Chloe whispered. "I had my doubts when Saul first told me he wanted to find a werewolf babysitter, but I'm glad to have her. She's amazing."

"I still can't believe she does it for free with no expectations of compensation."

According to Chloe, some shapeshifters like Nuri were born as animals, only they learned to walk as humans at some point in their adult lives. Nuri lacked appreciation for technology and had simple desires. Family. Peace. Belonging. She lived as part of Saul's pack.

Quiet as thieves, they moved into the neighboring room and used the sink to wash the makeup from their faces. Afterward, they changed from their finery into pajamas and settled on the couch in front of the television.

"Why didn't you warn me you made lunch plans with Teo?" Marcy asked, interrupting their movie with her abrupt question.

"I didn't," Chloe laughed. "I think he was only trying to put Helena in her place. Did you see her expression? She looked like she'd sucked on a lemon."

"What if he was serious?"

"Trust me. Teo has better things to do than to hold our hands at his resort," Chloe assured her.

Chloe was right. The next day passed without Teo's presence for a shared lunch by the cove. Despite her disdain for the arrogant dragon, Marcy couldn't help but feel let down by the ruse.

Chapter 3

Waves crashed against the white sand shore as Marcy captured the foaming tide with paint. At first, she'd sat beside Chloe with a collapsible watercolor easel while Astrid made castles in the sand. The child made the perfect artist's subject until she'd passed out. While Marcy finished the painting, Chloe sat nearby beneath an umbrella with a sexy paperback novel in her hands.

"Ugh. Hey, Marcy? I'm going to take Astrid back to our room. I'm feeling a little tired myself. Watching her run around wore me out."

"All right. I want to finish this painting first. Guess I'll see you guys for dinner?"

"Sure." Chloe gathered Astrid into her arms and plucked their blanket from the sand. With them gone, Marcy had no distractions from the creative scene coming to life on her easel.

Astrid is such a beautiful little girl. Smart as a cookie, too. Marcy had been taking pictures of the child since her birth, saving the couple any need to hire a professional photographer. It was only another of Marcy's hats: artist, plant enthusiast, blogger, candlemaker, and financial whiz. She had her own mother to blame for it by sharing a love of all things artistic.

A shadow fell over Marcy and her work. When she glanced up to her left, she saw a man standing over her with his hands in the pockets of his loose, white linen pants. A small, startled shriek rose in her throat until she recognized the chiseled features and intense green eyes.

"You scared the shit out of me!" Her heart pounded in her chest, a wild and frenzied rhythm

"My apologies. I did not wish to interrupt your work."

"Well, say something next time. It's kind of creepy to just stare at a woman."

"I apologize again."

Marcy tilted her head and raised one hand to shield her eyes from the sun shining over his head. "You're full of apologies today. I guess you felt like an asshole?"

"Indeed. I came to ask if you have seen my aviary."

"No, I haven't seen the aviary," she said in a clipped tone.

Another place where he'd no doubt attempt to rub his immense wealth in her face.

"You wish to be alone," Teo said. His words were as much an observation as they were an inquiry.

"I wish to know why the hell you've hovering by me," she mocked him, only to feel like a bitch when the words left her tongue.

"I would like to make amends for the poor impression I have made."

I'm going to regret this. He's hot, but all of the good looks in the world won't change the fact he's an asshole, Marcy thought sadly. *Or a dragon. Not like I really have a chance with him anyway.*

"Marcy?" Teo spoke in a soft tone.

"Why now?"

Five years ago, meeting Teo had seemed like an outrageous, impossible dream. Her best friend had fallen in love with an amazing dragon shifter who worshipped the ground beneath her feet, and the arrival of his friend Teo seemed fated until the black dragon opened his mouth.

"Chloe tells me you own a camera. You will want to bring it with you," Teo told her. "Meet me inside the hotel lobby in thirty minutes."

He left Marcy staring with her mouth agape while he walked away. *The nerve of him, ordering me to meet him. Fuck that. I'm not going.* She turned back to her watercolor, determined to blow Teo off. Five minutes later she packed her materials and stalked across the sand.

"Fine," she muttered to herself. "I'll go, but not for him. I want to see the birds."

Marcy traded her art supplies for her camera bag, took a quick shower, and pulled on her favorite sundress. The burgundy color flattered her tanned skin and dark hair. She considered it her armor, boosting her self-confidence so she could withstand Teo's aristocratic bullshit for another day.

She peeked in to see Chloe and Astrid snuggled tight on their bed, then she left the suite to embark on her day. As promised, Teo waited for her in the lobby where he stood out like a sore thumb. Female tourists took appreciative glances at him, clearly unaware the hunky specimen was the resort's owner. No man should look as good in white as he did.

"So where is this aviary? I didn't see anything on the map," Marcy commented. She adjusted the strap of camera case, aware of Teo's eyes drifting over her legs. If she had to pick any part of her body to take pride in, it had to be her legs — her tits a close second. Marcy's legs were thick but strong, her calves perfectly shaped when worn with heels to boost her height. Four inches would only nick the surface of the height difference between her and Teo.

"Of course not. Only attractions belong on the map. My private aviary is a sanctuary," the mysterious dragon said. He offered his arm to her, which she took with dwindling reluctance.

They took a dune buggy down one of the private dirt roads leading away from the resort grounds. Teo drove, offering another surprise. Marcy had expected him to summon a servant. The thirty minute drive took them deeper into the natural jungle, where Marcy spotted monkeys in the trees and wild capybara wandering beside the road. Teo slowed the vehicle long enough for her to take photos and to point out the animals she missed along the way.

The aviary took up a large tract of land. The metal frame gleamed in the light and supported the wire mesh stretched between each section. Semi-translucent glass composed the lower five feet around the entire structure.

"You may wish to remove your shoes. The heels will sink into the soft soil here."

After heeding his warning, Marcy padded on her bare feet behind him over cool ground with dense patches of grass and growth. It felt good beneath her naked toes. Teo unlocked the door and held it open for her like a gentleman.

Inside, brightly plumaged parrots perched on branches with thick foliage. Long legged pink birds strutted beside a small river, accompanied by a few native ducks. A trio of hyacinth macaws nested above a man-made pond located near the back of the structure.

"There's so many." Her eyes became as wide as saucers when she noticed a rare, blue macaw preening its feathers on a low branch. "You have a Spix!"

"Two," Teo murmured. "The fate of their kind angers me, and so I have spent some of my fortune to put an end to smuggling. From time to time I acquire a bird long past its prime and unable to survive in the wild. They are rehabilitated here and given a home. We buy them from irresponsible pet owners who would put them in tiny cages."

It wasn't what she had expected from him.

"That's wonderful, Teo. I mean it. Are your pair mates?"

Teo shook his head. "Not yet, but I hope they will change their minds. I try my best to give them a good life while here, but…"

"It's no substitute for the wild," she finished.

"No, it is not," Teo agreed sadly.

An umbrella cockatoo worked his way closer to them and studied Marcy from afar. She hung back while Teo reached out to caress its feathered fringe. "Why are you standing there? Come this way. They wish to meet you."

"I can touch one?"

"If they desire it, yes." When Teo turned to face her, a large macaw with ruby wings landed on his outstretched arm. The blue and green feathers accenting the red made for a striking contrast.

"Why don't they fear you? Chloe once told me animals can tell Saul is a predator. I've seen some give him a wide berth."

"They can. Most animals recognize me for what I am, but many adapt to my presence over time. I visit these creatures often and have gained their trust," he explained.

"But how? I'd be afraid you planned to eat me."

Teo shook his head. "Does a lion not eventually earn the trust of his human handler?"

"I always considered it to be the opposite, that the human earns the lion's trust."

Teo's quiet but brief chuckle almost escaped her notice. "No."

"Does he have a name?" She trailed her fingers down the soft feathers.

"This one I call Bailador."

"Dancer?" Marcy's brow shot upward.

"It suits him," Teo replied with a shrug. "When my servant tends the plants here, he often plays music. This one likes to bounce to the beat." Teo brought the bird close to his face and lowered his voice to a whisper, as if in conversation with the creature.

He's like a whole different person in here, she mused, intrigued by the change that had come over him.

Bailador hopped from Teo's arm to Marcy's instead. The sudden weight surprised her and she remained still as the bird sidled up her arm and settled on her shoulder. His claws tickled her bare skin, but she didn't dare to utter a complaint, even when he used his beak to groom through her hair. Bailador nibbled at the small clip pinning her bangs back from her face, but quickly lost interest when Teo placed a handful of large shelled nuts in Marcy's palm.

"*Nogal,*" the bird called in its croaky voice.

Marcy giggled. It made sense the bird would speak Spanish rather than English. "You want this walnut, hmm? Here you go."

The green-winged macaw took the offered treat in one claw and went to work on cracking the thick shell. Teo stepped back around the corner.

"Where are you going?" Marcy called to him.

Teo reappeared with a full-length mirror and tilted its angle on the stand until Marcy and the parrots on the perch came into view.

"I do not know the first thing about taking photographs with your device. I asked my servant to bring this for your use."

Marcy stared at him initially, then the laughter spilled out of her. "Teo, my camera has a folding tripod and a timer. I'm not a girl taking selfies in the bathroom for Facebook."

"Oh."

Once Marcy set up the stand, she made a few adjustments of the lens and deactivated the camera flash. She posed for at least a dozen pictures of herself and her new friend. Bailador cooed and rubbed his feathered cheek against her face.

"Will this do for your profile photograph?" Teo asked, his voice soft and genuine, catching Marcy by surprise.

"Yes..." She stole a peek at him. "Thank you. But... my camera does have a timer. Aren't you going to take a photo with me?"

"You are very welcome, but I do not take photographs."

"Why not?"

"I prefer paintings. It is a lost, forgotten art often set aside in the digital age due to the ease of using technology."

"Forgotten art? I've spent years taking photography classes to develop my skill. It's not as easy as point and shoot, Teo."

"I mean no offense," the dragon said, his prompt reply making her wonder how much she had frowned. "They are simply not my preference." His spine became stiff, and he froze like a wild animal under scrutiny by a hunter.

"Relax, Teo. It's okay."

"I did not mean to insult you this time."

This time, she thought. If his apologetic features didn't touch her heart, she would have teased him mercilessly and brought the implication to his attention. She didn't. Instead, she stepped close and raised her face to his smooth jaw for a quick kiss to his cheek.

"I forgive you for how you treated me."

"Thank you."

The discomfort didn't return between them. They chatted about his efforts to bring awareness to animal smuggling, his donations for environmental protection, and the purpose of the banquet she'd attended. While Teo didn't have Saul's awareness of technology, or share in his friend's love for it, he was willing to grant large amounts of cash to the people who ran his foundation.

"So how do you know they don't squander your money? I thought it was against a dragon's principles to give away cash. Lord knows Saul scrutinizes his accounts."

"My servant assists me with keeping up with the foundations expenses, but I will admit it is baffling at times. I can tell you the worth of my horde, every coin, every gemstone, but I do not understand digital money. "

"Why don't you let me look at the books and see your accounts."

"You will do this for me?"

"Yes. You're doing a good thing, Teo, and if someone is taking money from you, you deserve to know. It shouldn't be lining someone's pockets."

"Why do you suspect someone has stolen?"

Marcy bit her lower lip. "Well, it happens sometimes with big foundations like this. People embezzle once they're trusted and realize their theft may go undiscovered. You're dealing with millions—"

"Hundreds of millions," he corrected her.

"Exactly. Would you notice a few thousand missing here or there?"

He shook his head.

"Exactly. But I've been trained to look for this kind of thing. Let me into your files, if you trust me, and I can at least let you know if the people you work with are honest."

"I trust you. We will discuss this over dinner in full. Afterward, my servant will grant you access to the resort's administrative offices. He is overworked and will appreciate the assistance."

Is that how a dragon asks someone to dinner? Marcy sighed. "Sounds good to me." Her tummy rumbled noisily.

"I have been a poor host to you. I should have fed you at the cafe prior to this excursion. Come. We will go dine now."

As if on cue, Bailador abandoned her shoulder and flew up into the trees. Marcy watched after him sadly. She would have loved to keep a parrot for a companion, but her active career wasn't conducive to caring for a time-consuming pet. An animal so intelligent deserved more than neglect.

"I love birds," she sighed. Marcy brushed off bits of shell from her dress and hair.

"He seems to favor you as well." The gentleman dragon held the door for her and they returned to the dune buggy where Marcy stepped into her shoes before climbing back in.

"So," Marcy began during the drive back to the hotel, "you're this big acid-spewing dragon with a soft spot for butterflies and birds? I thought they would be bite-sized snacks for you. Like chicken nuggets."

Teo chuckled. "No. I may be a dragon, but I do not make a meal of every creature smaller than me."

"But Chloe told me you and Saul *enjoy* hunting together."

"We do. The thrill of the hunt sates our inner dragon and allows us to be who we are. But we are not beasts. The time of hunting for sport is long past, an age put behind us when our ancestors blended into human civilization. When I hunt, I take no pleasure in the suffering of any animal. I seek only to feed myself."

Marcy nodded. Biting her lip, she glanced away from him and toward the passing scenery. "Sounds noble, I guess."

"No. It is right."

"What about Brigid? She seemed to really get off on hurting other people. She wanted to kill Chloe and Astrid."

"Brigid was an exception, a bitch so cold even her own father failed to grieve her death for more than an evening. Could you imagine, Marcy? Held with such disdain your own parents would not mourn your passing?"

She shook her head. "No. Chloe and I were afraid for a long time her dad would come for revenge, but then Saul assured us it was okay. He never said why."

"Now you are aware. She was his daughter, but he did not condone her actions. She took us back to a time when we were not as… civilized."

Marcy picked Teo's brain further about dragons during the rest of the trip and he gave honest, candid answers to each question. When they arrived to the seaside restaurant, the hostess' eyes grew saucer-wide and she stammered when he walked past her.

"Mr. Arcillanegro, you didn't call ahead as usual. Your usual table isn't ready and—"

"Any table for two will suffice. Thank you."

"Yes, yes of course. Please follow me." She led them to a table outside in the fresh air beneath the shade of many trees. Fragrant blossoms perfumed the tiled deck, which was bordered by several examples of wild flora native to the area. An ocean bird lingered near, waiting for the chance to steal morsels from unattended plates.

Teo drew her chair from the table and seated her. Marcy stared, expecting him to sprout a second head.

What is going on here? He's not even the same dragon anymore. Is he really sorry about being a dickhead? Did Chloe change his opinion of humans?

"Tell me about the job you have decided to leave."

Marcy sputtered on her water and coughed until she was red in the face. "How did you know about my job?"

"Chloe told me she brought you to unwind after turning in your two weeks' notice."

"Oh."

"Why do you wish to leave?" Teo pressed.

"If you're into dull dinner conversation, then fine."

"I am interested."

"I've been with Burke's for years. So long I feel like I never really leave work. Even when I'm at home I'm always fielding calls, checking bank records, and writing up reports. The last time I visited Chloe in California I spent an entire day in my room because an 'emergency' popped up." She made quotes with her fingers.

"Does he not pay you well?"

"He does, but not well enough for all the work I do."

Dinner arrived soon after, including a bottle of white wine which Teo poured himself after dismissing the waitress.

"Are you going to eat all of that?" Marcy eyed the large, whole fish on Teo's plate. It still had its tail and head. Including the eyeballs.

"Would you like some?"

"No, I'm good with my scallops. It's only... Nevermind, I guess it makes sense in a weird way. You, uh, must have a bigger appetite."

Teo grinned.

They finished their meal with friendly conversation focused on Marcy's experience on the island so far and young Astrid. Teo suggested a boat ride and promised to have a personal tour set up for the girls the next day.

"You could come with us..." Marcy ventured after they'd left the restaurant and walked down a fern-lined path.

"I have business matters to attend to tomorrow."

"Oh. Okay." She sighed, silently berating herself for getting her hopes up.

Teo led her into the administrative building to a huge corner office. It was sparse and unappealing, its barren walls driving Marcy to make one conclusion: Teo spent little time, if any, inside the room.

"You must forgive me if your task is difficult, Marcy."

"It can't be too bad. If you and your employee keep orderly records, I should be able to make this quick. It might take a day or two."

Marcy overestimated Teo's diligence in maintaining his financial records. Unlike Saul who enjoyed monitoring his online bank accounts, Teo's were a disaster. With two resorts and a charitable foundation in his name, she'd expected to find some crossover of funds. What she didn't expect was to find a complete clusterfuck consisting of multiple accounts used for different purposes, shuffling money back and forth in large and small quantities.

"This is going to take days." Marcy sighed.

And she'd already given her word she would do it.

Chapter 4

Marcy and Chloe treated Astrid to a glass bottom boat ride the next day. As promised, Teo had one arranged for their personal use. Once the trio descended to the lower level of the boat, they watched schools of fish swim beneath the clear viewport in its bottom. The little girl clapped and grinned each time she spotted an underwater creature. The large sea turtle followed along beneath the boat for almost a half hour had been her favorite.

The following afternoon, Nuri occupied Astrid while the two women donned flashy dresses and danced at a beachside party. A live band played music while vendors operated a market with regional favorites. Later, as the sun descended below the horizon, they enjoyed a special indoor performance consisting of Latin music and outfits in vivid colors. The days passed in a haze of exhaustion, divided between family-centered activities for Astrid and adult fun for the two friends. Somehow, Marcy found the time to return to Teo's office early each morning where she crunched numbers and traced bank transactions prior to her outings with the girls.

Two days after they visited the aviary, Teo popped in before lunch and leaned over the desk to gaze down at her. "I wish for you to paint me. Take a break from your labors at my computer terminal."

Marcy let out a laugh at the incredulous request. "Paint you?"

"Yes. Why does this amuse you?" Teo asked.

"You're serious?"

"Why would I lie? I have watched you paint and desire a portrait for the upcoming charity auction."

Marcy bit the inside of her cheek. "I only paint nudes for charity," she quipped with a grin on her face, joking. And then she remembered he was a man, and not only a man, but a shifter and completely at ease with nudity and likely to take her seriously. *Shit.*

"Excellent. I look forward to seeing my likeness crafted by your own hands. It will be an amazing piece of work."

Marcy inhaled a breath. He was a dick for calling her bluff, but she wouldn't back down. Squaring her shoulders, she met his gaze head-on. "I need to return to my room to get my supplies."

"We will meet again here."

"Where ya goin'?" Chloe asked. "God, I'm tired. I feel old and crusty today. Just plain exhausted."

"You can't get pregnant again, right?"

Chloe hurled the pillow at her. "No! Geez. I can feel bad without being pregnant."

"Hey, I'm returning the favor for all of those times you tormented me, chica. It's okay to be tired and to rest on your vacation. Why don't you call Nuri to watch over Astrid and get some undisturbed rest for yourself?"

"Good idea," Chloe murmured. "I need a vacation from my vacation. We hit the tourist spots so hard in these first few days. So where are you going?"

"Uh. A guy saw me painting down by the shore and wants to sit for a portrait."

"You do portraits now? He must be hot." Chloe whistled and sprawled across the bed with her phone.

"I guess so." Marcy smiled. *If only she knew.*

Marcy returned to the office to find the room transformed. A few laborers were on their way out the door as she entered to find paintings hung on the walls, sheer curtains over the windows, and new furniture. The old desk had been replaced with one of gleaming wood, a chaise upholstered in black silk brocade with burgundy throw pillows sat against the western wall, and a trio of flowering plants were clustered in a corner. The pots holding them were as beautiful as the plants themselves, glazed in bold colors.

"What the hell happened while I was gone? That was only like thirty minutes!"

"An hour," Teo corrected. "Is it not to your liking?"

"It's... wow. It's great, really. It surprised me a little, is all. So um, give me a second to set up."

Male nudity wasn't anything new to Marcy, but Teo's delectable body stole her breath. Hard muscle composed his torso beneath a layer of brown skin with only a few flaws. And even those flaws seemed to enhance his appearance. A few thin, narrow scars stood out upon his perfect back as upraised lines, reminding her of animal scratches. He tossed his shirt aside on the desk, pushed his thumbs into the waist of his shorts, then pushed them off. They tumbled to his bare ankles and Teo stepped free. Apparently dragons went commando.

Marcy tried to play it cool while she set up her easel and prepared her paints. His half-hard cock thickened, threatening to rise toward his navel.

Holy crap, he's huge. How the hell was he hiding that?

"Am I to your expectations?" he asked when her eyes lingered.

Marcy jerked out of her thoughts. "Did you have a pose in mind?" she countered, ignoring his question. The Latina leveled her voice to a neutral, professional tone and plastered a smile on her face. It was a job. A job for charity. Some bitchy old snob like Mrs. Valance would buy it for her personal collection for a cool couple of million.

"What would you suggest?" Teo's eyes never left hers as he asked the question.

How about in my bed? The wild thought flitted across her mind and left her feeling breathless for a moment. "Um, well, how about here. You're too tall to sprawl out seductively, but if we want to do something more manly how about..." Marcy guided him to the chaise and instructed Teo to sit with his side profile exposed. With the window beyond him, sunlight highlighted his features and gleamed over every ridge.

Marcy wet her mouth with a sip of water then began. She mourned that the tasteful pose obscured his cock. She'd wanted to touch it, to run her fingers over the sinewy length, and to taste him while watching his stoic features contort with pleasure. Her insides clenched.

Charity, she reminded herself. *I'm helping the...* "Hey, which charity is this for? Your foundation, or another?" Even as she reminded herself to maintain her own professionalism, her sharp eyes picked up his quickened breathing. He studied her closely with hunger in his green eyes then resumed facing forward.

"The Natural Earth Wildlife Fund."

"Ohhh. Nice choice. Is the auction soon? I can't finish this in one day, but I can get a good start on it."

"It is to be held on the final day of your vacation. Will you attend?"

"Sure. I don't have serious auction money, but it'll be neat seeing how high a price this goes for."

"You will be paid for your work, Marcy. I do not expect you to donate your time as freely as I donate my money. This is a vacation for you, a holiday to rest and unwind. You have given generously to me."

253

"Okay." She didn't argue. If Saul had taught her anything, it was to accept gifts from dragons when they were offered. They did not give them easily and took offense when denied the opportunity.

A few hours later, a text from Chloe indicated the end of their session. Her friend wanted to know where she'd gone.

"Wow, the time flew. That was actually kind of fun. Usually the guys we'd get in life drawing class were…" *Usually ancient grandfathers with saggy balls and not as fucking attractive as you.*

Teo approached her for a look at her progress. "This will be an excellent portrait. I have not sat for a painting in nearly a century."

"*¡Dios mío!*" A century? His comment reminded her of his age, which she'd quickly forgotten when distracted by his washboard abs. Thankfully, his cock had softened during the painting, no less impressive in its unaroused state than some of the hard dicks she saw while dating.

"You may leave your easel within the closet if you wish no one to see it." His warm hands descended to her shoulders, uninvited but completely welcome. "Thank you."

"You're welcome." She swallowed and regained control of her emotions. "When I finish painting your pose, I'd like to do the rest in the aviary and have some of the birds perch on your knee. If you think you can get them down. Maybe one of the Spixes or Bailador." She could already see the beautiful contrast of cobalt blue and scarlet red in her mind. Their bright color would be stunning against Teo's bronzed skin.

Teo dressed while she tucked her work in progress away in the spacious and empty closet, but it didn't matter. The image of his naked body was etched into her memory.

"I wish to see you again tomorrow."

"If we're going to finish your portrait, of course you'll see me again, Teo." She chuckled and glanced down to see another impatient text from Chloe. She and Astrid were hungry, and thus leaving to get dinner with or without her. Of course, she was welcome to join them at the seaside grill.

"No. I wish to see you for personal matters."

Her brows rose. "You mean like a date?"

"Yes."

Play it cool. Don't do cartwheels yet. "Okay," she said aloud. Her brown eyes locked to his green, before she forced herself to walk calmly out the office. "I'll see you tomorrow."

She returned to the suite as Astrid and Chloe were walking out the door.

"Just in time to come with us. So how was it? Will I get to see this mysterious portrait masterpiece?" Chloe asked.

"Oh, you'll see it soon."

There'd be no hiding it during the auction, but until then, her painting sessions with Teo were her little secret.

Chapter 5

With Marcy alongside him on his arm, Teo led her into the tropical resort's restricted area. The trees grew thick and lush on the opposite side, beginning at a considerable distance from the gates. They provided perfect shade from the unyielding summer sun. She touched a few silken petals in passing and sighed once they wandered under the living canopy.

"I asked my servant to gather several specimens from the island as souvenirs of your time here. They will grow as beautifully in your home as they do in the wild."

"You never refer to him by name. Does he have one or is he only 'my servant'?" Marcy teased. "Is this customary? Will I be 'the human' next? Should I refer to you only as 'the dragon' so I can fit in?"

Red hot color swept over the apples of Teo's high cheekbones. "He does have a name."

Is he blushing? I made him blush! "Which is...?"

"Kekoa."

"See. Was that so hard?" she trailed her fingers over his huge bicep. His muscles seemed chiseled from stone.

"Not at all," he murmured. His low voice was a seductive caress to her ears. It melted her insides, and clenched her pussy with anticipation.

Marcy couldn't believe she'd put condoms in her bag, but it was better to be safe than sorry. They both wore swimsuits with the intention of walking the beach together after their lunch date. Chloe and Astrid were attending a series of mother-daughter art projects at one of the activity centers, freeing Marcy for most of the day. Prepared for anything, Marcy carried a souvenir tote bag on her shoulder with her camera, a couple lenses, a towel, and a change of clothing.

"We are here."

Colorful, thick pillows covered the ground in an open cabana before them. Beside it, a bucket held a chilled bottle of Prosecco. Their date location was charming yet simple. Marcy's brows rose. "Did you have one of your employees arrange this?"

"No. I did it. Chloe told me you have a fondness for dragon fruit and other rare delicacies." He gestured to a carved wooden bowl piled high with papaya, pink dragon fruits, and strawberries alongside others Marcy didn't recognize.

Marcy removed her shoes and lowered herself to the cushions. Each one cradled her body like heavenly clouds, molding to her curves, pliant, but firm enough to support her lazy sprawl. Her beach coverup shifted to her mid-thigh and she had the pleasure of watching Teo's eyes rove over her legs.

He surprised her with a small cooler of cocktail shrimp and sauce, then surpassed her expectations again when he sliced the various fruits and offered her tidbits with his fingers. The time passed in pleasant talk about their surroundings and quiet observations. Marcy lifted her camera and snapped a few shots of the occasional monkey wandering near to investigate them. One had a baby clinging to its back, prompting Marcy to coo at its cuteness.

"It is a shame you are barren. I have seen you with Astrid and you seem quite capable with her."

"Barren?" Marcy queried, voice rising in pitch. "Why do you assume I'm barren?"

"Is it not a human woman's place to be in the home with her offspring? I assumed your failure to acquire a mate indicated you were barren."

So I have to be sterile to decide against having a husband and kid? What the fuck? "Screw you and your sexist bullshit," Marcy hissed at him between her teeth. She crawled to her feet in an impetuous decision to stalk away. Teo rose to pursue her.

"Wait—" Teo reached out and grabbed her wrist. His fingers were like iron bars molding around her limb, anchoring her in place and also cutting off the circulation to her hand.

"Ow!" Her other hand came up and smacked his cheek, stinging her palm.

"I barely touched you!" he growled back at her.

"You are a dragon! Did it ever occur to you I'm not as sturdy because I'm not a supernatural creature? You can't grab humans on a whim, even Saul knows better." *And why does something about his incredible ignorance to his own strength turn me on?* "Is that the first time you've touched a human woman like this?"

Teo's silence was an answer in its own right. She peered up at him through the difference in height, barely reaching his chest. "Yes," he gritted out after a delay. "And you have my apologies for any pain I have caused you."

"Only you could make an apology sound like you're being asked to drink *snake venom*."

Teo glowered down at her. He opened and shut his mouth a few times, comically searching for a retort, only to glare at her in silence instead. The muscle in his cheek jumped. "You are infuriating."

"And you're—"

His lips crashed against her mouth. With no warning given, Teo's ferocity caught Marcy off guard and her fingers flew to his shoulders to push him away. They curled into his shirt instead then she smoothed the garment back from his body and down his arms.

Marcy snatched at the velcro closure of his board shorts and tore it open. His shorts fell to his ankles a moment later, revealing Teo in all of his nude glory to her again. She broke the kiss to stare down at his erection, and when she dared to skim upward over his perfect torso to find his face, she found him watching her intently with a hint of a rise to the corner of his mouth.

"You did not answer when I asked before. Am I to your expectations?"

"Who says I expected anything," Marcy fired back, but her slowly exhaled breath betrayed her. She ran her fingers slowly over his abs, tracing the dips of his muscles and the hard planes making his six-pack. She didn't dare to touch his cock, no matter how it swayed in front of her, enticing and larger than any she'd seen in all of her sexually active life.

Teo peeled the clothes from her curvy body and dragged her swimsuit down her thighs. On his way back up, he kissed the top of her slit and lingered. She tangled her fingers in his immaculate mane of black hair and cried out when his tongue split her folds. A spark of electricity combusted and spread through her nerves like fire. Teo coaxed her down to the pillows with ease then his dark hair fanned over her thighs as his tongue performed an intimate dance, darting between her lips.

Holy shit, he knows what he's doing.

Teo circled her clit with his tongue, then sucked the swollen nerve bundle between his lips. Her hips jerked up and she cried out an impassioned plea for more. His hand smoothed up and down her thigh, squeezing and palming her flesh. By the time his mouth made its ascending path to her breast, both nipples had tightly budded, hard as pebbles beneath his exploring fingers.

"Are you ready for me?"

"Fuck yes," she breathed out. "Just… wait a second."

Marcy dragged her tote bag closer and fumbled inside. She removed a condom and ripped open the foil before raising her eyes to find Teo staring at her, his inquisitive features filled with lust.

"What is that?"

"It's called a condom. I put it on your—"

Teo snorted. "I know what it is and where it goes. Why must we use one?"

"Uh… because if we don't, we'll end up like Saul and Chloe. Because as far as I know, I am *not* barren."

"Is the thought so displeasing?"

A kiss to his firm pectoral muscle provided an excuse to remain quiet. Marcy took the lead and slid the latex ring over his cock. He pumped in her hand, a groan leaving him as his fingers slipped between her own bare thighs.

"I need to be inside you," he said, voice thickened with lust. "I want to feel you." Two digits stroked her outer folds then curled to test her wet channel. Marcy shuddered and yanked him back down to the cushions with her.

With her legs around his waist and her dark hair spread over the cushions, Teo lowered his manly bulk to her body. His dick bumped against her inner thigh until Marcy reached between them and guided him within her slick entrance. He surged forward, burying himself until their pelvises met. They moaned together in blissful harmony at the completion of his next stroke.

"You *are* to my expectations," Teo whispered huskily against her ear. "Perfect."

She shivered and pressed one heel to his ass, urging him deeper. Her snatch was so wet for him that he slipped in and out without difficulty, clapping their bodies close on each thrust.

Her dragon lover took his time, unhurried and unrushed. The sweet penetration stretched her to the limit until her eyes rolled back in her head and a guttural groan parted her lips. The base of his dick rubbed her clit, bringing her close to orgasm. He took her to the brink and held her over the edge.

"I'm so close, Teo. So close." The tightening sensation in her core lingered and blossomed, an unbearable tease she endured.

He drove into her harder. With his weight propped upon one elbow, Teo gazed down at her luscious body. Her squeezed one weighty breast in his other hand then curved his spine until his lips reached the tip. Her pussy tightened around his dick, eliciting a growl from his throat.

"You feel amazing," Teo hissed between his teeth. "Better than… than…" God, she wanted him to finish his sentence, but he never did. He drove into her harder, jostling Marcy until her breasts shook and

259

trembled.

His pounding thrusts hurled her into an intense orgasm that curled her toes and tightened every muscle in her body. As she cried out in ecstasy Teo didn't slow until his own grunts announced his release. For a moment, Marcy loathed the condom between them, denying her the hot rush she craved.

Teo lay heavily over her, his face buried against her sweaty throat and his chest heaving. Marcy wasn't any better. Her exhausted body protested any idea of moving from beneath him, limbs too weak to even nudge the dragon off of her.

After their heaving breaths quieted, Teo rolled to the side onto his back. Marcy slid the condom off of his softening length and tucked it neatly into the torn package. Without a trash can at hand, she placed it into her bag, only to be drawn into her dragon's arms and held close.

They chose silence over awkward pillow talk and after-sex conversation, caressing each other, kissing, and nipping playfully until a second condom was needed. She didn't think it was possible for sex to be any better than their first time, but Teo's relentless pace proved otherwise. At the end, Marcy couldn't do anything but succumb to the blissful peace of sleep.

She awoke to the slanting rays of the late afternoon sun shining on her face. Teo wasn't beside her but she spotted him at the nearby spring. He had dressed, so she slipped into her own before wandering out to join him.

"Was your rest pleasant?"

"It was. Did you sleep?"

"For a short while. Your phone has been ringing. Chloe, I believe."

Marcy swore under her breath. "Crap, yeah. We had plans for dinner and drinks with someone from Saul's studio."

"Then we should return."

"Okay…" Marcy had expected something different. A request to stay maybe, or his usual careless directive. Instead, Teo offered his arm and led the way back toward the resort grounds. As before, he pointed out several animals as they passed through the natural landscape.

"I could have sworn I saw a jaguar moving past those trees," Marcy whispered.

"You did," Teo replied, unconcerned. "I have several on the island."

She turned her face up and stared at him. "Is it safe?"

"It is why areas are restricted, Marcy. They cannot reach the resort and they offer no danger to me." He paused, seeming to consider something, then looked down at her. "Please promise you will not wander alone in search of me."

"Er... sure thing." She had no desire to wind up as cat chow.

Teo punched in a code at a locked gate, waving Marcy through first. The change between sides was subtle. The path widened and transitioned from loose dirt to hard-packed gravel, the plants arranged with an eye for aesthetics rather than growing where they would, and voices drifted on the breeze rather than the chitter of insects and monkeys.

"Um, so... we'll meet in your office to finish the painting? I promised to help Astrid with the sandcastle contest in the morning but I'm free the rest of the day."

"Yes, of course." He leaned in and brushed a light kiss against the corner of her mouth. The simple, affectionate gesture ignited sparks down the length of her spine. "Enjoy your time with Chloe."

When they parted at the hotel, Marcy pinched herself repeatedly. The dream didn't end, a sign her sensual evening with Teo truly took place. Then again, the sore and aching feeling between her thighs was the only proof she needed.

Chapter 6

Marcy arrived to an empty office the following afternoon. A note left on the desk informed her their portrait session would have to wait. Teo had gone off the island for business matters and wouldn't be back until tomorrow.

Disappointment washed over her, leaving a sour taste in her mouth. Rather than return to the beach, she sat behind the desk and booted up the computer. She figured she may as well work on the financials while she had the time.

Once she studied the suspicious account activity and totaled the numbers, Marcy shook her head. Without speaking to Teo, she couldn't verify fraudulent from approved purchases.

Marcy tapped the speed dial button on the intercom phone. A small tag beside it read 'Kekoa'.

"This is the residence of Teotihuacan Arcillanegro. How may I serve?"

"Kekoa, right?"

"Sí, señorita. How may I help you?"

"I have a list of unknown account numbers I'd like to run by you. I need more information, and Teo mentioned you manage most of his finances."

"I will log onto the computer from our home network to assist you."

What a sweet guy, she thought. Conversation between them painted a favorable portrait of Teo's mysterious house servant. Like Saul, Teo also had a shapeshifter in his service, but he'd never elaborated by telling her more about Kekoa's nature.

Once he logged on to the chat program linking the office and home computers, she sent him a list of account numbers and waited for his feedback.

Kekoa: I am familiar with all of these, save for three.

Marcy: I take it that it's unusual for money to disappear to random accounts?

Kekoa: Yes. The first five accounts are private donations to local animal shelters. We give money to them. This next account is to help needy families. Teo dislikes the idea of starving children, so he gives secretly to a few organizations.

Kekoa rambled in text about the good deeds of his master. A smile crept onto Marcy's face. *He loves him.* Together, they eliminated most of the transactions Marcy flagged and Kekoa promised to look into the rest.

"Ugh, I can't believe he went through all this trouble to build a resort business and didn't hire an actual full-time accountant," she muttered to herself after Kekoa logged off. She opened a calculator program and totaled up the missing funds.

Her hunch was right; Teo had lost hundreds of thousands of dollars, spread out over a gross amount of time. Without full access to his accounts, there was nothing to do but catalog a list of the offending transfers.

Marcy took the time to package her findings, lingering in the office with the hope Teo might return at any moment. He didn't, so she left his office before she risked missing her surf lesson on the beach.

***

A young, dark-haired man approached Marcy on the beach the next morning where she lay on a blanket to recover from the previous day's strenuous activities. Under his open, white shirt, he carried the build of a Pacific Islander, thickly muscled and sturdy in frame. Unlike Teo, he wore his hair short.

"Greetings, señorita. I am Kekoa. Master Teo would like to see you in his office if you are free."

"Nice to finally meet you, Kekoa. Sure thing. Could you help me gather my things?"

"Of course."

With Kekoa's help, Marcy packed her belongings away and folded her beach blanket. He carried everything, including the personal tote bag filled with her snacks, laptop, books, and change of clothes.

The blue Spix was the first thing Marcy saw when she stepped inside Teo's office at the administration complex. The bird perched on a stand with a half-eaten peach clutched in one claw. Beside Teo's desk, her easel awaited her, paints positioned in a neat row with her supplies and fresh rags.

"Good afternoon, Marcy." Teo sat behind the desk with his intent

263

gaze on the monitor. "Allow me a moment to complete this then I will sit for you."

"You brought the bird here. To your office."

"You wished to paint one, yes? So I brought her to you." He offered a small, brief smile. Almost shy.

Marcy's gaze caressed his body as he stripped, visually digesting every inch. Teo took up the exact same position as before on the chaise. The parrot answered his call and perched on his bent knee.

Something's different. He's so quiet. The conversational dragon of the first portrait sitting said little and spoke only when addressed.

"Is something on your mind?" she asked.

"Yes."

"I'm a good listener," Marcy prompted.

"It is nothing," he assured her.

"Okay. Well, if you're not going to talk, do you mind if I put on some music?"

He waved a dismissive hand toward the computer, so Marcy crossed behind the desk and found the satellite radio. Within moments, peaceful and relaxing music filled the space.

"Your belly has rumbled twice," Teo interrupted her hours later. "Have a break to order lunch."

"I brought one with me," Marcy said.

"I insist. There is a menu beside the computer you may use to this purpose." With the exception of his generous offer, Teo remained aloof, a quiet, distant man sharing the office with her. A stranger.

Does he regret it? Did he use me? A dozen other thoughts niggled into Marcy's mind until she dismissed them and placed a delivery order for lunch on Teo's dime.

"Would you like anything?"

"No. I hunted and will be fine for some time yet." Teo stroked his fingers down the parrot's wing feathers and offered the bird a nut.

Okay... What crawled up his butt? Marcy sighed and gave up on the attempt to spark conversation. She added a few more details to the artwork while she waited for her meal, which arrived in under ten minutes. She'd never get enough of the café's scallops, but the uncertain mood between her and Teo ruined the taste. Her appetite suffered during the silent lunch. Eventually she put her leftovers in the small fridge behind the desk and moved back to her easel. Painting, at least, occupied her mind and made the passing hours seem to fly.

"All done." Marcy applied a last paint stroke then set her palette aside. It was, without a doubt, the best watercolor she'd ever put to canvas.

Some rich bitch is going to have this. A small stab of jealousy struck her at the thought. She had depicted the stoic man in natural colors, utilizing a photorealistic style to highlight his strong jaw and handsome features. His Spix added a bold splash of color against the brown skin painted on canvas.

"You have great talent." Teo had already pulled on his clothes. "Will it be dry in time for the auction Friday night?"

"Er…" *Fine, he wants to be all professional about this. I can do the same.* "Yes, it should be fine once I seal it. It will need a frame though."

"Already ordered. Kekoa will deliver it tomorrow."

"I prefer to mount and frame my own work."

"As you wish. Do what you must and I will compensate you. Now then, I see you made many organizational changes with my accounts. Are my funds secure?"

His sudden jump from one business matter to another baffled her. He hadn't touched her once and he barely even looked at her.

"Not so much. You're missing large chunks of money, Teo. I've flagged over three dozen different transactions where the numbers don't add up. Each is for a small amount, by your standards anyway — sixty dollars here, a hundred there. They're interspersed in with hundreds of other transactions between your many charities but the bulk of them are drawn from the main umbrella organization."

"Do you know who the thief is?"

"No names, but I do have account numbers. There are three of them in offshore accounts. I don't have the needed access for determining who it is, but there's enough evidence here to report so an investigation can be launched. Kekoa had no record of them. Your friend is very overworked, so please don't blame him."

The quiet dragon regarded her with a tense expression, his jaw clenched. "I do not blame Kekoa."

"Good. I've seen tricks like this before and heard about others. Whoever hit you has stretched this out over a long time, Teo. I only traced it back about a year, but it may have gone on for even longer…" Her voice trailed as she took in Teo's features. He looked scary.

"I should have known better than to trust a mortal with any extension of my horde. This is typical of human monkeys; thieves and liars, taking what is not rightfully theirs!"

"Excuse me?" Marcy stiffened. "Human monkeys? You're calling humans monkeys now?"

"You are right. I've paid an unfair insult to monkeys when humans are rarely more than parasites infecting this Earth," Teo rumbled. His high cheekbones were flushed with color.

"Right. I think it's time for me to go. Here, I printed it all out and highlighted the accounts for Kekoa." She passed over a thick manila folder with a thumb drive taped to the outside. "Everything is also saved on the flash drive there and on a CD I locked away in your drawer. Multiple backup copies never hurt."

"I did not include you in my generalization, Marcy. Your kind are not worthy to have you among their number."

"Save it. This human monkey has a date at the bar."

Marcy claimed her supplies and collapsed her easel without another word to him. Teo stood tall and straight, his face an impassive mask. He gave her no argument. Once she stalked to her suite and jumped into the shower, she scrubbed dried ocean salt and remnants of sand from her skin. She donned the perfect short and flirty dress for a night at the bar.

Maybe she didn't have a date, but she'd be damned if she waited around for a spoiled dragon.

Chapter 7

"Have you seen Teo around anywhere?"

Marcy snapped her gaze to her best friend. "No. Why would I have seen him?"

"I figured since you try to avoid him you'd have noticed if he was around," Chloe replied. She snagged two glasses of wine from a passing waiter and handed one to Marcy.

"Who knows? He's probably off hobnobbing with someone or counting his treasure, or something equally boring." Marcy absently adjusted her dress strap and avoided eye contact. She would have worn the same cocktail dress again as the first night, if Chloe hadn't insisted it would be a fashion faux pas to wear the same thing twice. They made a stunning pair in similar little black dresses.

"Oh well. True, I guess. Saul likes to go count his rubies whenever we have a spat. Anyway, the auction is about to start up."

The banquet hall had been transformed. Neat rows of velvet-cushioned chairs had been filled by the wealthy and influential guests. Marcy and Chloe took seats toward the middle of the room and were offered fresh champagne glasses.

Teo's organization had acquired everything from priceless works of art to decades-old movie props. Rare wine vintages went for thousands of dollars in bidding wars between members of elite society. Their elusive host arrived when the last bottle sold and he personally delivered it to the winning bidder.

"Next up, a portrait," the auctioneer announced as two men carried in a large cloth covered rectangle and set it on a waiting easel. He pulled the covering with a flourish. Quiet murmurs filled the room and more than one lady sighed in sheer appreciation. Several glanced from the intimate portrait to the man who had inspired it. Teo stood at the side of the room, impassive as ever.

"You painted *Teo*?" Chloe hissed, leaning in close against Marcy. "You told me a guy approached you on the beach."

"Which was true. Teo is a guy and he asked me to paint his portrait for this," Marcy mumbled back. The bidding had started in earnest with several ladies already driving the price up to $200,000.

"He's *naked*."

"You can't see anything."

Chloe stared at her then raised her hand.

"Three hundred thousand for the lady in the back," the

auctioneer called out.

"Chloe!" Marcy shot her friend a scandalized look and grabbed her arm, pulling it back down. Someone further up took over the bid at a half-million.

"What? I thought you might like it," Chloe teased. "Or maybe I'd give it to Saul. They're so close he might actually *like* it."

"You bitch." Marcy's shove barely budged Chloe. The dragon's blood flowing in her friend's veins made her more formidable than any human. She couldn't shift like her husband, but her body had undergone irreversible changes during pregnancy, making her stronger and faster.

"Why didn't you tell me?"

Marcy didn't answer. *Because I… didn't want to get your hopes up. I didn't want you to think one day I'd be immortal and forever-young like you, with a man who actually gave a damn about me for more than five minutes.* She sighed. "It was for his charity work. He's still a human-loathing asshole and I wouldn't piss on his flaming corpse after Saul breathed on him."

Chloe twisted in her seat to face her. One of her fair hands lowered to Marcy's bare shoulder. "What did he say to you? Did he insult you again? I swear, I'll find him and kick his ass myself if he—"

"He didn't insult me personally, chica," Marcy interrupted. "Anyway, I don't want to talk about it. It's very obvious he's still the same jerk."

"Okay." Chloe sighed and settled back in her seat. The blonde didn't bid again on the painting, and eventually the marvelous piece sold for a little over a million dollars.

A million dollars, Marcy thought, awestruck. *My painting sold for a million dollars.* The bittersweet moment of watching her donated work sell for such an astronomical amount was spoiled by Teo's changed personality. She had been a fool to trust him. Still, tears streamed down her cheeks until she and Chloe attempted to dab them away.

The next item went on the block, followed by another outside of Marcy's range. Eventually, she raised her hand for a necklace once owned by Italian actress Sophia Loren but the price jumped above her budget within five bids.

"Do you want it?" Chloe whispered.

"Not enough to empty my entire savings account," she replied.

One hundred thousand. Two hundred and fifty thousand.

Chloe raised her hand. A woman adorned in a fur stole shot them both a dirty look and raised her own bidding paddle. Jewels gleamed from her ears, wrists, and neck.

"Chloe, no."

"You love her." She raised her hand again. "We used to spend entire nights watching the same movies over and over during sleepovers."

"Chloe, we were like twelve. I don't love her enough to spend a half million dollars. I liked the Backstreet Boys and N'Sync, but I don't see you buying me Lance Bass as my manservant. He's probably cheaper than—"

"One million dollars. Do we have another bid from Mrs. Drakenstone?" the auctioneer asked.

Their wealthy opponent's husband nudged his wife in the ribs and shook his head. She gave him an offended look in return, her mouth falling open.

"Guess they realized who they were up against." Chloe raised her hand again.

"Sold, to the lovely Mrs. Drakenstone!"

"You can consider this your birthday present. I had a peek in advance at the auction list and phoned Saul about it a couple hours ago. It's from both of us."

Kekoa approached with a wrapped jewelry box. He bowed to the women, placed it in Chloe's hands, and left after a polite greeting. Chloe passed the square box to her friend and kissed her cheek.

"Love you. Now let's pluck some food from those little hors d'oeuvres trays the servers are carrying."

Marcy clutched her new necklace close to her chest, still in a state of disbelief. Chloe had spent an exorbitant amount of money on her without batting an eye. "I can't believe you did this."

"Pfft. *I* can't believe our time is over. This has been an awesome time, Marce. I'm glad you came with me."

Sniffling, the Latina tried to fumble a cloth from her handbag to dab the tears from her cheeks. "Only you would make a million dollar purchase seem like buying a box of Skittles. I'm glad I came along, too. We need to do this again sometime, but uh, somewhere different."

"Paris?" Chloe suggested.

"Forget Paris. Florence, Italy."

Chloe's grin widened. "You wanna go wine tasting."

"That and I'm a sucker for a good pasta. You see these hips? They didn't get this size on their own," Marcy joked.

"So, we'll do some research to see when the best time of the year is to visit Italy. We'll make it another girls' week out," Chloe decided as they meandered toward a server. Once they helped themselves to the delicious, savory finger food, they continued on their rounds to hob nob.

"Saul wants me to pretend to like the people here. He encouraged a lot of film makers and studio execs to come for this, so I'm doing his work for him," Chloe explained.

"How's he holding up anyway since he's without his favorite ladies?"

Chloe rolled her eyes. "He texts every night to say how much he misses us. Astrid is going to totally be a daddy's girl when we return. I'll cease to exist."

"I can't believe you didn't have Mahasti take you back for a romp or two."

Chloe shook her head. "You know what they say. Absence makes the heart grow fonder. We have a long time ahead of us."

"Yeah. You do." *And I'll be gone.* The morose thought threatened to ruin her mood, so Marcy shook it away.

The remainder of the auction took less than an hour. Marcy had never seen so much money waved about in all her life. Their table companions from the first night, Archibald and Helena Galway, walked out with a Ming Dynasty ewer for nearly three million. Teo's charity would be off to an amazing start. The two friends spent another hour mingling before they headed back to their suite, arms linked. Marcy had filled her tummy with fancy appetizers and had a pleasant buzz.

"They have the best chocolate martinis here," Marcy mumbled as they kicked their strappy heels aside and flopped onto the sofa to rest. Her feet ached from the time spent socializing with wealthy business moguls, but she'd ended up passing out her business card to a few Los Angeles executives.

"Running my mouth so long exhausted me. I'm gonna crawl into bed next to Nuri and Astrid. Mahasti's coming for us at 3 PM, so there's time to hit any last minute attractions if we want."

"I know, I know. I think I'm attraction'ed out though."

Once Chloe had gone to bed, Marcy took her birthday gift to the mirror and opened the box. The necklace gleamed against her naturally bronzed skin tone, the brilliant ruby as lovely in person as it was in photos.

A folded piece of cream colored paper fell from the lid as she put it away.

Marcy,

I would like to meet you at the Surf N' Turf Cafe at noon for lunch. If you choose not to come, I will understand, but I ask you to grant me this chance to make amends for my poor behavior.

Teo

Marcy wadded the paper and tossed it into the trash. A few minutes later, she fished it out the can and smoothed it flat again.

"Noon, huh?"

Would it hurt to hear him out? There was only one way to find out.

Chapter 8

Marcy lingered in the cafe's doorway, half hidden behind a hibiscus tree. Everywhere she turned on the island there were flowers, whether planted in vibrant pots or growing wild. It was her favorite part of the resort.

The dragon sat alone at a table for two, his spine erect and features stern. He didn't resemble the jovial figure who laughed and granted her a personal tour of the island's untamed wilderness. The memory of their stroll through the floral growth gave Marcy cause to linger and observe him quietly.

She had yet to see Teo in anything unflattering. His casual khakis and unbuttoned powder blue shirt struck her as more laidback than the dragon they clothed. From afar, she admired the brown strip of skin between both halves of the open shirt, as well as the way shafts of yellow sun highlighted his high cheekbones. He appeared lost in his own world, gazing through the window with a concerned expression on his face.

"Penny for your thoughts?" she asked as she approached.

Teo rose smoothly from his seat. "You came."

"You invited me," Marcy countered.

Pulling out her chair like a proper gentleman, Teo ensured Marcy's comfort before retaking his own seat. "Would you like something to eat? The scallops were pulled from the water this morning."

"Teo. It's a cafe. I came for coffee and a brief talk, not more rich people scallops." Her belly rumbled a second later in defiance of her statement. "Okay... I'd like the scallops," she recanted. They were as addictive as cocaine.

A crook of his finger summoned a waiter in an instant. Teo relayed the order for the both of them then dismissed the server.

"Okay so..." *Cut to the chase, girl,* Marcy chided herself. An afternoon of amazing, jaw-dropping sex didn't mean anything. "Do you plan to tell me why I'm here?"

"I owe you an apology for my behavior. As I mentioned in the note, there is no excuse for how I spoke to you. I was angry, and the violation of my trust hindered my judgment. I ask you to forgive me," Teo said.

"I... I guess if someone stole so much from me, I'd rant and rave a little too. But you were being an asshole before then," Marcy pointed out.

"Yes. I was. I had many things in my thoughts. I am a quiet thinker, Marcy, and do not often voice what is on my mind." He leaned forward and reached to take her hand across the table. His voice lowered, the next statement for her ears alone. "We dragons often take time to consider matters of extreme importance without realizing the world continues to move around us."

"See, if you had said so from the beginning I would have at least had some warning." His touch barely blunted her wariness, and through sheer will, Marcy kept her shields raised.

"I understand."

She stared and waited, expecting some dismissive or haughty words to follow. When none came she cleared her throat and reached for a glass of water with her spare hand.

"Do you plan to tell me what took so much of your concentration that you couldn't open your mouth to talk to me?" she ventured after the waitress delivered her meal.

"Yes. I pondered many things, including our existence together and whether you would allow me to pursue you. I asked myself if I wanted a human, and if I should invite you to stay with me," Teo said.

"Stay with you where?" Marcy withdrew her hand. She spread a linen napkin over her lap then took a bite of her food.

"My home."

"You want me to come to your private residence?" Mercy folded her arms and leveled her eyes at him in disbelief.

"Should that come as a surprise for you?" Teo's bright green eyes mesmerized her, too brilliant a hue against his deeply tanned skin.

She bit her lip and considered her options. With Chloe planning to return home to her husband, Marcy had no reason to remain on the island. She folded her arms against her chest and gazed into the sunlit afternoon.

Temptation and the memory of his lips warred against the common sense telling Marcy to leave. A smarter woman would run away screaming and never return to the billionaire's retreat. Or maybe, a smarter woman would investigate the matter to make an educated decision. "I don't know. Maybe I'm ready to return to work. I've had a great two weeks here with Chloe."

Teo raised both brows. "What matter of importance awaits you greater than my offer of hospitality?"

Marcy shook her head and rose from her seat. Her bouncy skirt

273

shifted around her mid-thigh level, shorter than anything she'd ever worn besides a swimsuit. Chloe had talked her into the impulse buy from one of the resort's shops, but the hope of Teo seeing her in it had prompted her to wear the sexy garment. Deep down, she'd hoped he would see her off.

"No, thanks. Your island is gorgeous, but I need to get back to my life at home. Goodbye, Teo. It's been nice, and I'm glad I helped you out with your business matters."

The dragon abruptly rose from his seat. "Please."

Marcy paused mid-turn and glanced over her shoulder to him.

"Please, Marcy," he said again. "Come back, enjoy your meal, and then stay with me."

Something about his earnest expression gave her reason to stop, but most of all, he'd said the one word she had never heard from his lips. A word she doubted he spoke often at all to anyone.

"All right."

***

"I'm not going back with you to California."

"You want Mahasti to drop you off at your apartment?" A line creased Chloe's brow.

"No, I mean... I'm staying here for another week."

"Oh! I'll have VIP Services charge us for another week."

Marcy nibbled her lower lip. Anxiety fluttered in her belly until she considered calling the entire thing off. For as long as she and Chloe had been best friends, they had shared everything with each other from first kisses to losing their virginity.

"I don't need the room for a week. I'll be at Teo's house."

"Why the hell would you want to stay at Teo's place?"

Marcy cleared her throat and glanced back at the bed. Astrid lay sleeping with a peaceful expression on her youthful face. Her blonde curls fanned over the pillow and a couple tickled the darling child's rosy cheeks.

"It's a long story."

"So summarize it and make it a short one," Chloe encouraged her.

"I kind of had sex with him."

Chloe took one look at her friend, resembling a deer caught in the headlights, then her eyes gradually slid toward her sleeping child. In the next second, she grabbed Marcy by the hand and dragged her into the next room of their suite. Anti-lock brakes wouldn't have saved the Latina from the conversation looming ahead of them.

"What the hell happened? Were you drunk?"

"No... I... It just happened, all right."

"Cocks don't spontaneously just happen to be inside you. Come on. Dish."

Marcy sighed. "It was phenomenal. I mean... I'm pretty sure it was the best sex I've ever had. Which kind of depresses me when I really think about it."

Chloe stared. Her voice escaped in a harsh whisper. "You've lost your mind. What happened to him being a pompous asshole you wouldn't piss on if he was on fire?"

"Pissing on him is definitely out of the question now," Marcy stated dryly.

"Obviously. You've already rubbed your snatch on him instead."

After the ludicrous statement fell from Chloe's lips, the two women burst into a fit of uncontrollable laughter. Marcy giggled until her belly ached. By the end, they were leaning against each other in a half embrace, the last of their snickers dwindling as they caught their breath.

"Oh, sweetie. Are you okay though? Did he bond you to him? You don't smell any different to me."

"Bond me? No. At least, I don't think we've bonded. I remember how you described it, and I don't feel as if I can't be without him, that's for sure. I'd go back with you to California at the drop of a hat, but I'm..."

"Curious?" Chloe asked. "If you're only a little curious then I don't think you're bonded to him. If you were, you'd definitely know. Saul bonded to me the very first time. I was missing him from the moment I got home, like I'd made the biggest mistake of my life."

"Don't remind me. You sulked around like someone killed Felix in front of you. You were depressing to be around."

Chloe's blush pinkened her whole face. "I wasn't that bad."

"You were the biggest buzzkill ever. If you didn't agree to go seek him out, I would have bundled you up into my car trunk and kidnapped you across state lines to find him myself."

"Be safe, okay? I love you, Marce."

"Be safe?"

Chloe raised her brows suggestively and mimed putting on a condom. Marcy shoved her. "What? I'm just saying. Maybe I do make

275

fun a little about wanting you to... to be here forever with me," she confided, her voice dropping to a whisper. "But I wouldn't wish what I went through with Astrid on anyone unprepared." Chloe wiped her cheeks quickly with the back of her hand. Human bodies weren't meant to bear anything but humans. The incredible duration of her pregnancy had weakened Chloe severely. She came close to hemorrhaging to death, and the scarring to her womb ensured she'd never have another child.

"This is a real bummer of a topic, chica. I'm only 34. We have decades together. And if I do have a kid one day, I want it to be because I'm ready and I want a baby. Not because it's some fast track to achieving immortality. You and Saul are different. You were meant for each other. I can see it in his face every time he looks at both of you."

"I love him so much, I only want the same for you. Teo is an asshole and..." Chloe shook her head a few times. "You can handle yourself. Ignore me. If he's out of line, I have faith you'll put him in his place."

"I will, and I have."

Chloe's brow wrinkled. "Okay, fine. Enjoy hot dragon sex in the meantime. When you're ready to join us in California or get back home to Texas, send me a text and I'll have Mahasti come for you."

"Sounds like a deal. I promise, if he does anything I don't like, I'll put him in his place."

Chapter 9

Prior visits to Saul's mountainside estate had prepared Marcy for a sprawling mansion tucked within an island. What she found instead provoked contradicting feelings of pleasure and disappointment. Teo didn't live in a majestic manor; he dwelled in a spacious bungalow nestled between the trees. Solar panels gleamed from the roof as they approached the modest one-story home.

Marcy lingered on the stone walkway and tried to find bits of Teo in the architecture. "I thought it would be bigger," she admitted.

"Is my home dissatisfying?"

"No," Marcy blurted out quickly. "It's very nice. I thought you'd go for large and roomy like Saul." *Where the hell does he keep his hoard around here?* she wondered.

"Hahaha, no. This is a home for my servant and guests such as you. Oftentimes visitors come when it is necessary to pretend I am human."

"So... you sleep in your hoard."

Teo nodded, confirming one was nearby but out of her sight. She didn't think it could be below ground under the house, so she twisted to scan the surroundings. A tall peak covered in thick green foliage rose up from the center of the island, dominating the skyline.

"It's there, isn't it?" *I hope that's not some sort of volcano.*

"Astute observation, Marceline."

"I will go home if you call me Marceline."

"Saul addresses you as such."

"Yeah, well, he's allowed. No one but Saul and my mother call me Marceline." *Even if it actually sounds sexy coming from you, big guy.*

While lacking the wealthy design of Saul's multi-million dollar estate, Marcy found a certain charm to its quaint interior. She removed her shoes and stepped forward as Kekoa hurried to meet them.

Teo and his apparent manservant spoke in a flowing, lyrical language she didn't understand, then the man stepped forward to take her bag. She shook her head and waved him off after a friendly smile.

"What language was that?" she asked once Kekoa was gone.

"Hawaiian. I met him on the island of Maui nearly fifteen years ago. He was a child then."

"So his mother allowed you to just take her baby?"

"His mother had been killed for her teeth and her fins."

"Oh." She hadn't expected such a sad story.

"Did you believe I had stolen a child?"

Chagrined, Marcy nodded and let out a brief, nervous chuckle to relay her discomfort with the situation. Every time she thought she had a bead on him, he proved her wrong.

Am I looking for flaws so I have a reason to ditch him and tell Chloe this was a dumb idea? The thought flit through her mind, a sudden realization that twisted her insides. She was trying to doom Teo to fail before he ever had his chance.

Teo surprised her a third time with a personal tour. Part of her had expected their path to head to the bedroom straightaway, certain he'd invited her only for the sake of fulfilling his long-forgotten sexual appetites.

"I entertain many business partners and humans here, so you will find no shortage of human comforts. Through this doorway, you will find the kitchen. Kekoa is an excellent chef, and capable of making whatever you require."

Marcy nodded and followed at his side, hoping to walk off the antsy feeling churning in her gut. "What about the bathroom. Do you have a big tub like the ones at Saul's manor?"

"I have better, and will show you soon once we take a tour of the island. First, you must be rid of this suitcase." Teo took her by the hand and led her to his private bedroom. Again, he took her by surprise, his lack of opulence contrasting the extravagant displays in Drakenstone manor. She stared with wide eyes at the simple king-size bed, ivory walls, and the cool, Caribbean-blue accents adding the occasional splash of color. An enormous sliding glass door yielded a fabulous view of the island's white coral shoreline.

Teo gave her ample time and space to unpack then resumed their tour. The household design strove for quality over quantity, with a small number of spacious, tastefully decorated rooms. He introduced her to the bathroom where a magnificent shower awaited her beside an enormous, square-shaped tub. Water rained from above at a speed and force determined by the user.

Dragons seem to love water, she thought.

The tub didn't surprise her, but his movie room did, as if he and Saul were in competition to have the best home theater. When he opened the door and led her inside, Marcy's eyes widened at the twenty-foot-wide curved screen. She descended the stairs and marveled at the sheer size. In lieu of traditional theater seating, the front row had a roomy lounger large enough for two.

"You have your own movie theater?"

"I enjoy them. Saul sends many to me once they are prepared for the movie theaters. I own every production he has ever made." A rare smile crept over Teo's face when he spoke of his friend.

"That's... actually pretty awesome," Marcy said. "You guys are so close."

"I have known Saul since he was a young cub. Our mothers were very close friends. Are very close friends." He frowned. "His mother sleeps, but we hope she will awaken within the next century."

"The next... century?" Marcy's eyes grew a little rounder as he took her into the next area. The spotless kitchen needed a woman's touch, dull and lifeless. She opened and closed the cabinets in passing to find a variety of exotic spices. The stocked fridge held exquisite cheeses, yogurt, bottled fruit juices, and packaged deli meats. Marcy eyeballed a carton of yogurt. *He has my favorite flavor.*

"The loss of a bondmate is devastating. She will remain in hibernation until the pain has dulled," he explained. "Until then, we wait for her to return to us."

Marcy shut the fridge then slipped her fingers into Teo's hand, pleased when he delivered an appreciative squeeze in return.

"Enough of sad things. I have one final thing to show to you," Teo said.

Once they were outside with the cool stone beneath Marcy's bare feet, Teo led her through a set of wide glass doors onto a stone walkway. Lush, untamed plant life bordered either side, while colorful orchids provided bright dots of color from hanging vines. Palms, bamboo, and multi-colored hibiscus created a private escape and perfumed the balmy air.

"It's so beautiful. So... why did you ask for me to join you? What do you want from me, Teo?"

"I can no longer say," he confessed. "I know when you are with me, I enjoy your smile." His fingers rose to touch her cheek, only to slide down and cup her chin. "You are different from any human woman I have met with exception of Saul's mate."

Marcy's heart skipped a beat. "How are we different?"

"You are like female dragons. Fierce and strong. You do not bend to us." His mouth lowered to her collarbone.

"I think you'd find most women aren't meek sheep if you actually paid attention to them."

"Why would I wish to pay attention to anyone but you?" Teo's words husked against Marcy's ear in a gentle breath then the warm play of his fingers molded to her ass. He coaxed her closer until they

279

were flush together, trapping his cock between their bodies. His flowy beach attire disguised nothing.

"You would be exquisite wearing nothing more than your new necklace." His lips lingered over the fluttering pulse point at her throat.

"I want to see you again first." *And enjoy the view.*

"As you wish, Marcy." Teo stepped back from her and shrugged out of his shirt. His pants fell next, confirming her suspicion that he never wore undergarments. "Your turn."

"Out here?"

"This is a private island and my personal refuge. You are safe here, Marceline."

God, my name shouldn't sound so sexy. In his low, sensual voice, it became easier to tolerate the offending name. "Okay. Fine." With warm cheeks, she removed her dress and set it aside on a low hanging branch.

"And those," Teo murmured. He curled his fingers into the waist of her panties. The touch made her shiver in anticipation. Crouching low, her lover dragged them down her thighs and exposed her to the humid jungle air. His lips pressed against her pussy, a teasing kiss that caused her to grasp a handful of his hair.

"I'm starting to think you want me naked so you can have your wicked way with me."

Teo's chuckle huffed warm air across her swollen clit. Marcy's grip on his hair tightened and her knees went weak. Her dragon's teasing continued in an upward trail of slow, nibbling kisses. His teeth grazed over her hips, his tongue dipped into her navel, and then he lavished each breast with a suckle before moving up to her neck and finally her lips.

"Come. Let me show you my home," he whispered. Marcy had better ideas in mind, ones which included becoming acquainted with his bed, but his eager expression swayed her.

"I'd love to see your home, Teo."

Unhindered by clothing, the pair walked hand in hand down the pathway snaking between the trees. A golden face popped out of the bush to watch them. More jaguars.

"You have a fascination with jaguars, I see."

"Many have found refuge on my islands. They come from places where they were kept as pets or mistreated. Here, they are allowed to be free creatures again with no cages to hold them captive."

"Will they hurt me?"

Teo shook his head. "Doubtful. I will acquaint you to each of them as we cross paths. The one in the woods is Aurelio. Sooner or later, he will become curious enough to approach you. Treat him with respect and he will return it. Philomena is his mate, and you will cross paths with her at some point. She is friendlier and more trusting. It is unusual for jaguars to form mated pairs, but these two have chosen not to separate."

Something tickled Marcy's skin. She shrieked and jerked back and to the side, reflex raising her hand to swat her bare shoulder. Teo caught her wrist with a gentle touch then kissed her knuckles.

"It is a butterfly, Marceline, and means no harm to you."

Her chest heaved with frightened breaths, but the delicate insect on her shoulder hadn't moved.

"It scared the hell out of me."

"It is said among our kind that butterflies are messages from the ancestors, smaller pieces of their souls guiding approval to their descendants. When a butterfly visits, we know we remain in their thoughts."

Marcy blinked up at him. "That's beautiful," she murmured. The blue morpho lifted off and fluttered high into the canopy. She watched it go, wearing a quiet smile on her face.

The peace was short-lived. Marcy didn't realize Kekoa was behind them until he spoke up. "Master, I have brought drinks. Also, a phone call for you has come from Galway's lawyers regarding the theft—"

With a startled shriek, the feisty brunette leapt into the bushes and out of sight, her big breasts quivering every second of her frantic effort to take shelter from Kekoa's eyes. She leaned her head out from behind a wide tree to find the shifter and her dragon staring at her, peculiar expressions on their handsome faces.

"Señorita, are you well?" Kekoa asked. He held a pair of glasses in his hand, filled with a colorful, tropical concoction of some kind.

"I'm perfectly fine," she gritted out between her teeth.

Kekoa and Teo spoke at length about criminal charges until the servant collected the necessary information. Once he was gone, the dragon turned to face her and offer a glass.

"Why did you hide when my attendant arrived?" The genuine curiosity in his tone prompted Marcy to peer at him with mirrored confusion.

"Because I'm *naked.*"

"As am I. What does it matter?"

"It matters because I. Am. Naked." Marcy ground out. "I'm not

281

sure if the rest of your dragon buddies failed to tell you this, but most of us people don't wander around freely without a stitch of clothing on."

Marcy grabbed her dress and hurried down the path back toward the house, Teo hot on her heels.

"My island is completely private. Kekoa and I are the only ones here who can see you." The point flew over his head. In a way, it was almost adorable that he didn't grasp the problem with their situation.

She didn't stop until she reached his bedroom and the privacy it offered. She took a long sip from her fruity drink before she turned around and faced her wary, bewildered dragon.

"I do not understand the issue."

Marcy sighed. "Look, let me make this crystal clear for you. I've agreed to let *you* see me naked. Not your help, no matter how cute he is."

The corner of Teo's mouth twitched, threatening to rise into an actual smile. "You think Kekoa is cute."

"Don't you change the subject." Marcy poked him in his chest to punctuate her words, only to lay her palm flat against his chiseled pectoral muscle. She stroked him afterward and slid her fingers down to his abs. Why was he so irresistible?

Teo frowned. "My apologies, Marceline. Kekoa is accustomed to bringing refreshments before or during—"

"You have your attendant bring you drinks and snacks while you're fucking?" Marcy asked incredulously.

"Executive meetings," Teo finished. An awkward air hung between them, as heavy as the leaden lump forming in Marcy's belly. "I have never indulged in this home."

The quiet deafened her, an awkward lull severing what could have been playful conversation. "You will now." Marcy eased the tropical cocktail from his hand and took a deliberately long drink. "Do you trust me?" she asked.

Teo's silence provided the only answer she needed. Marcy's elation popped.

"Right. I guess I shouldn't be surprised," she sighed. Why had she agreed to come?

"If I did not trust you, would I bring you to my home?" he asked evenly. She picked out a hint of strain to his voice, something unfamiliar.

No, it wasn't unfamiliar. It was pain. She'd hurt his feelings.

"Teo, I'm sorry. I'm not being fair to you," she murmured. "I haven't been fair since we arrived."

He grunted and declined to respond again.

"Let's play a game."

Her challenge piqued his curiosity. "Do you wish to play cards? Chess?"

Teo's ignorance made Marcy giggle. "Not that sort of game."

"Then what do you wish to play?"

"The kind of game where you do everything I tell you to do," she clarified, flashing him an impish smile. "Which is why I asked if you trust me."

Teo eyed her with skepticism. "It does not resemble any game I've played, but I will acquiesce."

"Good. Now, go lay down."

He did as she requested, though a frown furrowed his brow as he played along. His willingness to humor her counted in his favor.

Marcy knelt beside him on the mattress, and with a bit of leather, she secured Teo's wrists above his head. Even tied to the bed, the regal presence about him never faded.

"I could snap these cords at any time," Teo muttered. He glanced to the left and right at the leather binding his wrists to the headboard.

Without a stitch of clothing on him, Marcy returned to her original assessment of Teo, the one she'd made years ago during their first meeting. He looked like an Aztec warrior, his body built with strong sinew and muscle beneath flawless golden brown skin. His dark hair fanned against the pillow behind his head, sleek and smooth as silk.

"Do that and I'll just have to put my clothes back on and leave." Teo appeared torn between obedience and rebellion. The tension left his muscles as she circled his left nipple with the tip of her finger. "Much better. You can surrender a little of your control to me, can't you?"

"I want to be inside you."

"And you will be, very very soon," Marcy promised. She craved the way he filled her pussy, stretching her just right. "You have one job, Teo. If you break those leather cords, our game is over. If you're good…" She dipped her head and traced her tongue over his swollen length. When she reached the tip, she circled the smooth head. He shuddered and tensed anew. "I'll reward you."

"You are a vixen," he accused.

"Your vixen," she replied. Teasing Teo became her favorite game, a finely balanced line of exploring his body and denying her own

283

desires. Once Marcy suppressed the craving to have him inside her, she straddled his thighs and placed her lips against his taut abdomen. Her fingers danced over his skin, tracing the dark treasure trail dividing his chiseled abs until she reached the silky black triangle surrounding his cock. It twitched in anticipation.

"I want to learn something new about you, Teo. Tell me something you want. Something you've had on your mind," Marcy whispered. Bent above him, her worshipful pose placed her lips in the perfect place to seal at the base of his shaft. She teased the eager thump of his pulse then kissed his heavy balls.

He released an unintelligible moan.

"Tell me," she insisted. Her fingers skimmed his cock, finding him as rock hard and ready as she remembered. She pumped him twice in her fist and chuckled when he began fucking her hand. She released him. "Tsk, I didn't say you were allowed to move."

"Marcy—"

"You're being a very bad dragon. I think you want me to go back to the main island."

"No," he groaned up to her. His belly tensed and sweat beaded his brow. Her tortured lover was at her mercy, the difficult past long behind them.

I tamed a dragon, Marcy thought, fascinated by the longing in her lover's expression. "There has to be something you've wanted."

"I've wanted… I want you to take me in your mouth," Teo pleaded.

"Is that your wish?" she teased, emulating his speech.

"Yes!" he shouted. "Please."

The word "please" from Teo's lips became the sexiest word to ever grace her ears. She shivered in delight and dipped her head again, bringing his cock within reach of her mouth. With her fingers around the base, she angled him toward her lips and glided her tongue over the veined underside.

Just when Teo's body rippled with tension and threatened to break the cords, her lips parted to take the soft tip between them. Her tongue circled his crown, teasing a droplet of precum from his slit. One inch at a time, she took his majestic dick until half its length disappeared. She slid off of him with a noisy pop.

"I want to touch you," he groaned. "I want to touch you and m—"

"Fuck me," she breathed down to him. "Humans don't mate,

Teo. Say it."

Marcy teased her lips over his sensitive tip again, drawing a shudder from his body. "No. I want to... I want to make love to you," Teo breathed.

The unexpected admission stung Marcy's eyes with tears. "I want the same."

"Then untie me."

"Not yet. Soon," she promised.

After Marcy rolled the condom over his cock, she lowered her body into place, allowing him to fill her in slow increments. The sensation of being stretched felt as wonderfully delicious as their first time.

"Marceline," he groaned. "I *need* to touch you. Free me from these bonds."

"Snap them," she ordered.

Teo popped the bindings and took ahold of her hips. She remained atop him in the dominant position, but his fingers curled over her brown skin and secured her in place. They moved together, and within seconds, found their frenzied rhythm. Marcy bounced atop his pelvis, plunging his dick in and out.

"Stop, stop," he gasped, holding her in a white knuckled grip. Marcy froze atop him and leaned forward on her elbows. Smoldering green eyes gazed back at her when she kissed his lips.

"What's wrong?"

"I am... not ready to finish."

While Teo recuperated and came down from the approach of his early climax, Marcy traced her fingers over his smooth pecs. He touched her in return, curious and even delighted as he squeezed one full breast in his hand.

"Slower," he murmured against her nipple. "I wish to savor every minute."

The rest of their time passed as a sensual haze. They didn't fuck; they made love sweetly, slow, dragging out each thrust until they reached their limit. Marcy came first when the inquisitive dragon's thumb sought her clit, rubbing her until orgasm clenched her pussy tight around his dick.

Teo loosed an unintelligible moan and held her tight. Every muscle stood out in sharp definition as he tensed and ground against her. They both sank to the sheets in a sweaty heap of tangled limbs.

"Holy shit," she gasped when she had enough breath. "That was amazing."

"Were you not pleased before?"

285

"Mmm. No, I was plenty pleased, but you did some new stuff this time around."

"I learned from videos," he confessed. "I wanted to be pleasing to you, so I watched many."

Marcy erupted into a fit of giggles.

"You find me amusing?"

"I find the idea of you watching pornos in your private movie theatre amusing. I find you—" She dipped forward and kissed him. "—Impossibly sexy."

"Then let me show you more," he whispered, a husky promise.

Marcy gladly offered herself up as his captive audience.

***

Marcy stirred to the sound of Teo returning to the bedroom with a tray. He served her midnight breakfast in bed, her meal beneath a silver cover. He'd also poured her a tall glass of OJ and provided a small dish of sweet jam.

"What's all this?"

"I wanted to surprise you," the proud dragon informed her. "You were asleep, and Kekoa is not here to cook our dinner. I dismissed him to act in my stead regarding a few matters. We understood it brought you discomfort to roam nude while he was present."

Sweet! Finally, a man who can cook. Matt had dismal luck in the kitchen, and the boyfriend before him had talent he was too lazy to share. Teo's eagerness to provide for her touched Marcy deeply.

She raised away the silver lid to inspect the contents of her plate. Undercooked scrambled eggs sat beside oily French toast. The bacon was almost raw, crispy in the middle and white at the ends, drowning in its own grease.

She didn't smell cinnamon under the pool of maple syrup drowning everything. In fact, she thought she smelled garlic. Teo's earnest expression prompted her to try a mouthful of toast.

Oh my God. It's awful. Do I taste Worcestershire sauce?

Marcy struggled to keep the unappetizing bite of food in her mouth and chewed until her eyes watered. Defeated, she spit it all into her napkin. Only a masochist could have swallowed it down.

Teo's smile faded. "What is wrong?"

"What did you put in this?"

"Kekoa told me garlic is good on everything."

"Not on French toast, baby. No." One look at his crestfallen expression encouraged her to try the eggs. They were saltier than the ocean. "Ugh, no."

"But Chloe says my eggs are good."

"Chloe *lied*."

"But her plate was clean."

"Teo, baby, I am pretty sure she dumped her plate when your back was turned."

His downtrodden features reminded her of a sad puppy. Even pouting he was adorable.

"Hand me my robe, sweetie?" Her sulky dragon handed her the requested garment and she donned it before heading into the kitchen. Marcy emptied the unsalvageable mess of eggs and bacon into the trash then she helped herself to his fridge.

"Come here," she called him. "You don't watch what Kekoa does in the kitchen, do you?"

"I have never had reason to learn." Teo eased into place beside her.

"Then you'll watch me today. Thank you for cooking for me. I do appreciate it *greatly*, but you're going to learn the right way now." Her kiss to his forlorn face, sweet and brief as it was, restored some of the enthusiasm she'd stolen with her honesty.

"You are welcome, my love."

Once she spread fresh bacon over the broiler pan and placed it in the oven, she whipped eggs, milk, sugar, and cinnamon into a bowl for the French toast. She walked him step by step, both surprised and pleased with how easily Teo took instructions.

"What you use to season one meal doesn't necessarily season another, okay? What you put on the toast would have been great for say, a burger or a steak."

Teo surprised her the next day with another meal, a perfected clone of his failed attempt. He did it again for dinner when he served perfectly seared steaks and baked potatoes loaded with cheese. The contrast between meals confused her until Teo confessed he'd overheard her lamenting Kekoa's absence over the phone to Chloe.

"How the hell did you learn to make steak when I had to teach you to cook eggs and toast?"

"I watched Food Network."

"Let me get this straight. You watched porn, but you never watched a cooking show until now... and you did so because you overheard me telling Chloe I'm starved?"

"I have never needed to cook for anyone until now."

"Yeah, well, as quick as you pick things up I think I may have to sit you down for a Food Network marathon. You'll out-cook them all in no time."

The smile Marcy had come to love returned to his proud features.

And then she realized it wasn't only his smile she'd fallen in love with.

Chapter 10

The days passed in bliss and passion, establishing a deeper friendship where there had been only lust before. They snorkeled in the crystal blue water, cooked together, and spent every night wrapped in each other's arms.

At the end of their first week together, Marcy phoned her boss in Texas. She couldn't tear herself away from Teo to return the plain world of finances and numbers.

"Marcy, is everything okay? Are you well?" Howard's concerned voice filled her with guilt.

"I'm not hurt or sick. I'm just..." Marcy glanced toward the prowling jaguar at the edge of the veranda. One of Teo's juveniles crept out and crawled onto the lounger to join her. "I'm still in the islands. I've never lied to you, and I won't now. I met someone very special while here so I'm not sure if I'll return in a week."

"A man?"

Marcy glanced at Teo. He sprawled beside her with a magazine in his hands, researching resorts around the world. If he paid attention to her end of the conversation, he didn't show it. "Yes," she replied.

"Marcy, please be careful, sweetheart. So many things happen to young girls vacationing away from home these days, especially when strange men are involved," Howard fussed, a perpetual father figure who looked out for her more than her actual dad.

"I met him a few years ago, but we're just getting acquainted for real this time," she assured him. "Do you remember my best friend Chloe?"

"How could I forget Chloe? What a wonderful girl."

"Well, I met him through her husband. They're best pals."

"Ah, I see."

"He owns the island and the resort," Marcy added quickly.

Howard choked. She imagined him in the midst of a brandy sip. "He certainly sounds successful, Marcy. I am happy for you. Please, take as long as you need. I meant it when I told you to do what was best for you."

"Thanks. I appreciate it, Howard." Marcy took in a deep breath and slowly released it. "Lately, I'm feeling like I should start my own business as a financial consultant. It's possible I won't be coming back to the company *at all*, and I thought you deserved to know."

"I feared you might say that. I'll begin to conduct interviews for your position while hoping it won't be necessary. Take care of yourself, Marcy. You're more than my employee. You're a friend."

"Thanks, Howard." *Ouch. I guess Katie isn't working out after all. So much for her claims about being able to do my work standing on her head.*

Clad in only a thin silk robe, Marcy crawled onto Teo's lap and straddled him. When out of the office, he devoted his free time to a lazy lifestyle of books and socializing with the animals near his home. She also learned of his nocturnal lifestyle, meaning their days of activity weren't natural. As they spent time together, her dragon grew lazier and more exhausted during the mornings.

"What would you like to do today, Marceline?" he asked.

"You don't have to do this for me. If you'd rather sleep, I can wait until the afternoon when you're more coherent."

"I slept during the night," Teo said.

"Poorly. I felt you moving a few times. You were so restless." She wrapped a lock of his dark hair around her index finger then ran her fingers through the rest of his tidy mane.

Teo shrugged and waved off her concern. "It is nothing. An adjustment is all. Now, will you answer my question and tell me what you would like to do?"

"Well... there is one thing."

"Anything," he vowed. His hands slid over her hips, traced her ribs, then traveled down again to cup her ass in his palms. Her dragon pressed her against the hard tension beneath, jutting from his naked crotch.

As much as I love it that he never seems to wear clothes here, he really makes it impossible to hold a conversation. Marcy raised her hips before he could slyly reintroduce his cock to her body. Sex would only distract her. "I want to see *you*. I want to see you in your natural body."

Hesitation flit across his features, accented by his prolonged silence. "Why?" Teo asked after a few awkward seconds passed.

"If I can adapt to walking around your island naked, you can show me who you really are, Teo."

"You are wearing a robe."

"But with nothing beneath it," Marcy pointed out. She gave him a cheeky smile. "Anyway, I want to see you. Fair is fair."

The confusion faded, transitioning between caution and bewilderment to something foreign and different from what Marcy had become accustomed to as she learned to read him. Modesty. Her dragon was shy.

"Of course," he murmured before he lifted her from his lap and stood. "You will want to come with me to the beach."

What the hell got into him? Is he shy or something? she wondered. Their path took them away from the bungalow and through the heavy growth, between trees, over mossy soil, and through the natural fauna that made up his exotic paradise. As they stepped barefoot onto the sand, Teo turned to face her with the same strange expression.

"You are sure of this?"

"Yes.

"Most humans become terrified at the sight of a dragon."

"Teo. I was there when Chloe fought Brigid. Hell, I was there the day Brigid and Saul went toe to toe on his lawn. I'm sorry, but the dragon-seeing cherry was popped five years ago."

A low chuckle escaped the nervous dragon. "It is not the same. When Saul and Brigid revealed their forms to you, you were not alone. You were safe with others present, yes? When Chloe faced Brigid, Watatsumi, Mahasti, Leiv, and even I stood beside you as guards. When a lone human faces a dragon, something happens. It overwhelms the fight or flight instinct."

"I won't run from you, and I don't have a dragon-slaying sword at my disposal. If we're going to try to make something of this… then I want to see all of you, Teo. I need to appreciate both sides of you, man and dragon."

"As you wish." Without further argument, Teo turned and strode away from her, revealing his muscular back. Marcy's appreciative eyes drifted over her dragon lover to his perfect ass, his bottom rounded and tight with adequate muscle to give it shape.

When he turned to face her again, an abrupt change overtook him. Pitch black flowed over his brown skin as his body elongated and grew. He jumped up in size and, with a flash, two enormous wings snapped out at his sides. Dragon lore and historic art depicted creatures with scaled and leather appendages, but it was untrue. Saul and Teo each possessed a glorious set of feathered wings.

Two golden-brown, corkscrew shaped horns twisted back atop his head. His eyes remained the same, large, green, and surprisingly docile. Filled with the same warmth she saw when Teo opened up to her.

Big. He's so big. He's so big. But I'm not afraid. I can't be afraid because he's my Teo. He's still the same man.

Marcy's heart pounded, filling her head with the sound of rushing blood. The world around her spun out of control until she stumbled back a step. She fell into his outstretched claw. The pad of his

291

monstrous appendage reminded her of a cat or dog, pliable but covered in coarse, leathery skin. Each of his four digits was splayed to point the sharp claws away from her.

"I have frightened you." Teo's voice rumbled from him in a deeper, booming timbre.

"No. You're… you're gorgeous," she blurted out. "I didn't expect you to be so large."

"Many humans flee when they are face to face with a dragon."

"Obviously I'm more than human," she quipped, voice dry despite her attempt to infuse it with humor.

Marcy reached out with one hand, only to withdraw and lower it back to her side. "May I touch you?"

"I am yours. Would you ask to lie in your own bed, or to wear your own shoes? You may touch me to your heart's content."

Marcy glided her fingers through his shaggy, rust-colored mane. He smelled delightful, like fresh soil and earth, a hot day after a brilliant summer rain.

"You are truly unafraid?"

"Truly," she murmured. Both hands rose to touch his inquisitive face. At such close quarters, he could have gobbled her up in a single bite. She refused to feel daunted by his massive teeth and kissed his velvety snout. "I won't fear my own dragon."

"Yours," he rumbled in approval.

"God, your skin is so soft here." She slid her palm over his face, unable to miss the way his green eyes drifted shut, or the motor hum emanating from his chest. *He purrs like his jaguars.*

Closer inspection revealed his feathered wings weren't solid black as she'd initially assumed. His dark plumage had a sheen to it that reminded her of an oil slick on water. Subtle shades of green, blue, and red shimmered against the ebony.

Marcy moved around him to inspect his powerful body. His huge claws pressed into the damp sand, leaving massive indents in the ground. She trailed past him with her fingers drifting his sides. Teo's muscled build reminded her of a reptile in some ways, but the heat radiating from his body identified him as something else. A ticklish something else, who flinched from her fingers.

"Are you ticklish?"

"I am not."

Marcy repeated it and he wriggled away from her onto his side to escape. "You are!"

"No, stop!" Teo's thump into the sand nearly threw her off balance. He shook the shoreline with his massive weight and made her stumble against him with both hands on his body.

Something childish overcame her. She had a dragon at her mercy, writhing like a petulant child. She traced her fingers over his ribs and tickled him again, reducing her stoic and masculine dragon to the likeness of a puppy in seconds. He never hurt her. Never threatened her. He took it with laughter that sent chills up her spine, a deep rumbling voice contrasting his usual haughty arrogance.

"No one has tickled me since I was a cub."

"Well I have." She stuck her tongue out at him. "I have a secret weapon for the next time you piss me off. I don't need a dragon-slaying sword to put you in your place."

"I will try to avoid pissing you off, Marceline. To the best of my ability, I will try."

"Now become my Teo again. I think I want to kiss you, and I want to do it without the giant teeth."

In the span of a heartbeat he went from beast to man. Wet sand clung to his naked side, prompting her to brush it away with one hand. He enfolded her in his strong arms and yanked her close. His mouth descended to her lips in a surprisingly tender kiss, parting them with the first stroke of his tongue.

"I wish to take you for a date," Teo whispered at its end.

"A date?"

"I want all of my employees to see we are together. Come with me to the main island. Please."

"Teo, I don't care whether or not they see us. Just take me out to take me out."

"But I do care. Am I not allowed to be proud of you? To wish for everyone to bask in the joy you have given me?"

Unable to argue his logic, Marcy surrendered with a sigh.

"I have been lonely for so long as a result of my own foolish choices. Come with me, Marceline. Please."

The magic word made her smile. "Mm, you mean those choices of wanting a submissive black dragon?" she teased.

He chuckled softly and rubbed the back of his neck. "I see Chloe is unable to keep a secret. Yes, those choices," he confirmed. "You are unlike any dragon. My earlier ideas were misinformed."

"Can I ask why you thought you wanted one?"

"The females of my kind do not give up power willingly, Marceline. They crave control, and as males, we have no choice but to obey."

"Seriously?"

"Dragonesses are fewer in number. To attain a mate and keep her by your side, you must do all you can to please her. Give in to her every whim. Brigid, for example, would never allow a man to find his pleasure first."

"I like watching you come, but it's impossible to do if I'm distracted first." Marcy stared at him. "Your kind are so different from our society I guess, where men have all the power."

"Indeed. While all are not like Brigid, the exceptional females are difficult to find and often taken. For a time, we indulged in temporary breeding contracts to procreate without bonding to replenish our numbers after the dark ages. Females wanted cubs without the bond."

"Do you…?"

"Have a child?"

"Nevermind. None of my business." *And I really don't want to know unless it swoops in to eat me for stealing its daddy.*

"Marcy." Teo kissed her. "Once, I tried. But without a soul bond between dragons, breeding is a difficult thing. I am childless."

Marcy exhaled a relieved breath. "I mean, not like it matters if you do or anything. I love ancient dragon kids." *Great. No jealous or judgmental stepchildren in my future.*

Once clothed appropriately, Teo prepared the boat but placed Marcy in charge of its navigation halfway to their destination.

"Teo, wait. Stop! I don't know what I'm doing here."

"There is no better time to learn," he assured her.

"Not all of us are dragon-fast learners," she grumbled.

Despite Marcy's concerns, she didn't capsize the boat, drown them, or crash against invisible obstacles in the water. Their arrival to the resort was met with enthusiasm from the staff. His employees greeted the couple with respect and handled the mooring lines for him.

"What would you like to do?"

"Well, I've already seen all the attractions. Maybe dinner. Oh, and dancing." Marcy seemed to consider the last bit and slanted a curious gaze at him. "*Can* you dance?"

As an answer, Teo tugged her in close by one hand and dipped Marcy back. "If dancing is your wish you will not be disappointed."

Hand in hand, they walked along the beach looking like any other lovers out for a stroll. They shared a daiquiri served in a coconut shell and talked about Teo's plans for the island. He dreamed of expanding his vision and creating several more eco-friendly resorts across the world.

"Picture, sir?" A chipper voice called over, belonging to a young woman in a Staff Polo shirt.

Marcy lifted a hand to shade her eyes and smiled at the approaching staff photographer. She, Chloe, and Astrid had pictures from all over the island thanks to the roving photo crew.

It's a shame Teo dislikes having his picture taken. The thought was a sad one in many ways. "Oh, no thank y—"

"Yes," Teo interrupted. "I would like a picture with you, Marcy."

Touched beyond measure, she leaned in close to his side, tilted her face for its best angle, and smiled for the camera. If this was going to be her only picture of Teo, she wanted it to be a good one.

"Here's your ticket, Mr. Arcillanegro. It'll be ready in an hour."

"Gracias, Adelaide."

"Do you know everyone by name?" Marcy asked when they were alone again.

"All those in my employ, yes." Teo looked down at her. "Does this surprise you?"

"A little, considering you always called Kekoa 'my servant' or something of the like until I mentioned it."

Eventually, as the sun began its descent toward the horizon, her dragon led her into one of the fancier restaurants on the island. They ate by candlelight and enjoyed glasses of red wine with their pasta dishes. Marcy passed on dessert and pulled Teo toward the dance floor instead.

As with everything he did, her lover moved with grace and finesse. He held Marcy close and guided her across the empty space. The smooth strains of Latin jazz encouraged slow, swaying steps. Teo dipped her back low over his arm and pressed a gentle kiss against her collarbone in a very public display of affection.

"I think I'm ready to go back to your place," Marcy whispered. The many eyes on them kept Marcy from following through on her desires. Their dance left her with the insatiable need to have Teo naked and close. To move against him, flesh to flesh, bodies joined as one.

Teo's nostrils flared. He said nothing, but drew her from the restaurant without a backward glance. They didn't stop until sand was beneath their feet and there wasn't a single soul in sight. With the darkness concealing them on the beach, Teo stripped from his clothes and transformed.

"Would you like to fly, Marcy?"

"Oh my God, yes." Marcy had flown on Saul, but this was Teo. *Her* dragon. Without another word she gathered his discarded clothing then scrambled up onto his back. As a dragon, his leaner frame made him narrower than Saul through the shoulders. Straddling the base of his long neck reminded her of riding a horse.

After he stepped into the waves and whipped the sand to clear his tracks, Teo snapped out his wings and took off to soar low over the water. The distance requiring twenty minutes by boat took only five on dragonback. The salty air whipped through Marcy's hair but not once did she feel afraid.

"Flying is awesome," she cried out after they landed. She hugged his neck before she slid off then rounded to his jet-colored face. "*You* are amazing."

"You have no idea how it pleases me to hear you say so."

"Shift back into my naked man and you could show me," she suggested, pulling him along toward his beachfront home.

Before her feet could touch the stone path leading to the door, Teo's arms wrapped around her and drew her back to face him. His fully erect cock pressed into her belly.

"I can… I cannot make promises my dragon half won't claim you if we make love again, Marceline. The urge is too strong." He dragged in deep and heavy breaths, resembling a wild animal more than a man.

Marcy smoothed her fingers over Teo's brow then through his dark strands. "What happens if I let you?"

"I will bite you and gift you the Dragon's Brand. It symbolizes my vow to give myself to you, and once done, it means we are bonded. I become forever yours as much as you become mine."

His promise kicked Marcy's heart rhythm into overdrive. She swallowed the dry lump in her throat and considered the tender way he had treated the animals in the sanctuary. The way he tended his personal garden. The kindness he had shown to Kekoa by rescuing an orphaned boy. Teo's gruff attitude and overbearing arrogance were a result of upbringing, not a true reflection of the kind spirit beneath.

"Is it irreversible? It's not like marriage, is it? Once we're bonded, there's no going back?"

"You have seen Chloe's. If you were a dragon, you would bite me in return, sealing our souls as one. But you are not a dragon. If you come to loathe me, I can set you free," he said quietly, "but I would hope you remained alongside me. Be my mate, Marceline."

Faced with the biggest decision of her entire life, Marcy gazed up at his solemn features. Her fingers traced through his dark hair and smoothed it back from his shoulder. "I want you, Teo. I'll be your mate."

They moved at the same time, hands greedily reaching for each other. The straps of her dress snapped beneath Teo's impatient touch. He dragged the material down her body and ripped away her panties as if they were made from tissue.

Fuck that's hot.

Teo swept Marcy from her feet. Moments later, she hit the bed face down, sprawled on her belly. The path to his home and bedroom had been a blur.

"Teo?"

The man behind her growled, no longer the cool and sophisticated dragon she'd tenderly made love to in the cabana or teased in this same bed. Foil ripped then strong hands dragged Marcy onto her hands and knees. He touched her, testing, fondling her pussy, and gliding his fingers over her wet slit. She'd never been more prepared for him — and he knew it. In a thrust, he seated his cock to full depth within her waiting channel.

From anyone else, Marcy would have discouraged the dominating position. From Teo, it felt as natural as breathing. She groaned his name and fell onto her elbows with her bottom raised to the air. Teo dragged out until the tip remained then snapped his hips forward again. He became an animal, frenzied and lost to the sensation of burying his dick in her folds. Nothing else mattered but the primal joining of their bodies.

Teo's palm molded to one weighty breast and squeezed. "Perfection," he growled, deep in his chest. "Every inch of you is perfection."

The sheets bunched beneath her grasping hands and one corner pulled free from the mattress. Another hard thrust inched her forward and threatened to lift her knees from the bed. The headboard slammed. Unconcerned, Marcy surrendered to her own needs and moved wildly to the feverish rhythm he set.

"Be mine, Marcy. Tell me you are mine."

"I'm yours, Teo," Marcy choked out. "And you're *mine.*"

Delighted with the affirmation of their union, her dragon speared her again, hilting at complete depth. As her walls spasmed, contracting in the throes of orgasm, Teo's teeth closed around her shoulder and introduced her to a sharp, blinding pain that threatened to consume her. The intensity was only matched by the climax mercilessly throbbing in her core.

"Teo!"

Her mate's feral roar blended with her scream. Pushed to the brink of oblivion, Marcy's body could no longer differentiate pain from her pleasure. Every nerve ending was aflame, threatening to consume her in a blaze of ecstasy. Another orgasm rocketed through her like fireworks on a cloudless night, then her world spiraled out of control.

"Teo!"

"Accept it," he growled. "Accept me as yours."

"I do, I do, I love you!" Marcy wailed. Hungering to taste his lips, she turned her head to the right and found her intuitive lover waiting for her. Their lips met with urgency, and despite the latex sheath, she knew he'd climaxed. She longed to feel the hot pulse of his seed and the bloom of warmth it would bring.

The orgasm didn't stop, a relentless and steady series of contractions. "Teo?"

His arm curled around her waist, securing her against him. Each back stroke, every thrust, renewed the chain of molten sensation pooling in her core. Marcy thought for certain she'd be the first woman to ever die from absolute rapture.

"I will always treasure you, Marceline," were the last words to caress her ears before she screamed in pure lust at the tail end of his last ardent stroke. Her walls shuddered around him, a merciless and explosive bliss on repeat that reduced her to a writhing pile below her mate.

Eventually, Marcy moaned from the bed where she lay face down amidst the cushions and silky comforters. Their cool touch felt good against her naked skin. Despite his views toward nudity, Teo had covered her. The sweet gesture and acceptance of her rules brought a smile to her face.

Did I pass out? What the hell? She raised her head and sighed, reluctant to move from her nest. "That was amazing," Marcy murmured. "No wonder Chloe never stays away from Saul for longer than a couple weeks." She pushed up on her elbows and scanned the room for Teo, finding him by the window. Her bronzed god watched her with a relaxed smile on his face.

Once her weak, trembling legs cooperated with her decision to leave the bed, Marcy crossed to her mate and joined him at the window seat. He curled his arm protectively around her waist to secure her on his lap, then she pressed her ear against his chest and listened to the slow drumming beat.

"This is the happiest I have felt in all my life," Teo murmured against her hair. "Thank you."

"You don't have to thank me for making you happy, silly."

"But I do. You have changed my life, Marcy, and there's something I'd like to show you."

"What is it?" She drew on her silk robe.

"What is mine is now yours, Marceline. I would show you all of it."

Teo led her outside into the balmy evening air and shifted. Marcy never tired of watching the transformation, loving admiration shining in her eyes. She took her time, moving around him, and trailed her fingers over his soft skin. His feathers ruffled beneath her touch.

"Sometimes I wonder if the past five years have all been some crazy dream," she mused. "I worry I'll wake up and Chloe will still be living with me and dating that douchebag ex of hers, and I'll still be stressing at work."

The dragon's rumbling chuckle raised goosebumps on her arms and stirred the sand beneath her toes. "No, it is not a dream. I am quite real, and completely yours. As is Saul's devotion to Chloe."

"I know." She kissed his long snout. "I am incredibly blessed to have you."

Marcy moved around to his side and claimed her place on his back. Only after he was certain she was secure, Teo flapped his powerful wings and lifted them into the air.

They flew, circling twice around his island before Teo turned toward the rocky peak dominating the skyline. Up close it was larger than Marcy had anticipated, a sheer wall of rock she doubted even Chloe could climb with her best gear. Trailing wisps of fog clung to the thick foliage.

A backstroke of his wings slowed their descent onto a small ledge, where large green ferns covered the entrance into his lair. Marcy was forced to dismount and follow inside on foot, the crevice was so narrow. She watched, amazed, as Teo's bulky form twisted inside with ease.

"Doesn't it hurt scraping against the rock?"

Teo's rumbling chuckle echoed against the walls. "No. It feels nice against my hide." To emphasize his point, he rubbed against the smooth worn stone.

"Like a bear against a tree."

"More or less." The black dragon shrunk down, becoming a man once more. He offered out his hand, which Marcy readily took.

"Come."

Stories spoke of dragon hoards, but even their close description couldn't match the beauty of seeing one in person.

Saul's treasure room was organized chaos, his hoard separated into distinctive piles. Teo, on the other hand, preferred a single large collection. Coins of all sizes glittered amidst scattered jewels and ancient relics.

"Dios *mío*," she breathed, taking it all in. "Do you swim in that pile?"

A wide grin split Teo's face. "No, but I do often use it as my bed."

"Meaning you'd be sleeping here if I wasn't on the island."

Teo's enigmatic smile gave her the answer he wouldn't speak aloud. "Do you like it?"

"It's amazing, Teo. A mess, but amazing all the same."

He snorted. "What use are neat stacks when they only fall over at the brush of my tail or wings? This is for my enjoyment. Not for mere admiration."

Marcy still couldn't shake the image of him swimming through his massive wealth, no matter how much he denied it. She easily pictured him rolling through the mess and playing with rubies and diamonds the way a child would play with marbles.

"Seriously?" She bent down and snagged a handful of coppers from the floor. "You hoard pennies?"

"You might be amazed, Marceline, at how swiftly such paltry sums add up."

"I'll be sure to raid my couch when I get back home," she mumbled, her attention caught by a feathered headdress. "Is this Aztec?"

"It belonged to my father."

"It's beautiful. May I?"

"Touch whatever you wish."

With great care, Marcy lifted the beautiful accessory from the stalagmite where it had been resting. The feathers retained their bold shades of blue and green. She carried it over to Teo and gestured for him to lean down a bit, then she settled the crown on his head.

"Just as I first imagined you," she sighed, breathless at the sight of him. "You made me think of an Aztec warrior from the first moment I saw you crossing Saul's lawn."

"I did not live up to that honor."

"No, you didn't," she agreed, smiling. "But you've made up for it."

Teo leaned down and kissed her, claiming her mouth in a slow and sensual kiss, with a tenderness their bonding had lacked. Marcy's knees wobbled and her toes curled, his kiss felt in every fiber of her being. Her face remained tilted upward toward his after their lips parted and her lashes fluttered open.

"I'd like to sleep with you. Here. In your true shape." She placed her hands over his muscled chest and looked deep into his eyes. "I want to sleep with my dragon."

"Whatever you desire."

Chapter 11

Money, Marcy determined, did not make a comfortable bed, but a dragon as her pillow had more than made up for any discomfort. They awoke to the sound of bird calls outside and the soft, distant rush of waves crashing against the shore. After urging her to pick something for herself from his collection, Teo carried her down in a lazy, spiraling glide. They landed seconds before a gentle rain began to fall. The warm kiss of misty rainfall felt incredible, an improvement over the persistent dry heat of Texas.

With overcast weather trumping any plans for outdoor activities, Marcy suggested an afternoon of cinema. Teo's personal movie room made any film a thrilling experience, especially the ones from Drakenstone Studios. The panoramic screen and interactive seats made her feel like she was in the scene.

Together they watched Saul's newest release, which hadn't even hit the theatres yet. With a bowl of popcorn between them and a fruit platter, they enjoyed the fantasy adventure.

"Would you like to watch another?"

"Actually," she said, a saucy grin turning up her lips. "I'd like to see one of your educational films."

"Er… what?"

Marcy laughed and crawled over the armrest into his lap. "Your pornos, Teo. Let's watch one together."

He blinked owlishly up at her, but his nostrils flared and his cock twitched beneath her bottom. "I did not think such was done."

"Oh, it's done." She leaned down and kissed him sweetly. "Consider this a human biology lesson."

A lesson which took the rest of the afternoon and evening. During which, Teo's eagerness to take the submissive role in the bedroom became apparent. She challenged him in bed, teased him with a downy feather from his own wing, and pushed her new lover's sexual limits during their exploration. Through it all, he was her eager student, only accustomed to intimacy in his natural form. As a human, he craved her every touch.

The following morning dawned bright and offered perfect weather for a swim in the cove. Teo cut through the water as efficiently as a dragon as he'd flown through the air on his wings.

Marcy straddled his back and held on tight as he took her in short dives beneath the waves to explore the colorful coral formations below. As with the wildlife on his island, the local sea creatures had become accustomed to his presence. They didn't flee for cover as Marcy expected.

Another day was spent on the main island enjoying the attractions. The moment Marcy learned Teo had never built a sand castle, she dragged him to the beach where his guests enjoyed the sun and surf. As the sun began its descent, Marcy manned the boat's helm and took them back home.

"Did you have fun?" she asked once they were settled inside with their clothes stripped away.

"It was better than I expected," Teo agreed. "Better still now we are alone, away from the noise and prying eyes."

Leaning over her in the bed, Teo nibbled the sensitive spot on Marcy's throat. Their joint explorations had acquainted them with the subtle nuances of each other's bodies: where to touch light, where to knead with more pressure, and which areas turned them into a ball of putty.

Distracted by his kisses, Marcy fumbled for the adjacent box of condoms. Foil packets spilled over the floor and scattered, then she raised her hips and moaned. Part of her wanted to feel him skin to skin, to let him experience her inviting clench without the layer of latex between them. Something feral within her demanded to claim Teo as thoroughly as he claimed her. In the end she prevailed through the struggle and smoothed the ring over his cock.

"Why must I continue to wear this ridiculous sheath? It is time to conceive our child, Marceline."

"What?" His words may as well have accompanied a bucket of ice water.

"To mate as was intended by nature. Is there no better time than now?"

"Uhh, yeah, like never," Marcy replied, bewildered.

A low growl rumbled in Teo's chest. "You cannot be serious. We came to an agreement in which you swore to be my mate. You accepted me."

"Wait, hold on, wait. I never agreed to bear you a child. I never agreed to that."

"What did you think I was asking of you when I asked you to allow me to mate to you?" Teo's green flashed with anger only to dim moments later. A furrow creased his brow. "Marceline, if we do not... what point is there to being mine if I will lose you?"

303

Marcy shook her head. "We didn't discuss making a child. That's where I draw the line. I adore you, but I'm not going to subject myself to what I helped Chloe through. She almost died. She had an excruciating, horrible birth, Teo. Her uterus *ruptured*. If you want me, you get me for a human's life span."

"Marcy—"

"Don't *Marcy* me," she snapped. "What? Don't like the idea of me growing gray and old because then I won't be so fun anymore? Is that it? No one wants to have sex with a grandma."

Teo quieted.

"I'd be too human then, wouldn't I? Another monkey. So there we have it."

Her dragon remained silent.

Marcy and Teo didn't speak for the rest of the day. He shut himself away outside in the wilderness and left Marcy to the hospitality of his home. Kekoa arrived to engage her in conversation, but his conflicted feelings of fondness for Marcy and loyalty to Teo sent him back into the waves. He didn't want to judge either of them.

I'm alone here. Is this what I can expect any time we don't agree? Being left alone and isolated?

Without him there, Marcy sprawled outside in the shade with Philomena stretched out alongside her. The jaguar rubbed her face against Marcy's cheek and purred.

"I must smell like Teo now, huh? Is that why you love me so much?" Her fingers slid over the jaguar's furry head and stroked her ears. One of the cubs came up to join them next. He batted Marcy's hair and rolled across her lap. "Hello to you, too, Chapo."

Despite the company of the jaguars, Marcy was lonely. It reminded her too much of her empty apartment and days spent without friends. She missed Chloe. She missed going out on her own.

Most of all, she missed Teo. On the second day, Kekoa cooked for her and took her out to the main island. She caught a performance and visited the aviary, but it wasn't the same without her dragon by her side.

Her mate returned on the third morning, nude and gleaming from head to toe. His dark hair lay wet against his shoulders when he strode into the bedroom to find her.

"Why are you packing your belongings?" Teo asked.

Marcy's open suitcase lay over the enormous bed, half-filled with the clothing she'd stored into his closet. "I'm going home."

"Home?" The smile dropped from his face. "I do not understand."

"Home. I need time to think about this. Maybe we jumped into it too fast without thinking things through. Without talking about what we both wanted."

"Are we unable to talk now? Is this not a talk?"

"I need to go for a while."

"But why?!"

"Space," she replied in a clipped tone, unable to look at him.

"Did I not give you space?"

"You walked away without telling me a thing. I'm at least informing you I plan to leave and where I'm going."

"You will not return. You do not plan to return."

"Don't tell me what I plan to do, Teo. I know my own fucking mind. I just need some space away from this, away from you, to think about things and what we've done here."

"You must stay and speak of this with me."

"You have a lot of nerve to insist I need to stay here when you left me alone for two days."

"I allowed you time to think. Time I felt we both needed."

"And now I'm taking some more time to think. Just as you did."

"I did not leave to another country!"

"Who knows where you went off to? I sure didn't," she snapped back at him. "I need to go home and handle some things and that's all there is to it."

"I can make you stay."

His words held truth and they both knew it. He was a dragon and she was only a human woman. If he chose to hoard her away like the rest of his treasures then there was nothing much she could do about it.

"Force me, Teo, and you'll lose me forever," she said in a soft voice. With all her belongings packed, she zipped up her luggage and headed out the door.

Teo didn't stop her.

Chapter 12

"You're certain about this?"

"It's time, yeah." Marcy smiled at her long-time employer and held out her hand. Howard pulled her into an embrace instead.

"You'll always have a place here with us, Marcy, if you ever change your mind. Even if that doesn't happen, don't be a stranger."

"I won't, I promise."

Marcy left the building feeling lighter. Her substantial savings and numerous talents meant she didn't need to worry about work right away, but she didn't want to get lazy either. Between all the contacts she'd made at Teo's resort and a few from work, she was confident she could build a small clientele base. Going into business for herself was a longtime aspiration, and it had taken cleaning up Teo's tangled accounts to make her realize she could handle it.

Her apartment was quiet when she unlocked the door and stepped inside. Too quiet, almost. The bright, open space felt barren without her best friend there living with her.

At least I can turn her old room into a dedicated office, she thought.

The ring of the phone broke the depressing silence. Marcy smiled faintly down at the Caller ID window, wondering if Chloe's new abilities included knowing when someone was thinking about her.

"Hey, Chloe," she answered. "Recovered from your vacation?"

"Are you kidding? Astrid is ready to go back for another glass bottom boat ride."

Marcy laughed. "Those were fun, I agree."

"So how are *you* doing?" Chloe asked. "You never called and said you were coming back home."

She heard the worry in her friend's voice clear as day. Marcy swallowed thickly, tears threatening to well in her eyes. "A lot happened, chica."

"Do you want to talk about it?"

Starting at the beginning, Marcy let it all spill out, from Teo's back and forth behavior to his threat the day she packed her bags.

"So I left. I asked Mahasti not to mention anything to either of you."

"Oh, sweetheart," Chloe whispered into the phone. "I'll be right there. She's bringing me now."

Before Marcy could hang up the phone, Chloe was there in a puff of jasmine-scented smoke, tendrils of the genie's magical essence wafting through the apartment. The two friends met halfway and collapsed against each other. Their limbs tangled in a tight embrace and they sank to the couch where Marcy wept against the other woman's shoulder. Uncontrollable sobs shook her body, and through it all Chloe held her tight.

"He... he didn't even care I was leaving. He didn't say please. Instead of asking to come with me, he threatened to make me stay like I was another gem in his treasure pile."

"I promise you, Marce, everything you feel, he experiences double."

"What makes you think so?"

Chloe hesitated. "I knew to call you and check on you because... Teo called Saul. He's devastated and blames himself for trying to pressure you. I wanted to make sure you were okay."

"What did he say to Saul?"

"I didn't eavesdrop in on the call, sweetie, so I can only repeat what Saul told me. Apparently dragons have their own bro code, because that's all he'd say."

"Figures. Shit. I don't know if I did the right thing anymore. I don't want to second guess myself but now I'm home, none of this feels worth it. I was *happy* with him."

"It isn't too late to go back to him. Saul told me he never once considered not taking me back after I ran him away the way I did. It takes a while for a bond to break."

"No, Chloe. He isn't Saul, and I'm not you. I'm not the one in the wrong here. Why can't he love me for me without wanting to permanently change me?"

Chloe sighed gently and smoothed her hand up and down Marcy's back. "Do you remember what I said about being pregnant with Astrid?"

"You said it was worth it."

"To me, it was. But if you don't want to do it, Teo needs to respect your choice. You did the right thing for *you*, Marcy. Teo, Saul, and even I realize that."

"Then why do I feel so awful?"

"Because of the bond, and because you have feelings for him that transcend that bond. Everything about loving them is... it's more intense than anything I ever felt as a human. You feel awful because... I think you're experiencing his pain, too."

"It sucks," Marcy blew her nose into a tissue. "It's like he only wants me if I'll pop out babies. God forbid he be attached to a plain, unspecial human."

"Oh sweetie, there's nothing unspecial about you." Chloe squeezed her again. "Maybe the problem is you're both looking at it in absolutes. You won't consider a child and he wouldn't consider a bond without one. Maybe... you both need a compromise."

"Like what?" Marcy asked, sniffling. "I feel like an idiot for crying. I didn't even cry over Matt or anyone else. What's wrong with me?"

"Marce. There's nothing wrong with crying and letting out emotion."

The Latina nodded her head and scrubbed her cheeks with one wrist. "Okay. A compromise. How do you compromise on something like this?"

Chloe smiled sadly. "See things from his point of view and give him the chance to see things from yours. You said it best, girl. You're only 34. Maybe five years or ten years from now, you'll feel differently. Maybe you won't. Ask him if he's willing to accept a compromise and take it one day at a time. Don't walk away from each other for days and waste what precious time you do have."

Eventually, the tears subsided and left a dull ache in Marcy's heart. She sighed and looked down at the picture frame on the coffee table. In the photograph, Marcy was attempting to flash her most alluring smile while Teo held her close for the camera. She hadn't noticed until later that he was smiling. It was a faint, fragile thing, no doubt his attempt to maintain a straight face.

She'd made him smile on their date. She'd made him smile so many times after. Marcy would never forget the elation on his face in the moments after their bonding.

"Do you want to come home with me tonight?" Chloe asked.

"Yeah. I don't want to be here alone. I'm so fucking tired of being alone," Marcy admitted, shaking her head sadly. She'd been lonely ever since her best friend in the world moved away, and no amount of teleporting to see her was enough to make up for the distance in their friendship.

"Why don't you move in with us? We have the room and Saul won't mind. Astrid would be overjoyed to have her tía with her every day."

"I'm not sure."

"Give it some thought. Mahasti?"

"I am here," the genie's voice whispered into the room.

"Take us home."

The djinn magical transport didn't leave Marcy as dizzy as it usually did. Or maybe it was because her head was already pounding and heavy from her cry-fest. They appeared in Chloe's solarium where golden beams of sunshine angled through the floor to ceiling windows and warmed Marcy's cool skin. Potted plants in multiple varieties added colorful splashes to the bright, feminine space.

"Chloe!" Saul's voice boomed, a telltale sign of drawing power from his dragon half. "Chloe! Come quickly!"

"Just a sec, hon!"

"Hurry or you'll miss it!"

"Go on, chica, I'm right behind you," Marcy encouraged. Chloe hurried off to the next room and soon she was squealing in excitement and calling for Marcy to join them.

"All right, all right, I'm coming." Swiping the last tear streaks from her face, Marcy crossed the room to join her friends. "Now what's so — oh my God!"

A small dragon, roughly the size of a German Shepherd, chased a ball across the playroom floor. Astrid's soft skin was golden in color, brighter than her father in his dragon form. Pin feathers lines her small wings, interspersed with small tufts of pale white down. Saul beamed proudly while Chloe had her hands clasped over her mouth, joyful tears streaming from her eyes.

"Oh I wish I had my camera," Marcy whispered, afraid to ruin the moment. Within seconds her wish was granted and her photography bag materialized at her feet.

Having a djinn around really is handy. Geez.

"How? When?" Chloe asked her husband.

"A few moments before you and Marceline arrived. I was about to call," Saul replied. "A true dragon shifter and unique among my kind."

"She's gorgeous." Marcy snapped a few quick photographs as Astrid pounced a stuffed dragon. The miniature dragon abandoned her toy and approached Marcy, sniffing.

"Tía smell like me!" Astrid cried. She nuzzled in close against her aunt.

"Nope, I'm still me," Marcy quipped. "Can you sit over here and let Tía Marcy take pictures of you for your photo album?"

Astrid posed long enough for Marcy to take several pictures, and then the excited child bounded outside onto the balcony. Saul intervened before she tried out her developing wings. He caught her by the tail and promised flying lessons after her feathers grew in. They all spent the rest of the afternoon playing until, exhausted, Astrid shifted back and asked to take a nap. She curled up on the loveseat and drifted off.

"What did you mean by unique?" Chloe turned her questioning gaze up at her husband. "St. George was a halfling like her."

"Indeed he was, though I am uncertain if he ever took dragon shape. Watatsumi might know," Saul replied. He rubbed his chin and appeared deep in thought. "Beyond that, I have never heard of a gold dragon among my kind, my love. It will be interesting to discover what abilities she develops as she matures."

"Is your dragon council gonna be okay with that?" Marcy sank back against the cushions and tucked her feet up.

"They have come to a neutral standpoint regarding Astrid."

Chloe rolled her eyes. "What he means to say is, they're claiming to be okay with it since Astrid is being raised by a dragon. Hopefully it keeps her from growing up to become a dragon-hunting monster."

Marcy glanced at Astrid. "She couldn't hunt dragons without the sword, I thought."

"Yeah well... about that," Chloe began. Her eyes shifted to her husband.

"Watatsumi insists we should give the sword to Astrid on the day of her 25th birthday," Saul explained. "He has foreseen something, and assures me all shall go well as long as Astrid receives it."

"Right. That's not ominous at all," Marcy said.

Saul chuckled. "Welcome to our world."

Chapter 13

Marcy couldn't rest. She tossed and turned in bed, enduring a difficult sleepless night. When rest didn't come, she kicked off the sheets, grabbed a book from the shelf, and began to read.

Chloe and Saul must be asleep by now... She sighed. It wasn't the same, the time long past when she could knock on the door past midnight and intrude on her friend to talk. As much as she enjoyed the comfort of living with her best friend, she felt like she'd imposed on them. To make up for it, she had taken up babysitting duties to give Nuri and Chloe a break. Caring for the half-dragon child gave her a chance for introspection.

Would it be horrible to become a mom?

Could she live up to the standard her own mother had set?

Chloe was right. Living her life in black and white absolutes was the fast track to missing out on new experiences. Teo wasn't the only one at fault — she'd shut him down without even hearing him out.

On top of her heartbreak, Marcy was also experiencing the worst case of generalized anxiety she'd ever suffered since graduate school. She paced in her room, did lunges across the floor, then struggled through half an hour of yoga before she surrendered the attempt to de-stress. The site of her mark from Teo ached where his teeth had left a deep purple bruise.

Weird. It hasn't bothered me since he did it.

Helping herself to the kitchen, Marcy brewed herself a steaming tumbler of tea. She snagged two cookies from the jar on the counter on her way outside to the veranda. With sunrise a few hours away she was determined to stay up and capture the splendor on film. At least her insomnia would be put to good use.

"Marcy, hon?" Chloe appeared when she reached the bottom of the tumbler.

"Yeah? I thought you'd be asleep."

The blonde shook her head then leaned out of the door to smile at her. "Not yet, but there's a visitor for you."

Marcy's breath caught in her chest. She didn't need Chloe to tell her who was there, she knew. Her heart had been racing for the last five minutes, pounding at an unrelenting pace.

"Marceline, may I join you?"

"Yes." At that moment, Marcy realized the anxiety she experienced belonged to Teo, as it was written all over his face. He wrung his hands together and hung at the open doorway, the very example of a contrite dragon.

"Teo…" *I want to be with him forever. I don't want a human lifetime with him. I want more. I've been the one who's scared,* Marcy realized. Hot tears spilled down her cheeks and she quickly tried to wipe them away.

"I have been miserable without you, Marceline."

"You have?"

Teo took a hesitant step forward. "Of course. You are my mate and my actions drove you away. You were in the right to leave."

Admission of wrongdoing ranked high with saying the word please. Marcy rarely, if ever, expected to hear such a thing, and yet Teo freely spoke the words, without coercion.

"Teo, I'm sorry." She closed another foot of space between them.

"Why do you apologize when I wronged you? I urged you to make a choice you were not ready to make."

Marcy smiled sadly. "I wronged you, too, when I fibbed. I do want… I do want to be with you for a long time, but I'm afraid we'll be doing this for the wrong reasons. I want to make a baby because it's something we both want, when we're both ready."

Teo took both of her hands, lacing their fingers together. The palpable relief on his face touched Marcy to her soul. "Okay," he agreed.

"Okay?" She arched a brow and wondered if she was hearing things.

He nodded. "I accept. I will accept any choice you make, my love. Your years may be a drop in the bucket for me, but I would take that over a life that is dry and void of you at all."

"Before we discuss anything else, I need you to tell me something, Teo. You were a complete jackass to me the first time we met. Why? What did I ever do to you, and why did you change now?"

A flush crept into his bronzed cheeks. "I have a confession, my love. When we first met that fateful day in this very house, my heart recognized you immediately."

"What?" Marcy's voice cracked.

"I knew then you were fated to be mine and I acted poorly because of it. I was insulted a mere human woman snared my heart as no dragon ever had."

"So you were an ass because you wanted me?"

"Yes," he answered without excuses. "I behaved childishly. When you came to the island, I was happy to have another opportunity to make things right between us. You've shown me humans can be trusted… and loved. I forgot for a moment when I realized the Galways were stealing from my foundation, but I never meant to hurt you."

Marcy could hardly believe her ears. Five years wasted because he had been too proud to take a risk on her. At first, fury churned in her gut, but then she remembered what Chloe has said and tried to look at it from Teo's perspective.

He had lived countless years, aware of his superiority over the hapless humans. Finding himself yearning for one must have come as a shock. Choosing his lifetime mate wasn't as easily done as picking up a car off the lot. He had taken his time to consider it.

"And you disappeared on me at the island," she continued. "Can you promise not to take off again?"

"Should I need time away to think, I vow on my ancestors that I will tell you first."

Marcy closed the remaining distance between them. "So what happens next?"

The proud dragon lowered himself to one knee and held out a small black velvet box. Marcy's heart stopped, or at least it felt that way. Warmth rushed through her, fire coursing through her veins, but she froze on the spot, unable to move.

"Marry me, Marceline."

"I thought you didn't believe in that stuff," she whispered, her voice tremulous.

"Marriage may mean nothing to dragons, but you are everything to me. I will do things the human way, because nothing else matters if you are far from my side." Teo's solemn features gazed at her from his lower position. "And if you should choose against bearing a child for us, I vow to value every precious second fate gifts to us."

He opened the box and once again Marcy caught her breath. She struggled with remembering how to breathe, each little gasp quick and shallow. A salty tear slid down her cheek and caught against the corner of her mouth

Nestled against a white velvet cushion was the most stunning, heartfelt ring she had ever seen. A Tahitian black pearl gleamed in the center of a setting resembling a hibiscus flower, each petal studded with pale pink diamonds. The platinum band slid onto her finger - a perfect fit.

"Yes," she mouthed, too overcome with emotion to find her voice.

Chapter 14

Saul's yard had been transformed into an outdoor cathedral, complete with rose covered arches and a grassy aisle lined with potted orchids. Guests would be welcomed to take them after the festivities, a small gift from the bride and groom.

Marcy fretted over her reflection. As far as she was concerned, she had the best hair stylist and makeup artist in LA. Mahasti's work was flawless, perfect to the last detail.

I feel like a whale in this dress. Is it really pretty? Who am I kidding? I'm gorgeous. It's not like I need breathe for the next hour or so. Maybe I should have Mahasti loosen the laces a little if I want to eat at the reception.

"Are you ready?" Chloe slipped inside the gauzy tent and stopped in her tracks. "Oh, sweetie, you look stunning."

Marcy turned away from the mirror and smoothed her trembling hands over the skirt of her gown. The sweetheart neckline and corseted bodice flattered her generous bustline, emphasizing her waist and curvy hips. "I feel like a princess."

"You look like one," Chloe assured her. "Here. Teo asked me to give you this as a finishing touch."

Chloe stepped over to her best friend and tucked a single, pink hibiscus flower into her hair over her left ear. Marcy reached up and touched the silken petals.

"Is my mom seated? I didn't think she'd ever leave after giving me Abuela's old cross."

"Yup, she's with Dad and Annette," Chloe confirmed. "Your brother is waiting outside the tent to walk you down the aisle."

Marcy drew in a deep breath, her insides quivering with excitement. "I'm ready. I want to have a peek at everyone first."

"Um… maybe we should just get you outside for the wedding. I have something to tell you, but I don't want to make you nervous before your big moment."

"I'm already so nervous I could puke, chica. Just tell me. Rip it off like a Band-aid."

"It's their mothers," Chloe whispered, parting the tent for Marcy to have a peek. "They both showed up about two minutes ago as I was passing by. Saul and Teo have been staring at them, but…"

"Everyone's waiting on you to give the signal for the wedding to begin," Marcy finished. And the guys were stuck waiting at the altar.

"I still can't believe Ēostre is here." Chloe let out a shaky breath.

"Teo told me his mother would be here, but not Saul's." Marcy's belly would have flopped if the corset boning didn't anchor it in place. It became a lead weight instead, an oppressive burden in the center of her body threatening to bring up the tiny sandwich and sips of tea she'd had for breakfast.

"Saul wasn't expecting her to wake from her long sleep for at least another fifty years, if not longer."

"I've seen Ēostre's photograph in your house. It's really her." Marcy bit her lower lip and studied the fair-skinned, regal woman in the moonlight colored dress. Every inch of her screamed sophistication but there was also a sadness in her face. She sat beside Marcy's mother-in-law to be, an ethereal vision with flowing golden hair. Both female dragons were polar opposites, closely resembled by their handsome sons.

"At least we can meet the in-laws together," Chloe said, attempting to lighten the mood.

Why does that seem scarier somehow? Two mother dragons meeting the humans their sons fell for. Panic fluttered in Marcy's stomach. "Teo's mom looks like a classical actress or something. She's gorgeous."

"Not more beautiful than you on your wedding day. Don't you forget that."

"Oh my God," Marcy squeaked. "What if she hates me? What if she thinks a human isn't worthy of her son? I can barely pronounce her name!"

"Marcy, hon, relax." Chloe pulled her away from the tent's entrance. "All that matters is what Teo thinks, but it won't hurt to rehearse her name a few times. Say it with me. Xochiquetzal. Girl, you got this. If you can say that mouthful of syllables she named your husband, you can say her name."

They practiced calm respirations and speaking dragon names for another five minutes before a pleasant voice called from beyond the tent. "Knock, knock."

Chloe and Marcy shot each other uncertain gazes. "Come in," Marcy replied.

The curtain parted to admit the ancient dragoness soon to become Marcy's mother-in-law. Xochi's gold dress flowed like liquid against her bronzed limbs, but the smile she flashed Marcy was radiant and genuine. "Ēostre and I both wished to meet you, but I feared the both of us would overwhelm at once."

Up close at a conversational distance, the similarities between mother and son became more apparent. He had her high cheekbones, her flawless complexion, and the same vivid green eyes. She wore her black hair in an elaborate semi-updo, held in place by a few sparkling ruby clips.

"I apologize for my mate's absence from the festivities," Xochi said to her. "As I understand, it is tradition among humans to don something borrowed and something blue. I would be honored if you accept both from me."

"I…" Marcy must have looked like a deer in the headlights because Chloe nudged her gently from behind. "Thank you, Xochiquetzal. I'd be honored."

"Xochi is more than fine," she assured Marcy.

Oh thank God! Marcy smiled. "Xochi, then."

The elegant dragoness opened a small clutch bag with an expensive designer label then offered a slender box to Marcy. "Something blue for you, and my gift."

"They're gorgeous, Xochi." Marcy held up the chandelier-style earrings. Polished beads of obsidian paired with sapphires and pearls for a stunning tiered drape.

"I hoped you would like them. Now, this one I should like returned after the wedding. This bracelet belonged to my mother. She plucked the oysters from the deep herself, fascinated by the treasure they offered."

Pearls, Marcy determined, were favored in Teo's family. Chloe helped her clasp the double strand around her wrist.

"Perfect," Xochi declared. Without hesitation, she stepped forward and kissed Marcy's cheek. "I look forward to having you as my daughter."

The regal woman stepped outside to return to her seat, leaving Marcy stunned. Chloe hugged her then did some quick, last minute adjustments to Marcy's veil.

"She liked me," Marcy whispered, stunned.

"Of course she did, silly. There's nothing about you to dislike," Chloe replied.

Marcy let the worry wash away with her next exhaled breath, excitement replacing the jitters. *Teo is outside waiting for me,* she thought, and the blooming warmth of happiness in her chest spread out to her fingers and her toes. "Ok, let's do this."

Chloe grinned. "Count to five, then follow me out."

One, I'm beautiful in this dress. Two, I love Teo. Three, I'm marrying a dragon. Four, today is my day. Five… I have never been so happy.

Marcy emerged from the tent.

I will not pass out on my wedding day. I will not pass out.

Leiv had surprised them all by volunteering to play the piano. His skillful fingers began her wedding march once everyone took their places. Among the human revelers, family members, and business associates, members of the supernatural world littered the seats in the audience.

All of her family, save for her estranged father, awaited her on the bride's side of the aisle. Her former employer and his wife smiled at her from their seats, as supportive following the end of her employment as he had been during their years together.

Teo waited for her at the end of the aisle, a proudly beaming man in an immaculate white tuxedo jacket. His black hair flowed in sleek weaves over his shoulders, and he'd never looked hotter.

Marcy's heart raced with every step.

As Maid of Honor, Chloe went down the green aisle first and joined Saul at the front. Astrid followed behind her, the world's cutest flower girl in her cream and gold dress.

Marcy's older brother Alejandro led her the entire way. He kissed her cheek before passing her hands to Teo.

The priest, an old man in his late sixties, spoke briefly about the importance of marriage then asked the bride and groom to exchange their personal vows.

Teo lifted Marcy's hands to his lips and looked deep into her eyes. "On our wedding day, my dear Marceline, there are many things I wish to say to you. My life became irreversibly changed from the moment I met you five years ago. You are the air I breathe and the sun to lighten every dark path. You are worth more to me than any amount of treasure and all of my wealth. Without you, I could not be poorer."

There goes my makeup. Yup. It's gone.

"When we first met, Teo, I knew you were unlike any other man I'd ever met. Those weeks with you on the island showed me your heart. Your kindness and your empathy. You filled my empty life with happiness and joy, and I couldn't love you more for it."

Their friends and family ceased to exist when she and Teo kissed. Saul cleared his throat and the pair parted with flushed cheeks and embarrassed smiles. Instead of rice their guests threw rose petals or blew bubbles.

Afterward, their guests moved to a secondary tent with banquet tables beneath and a wooden dance floor lay on the ground. A string quartet played soft music. Their four tiered cake was a confectionary

317

masterpiece of icing and tropical flowers.

"Before we all dine, I wish to share a dance with my Marceline," Teo announced. He kissed Marcy's hand and drew her with him to the large open space in the center.

Everyone watched them and several cameras flashed from various tables. Their hired wedding photographer crouched down a few feet away as Teo pulled her into his arms for a slow waltz. After a few minutes, other couples joined them, with Saul and Chloe leading the way. Thor escorted Saul's mother and Watatsumi accompanied Xochi.

"What is so funny?" Teo murmured against her ear.

"All these dragons," she whispered back, "and my family has absolutely no idea."

"One day, we will tell them the truth." A soft kiss against her brow followed his promise. "When you are ready."

She wouldn't be able to hide the truth from her family forever, but for today, she would let them continue on in blissful ignorance.

"Look, Maximilian has asked one of your many cousins to dance." Teo directed her gaze to the handsome, auburn-haired dragon as he twirled a dark-haired young woman across the floor. The male dragons in attendance had a common trait, sporting broad shoulders and tall frames. Marcy's human guests, unaware of the predators in their midst, swooned over them all.

"So he really doesn't harbor any ill-will about Chloe killing Brigid? You made it sound like he doesn't care, but he looks..." She had yet to see a true smile on Maximilian's face. He carried the mature features of a man in his mid-forties, revealing touches of silver in his neatly trimmed goatee.

"No, I may have exaggerated. He *is* saddened, of course. Brigid was his only offspring. But he also understands she instigated by challenging Chloe. It could not be avoided, and Brigid had a reputation for cruelty."

"What about the others?"

"Some are worried mingling will reveal our kind. Others, like Maximilian, are of the belief we cannot stay hidden forever. The Council has called a meeting a month from now, but this is not the pleasant talk we should be having on our special day, my love."

"Sorry." She lifted onto her tiptoes and kissed him. Applause and friendly cheers erupted all around them.

"Save it for the honeymoon!" Alejandro called out, a sentiment which Saul seconded. Marcy's brother and her best friend's husband had hit it off since his arrival at the estate.

The rest of the evening passed by in a joy filled haze. Chloe introduced Marcy to her own mother-in-law and while Ēostre's welcome was less warm than Xochi's had been, it was equally genuine. Toward the end of the evening Teo and Marcy cut into their cake and fed each other small bites.

Their loved ones sent them off with hugs, kisses, tears, and well wishes. Then Mahasti swept them away after the limousine was out of sight.

Teo surprised her with a Tuscan villa in the Italian countryside. Marcy had learned early on to expect extravagant gifts as dragons rarely did anything small. The magnificent home held familiar furnishings from her Texas apartment and Teo's island home.

"I have another surprise for you."

"Another? Teo, this house is more than enough. Too much."

"I promise you will be pleased."

An easel covered in red silk waited for them in the bedroom.

"My wedding gift to you, my bride." Teo removed the protective sheet from the canvas to reveal the million dollar watercolor portrait.

"My painting!" she cried, raising both hands to her mouth. "But we auctioned this!"

"Once it was entered into the auction rolls, I was unable to remove it. However, I couldn't bear to think of another person possessing your work and paid a colleague to purchase it."

Tears came to Marcy's eyes then she threw her arms around his shoulders and hugged him. She giggled at his exaggerated kisses and leaned back to gaze into her husband's green eyes. "I'm so glad you and Saul concocted my vacation."

Teo's eyes widened. "You knew? You are not upset?"

"No, silly. It makes me happy. *You* make me happy."

Teo cast his gaze toward the bed and his lips turned up in a devilish smile. "I brought the fuzzy cuffs."

"Mmm. Did you bring our riding crop, too?"

"How could I forget?"

"Well, you haven't been a naughty dragon." Marcy trailed her fingers over his chest, freeing his shirt buttons as she went. "In fact, I think my very good dragon deserves a reward."

Epilogue

4 YEARS LATER

"I still can't believe Maximilian is running for Governor of California." Marcy sipped her lemonade, settled down in comfort on a chaise with pillows propped up all around her. A cell phone beside her bowl of snacks connected to the small Bluetooth clip curved around her ear.

"The Council feels as you do," her husband replied. By his dry tone she could easily picture his face. "Dragons have always been in politics, but they worry about this modern age. He will draw attention to himself and all of us."

"Then maybe in this modern age it's time to come out into the open. What's the world going to do? Send cruise missiles after you? You guys own them."

"Several have voiced the same opinion, Watatsumi among them. My mother and Ēostre have taken his side, but my father is vehemently against it. Many of the older dragons despise the thought of revealing themselves."

"Why do they hate it so much?"

"If we are in the open, we cannot manipulate humans as easily. Besides, this affects more than dragonkind. Once we are out, humans will realize magic exists. It is not a choice for us alone to make."

"I guess I can understand. The dragons alone shouldn't make the decision."

"Exactly. Maximilian and Ēostre have called for a great Conclave to convene, with the leaders of the many shifter tribes."

"Those two have certainly been working together a lot."

"They share many views and Ēostre has always been involved in human politics. Maximilian has asked her to run his campaign."

"Aunt Marcy, Aunt Marcy!"

Teo's warm chuckle caressed Marcy's ear. "I can see you have your hands full. We will return by this eve. I love you."

"I love you, too." Marcy returned the sentiment just as Svetlana rushed onto the chaise and nestled in against her side. Chuckling, the Latina ran her fingers through the little girl's wavy hair. "Are you in trouble, little one?"

The child shook her head quickly then buried her small face into Marcy's shirt.

"I think you are. Where's your mama and papa?"

"Papa with the bees," Svetlana confided. Mahasti and Leiv's little girl resembled her mother the most, inheriting the djinn's thick black hair and brown sugar complexion. She had Leiv's warm chocolate eyes and personable nature. The couple was eager to see if she had also inherited her father's ability to shift.

"I caught these little troublemakers in the pasture, scaring the goats again," Chloe announced, chuckling as she stepped into view hand in hand with her own child.

Astrid skimmed her bare toes over the ground, sulking while she directed her big blue eyes to the grass at her feet. "It's my fault. I told her it would be fun if we chased them and pretended we were Daddy and Uncle Teo."

"Those goats are our food, sweetie. They're not toys, and they're not there for you guys to terrorize. Your daddy and uncle respect the animals and never hunt for sport. They hunt when they are hungry."

"I know," Astrid mumbled. She turned her apologetic face up to Chloe and frowned. "I'm sorry, Mommy."

"It's okay. Just don't do it again. One day, you'll be a big dragon, too, and you can hunt with your Daddy. But you should never have fun making an animal afraid of you."

"Okay. Can Svetlana and I go to help Uncle Leiv with the bees?"

"Wanna help Papa," Svetlana said.

"Only if you listen to everything he tells you. If he says no, you both better come back to me right away. Got it?"

"Yay!"

The kids scrambled away to become pests, practically hand in hand.

"She's getting so damned tall, Chloe. Look at her."

"I noticed. There's barely anything written about dragon halflings, so we're wondering if the slow childhood aging is over and she'll sprout up like a normal little girl after all."

"Well, she *is* almost nine."

"At least you and Teo will have our experiences to tell you what to expect. What about your little guy in there? Did you both settle on a name yet?" Chloe dropped her eyes to Marcy's round belly.

"We did."

"Well are you going to tell me or not?" Chloe demanded.

Marcy chuckled. "We decided to name him Javier Rafael," she

321

said. She ran her fingers over the curve of her belly and sighed. "Is it an okay name?"

"Fantastic." Chloe refilled Marcy's lemonade glass and sat down.

"How do you feel about it? It's almost time… you look about how I did when I was ready."

"I guess watching the two of you have kids finally got to me and made me baby crazy enough to risk it."

"You're going to have the best healers by your side. Promise. Saul told me there's no one better than his mother."

"I know. It doesn't change how scared I am but… I can't wait to meet him."

Female dragons carried their young for nearly two years, a gestation duration not shared by humans. Chloe had carried longer than the standard nine months, and still delivered a baby of just above average size. Despite that, Marcy felt more like a whale than ever as she approached the middle of her eleventh month. Her body was exhausted.

Just one more week. One more week to give her son the time he needed to develop. She'd spent most of the last two months bedridden while Teo dedicated his waking moments to her happiness and comfort. Just one more week. Marcy was already loved by one dragon, and in only a few days, she would share her affection with one more.

Taming the Dragon Bonus Chapter: Teotihuacan

Teotihuacan, resort owner and centuries-old dragon, paced the floor of the administrative office with a phone cradled between his shoulder and ear. "This is a ridiculous plan," he bit out in a terse voice.

"You had absolute faith in this plan two days ago. Why has your mind changed?" Saul asked.

Teo paused to glance at the security feed, his computer monitor displaying rows of tables beneath fancy cloth. He'd personally prepared each centerpiece as gifts for his guests to take home if they chose.

It was his gift, after all, a natural born talent of earth dragons to imbue vitality in the plant life around them. He could coax the tiniest seed into a vibrant flower within minutes.

"She loathes me."

"She has not spoken with you in years," Saul said.

"She will remember the times we have crossed paths in your home."

"Marceline is an incredible woman of intellect and integrity. She will forgive your past transgressions," Saul insisted. "Hang up and go speak to her or else."

"Or else what?"

"I will come and raze the entire island to the ground with such intensity that no amount of dragon's magic will resurrect your flowers," he growled into the phone, his best imitation of an angry, ancient wyrm.

The silence between them lasted for five seconds until Teo burst out laughing over the line. "It will be no more impressive than the tantrums you once threw as a child."

"I thought you could use the laugh, old friend. Chloe and I have done the most difficult work, although I do not believe my wife realizes our plan. You need do nothing more than appear and sweep your woman off her feet."

Teo laughed until his sides hurt then sank into the desk chair to watch the women in the monitor. *Sweep her off her feet?*

Marceline appeared as radiant as she had the first day he'd met her. The camera revealed her in deep discussion with some rich prick he couldn't recall inviting. The man's eyes watched her bosom closely, as if the words came from her tits instead of her mouth.

Teo growled, a low rumble vibrating in his chest. "I will call you soon with news of my success," he declared. He hung up without waiting for Saul to acknowledge him and marched from the office to greet his guests. Fashionably late, he swept into the room with a charismatic smile in place.

People waved him down at once. They all wanted the same thing — to garner his favor — but Teo had time for none of them. He weaved through the room, focused on his goal. Marceline was the only human in the room who mattered.

Luck seemed to be with him. Within moments of greeting Chloe and Marcy, another guest stole Chloe away.

And then he stole Marcy, too, coaxing her into the special garden and attached butterfly habitat. Her eyes widened as she took in the surroundings, and for one brief moment, she warmed up to him.

Then he ruined it in a single breath. With one ill-thought statement.

Fuck, Teo thought. As she strode away without looking back at him, the disgruntled dragon realized his error.

Hours after his failure, Teo retired to his personal island and stood at the shoreline, wondering how to take the next step. He paced along the sandy bank, absolutely nude from top to bottom, his fine tuxedo shredded in the water just beyond the resort's sea shelf. The refreshing swim in his dragon form hadn't helped to ease his mind, and if he phoned Saul, he suspected his friend would tell him to try again.

Of the hundreds on my island, she is the only one who expects nothing from me, and yet I want nothing more than to gift her with the finest jewels.

A dragoness would be content to accept precious gemstones and gold coins from him in exchange for her favor, allowing him the chance to later get to know her, and possibly earn her affection.

But many human women — Marcy included — led lives that seemed backwards to him, disinterested in a man's wealth until they had bonded.

Then they had the audacity to want to give equal financial support!

Such an absurd notion. Nothing should matter but the size of my hoard and that I am willing to provide for her.

And yet, it pleased him greatly to know she could find interest in him for more than his vast wealth — that she wouldn't be yet another gold-digging mortal searching for a favor.

Soon, I will try again. I will give her the time to forgive tonight's blunder, and then I shall make her mine.

***

Teo did not drown Marcy with priceless jewels, but he did discover every second of her time to be as valuable as the relics in his cave. He lived for the moments when a smile touched her lips, and he eagerly searched for reasons to bring them together. He escorted her to his private aviary where his delicate, feathered friends took an instant liking to her.

Later, it seemed only natural to entrust his wealth to her as well. He left her in his office with access to his account records.

He waited for her to call, but it never happened.

"Why do you remain here when there is a beautiful woman awaiting you?" Kekoa asked. "Does your heart no longer call to her?"

"It does," Teo admitted. "But she does not appear to be interested." He clawed the damp sand and muttered under his breath. For the first time in as long as he could remember, the crashing waves against the rocks and sandy shoreline failed to soothe his spirits. Wandering his personal island always brought him joy after a swim.

Kekoa laughed at him.

"What?"

"You truly know nothing of human women."

"And you do?" Teo shot back.

"I know they favor attention and play hard to get. I know women of quality value time over petty gifts. Give your *words* to her. Seek her and show her your attention hasn't waned."

Teo grumbled. "Two days have passed. How could my attention diminish in a mere two days' time?"

Kekoa rolled his eyes and sat beside him on the beach. "Trust me. Time passes more quickly for humans. She is not one of your dragoness bitches."

Teo growled and fixed Kekoa beneath a withering stare.

His friend raised his hands, pleading for peace. "The one you had here for a visit ten years ago, and the red I glimpsed in California, are all I have to go by. They didn't set a good example of your species."

"Fair enough. Very well then. What do I do?"

"Allow her to see more of you beyond the image you portray to the world. To your guests. Let her see the real you." Kekoa glanced at him. "And if that fails, human women appear to have an unnatural weakness for abdominal muscles. Flash your pecs at her once or twice and that should do the trick."

Teo stared at him.

Ultimately, he commissioned Marcy's artistic talents for a portrait, combining all aspects of Kekoa's advice into one endeavor.

It's been decades since I've had a portrait painted. Of course, I've always worn clothing of some sort as well, he mused. Moments after making plans to meet Marcy in his sterile, boring executive office, he cursed himself.

Teo went to the intercom and beeped his secretary. "I need this office furnished within the next half hour."

"Furnished?" Judy asked?

"Yes," he said impatiently. "Curtains, carpets, paintings. Things a woman would find attractive."

"Thirty minutes isn't enough—"

"Make it enough," he replied curtly before ending the call. Later, he'd apologize for his abrupt and rude behavior, but now, he had work to do. With help from Kekoa and a few of the other resort employees, they were somehow able to find furnishings and decorations in a miraculously short time, Teo himself even helping to arrange the room to his liking.

When Marcy entered a transformed room with personality, he couldn't wait to be rid of his clothing. Anticipation had made them stiff and uncomfortable against skin yearning to be free. His cock had already begun to tense, on the verge of achieving erection.

Marcy's eyes traveled downward to his dick. Her prolonged attention yielded a hot flush of masculine pride, then his cock twitched and swelled even further.

He ached, but most of all, he wanted her to find happiness in looking upon him, to feel equal pleasure to what he enjoyed whenever she entered the room.

"Am I to your expectations?" he asked.

Marcy abruptly swept her attention to his face. "Did you have a pose in mind?"

Teo's enthusiasm deflated. *Was Kekoa wrong?* he wondered. Marcy did not seem infatuated with his abs *or* the rest of him. He felt ridiculous and inexperienced with human women, and frustrated she did not reciprocate his interest by shedding her clothes as well. It was a foolish notion, expecting her to be as free with her body, but it hadn't changed how much he'd hoped to make progress.

"What would you suggest?" He held eye contact with her, refusing to show his disappointment.

At the end of their session, Teo reluctantly donned his clothes and searched for a way to prolong their time together. It came to him in a stroke of genius.

"I wish to see you again tomorrow."

And tomorrow couldn't come quickly enough, once she agreed. Teo floated through his day with dreams of confessing his feelings to Marceline.

Later, as he and Kekoa reviewed the construction progress of the island's new aquatics center, he absently muttered plans out loud.

"Tomorrow I will bond with her," he told Kekoa. "I believe you are correct. If money is the route to earning a dragoness' love, then certainly one's physical attributes are the way to impress a human woman."

"They like big cocks," Kekoa agreed. "You defend your female dragons quite readily but have poor experiences with them. Why?"

Teo sighed. "Loyalty, perhaps. Saul has no such qualms when it comes to speaking his mind about the fairer sex of our species, but I have always felt differently."

"Can you blame him?"

Thoughts of Brigid came to mind, making Teo laugh and shake his head when he recalled her air of superiority. "Ixchel was not as bad as Brigid. She did not mean to pay you insult, Kekoa, but you were a child then and it is unlike a female dragon to show affection to cubs not of her own flesh and blood,' he explained.

"You liked her." Kekoa leaned forward, curiosity on his brown face. "Enough to be her mate?"

"I did," Teo admitted. "Black dragons are a rarity among my kind, our females even fewer. I had hoped our year together would... inspire feelings between us beyond the contract to conceive young."

"She treated you badly," Kekoa said. "I loathed her for that more than I hated her for the things she said to me."

Teo snapped his head around to look at his friend. "What things did she speak to you?"

The wereshark hesitated, and spoke only when Teo gestured for him to continue with an impatient movement of his wrist. "She told me I was unwelcome and that if not for your pity, she would have eaten me. I was to leave once the cub was born, as you would no longer have an interest in guarding my life."

A bolt of fury streaked through Teo, knotting his stomach with

327

anger. He clenched his jaw. "You didn't think to bring this to my attention?"

"Forgive me, Master. I thought you were aware."

Teo gritted his teeth and set one hand on the young man's shoulder. "No. At no point was I ever aware of her abusing you while beyond my hearing. You were a child, Kekoa. A child. You were my responsibility. I brought you here to this island to protect you, and had I known…"

I would have made her dwell on the mainland in one of my other homes. Visited her there for our matings. I would never have brought her home to upset you.

Kekoa nodded his head. "I apologize. I should have told you. Ah, I should go and conduct the interview scheduled for this evening. Already, there is a vast amount of interest in this new compound. Forgive me for becoming distracted."

"Ah, yes. That man." Teo crinkled his nose in distaste. A well-known doctor had applied for the position of director over the aquatics center, and while he was as sharp as a tack, Teo's feelings toward him remained undecided.

"I will prepare the cabana in the morning." The young man stepped away from the metal frame dedicated to the facility's future shark tank.

"Kekoa?"

The young man paused to glance back at him. "Yes, Master?"

"Teo. Call me Teo. Take the evening off to go spend time with Dante. I insist. He mentioned a desire to have company out on the reef and I mentioned you may have an interest in showing him the reef. Enjoy yourselves. *I* will handle Doctor Castlebury. If he is as eager as his cover letter implies, he will not mind waiting a half hour or so for my arrival."

"But your plans—"

Teo waved him off with a hand. "I will manage."

"Thank you… Teo." Kekoa tested the word out, as if it felt strange to his lips without the preceding title. "Tomorrow, we will meet at the private cabana. I have an idea." Smiling as he waved, he then turned and strode away to search out his new friend.

And Teo was left to his own thoughts, filled with hopes of earning Marceline's heart.

***

Teo was not prepared for the intensity associated with falling in love, and underestimating it nearly cost him everything he had fought to build between them. As days passed and they eventually bonded, it seemed only inevitable he would chase her away again.

He spent the first few days in disbelief, waiting for her to return. When the longing for Marcy surpassed his pride, he phoned Saul for advice.

"An angered woman requires time," Saul cautioned. "Did you apologize after upsetting her?"

"No, of course not. I did nothing wrong."

Saul made an exasperated sound and groaned into the phone. "You've broken one of the simplest rules of having a human woman," he grunted out. "You must apologize to her at once."

"Why? What wrongdoing have I committed, save for giving my expectation of having her for more than a passing moment of my life?" Teo inhaled a deep breath. Few things frightened him like the potential loss of his new mate to old age.

"If you require me to answer this for you, Teotihuacan, then you do not deserve her," Saul said simply. "Consider her feelings and place yourself in her shoes. How would you feel if she were to command you to give up your dragon shape and live a mortal life?"

"I would n—"

"Have you not asked her to do similar?"

Teo remained quiet.

"To accept your seed and bear your child is to forsake her *humanity*, Teo. Neither dragon nor human, she will watch all of her friends, family, and loved ones die."

"Saul…" Teo sagged in the seat and gazed across the sand into the crashing waves. "I have been a fool."

"A lovestruck fool," Saul said gently.

"What must I do?"

Saul chuckled into the phone. "Marceline is a fiery creature with strong opinions. Stubborn. Give her time to cool and consider how you might apologize."

"You have the talent for words," Teo grumbled. "What would you say in my place?"

"Marceline, I have behaved as an idiot. An absolute buffoon. I beg your forgiveness and promise I will never foolishly give commands regarding your body and well-being again."

329

"Asshole," Teo grumbled. "I wanted flowery words."

"Save the flowery words and voice your feelings. Speak to her from your heart."

Words from my heart. How do I tell her that with her beside me, my heart feels as large as this vast ocean, and without her, it is as empty as its surface?

"I will ask Chloe to speak with her," Saul offered.

"I… feel lost without her," Teo finally admitted. "She has taken part of my soul to Texas."

"Then tell her so. Give breath to your thoughts and let her know she is loved, once you are ready."

Teo disconnected the call and thought back on his friend's words. Saul made it sound so easy — *too* easy. He wasn't sure Marcy would forgive him.

Restlessness drove him to the beach. The sun had barely begun to set when Kekoa wandered down from the quiet house.

"Saul called back," Kekoa informed him. The dark-haired wereshark came to a stop beside the pensive dragon. "He asked me to let you know that Marcy is staying with them for a time."

"Good… That is… It is good." Teo paced back and forth across the sun-warmed sand, torn by indecision. *Of course she would go there. She and Chloe are close friends.*

"Is everything, well?" Kekoa asked, brows knitted together.

"Y—no," he answered truthfully. He wouldn't insult Kekoa's intelligence with a lie when his faithful servant had witnessed the final tense days of Marcy's stay with his own eyes. "Marceline left me."

"I am certain she only needs time to cool off," Kekoa assured him. Teo wished he shared the sentiment.

"Do I call her, Kekoa?"

"Some words are better said face to face."

"What if she has no wish to see me? She has been gone for many days without word."

Kekoa chuckled, earning the dragon's glare.

"I find nothing amusing about this," Teo muttered.

"Forgive me, my friend." Kekoa attempted to school his amused expression, but failed. Another chortle escaped. "It is a new side of you. A good one."

"You think I am a fool," Teo growled.

"No, I think you are a man in love. A dragon in love. It is new for you. Good, even."

"It doesn't feel good." Teo kicked at the sand and turned his face into the salt-scented breeze. The cool air brushed against his cheeks and stirred his dark hair.

Each passing day without Marcy beside him was pain more than he could bear.

"If you truly wish to know how she feels, go to her," Kekoa urged. "Look her in the eye and tell her what's in your heart."

"Saul said the same thing."

Kekoa's broad grin widened further. "Ha! I am wise as a dragon, then. Or he is as smart as a shark."

Teo snorted and clapped his friend on the shoulder. "Very well, I will go to her." *And hope it is not too late to undo my foolishness.*

About the Author

Vivienne Savage is a resident of a small town in rural Texas. While she isn't concocting sexy ways for shapeshifters and humans to find their match, she raises two children and works as a nurse in a rural nursing home.

To get on Vivienne's mailing list for news and upates, go online and visit http://eepurl.com/boj0p1

Made in the USA
San Bernardino, CA
01 April 2016